The *j...*

'Not many books make me laugh out loud, but *The Perpetual Astonishment of Jonathon Fairfax* is one of them... A comic gem.'

Francesca Brown, *Stylist*

'It cleverly combines intrigue with comic, astute observation which made me laugh throughout.'

The Bath Novel Award (2014 shortlist)

'You can't help being tickled.'

Alfred Hickling, *The Guardian*

'Shevlin was rightly picked up by the literary agency that represents the likes of David Nicholls. ... the comic hero is caught up in a murder plot that unravels into a political thriller, which is by turns absurd and engaging.'

Ben East, *Metro*

'*Jonathon Fairfax Must Be Destroyed* is funny, it's daft-yet-relatable, it's still a nerve-jangly thriller and it moves at a cracking pace. In fact, if you're stuck in a bit of a reading rut, it's just the palate cleanser you need.'

Emerald Street

About the author

Christopher Shevlin dressed as a cowboy every day until the age of six, making him the most heavily armed child in Doncaster – no small achievement. Other facts about him include these: he distrusts condiments; he dreams in high definition; he briefly worked as a labourer in Tel Aviv, earning the nickname 'astronaut' for his incredible slowness of movement; he has twice performed at the Edinburgh Fringe; he once dug a grave.

His pen is available for hire, along with his writing advice and teaching. He has run a *Guardian* Masterclass, taught bankers to write, invented a giant outdoor board game, ghosted articles about diverse and intermittently fascinating subjects, prepared speeches, and written scripts for BBC Ideas. He also wrote *Writing For Business*, which is part of Penguin's *Writers' Guides* series, as well as the hilariously outdated *Simple Guide to Email*.

When life is hard, he has always turned to books for comfort. His favourites include his battered old *Jeeves Omnibus*, Douglas Adams's *Dirk Gently* books, *1066 And All That*, the *Molesworth* books, and *Augustus Carp By Himself*. His ambition is to write books that are even a tenth as comfortingly odd.

His first novel, *The Perpetual Astonishment of Jonathon Fairfax*, was shortlisted for the 2014 Bath Novel Award and became an Amazon UK bestseller. His second novel, *Jonathon Fairfax Must Be Destroyed*, was also a bestseller, reaching number three in Amazon's UK chart, but was only longlisted for the Bath Novel Award.

To find out more about Christopher Shevlin, his books, and the disturbingly assertive squirrels of Helsinki, please visit:

www.christophershevlin.com

The Spy
Who Came
in from
the Bin

CHRISTOPHER SHEVLIN

ALBATROSS

Published by Albatross Publishing

Copyright © Christopher Shevlin 2020

ISBN 978-0-9569656-5-3

Revised edition, February 2021 (3f)

www.albatrosspublishing.com

www.christophershevlin.com

Thank you

I wrote quite a lot of this during the Covid lockdown, so I don't have so many people to thank this time.

Nevertheless, thanks to my friends in Berlin for making me welcome when I went back to do a bit of research – Linn Hart, Paul Hawkins, Adam Fletcher, Julia Jorch, Kate McNaughton, Stefan Rother, Rich Baxter, Stef Jakobi, Jack Kinsella, and Manuel Meurer. Thanks too to the real Gabi and Hanno, with their real beautiful thatched cottage, and to Matthias Gottwald, for my author photos and the loan of his name.

Thanks again to Scott Pack for editing it, and Paul Hawkins for designing the covers. Also to the excellent Samantha Meah for having me on her radio show.

And thank you to every reader who has ever sent me a message of any kind. Authoring can be a lonely business, and it makes a huge difference to hear from the people on the other side of the page.

Thank you all.

Part One

The Fairfax Identity

Tuesday

1

Berlin, March 2003, around breakfast time

Berlin in the early twenty-first century was not like other cities. But it was not so different that a man could be found unconscious in a bin without attracting attention – especially a man wearing a shirt, tie and neatly pressed trousers. Berlin is a dressed-down sort of city.

It was Kurt who had seen the man tumble out of the heavy metal bin and into the waiting mouth of the rubbish truck. It was early morning, and the orange truck clanked and beeped beneath a pale, cold sky. The dirty metal teeth of the truck's compactor bit down.

'*Stop!*' shouted Kurt, forgetting for a second that his own hand was on the control. He released the button and the teeth halted.

Nearby, Mannie stopped rattling another huge bin over the cobbles.

'*What is here loose?*' said Mannie, in German, of course.

'*There within is a bloke,*' said Kurt.

'*Shit. Lives he?*'

'*I know not. Help me.*'

Kurt turned a heavy switch, then he and Mannie climbed up onto the metal access plate and reached into the back of the truck, among the water bottles, milk cartons and potato peelings that people really should have sorted into other bins for recycling and composting, instead of shoving them in unthinkingly with the used tissues, old toothbrushes and smartly dressed men. They grabbed the unconscious man, hauling him in with their big dirty gloves. Then Mannie got both arms around the man's chest, Kurt gripped the man's knees and they gently schlepped him down onto the stone pavement.

'*Breathes he?*' asked Mannie.

'*I know not. Call you help.*'

Mannie pulled off his glove and dug in the pockets beneath his overalls for his phone. Not finding it, he hurried off to the cab of the truck.

Kurt put his ear to the man's mouth, listening for breathing. The last thing he needed was for this man to die. He was already under disciplinary measures for a misunderstanding about some carpets.

He listened again. Nothing.

He pulled off his gloves, trying to remember what he was supposed to do. No obvious wounds, no bleeding. He put both hands to the man's chest and pressed down.

Once. Twice.

Next he would have to breathe into the man's lungs. But for how long? He held the man's nose tight between his fingers. Two seconds? Yes. Two.

'Yack, unk,' said the man. Then, in English, he said, 'Um, sorry. Could you stop doing that?'

'He lives!' Kurt called, in German.

'You live!' he said to the man, surprised at how quickly the English words came to him. Then he remembered something: 'No. You are living. Correct, or?'

The man seemed confused by this, but Kurt was sure that was the way they'd been told to say it in school.

Mannie returned from the front of the truck, his phone in his hand and the driver by his side. *'A sick-wagon is on the way,'* he said.

'He is English,' said Kurt. 'He is living.'

'He lives,' corrected Mannie.

'He is alive,' corrected the driver.

Kurt tried to regain the initiative.

'How many fingers?' he asked the man, holding up three.

The man looked confused. 'I don't need any, thanks,' he said. 'I've already got some fingers.'

'He has his head hit,' said Kurt.

'He has a brain-shake,' corrected Mannie, with authority.

'In English, it is "concussion,"' said the driver.

'How are you called?' Kurt asked the man.

'What is your name?' corrected Mannie.

'Who are you?' corrected the driver.

The man's mouth moved as though to answer, but no words emerged.

They all looked at him as he lay on the cobbled street in his smart clothes, neat but for a scrap of gherkin clinging to his tie. His face was as blank and characterful as a child's.

After a long struggle, the man finally managed to reply. 'Um, sorry. I don't know.'

2

The man was embarrassed to find himself lying on a pavement being stared at by binmen, so he tried to sit up. Abruptly, the light and colour drained from the world, turning it into a kind of splodgy brown mess that made him feel sick. That feeling of sickness swirled around until it was sucked into the enveloping brown, and he was gone.

When he opened his eyes again, all three binmen were crouching around him, looking at each other in alarm. When they noticed he was awake, they motioned him not to move.

The man looked into the cloudy grey sky. He saw the edge of the rubbish truck's orange roof, the underside of a binman's face, a yellow wall on which someone had painted a big red 'A' in a circle. Beneath him, through his thin shirt, he felt the pavement's small squarish stones. It was very cold, and he could feel his body shivering. Or he could feel a body shivering and knew it was somehow connected to whatever it was that was seeing all these things and containing these confused thoughts. Above him loomed a streetlamp, its head pointing to the earth, like a wilted metal flower. Everything felt a long way away. Then something thick and orange, smelling strongly of cigarettes, was laid on top of him, and he could feel it scratchy against his chin. The world went brown again.

There was a high-pitched noise. Something had changed. There were rattles and clanks. Voices he couldn't quite catch.

A hand on him. Then he had grabbed the hand and was trying to use his opponent's weight against him. This might have succeeded if his opponent had been, say, a small sachet of sugar. As it was, his opponent weighed around two hundred pounds and wore a white helmet and a padded brown uniform with high-visibility trim. He looked like a fireman, and his square, solid face seemed slightly sad and offended by the man's feeble attack. A stretcher lay beside him, and a large pink ambulance stood close by.

'Sorry,' said the man, abandoning his tiny assault.

His erstwhile opponent continued to look sadly at him, and with the help of another solid professional in a brown uniform, expertly put the stretcher under him, covered him with a blue blanket that didn't smell of cigarettes, buckled him in and picked him up. It was simultaneously cosy and terrifying.

'Thank you,' he said to the binmen.

'No problem,' said one.

'You are welcome,' corrected another.

'Don't mention it,' corrected a third.

Everything was very vivid now. The cold air on his cheek. The sky. The red 'A' with a circle around it on the wall, next to the earnest slogan, 'WAR IS BAD'. The street seemed a kind of dry canal formed of cobbles and yellow buildings. At one end, behind a big metal bridge, there loomed a huge astronaut, painted in black on the side of a grey building.

The firemen lifted the stretcher into the back of their bright pink ambulance, climbed in alongside him, turned on the world's most embarrassingly loud siren, and pulled off at great speed. Through the glass in the back doors, the man could see the disarray they left in their wake as they skipped through red lights and bounced over complex junctions.

As the journey went on, the man began to worry. Why had they buckled him into the stretcher? Why was the fire brigade driving ambulances around? Where were they taking him? What had he been doing in the back of a rubbish truck? Why couldn't he remember who he was or where he lived? And wouldn't real firemen be chatting to each other? The two sitting across from him were totally silent, their big faces still.

He must have fallen asleep again, despite the siren and his worries about the firemen. He woke as they were wheeling him from the pink ambulance into a large purple-and-white hospital. They moved his stretcher onto a kind of trolley in the large beige lobby, and handed him over to a new set of firemen. He thanked the first set as they moved off, but they just glanced at him in gentle silence.

The second set of firemen wheeled him to a corridor and told him to wait, then disappeared. A nurse arrived, unbuckled him, and asked him some questions in German. He dealt with this impromptu oral exam by looking blankly at her and stuttering. It was not that he didn't understand her questions – they were simple things like his name, date of birth, nationality and insurance details. It was that he was so disturbed at having no idea what the answers were.

The nurse tutted at him and marched off with the air of a teacher going to fetch the headmaster to deal with a particularly awful crime. Was that a glimmer of a memory? How did this work, that he knew about teachers, headmasters and the existence of Germany and its language, but nothing at all about himself, which should have been his specialist subject?

He sat on the trolley for a few minutes, feeling lost and afraid. Perhaps he should just leave. They were annoyed with him and he was obviously basically fine. His memory would no doubt gradually return, and it was likely to come back sooner out in the streets, where he might remember something, than in this strange and hostile hospital. Unless of course he worked in this hospital. That was also possible. Perhaps he was German. Perhaps he was a German doctor who specialised in treating memory loss.

He got up, intending to go, but again it was as though someone had turned the world's brownness setting up to maximum. A background sensation that he had thought was just part of the world broke loose and revealed itself to be a painful headache.

'Hey!' a voice called to him.

He sat down again quickly, guiltily. The headache and brownness sat down with him, reclining to a slightly less painful distance.

The voice said something to him but it was lost amid the brownness. He carefully framed a reply.

'Um,' he said. 'What?'

This time she spoke in English, fluent and easy, with a German accent.

'My name is Lisanne. I'm a doctor. So, you are having trouble speaking?'

Was that the problem? It was certainly true, but probably only because they kept asking him things he didn't know and making the world go brown when he tried to get up. He looked at her, paralysed by uncertainty about how to answer.

'That's okay,' she said. 'We're going to look after you.'

She laid her hand comfortingly on his arm, and the man was overwhelmed with gratitude for this little gesture. The hospital seemed to have concentrated all its powers of sympathy into this one person, leaving none for anyone else. Perhaps it was most efficient this way.

'First, what is this?' she asked, holding up a pen.

He goggled at her. Was it a trick question? Did she want the German word? He felt suddenly and obscurely betrayed. How could she help him if she didn't even know what a pen was?

She made a note on her clipboard.

'Can you smile?' she asked.

He goggled at her again. He seemed to be a person who was easily astonished.

'When?' he said.

'Now. Please smile for me. It is possible that you have had a small stroke, and the smile helps us to see if there is any difference between the two sides of your face.'

He tried, but he wasn't completely sure how to do a smile. The awkward mechanical hoisting of the two ends of his mouth seemed difficult to coordinate. It must be because he'd had a stroke. The left end seemed far higher than the right, but then the right put on a sudden burst of speed and seemed in danger of hitting his eyebrow. A stroke was the only possible cause. That must be why he knew that a stroke was caused by a burst blood vessel in the brain, but didn't know whether he owned a toyshop or had ever killed a man.

'Okay,' said Lisanne brightly, but with perhaps a note of worry in her voice. 'Now please close your eyes and raise both arms in front of you.'

This seemed a much easier request, but as soon as he began he realised that his right arm was hurting quite badly. It felt bruised, but perhaps that was just the stroke.

'Good,' said Lisanne unconvincingly. 'Now, please tell me what you are doing in Berlin.'

'Um.' He looked at her levelly, and again said 'What?'

'Just a neutral topic to check your speech.'

What was he doing in Berlin? What *was* he doing in Berlin? What was he doing in *Berlin*? He looked at her with growing panic.

He had absolutely certainly had a stroke. He looked up at Lisanne, who smiled encouragingly, as you might to an idiot. She was a good nine feet tall, around thirty, with blonde hair coiled in an old-fashioned way on top of her head. Despite her sympathetic smile she had the sort of chiselled face you might expect to find on a patriotic statue. He found it difficult to process all these conflicting attributes, especially when he didn't know who he was. Or what he was doing in Berlin.

'I will ask the Feuerwehr to move you to the next floor,' she said. 'We will do some more tests, just as a precaution. We will want to make a scan also, and it might be a good idea to take a medicine to thin your blood, just in case there has been a small stroke. You would need to think about this and give your consent. How would you feel about this?'

'Wub,' he said, unable to properly take in everything she had said.

And so he was wheeled to the next floor, where he was examined by another sympathetic doctor who told him that he had good lungs but that his legs were too white, which meant he must be English.

Then he was wheeled into a high-tech room that looked like the bridge of a spaceship, crewed by five beautiful and sympathetic female doctors who asked him more difficult questions, noting down his halting answers on their clipboards and encouraging him to consent to being injected with a blood-thinner and having a brain scan.

It wasn't until he was in the next room – secured to a padded bench, his head velcroed in place, with the electric whine of the mechanism bringing the bench into the huge white machine – that he suddenly realised he had allowed himself to be manipulated into taking drugs and climbing into a brain machine by attractive strangers on the thinnest of pretexts. He had walked into their trap, politely taking their poison and trotting into their device to have his brain wiped. Someone wanted him dead. Why else would he have woken up in a rubbish truck? Having failed to kill him the first time in the open, they had taken him to an institution to do away with him at their leisure. This was it: he was going to die.

Either that or he was a normal person who'd possibly had a small stroke and was being responsibly treated for it by caring and highly trained medical professionals. It was hard to know.

A couple of hours later, he found himself in the stroke ward, his amnesia having been, for the moment at least, forgotten. It seemed increasingly likely that he was in a normal German hospital and that no one was trying to kill him.

He was in a small but extremely adjustable bed, his right index finger connected by a clip to a machine that went beep every so often. The machine was also connected to an armband, which noisily inflated itself every twenty minutes, gripping him tightly by the upper arm as though it had something urgent to tell him. He was told he had to fast for twenty-four hours, which was going to be difficult because he was already so hungry that it felt like his stomach had begun to eat itself.

Apart from his own, the room had seven beds: two empty, and five occupied by much older men. One of them called 'Hallo!' every few minutes. But when someone came he had no follow-up conversation, and just sat there looking blank and expectant. The others were visited every so often by people in white coats who would draw the curtain and then do unseen things, speaking reassuringly all the while.

Soon, the other patients were brought food, airline-style, in small plastic trays with lids. The man was brought nothing. He powerfully wanted to eat the others' off-putting airline food, but it was not allowed. Perhaps they were trying to starve him to death. He would feel much easier if he could just get an absolutely definitive answer to this question of whether or not they were trying to kill him.

The bed was adjusted to an angle exactly halfway between sitting and lying down, so that he was neither alert nor asleep. And so he half-sat there, wearing a blue cotton gown that tied behind his neck and was open at the back, and he tried to remember who he was and what he did.

His life and personal history were just a fuzzy blank. And yet there were clues even in this. One encouraging point was that he had clearly expected to know who he was, which strongly implied that this blankness wasn't his usual state. Then there was the fact that his inner monologue was mostly English, and that any German words that popped up tended to either be followed by a clear English translation, or by a few possibilities surrounded by an overpowering doubt. Also, he had English legs and had clearly eaten on a plane at least once.

And then he found, so deep he hadn't noticed it – like the headache he hadn't noticed because it was everywhere – that there was a yearning in him, a powerful need for someone. There was someone who wasn't here, and he wanted that person to be here. And he didn't know whether this was a yearning for a specific someone, or a yearning for there to be someone. But it felt like a painful tender bruise in the centre of his body.

This train of thought was interrupted by another woman in a white coat. She was older, with glasses and dyed-red hair, and she spoke to him in German, asking him what a pen was, then telling him to close his eyes and hold his arms out straight. When he opened his eyes again, he saw her noting something sourly on a clipboard. Then she left, as though disappointed with his performance. This unexpectedly exhausted the man.

He lay back and drifted into another world, despite the machines that went beep, despite the thing on his arm with something urgent to tell him, despite his nameless yearning and his desperate desire for airline-style food, despite the many people striding about and drawing curtains, and despite the old man who forlornly called 'Hallo!'

A Bit of Wednesday But
Mostly Thursday

3

It was dark. Someone in a white coat was shaking the man's shoulder.

'*Young man?*' said the person in the white coat, in German. That was what they called him, because he didn't have a name.

'Hallo,' said the man, blearily rubbing his eyes.

'Hallo!' called the old man across the ward, helpfully.

The person in the white coat had a large lumpy face, as though someone had dropped a pile of wet clay on the empty front of a head. His glasses glinted.

'*I am Doctor Braun,*' said the white-coated doctor loudly, as though it were well known that sleep was unnecessary in hospital.

'*That is good,*' said the man.

'*What is this?*' asked Doctor Braun, holding up a pen.

'*It is a pen,*' said the man, who had at last come to understand what was expected of him in this situation.

'*Can you your arms so outstretch?*' said the doctor, holding out his arms.

'*Gladly,*' said the man, holding his arms straight out in front of him.

The doctor nodded and ticked something on a form.

'*So,*' said the doctor, '*you have the suspicion of a stroke. You must a time under observation remain.*'

'*Thanks,*' said the man. '*I understand. But I can myself nothing remember.*'

'*This can a symptom for a stroke be. We investigate this stroke. Make you yourself no worries. The signs are that you no stroke have.*'

'*Oh,*' said the man, confused. '*Thanks.*'

'*Good night.*'

'*Good night.*'

As the doctor turned away, the man noticed that there was a section of his form about languages, and that the doctor had ticked 'German'. It was the first thing the man had felt pleased about in his short remembered life.

Once the doctor had introduced himself to each of the other patients in the middle of the night and filled in some forms that had already been completed many times, he left with the air of a job well done.

The man lay awake, staring at the insides of his own eyelids, and watching as odd waking dreams projected themselves there – scrawls of colour, vivid shapes, then scenes, images, one melting into another, meaningless. There was a cat with one ear. There was again a feeling that he loved someone and she was far away. But maybe everyone felt like that.

At half-past six he was woken by a nurse. She asked him what a pen was and got him to raise his arms, which by now felt like a standard greeting. It almost felt rude not to also ask her what a pen was and if she could raise her arms. Then he was told to clean his teeth and wash himself all over using a bowl of very soapy water and two tiny flannels.

Shortly afterwards, a lady arrived with a book of pictures and German words. She asked him to look at the pictures and point to the right words. He hoped this surprise early-morning German exam wasn't going to be used to assess his mental development, but he lacked a means to convey this in German, and found he was too polite to switch into English. He could only pray that they wouldn't decide to put him in some sort of remedial institution for the rest of his life because of it.

Later that day, after a different kind of brain scan, he was brought lunch. This was by far the best thing that had happened in the man's short life. There was a slice of bread with something that both did and didn't suit the word 'ham'. There was a bread roll with butter, honey and a sort of chocolate spread that wasn't chocolate. There was a cup of horrible slightly minty tea that was the most delicious liquid he'd ever tasted. It was a sequence of glories, and it made him certain they were not trying to kill him.

After this he was moved to another ward, where he stayed for a few hours before being moved back to the first ward but in a different place. Doctor Braun introduced himself again, and then the man settled back into the routine of half-sitting while things went beep.

The next morning, he was woken at half-past six, asked what a pen was and told to clean his teeth and wash with two tiny flannels. There was an air of something momentous being about to happen, but in fact the half-sitting went on all morning. After lunch, he was allowed to walk to a room where a grey-faced nurse glued a little cap of electrodes to his head and then sat with him in companionable silence for a few minutes. It was, perhaps, not the life he would have chosen, but it was the only one he knew, and he was becoming increasingly comfortable in it, especially now he was allowed to eat.

And so it came as something of a shock when, later that afternoon, Doctor Braun brought him some news.

'Young man,' said the doctor, 'your wife is here.'

4

The man saw her approaching from the other side of the ward. She was short and neat, with bobbed chestnut hair and large eyes that locked onto his the second she saw him. She broke into a smile and hurried over.

'Jonathan,' she said, hugging him close, 'thank god I've found you.'

'Yes,' said the man. This sounded foolish and ungrateful. 'Um, thanks,' he added. This also sounded horribly feeble, so he added, 'Thank god.'

He had been hoping that when she arrived he would experience a sudden flash of recognition and his identity would click into place. This did not happen.

She moved back, still holding his shoulders, and looked into his eyes.

'They said you complained of memory problems – as well as the stroke. Do you remember me?'

The man looked at her. Her large eyes were green, and she wore a fluffy pink jumper with new jeans, little white shoes and a gold handbag.

She was entirely unfamiliar to him. He wondered whether anyone had ever given him advice about what to do when introduced to your life partner again for the first time since suffering total amnesia. It was a tricky social situation, and his two days' experience of the world had prepared him only to hold his hands parallel to the floor and tell Germans what a pen was.

'Maybe?' he said. 'I've forgotten absolutely everything. I don't even know my own name.'

'Oh, honey. You poor thing. We are going to get you through this. Your name is Jonathan, and you live with me in a beautiful apartment on Herder Strasse. I'm Amy. Now let's get you out of here.'

She looked around, but the doctors and nurses had discreetly withdrawn from the room, or perhaps just had things to do.

'Hallo!' called the old man from his bed in the corner.

Amy set her jaw and marched out of the ward, returning a few seconds later with Doctor Braun.

'So,' he said, 'please to fill this paper with your insurance details, sign on the bottom, and then you are free to take him home.' He handed her a clipboard and wiped his glasses.

The man was surprised to hear Doctor Braun speaking English. He had always felt it would be cheating not to talk to him in German.

'Where are his clothes?' asked Amy.

'A nurse will bring them immediately,' said Doctor Braun.

'And what about his amnesia? Do you know what caused it?'

He gave her a slightly puzzled look, as though her lack of medical knowledge had caused her to ask an odd question.

'He has problems to speak and answer questions,' said the doctor. 'This indicated a potential stroke – a little blood vessel in the brain that breaks or is blocked. So we run tests and give him EEG and FMRI scans, and keep him under observation two days.'

'And the result?'

He smiled as though shyly proud. 'We are pleased to say there is no further indication of a stroke. No physical problem in the brain. He is fine.'

'But he has amnesia.'

'Transient amnesia is common after a stroke.'

'But you said there's no indication of a stroke.'

'Yes,' said Doctor Braun, proudly.

Amy paused. 'Okay,' she said, 'so will his memory just come back? What's the soonest time a memory might return?'

'We would expect a few days, but you should consult a doctor about this.'

The woman called Amy glanced at his white coat and roomful of medical equipment. She seemed about to say something, but apparently thought better of it. Instead, she ticked something on the form and carefully signed her name.

'Thanks,' she said with a large white smile, handing the clipboard back.

'Well,' said Doctor Braun, turning to the man. 'Good luck for your recovery' – he glanced at the form in his hand – 'Jonathan F... How is this said?' he asked Amy.

'Forbes,' said Amy. 'Jonathan Forbes.'

A few minutes later, the man – who still couldn't get used to the idea that he should be thinking of himself as Jonathan Forbes – was standing with her in a hospital lift, heading to the basement where their car was parked. He wore his white shirt, which had been washed and now smelled like a small hospital, along with his tie, trousers, and shiny black shoes. Amy gave him one of her large smiles, which he returned shyly. Unable to meet her eyes, he looked again at his shoes. This was a difficult situation, being introduced to a total stranger and then expected to accompany her home and live with her for the rest of his life.

'Lift A,' said the lift, slightly patronisingly. *'Basement.'*

There was a metallic *bing* and the doors opened onto a large underground car park, all dark concrete and strip lights. The cold reached through the man's white shirt and ran its icy fingers down his back.

'We're over here,' said Amy.

He followed her till she came to a huge vehicle in lustrous grey, standing taller than him and with enough space inside for about seven large adults and their skiing equipment. It said 'Audi' on the back.

'Remember her?' asked Amy. 'You totally love this car.'

The man had, if possible, even less memory of his car than he did of his wife. He smiled apologetically.

'Relax,' said Amy. 'It's *okay*. It's not your fault you forgot everything. Just take it slow.'

He went and stood by the door, waiting for her to unlock the car.

'Listen,' she said, 'I really don't think it's a good idea for you to drive right now.'

The man looked down into the car and realised he was standing by the driver's door.

'Sorry,' he said, and moved around to stand by the other side.

'No problem. Like I said, relax.'

He got into the passenger seat and began a subtle wrestling match with the seatbelt.

'Did I drive a lot?' he asked.

'You *love* to drive,' she said, patting the red-stitched steering wheel. 'Seriously. And you *hate* when I drive your car. But today, sorry honey,

I have to.'

She softly boomed the engine, reversed the car in a swift swoop, and then glided forwards. They left the car park, turned smoothly right and joined a large road. Amy clicked a button on a machine marked 'Blaupunkt' and a voice began very softly wailing about some old-time loving it needed.

The car's heating had kicked in quickly, and now the man had the pleasing feeling of sitting in a bubble of warmth while looking out on a cold land. It was an overpoweringly odd sensation, seeing the non-hospital world for only the second time he could remember.

The road was a dual carriageway with grass running down the middle, punctuated by perfectly spaced trees that reached their naked branches to the dimming sky. The man felt surprised by the traffic but wasn't quite sure why: the road was neither empty nor full, and seemed to be carrying exactly the volume of traffic it had been designed for. The other cars were unglamorous, very unlike the sleek grey Audi in which the man was sitting. And the buildings on either side of the road matched the cars: functional, ugly, with plenty of space. The signs continued the same theme, with simple text on a coloured background saying either straightforwardly what the place did – bank, stationery, drinks – or proclaiming an odd name, like 'Edeka' or 'Renafan'.

The man felt suddenly that he should say something.

'How, er, how did we meet?' he asked, timidly.

'You know, standard kind of thing – but *so* romantic. I was out in a bar in Brooklyn and I see this cute guy looking at me. He sends over a drink, with a little note. I smile, a few seconds later there he is at my table and I just *melt*. The rest is history.'

The man was confused. 'I, um. I meant how did *I* meet you?'

She looked at him. 'You were the cute guy.'

'Oh! Right. Sorry. Got you.'

He looked out of the window again. The streets were almost aggressively well signed. At each corner, a signpost proclaimed the minor street – Havermann Strasse, Teterowe Strasse – and also reminded him of the name of the big road he was already on – now Buschkrugallee, the sign looking almost as though someone had just swept their hand at random across a keyboard. The street was filled with block after block of solid, plain, six-storey flats that reminded him obscurely of the big firemen with their blank, slightly sad faces.

The road narrowed, skipped over a river, passed a gang of sprawling car dealerships, and then ran through a little knot of much older flats with grand facades. There were a few empty spaces now, fenced in, with scrubby grass growing in them, beside buildings that seemed to end prematurely, as though they'd been cut off with a cake slice and hurriedly buttered over with concrete. 'Karl Marx Strasse', asserted the sign. An image flashed into his mind of a man with a monumental stony head, huge white hair and a beard.

'Karl Marx is a communist,' he said.

She laughed. 'You got that right.'

'It's strange that I can remember stuff about the world, and I can sort-of remember what German words mean, but I can't remember anything about me or my life. And it feels like there's a borderline where stuff in the world might give me a clue about who I am, and like my brain's almost deliberately making that foggy.'

'Oh, honey. Like I said, just relax, and don't worry about it. It'll stop being a problem soon enough.'

'Okay, thanks. I'll try.'

He looked out of the window again. The streets were filling up, getting weirder. They passed three kebab shops in a row. A fat man in a vest and sandals was riding a unicycle past people in black leather jackets and ripped jeans. Nearly everyone was either smoking or wearing a headscarf, but not both. Many signs were written in a language he didn't understand, and the walls were full of earnest German graffiti, like 'SOLDIERS ARE MURDERERS' or 'NOT FOR FASCISTS VOTE'.

'What did … What do I do for a living? What's my job?'

'You're in the import-export business.'

'Oh.'

There was a little island of silence, in which he completely failed to feel anything or have any associations with the phrase 'import-export'.

'So what do I do, day to day? What do I import-export?'

'Honey, you really don't have to worry about that right now. You do some pretty sweet deals. You go to a nice office in the … the financial district every day, you do a bunch of stuff that I don't fully understand, and you make a nice living out of it. You have a very nice life. Wait till you see our apartment.'

They drove on. Some of the older buildings looked like they'd been in a war that had only recently stopped – scarred, pockmarked, crumbling. Others seemed recently restored to imperial elegance, with gleaming stucco and elaborate balconies. The word 'currywurst' was everywhere, and he knew, without knowing how, that it meant delicious poor-quality sausages covered in paprika and ketchup.

They passed a building with a plane mounted on its front. They went beneath a huge flyover, then over a perfectly straight river, then past some unimaginative square buildings, a neat urban forest, and a huge and extravagantly ruined church, the holes in it seemingly soldered shut. And now there were well tended buildings all around, with glass and lighting that said they were expensive shops for rich people. There was a Rolls-Royce showroom, and the man immediately knew what Rolls-Royces were and what they meant.

And then, pulling off the main road, they drew up outside a grand but cosy-looking old building, its stone facade shining gold in the light of the old-fashioned lanterns on the street. It had an elaborate green-bronze doorway, and the balconies and windows were also inset with bronze. The man thought it was the most beautiful building he had ever seen, and he had seen plenty during their forty-five minute drive there.

'Home,' said Amy.

5

'Ta-da!' said Amy, throwing open the front door. 'Come on in.'

The man who had just discovered he was Jonathan Forbes walked in from the echoing stairwell. He entered through a doorway only slightly less huge and elaborately carved than the one on the front of the building. He and Amy had just climbed six flights of stairs, but the man noticed that neither of them was out of breath.

He was standing in a long hallway with a beautiful old wooden floor and a high ceiling. It was artfully lit, made cosy and inviting by lamps and Edison bulbs. A red and blue rug ran down its centre.

'It's lovely,' he said simply.

She laughed. 'Do you remember picking out that … uh, picture?' she asked, pointing to a print of two somehow atmospheric blue rectangles on a red background.

'Um, maybe?' He quite liked it. Jonathan Forbes must have good taste.

'You need to relax, honey. Come with me.'

She led him by the hand past a beautiful high-tech rustic kitchen and into a living room that was possibly even more cosily lit than the hallway. Large, high windows took up all of one side of the room. Outside, night had fallen suddenly and completely, as though someone had cut the cord suspending it above the city. The buildings across the way were also grand: handsome and softly illuminated.

Directly opposite one of the windows was a plump and invitingly weathered leather armchair, lit up by the lamp beside it. He was over-whelmed by how tasteful it all was. Could this really be his life?

'This is your favourite spot,' she said, indicating the armchair. 'Now, you sit here' – she gently pushed him into it – 'and relax.'

She sat on his lap and kissed him softly on the lips.

'I know I seem like this total stranger to you,' she said, 'and that must seem weird. But I can't help it.'

'It's, um,' he said, but she laid a finger on his lips and looked deep into his eyes.

'You wait right there. I'll go fix you a drink and slip into some-thing … a little more comfortable.'

She walked to the door, hips swaying. Her clothes already looked pretty comfortable, he thought. Was she going to come back wearing an old tracksuit? She gave him a little wave and then left, gently clos-ing the door behind her.

Despite having done nothing but half-sit for most of the past three days, the man was very tired. Fully sitting in this extraordinarily comfy armchair was exactly what he wanted. But he was deeply confused by his beautiful wife and their lovely home. He could see she was attrac-tive, and yet when she kissed him he felt nothing – and also guilty, as though he were betraying someone. Why was that? And why was there only one armchair? Did his wife sit over on the distant sofa? Why didn't they sit together? Or did she always sit on his lap? Wouldn't that be uncomfortable for her? Wouldn't it give him terrible pins and needles? Was he overthinking this?

He got up, hoping the movement would distract his mind from its odd worries. There was a television by the wall, and bookshelves beside it. He wondered what kind of books he read.

Zhoot!

There was a sound, muffled yet high-pitched. Was it the TV? It sat there, blank and aimless. He looked around. Oh. He had managed to damage the armchair. On the back cushion, right where he had been sitting, there was a neat round hole. How could he possibly have done that? Did he have a spike or something on the back of his shirt? He put his hand up to check. Of course not. Who has spiked shirts? And then he saw, on the glass of the window, an identical neat round hole.

Even as the next *zhoot!* came, he was no longer standing there idly wondering about spiked shirts and armchairs, but lying flat on the floor, eyes darting and limbs braced. His breathing was slow and controlled, his mind clear. He was being shot at, and he seemed to be dealing with it much better than he had dealt with the apparent normality that had preceded it.

Above him, exactly where he had been standing, there was another neat round hole in the window pane. Then the window pane shattered, and a second later the door slammed open. His wife stood framed in the doorway and it was suddenly terrifyingly clear that what she felt most comfortable in was a silenced assault rifle. It was aimed at the leather armchair.

She saw him on the floor, changed her stance and fired, but his foot had already reached out, without a thought passing through his mind, and kicked the edge of the door, sending it flying at her.

'Sorry,' he called, automatically – appalled that his foot had tried to smash a door into a woman's face.

The woman – his wife – parried the door with her gun, and he was up, barging the door out of the way, taking advantage of her parrying movement, continuing it, his hands on the gun, wrenching it from her grasp, then swinging back, sending her flying into the armchair.

'Excuse me, I am sorry,' he said, unable to help himself.

He slammed the living-room door, ran down the hallway, and grabbed the door to the flat, holding the assault rifle in one hand, checking instinctively that there was a round in the firing chamber. Then he was out, slamming the door behind him, and racing down the echoing stairwell.

Above and behind him, he heard the flat's door open and the sound of footsteps racing down the stairs. Two people, he thought: his wife and a well built man. He had no idea how he knew that.

The stairs were inconveniently huge, the bannisters ornate. There was no way to jump or swing himself over, down to the next flight. He sensed he had a definite top speed for running down stairs, and putting more effort in would only make him trip up. There was no way to go faster – unless … He hopped up on to the bannister and slid down it, slipping over onto the next bannister when he reached the roundel at the bottom. The footsteps above him became more distant.

He reached the bottom of the stairs, running through the tiled hallway. In front of him were the huge carved doors. One of them was even open. He had made it! He gripped the assault rifle tighter and sprinted for the door, through it – and then he was flying backwards along the floor, the assault rifle skittering from his grasp like a startled cat. An elbow had caught him across the mouth. In the doorway, silhouetted against the golden glow of the street lamps outside, stood a square-jawed policeman. The officer reached into his holster, took out a silenced pistol, and strode forward, levelling the gun.

The man raised himself from the tiled floor. His assault rifle was ten feet away, well out of reach. His brain was calculating instinctively. How long did he have? The policeman was almost at his feet, aiming.

'Ahem.'

It was the sound of a stern throat being cleared. The door to the man's left opened, revealing a steely-faced old lady in a worn pink dressing gown.

'That goes completely not!' she said angrily. *'This corridor is not–'*

And then she saw the gun in the policeman's hand. He raised it to aim at her, but she had ducked inside with surprising speed.

In that tiny slice of time, the man scissored his legs, knocking the policeman off-balance so that his body seemed to expertly bowl his head into the wall.

'Oops, sorry,' said the man, wincing.

From the staircase the sound of footsteps grew louder. The man got to his feet. The assault rifle lay beside the bottom step. But the man's wife appeared on the landing, now holding a small silenced revolver. He could hear sirens in the distance.

Without thinking, without even meaning to, he grabbed the unconscious policeman's pistol and raced through the door. Outside, flashing police lights were visible from the large road at the end of the wide cobbled street.

'Halt!' someone shouted. *'Police!'*

Following an instinctive protocol for handling the situation, the man ran away as fast as he could, into the Berlin night.

6

That same late afternoon, six hundred miles away in London, a young woman was sitting on a number 46 bus to Hampstead, staring disconsolately out of the window. Her name was Piper Palgrave. Piper was an unusual name in England, but her mother was American and her father didn't mind her sounding like she might be an oil rig, so there it was: Piper.

At first, Piper didn't pay any attention to the strange man in the over-sized overcoat who came and sat beside her. This was partly because London is full of strange men, but mostly because she was so deeply distracted by how awful she felt.

Piper had just emerged from her first therapy session – a thing she had spent the past two years putting off. That was how long her boyfriend had been missing. He was a freelance illustrator, and one morning he had set off for a meeting about possibly drawing some dogs, and had never returned.

When he'd first disappeared, she had poured all her worry and alarm into the search for him. Back then, she'd had help. But soon the authorities had given up, and gradually everyone else – without saying so – had come round to the view that he'd just … left her. She was sure this wasn't true, but it was such a worrying thought that it constantly haunted the margins of her mind. Her lonely attempts to track him down had become increasingly unrealistic and unhinged, mostly consisting of Googling ever more obscure variations on "missing thin man with brown hair who often looks surprised". Eventually she'd had to accept that she needed psychological help.

But now it turned out that the help was at least as distressing as the thing she needed help with. It consisted of sitting in a converted garage in Kentish Town, confessing her darkest thoughts to a man named Gordon who steepled his fingers and said a platitude precisely once every five minutes, in a voice of annoyingly practised smug calm, until she collapsed in a terrifying fit of uncontrolled crying and weird hysterical laughter and then got up and walked out.

That was why she was now sitting on the number 46 bus with her face all red and swollen and covered in mascara. She looked so bad that the teenage boys at the bus stop hadn't even mocked her. She felt emptied out, as though she'd been gutted by flames and extinguished by the fire brigade, leaving her a soot-blackened wreck.

From her seat on the stationary, shaking bus, Piper stared out at the world, blankly, registering it all without really taking it in. There was a scattering of lumpy backs. A man was propped up by the luggage area. Silly cars were parked in the street. A poster was telling her to be thin. Some more teenage boys, too cool to talk to each other, were listening to headphones. A big flag of newspaper was open in the seat in front of her. By the doors, a woman wrestled with a pushchair while her small daughter stood beside her saying 'Mummy' over and over again, with exactly the same intonation each time. And then, as the bus moved off, the strange man in the oversized coat turned to her.

'We may have some news about Jonathon Fairfax,' he said, his tone dispassionate, like a doctor's.

The strange man from the bus had wanted to come to Piper's house, but she didn't want that because, after all, he was a strange man from the bus.

Instead, they had come to a very small cafe where the plastic table-cloths were held on by metal clips and an icy wind blew in every time anyone opened the door. It was far from being the nicest cafe in Hampstead, but Piper didn't want to ruin any of the others by having a traumatic conversation in it.

The strange man from the bus sat opposite Piper, sheltering behind a large squeezy ketchup bottle and a laminated menu. He was a glorious confection of unimpressive attributes: a sparse and bristly grey moustache through which his upper lip could be plainly seen, greying hair brushed forward as though he wanted it to look like a wig, large glasses and a little nose, firm and hooked, which made an owl of him. To this he added shortness, a wobbly clump of fat that he carried between his chin and neck, as though he were afraid he might drop it, and an oversized overcoat of a shiny grey material, which could have been either polyester or finest cashmere.

'What will you have, my dear?' he asked her, blinking, his glasses magnifying a little quivering of the skin beneath one eye.

'A hot chocolate,' she said, forcing herself not to add, 'please'.

He nodded jerkily, as though he had only just caught the clump of fat under his chin in time.

'Do they come to us?' he asked.

'I think we go to the counter.'

The cafe was so small that just standing up took you most of the way to the counter. With difficulty, the strange little man squeezed himself around two sides of the table and then sandwiched himself between the back of Piper's chair and the glass counter.

'What'll it be, love?' asked the woman behind the counter, in that cheerful and carefree way you get when your cafe will make exactly the same amount of money every day, no matter what you do to your food, drink or customers.

'I should like a hot chocolate, a cup of tea and a small bottle of Perrier,' he said.

'Perry A? What's that?'

'A sparkling mineral water.'

'Fizzy?'

'Yes.'

'Alright, love. Sit down. I'll pass it over when it's ready.'

He paid her, laboriously squeezed himself around the table again, and resumed his seat.

'I appreciate that this is a delicate situation,' he said, 'and that it may be difficult to hear about someone who has been missing for so long.'

Piper said nothing. There was so much going on inside her that she was having to let her emotions fight it out among themselves down below, leaving her with an odd surface calm. Now, approaching from the distance, was an awful hope, and a kind of anger that went with it – an anger at what had happened and at the idea of going though yet another cycle of dreaming and disappointment.

The little man moved the vinegar bottle on the table, as though he were defending his bishop at chess.

'I would not like to raise your hopes too high,' he continued, 'and I can tell you very little – I know very little. But will you–'

'Hot chocolate?'

The woman behind the counter was calling to them. Piper stood and collected a hot chocolate, a tea, and a bottle of lemonade.

She sat down and sipped at her scalding hot chocolate, which burned the roof of her mouth. She gave no sign that this had happened, but ran her tongue over the skin there, which had already turned to rubbery ribbons.

'Who are you?' she asked.

'I am attached to Her Majesty's Foreign and Commonwealth Office. My name is Michaels.'

'Just Michaels?'

'Michaels, yes. That will suffice.'

'And what do you want me to do?'

'Firstly, has Mr Fairfax been in touch with you, recently?'

'No,' she said. The question would have made her cry, if she hadn't already exhausted her supply of tears thanks to her visit to her totally useless and distressing therapist.

Michaels watched her carefully, the skin beneath his eye quivering again, and she watched him back.

'You knew him well,' he said, 'that is, you *know* him well. It would be very helpful to have some insights into how he might behave in certain situations, in order to assist him.' He stirred his tea and looked regretfully at the lemonade. 'As I was saying, will you help us?'

7

After a couple of streets, the man – who was now seriously doubting whether he really was an import-export specialist called Jonathan Forbes – wiped the gun carefully with his tie and threw it into a bin outside a luxury hat shop. The instinct that compelled him to do this had come from a different part of him than the one which made him kick doors into women's faces and smash policemen's heads against walls. He now felt terribly guilty about both those things.

He ran on, down streets lined with grand old buildings, past shops selling luxury dog accessories and important ties, until he reached a wider road. The sound of sirens was gone, so he switched to walking, hands in pockets against the cold, moving quickly so he wouldn't lose too much body heat. Crossing the wide road, he moved into narrower streets of newer buildings.

All his instincts seemed to have gone quiet. Where was he going? Somewhere up ahead, he thought, was the urban forest they had passed, and that was probably as good a destination as any. Urban forests? Was that normal? He had no idea.

He had very little idea about anything. Just as he'd been getting used to being a stroke patient, he'd been wrenched away and had to adjust quickly to being a married import-export specialist. Now who was he? A man people wanted to kill. He couldn't help feeling offended by this.

Perhaps they had a good reason. Perhaps apologetically assaulting people was a habit of his. He might be a criminal, a murderer even.

The urban forest was just across the road now, but he had changed his mind about it. There might be some lonely dog walkers whom he couldn't help slaying. Instead, he walked in the other direction, past a colossal gold library. Then he came to a road thick with speeding cars, and walked along the dark, deserted and dilapidated pavement that ran beside it.

As he walked, he began to doubt that he was a murderer. He had, after all, just passed up several chances to kill people who were vigorously trying to kill him. So why else might they have wanted him dead? And who were they anyway? They seemed to be a team, in league with the police. They had somehow known he was in hospital and that he had lost his memory. The more he thought about it, the less likely it seemed that Amy really was his wife.

He passed the building with a plane on its roof, which turned out to be a technology museum. He thought about looking up the opening hours, so he could visit the next day, and then remembered that he would need to spend tomorrow evading assassins and police. He would probably need to spend all his tomorrows doing that. He was struggling to hold on to the reality of being on the run. Perhaps that wasn't surprising: almost his whole remembered life to this point had been spent lying in bed, fantasising about eating airline ham. Dealing with the threat of assassins didn't fit in with that at all.

By this time, he had reached a serene canal, lined with willows. There was an unlit path running along it, again deserted. He decided that it didn't make much sense to be afraid of the dark now, and he needed some serenity, so he walked, shivering, beside the water. Perhaps tomorrow he should go back to the hospital, tell them what had happened – and inevitably what a pen was – and see what they recommended. But it must have been them who had tipped off the assassins, mustn't it? He was so confused. He needed to sit somewhere warm and gather his thoughts.

For a while, his path was lit only by the moon. Then old-fashioned lampposts appeared ahead, casting a warm, golden light. They seemed to be welcoming him, beckoning him on. Now there were cosy flats on either side, then a beautiful old bridge, and restaurants. Hungry and tired, he checked his pockets and found he had just six euros fifty-seven cents in change, and a small bunch of keys.

He wandered on, moving away from the canal, past little candlelit bars which he found he wanted to go in. But no, he needed to save his money for food, and work out how to get through the night without freezing to death. This was incontestably a sensible point.

And yet, after a while, he found he had stopped outside a brown-windowed bar called Travolta. It looked quiet and low-key, and he could probably just go in and warm up without anyone noticing. His hands were shaking, and a little voice somewhere at the back of his mind told him that this was a symptom of shock.

It occurred to him that he probably couldn't trust anyone who claimed to know him – especially anyone who claimed to be married to him. Which meant that, for him, strangers were by far the most trustworthy people. No one trying to hunt him down after his escape would just wait in a bar several miles away and hope he would go there, would they? So this bar full of strangers was probably the safest place for him.

He walked in, took a stool a little way from the nearest clump of people and found himself pointing at one of the taps and saying, *'I'd have gladly a beer, please.'*

'Sure thing,' said the woman behind the bar in an American accent. This threw the man into panic and confusion. After all, the last woman who'd spoken to him with an American accent had tried to kill him.

'You okay?' she asked, looking at him with concern.

'I … I just didn't expect you to be American,' he said. And then, trying to cover his confusion, added, 'Is my German that bad?'

'Oh, I don't speak German,' she said cheerfully. 'Most people here speak English, or I just go by what they point at.'

The man smiled, again covering his confusion.

'So, you here on business?' she asked. Her teeth were large and she smiled often, so that she seemed always to be in the act of adjusting her lips.

'Why do you ask?' he said, still suspicious.

'Hey, relax. Just making conversation. You look like a businessman – dress shirt, pressed slacks. Two-fifty.'

'What?'

'Two euro fifty cents.'

'Oh, yes. I'm buying a beer, aren't I?'

'You sure you're okay?' she asked, looking at him sympathetically. She had caramel-coloured skin, curly black hair, and a mobile, expressive sort of face – very different from those of all the people who had tried to kill him.

'Yes. Probably. I think. Is there any food?'

'We've got bretzels, if you call them food.'

'What are they?'

She showed him some solid-looking twists of dark, hardened dough about the size of a small hat. They weren't appetising but he was hungry, so he took one.

'So, three-fifty, with the bretzel.'

He handed over the money.

As she gave him his change she said, 'So, am I right?'

'I hate to say "what?" again,' he said. 'But, what?'

'You a businessman?'

'Ah, er, yes, well …' He took a gulp of beer. It was cold and clean, tracing a passage down his throat and into his stomach, which seemed to have a direct line to the centre of his brain, piping up a supply of instant happiness and relief. 'Sort of,' he concluded.

'Sort of?'

'Um, I …' He took another gulp. 'Oh, fuck it. I've got no idea who I am.'

'What you mean like, identity crisis? Am I a businessman or, I don't know, like a shamanic drummer or something?'

'No, I mean I don't know what my name is, where I live, what I do, and whether I have any friends or family.'

'Seriously?' she said, giving him a sceptical look.

'Er, yes. Seriously.'

'Like the guy in that movie?'

'Possibly,' he said, not knowing what she was talking about.

'You know, the movie with that actor who's kind of hot but also kind of ugly? Often takes roles where he just wears an undershirt?'

The man smiled helplessly at her.

'Hey, Dave?' she said. 'Who's the actor in the undershirt from that movie about the guy who can't remember who he is?'

'What?' said Dave, who was shortish, fattish and English, with hair that stuck up like a shaving brush. 'Which one? There's tons of films like that.'

'Never mind,' she said. 'It'll come back to me.'

The man nodded.

'So how does that work?' she asked.

'What do you mean?'

'I don't know. Like, how long have you had this no-memory thing?'

'I was found in a bin two days ago.'

'Like a trashcan?'

'Yes, they found me when they emptied me into a bin lorry – I mean, a trash truck. Is that what Americans call it?'

'Is it? I've been here like three years. I forget. Garbage truck! That's what we say. So, at least you know you're British.'

'I think I am,' said the man. 'I have English legs.'

'Say "cuppa tea,"' she instructed him.

'Cup of tea?'

'Close enough. You ain't no Dick Van Dyke, but close enough. Anyhow, you don't look like you were in a garbage truck.'

'The hospital washed my clothes for me, but there are still a couple of stains.' The man raised his elbow to show her a yellowish mark.

'You need Frosch. Gets stains right out.'

The man decided not to follow up this tip, since the slight yellow stain on his elbow was not his most urgent problem. He took another gulp of beer.

'So,' she said, 'the hospital just let you out and you don't know who you are?'

He nodded. He considered telling her about the fake wife and the assassination attempt involving the police, but decided not to. After all, he was suddenly not entirely sure he accepted that those things had happened, and he was an eye witness.

'But you got *something*, right? An address, money, maybe some ID?'

'Um, no, not really. I've got three euros seven cents, half a bretzel and a set of keys.'

'No jacket?'

'No. Maybe that's where I left my wallet.'

'Nothing else?'

'Er, oh! A handkerchief.' He pulled out his handkerchief, also hospital-laundered and subtly stained.

'And they seriously just let you out to fend for yourself?'

'I sort of let myself out.'

'You need to go back there. Seriously.'

'It's a bit complicated.'

'What, insurance or something?'

He gratefully grabbed the excuse. 'Yes, that's it.'

'Oh my god, you poor guy.'

'It's all right.'

'So what are you going to do?'

'I don't know. Wait for my memory to come back? I don't know. That's why I thought I'd come in from the cold, and then I couldn't not have a beer.'

The woman broke off her sympathetic smile to rearrange her lips before giving a welcoming smile to someone else who wanted a beer. The man took another sip of his own, which was right up there with yesterday's lunch as the best thing that had ever happened to him. The more he heard himself talk, the less he thought he was a murderer and the more he suspected he was way out of his depth.

'So what's it like, having amnesia?' asked the woman, after she'd finished serving the customer.

'I don't really know. I haven't got anything to compare it with. Except that I sometimes notice that I expect things to be different than they are, or sometimes things seem sort of familiar.'

'So, how do you expect things to be?'

'Um, well, I expect everyone to not be German, so I can't have been here all that long.'

'I've been here three years and I also expect everyone to not be German. This is Berlin, like capital of Germany, but literally *no one* here is German. Like I said, I don't even speak the language.'

'Oh. Right,' he said.

'But you do speak the language,' she said.

'Some of them think I do. I think I do. So maybe I have been here a long time.'

'Maybe. And you said like some things are familiar, right? What's familiar?'

'Just little things. When you wanted me to say "cup of tea," that felt familiar.'

'That just means you've been around Americans. We're, like, obsessed with hearing you guys say "cuppa tea."'

'Cup of tea?'

'You don't do it right. I mean, I can hear you're British, but I really want the full' – she stuck out her elbows and did an odd sort of lurching dance as she said it – '"cuppa tea!"'

'You want me to be a pirate?' he asked.

She laughed. 'No! Is that what I sound like? No, I want *this.*' And she did the 'cuppa tea' dance again.

He looked around to make sure no one was looking, and then he tried to copy her. She shrieked with laughter, staggered backwards and then had to use the beer pump to support her while she finished laughing.

'That ... is the dumbest thing I ever saw. You are, like, an *idiot.*'

'But I just did what you did.'

'*That* was not what I did.'

They each did another couple of rounds of *cuppa tea*s, with the elbows, collapsing and having to wipe tears from their eyes.

'You want another beer?' she asked. 'It's on the house.'

'Oh, thanks very much.'

She poured it and set it before him. This was definitely not how he'd expected the aftermath of his first assassination attempt to be.

'Prost!' she said, raising a smaller beer of her own. He said 'Prost!' too and they clinked glasses.

'You have to make eye contact when you clink the glasses here. Otherwise it means seven years' bad sex – it's a German superstition. They get mad if you don't do it.'

'Oh, sorry,' he said, and did it properly this time.

'That's better.'

'Cockney,' he said.

'What?'

'That's what the "cuppa tea" thing is. It's cockney.'

'Right. Like I said, Dick Van Dyke.'

'No, I mean, I remember that.'

'Oh! *Right*. So has your memory come back?'

'No. Just this word "cockney", and then a load of pictures and associations. People in those black suits with all the silver buttons on them. And jellied eels. And up the apples and pears.'

'Okay. So, I am not going to get sidetracked into asking about what sound like rodeo suits. You said there are pictures in your head. Are you in any of those pictures?'

He thought about it. 'No,' he said sadly. 'I've still got no memories of doing anything before I woke up two days ago. Maybe the cockney thing wasn't a breakthrough at all. Probably I'd never forgotten about cockneys.'

And all of a sudden he felt overpoweringly tired, and very sad. It seemed like managing not to cry in the middle of this bar was the limit of what he could achieve. And again he desperately missed someone but didn't know who.

'Hey, Mister,' she said, 'it's okay. You wanna sleep on my couch tonight? I live right around the corner. I'm Karen, by the way.'

8

RRURRP-RRURRP RRURRP-RU–

Elsewhere in Berlin, a telephone rang in an underground room with glass walls and an open door. Franklin Sterling, sitting at the desk outside, overheard half the call.

'This is Channon.'

Channon had a good voice: dry, matter-of-fact, like a noble cowboy on an old TV show.

'Michaels,' said Channon. 'Hi …

… You made contact? Great …

… So, has she heard from him? …

… I see. You believe that? …

… She could be upset over anything …

… Tell her green tea and meditation work better …

… You are? Okay, well, the most important thing is to get the water temperature right …

… No, that ruins it. You want it around a hundred eighty degrees, which is what in centigrade? Eighty? …

… You do? I thought you guys had– …

… I guess so. Well a hundred eighty then. Listen, could you guys keep in contact with her? We may need to bring her over here …

… Thanks. Yeah, send it on to me. Oh, and I'd prefer it if …

… Exactly. It's pretty sensitive. People might misinterpret what's going on here …

… No …

… Two days. He missed a scheduled check-in and didn't show up to his regular assignment. With these assassinations, I worry that …

… A little on the nose, but yeah.'

Another telephone began to ring.

'Listen, Michaels, I have to go. Remember, one-eighty degrees. We'll stay in touch, okay?'

Friday

9

When the man woke the next morning he decided not to tell his body about it. He carried on lying motionless on the slightly-too-short sofa, his breathing unchanged, hoping to fool himself into thinking he'd never woken up. He waited for the drift back to unconsciousness, the only place where everything is always fine.

But as he lay, he became aware of a hushed argument. If it had been louder he might have been able to ignore it, but no one can resist listening to a quiet quarrel.

A muffled male voice with an unplaceable accent was saying, '… home and find once more on our couch some random fuckhead.'

Karen's voice said something that didn't make it through the wall.

'And why this has to be your problem?' said the male voice. 'He has lost his coat and his …' And then it dipped too low to hear, before ending, '… can stay here? No.'

The man moved, just fractionally, and every single muscle in his body reported pain. It was as though, at a departmental meeting of his limbs, someone had started a rumour that there was a budget for aches.

Again, Karen's reply was lost.

'Is not *your* bar,' said the male voice. 'Is only bar. Why I am only one who …' And then it dipped too low, sounding like, 'my-do-mem-bem-bing.'

Karen said something impatient-sounding.

The male voice replied, 'I say only I want to live in my apartment where I do not fall over a fuckhead each night when I come home. I am–'

And now unmistakably a putdown from Karen.

'No, *you* are idiot,' countered the male voice. 'This man, he has not even lost his memory. I put hundred euro on this.'

The man pulled the warm sleeping bag a little tighter around his face. Again, several of his limbs put in written applications for ache funding.

'For what I want talk to him?' said the male voice. 'I want only my apartment.'

Karen said something short.

'In this case maybe I find other apartment.'

Karen said something disbelieving.

'I go to work. Work. When I am back, he is gone.'

A door opened and the man, taking himself by surprise, instinctively sprang from the sofa and stood in what he assumed was a martial arts pose: knees slightly bent, one hand slightly further from his body than the other. He was wearing only a pair of hospital-laundered boxer shorts and some socks.

In the doorway stood the owner of the male voice: a jumble of spiky hair and aggressive beard, wearing a vest and an incongruous turquoise ski jacket.

'Um, sorry,' said the man who had no idea who he was, trying to stand more normally.

The aggressively bearded one looked at the man, sighed, shook his head, got a packed lunch from the fridge, and walked out of the flat's front door, slamming it behind him.

By the time Karen appeared, hair wayward and eyes red, the man had put on his shirt and trousers, and washed his face. He was still receiving regular reports of new aches and he felt terribly tired.

Karen's smile communicated cheerful friendliness and that all was well, but it was contradicted by her eyes and the rest of her face.

'Hey, Mister,' she said. 'How'd you sleep?'

He had slept like a man who'd recently woken up in a bin, been kept awake by a hospital, almost been assassinated by his wife, walked several miles and then drunk four beers on an empty stomach. Which is to say, oddly. He felt exhausted.

'Fine, thanks,' he said. 'How about you?'

'Good!' she said brightly. 'You want coffee?'

'I should go,' he said. 'I ought to … um.'

'Walk the freezing streets in just a dress shirt because you don't know who you are or where you live? I get why you'd be in a hurry to do that.'

'Well, when you put it like that, could I have a coffee, please?'

He sagged into a chair at the little round table by the window. And then he tensed, because it hurt when he sagged. Meanwhile Karen began some complex ministrations to an old beige coffee machine.

'So, I guess you heard me and Boris fighting?' she said over her shoulder.

'No,' said the man, but Karen looked around and he instantly reversed his answer for the sake of plausibility. 'Yes.'

She sighed. 'Don't worry about it. We're going through some stuff. Hey, you want a bagel that's maybe a little too old?'

'Yes. Yes please,' he said immediately.

'Okay, I guess someone's hungry.'

'Oh, er, that's me. I'm hungry.'

They ate old bagels with peanut butter and drank coffee from the beige machine. The man began to feel a bit better.

He looked at Karen chewing her old bagel, and noticed that sometimes, when she wasn't talking or reacting, her face would briefly lose all expression, leaving her looking slightly sad, lost and childlike. But then a moment later, she would come back to life – eyes widening, cheeks rounding in a smile as she started talking again.

'Okay,' said Karen, doing it again, 'so what are we working with here? Any new memories overnight?'

He shook his head. 'No, nothing since I woke up three days ago – apart from the existence of cockneys.'

'So what do you remember from when you woke up three days ago? I was thinking: that place where you woke up, wherever it is, is really the only thing that connects you to your old life – your real life. I guess when you arrived there you knew who you were. Do you know where it was? Remember anything about it?'

'I remember lying on a really uncomfortable street made of little square stones, and a man was holding my nose. I asked him not to, and then he asked if I wanted some fingers, which was weird. And then I saw the bin lorry, by which I mean the garbage or trash truck, and the binmen were all correcting each other's English. And there was a big building on one side and … a big building on the other side. Was one yellow and one white? Oh, and there was something spray-painted on a wall: a big A in a circle.'

'Okay, this is gold. Case closed.'

'Oh, really?'

'No, I'm being sarcastic. Berlin's full of cobbled streets, big kinda-yellow buildings and graffiti. What else do you remember?'

'You don't think the big A will help us?'

'It's the anarchist symbol. Try finding a building in Berlin that doesn't have one, or a big "Fuck Nazis" painted on it – which I can't help thinking is just a little too late.'

'Oh. There was an astronaut painted on a building nearby. How many of those are there?'

She stopped and looked at him. 'Seriously?' she said.

'What?'

'That's a famous piece of street art – it's up around Skalitzer. It's a huge hand-painted picture of a spaceman. How many did you think there would be?'

'I don't know.'

'Okay, well this is major. This helps. You sure there's nothing else that you're not mentioning? Like, did someone maybe give you a set of detailed maps and the exact address?'

He shook his head.

'Sorry,' she said, 'I'm a little cranky this morning. This is basically great news.'

10

Sterling paused outside the glass-walled office, then knocked quietly and walked in. Channon was sitting on his high-backed leather swivel chair in the lotus position, eyes closed, craggy face unmoving. Sterling put the tea quietly on the desk and was just turning to leave when Channon's eyes snapped open.

'How hot was the water?' said Channon.

'One-eighty degrees, sir,' said Sterling. He pulled the cheap thermometer from his pocket, as though it might back up his statement.

'The others all boil it,' said Channon. 'They think I won't notice, but I do.'

'I … yes, sir.'

'Sterling, right?'

'Right, sir.'

'This your first week with us?'

'I've been here a little over a month, sir.'

'A month? Don't ever get old, Sterling. At a certain point, time accelerates to light speed and you have to cling on by your fingernails.'

'I hope I don't take your advice there, sir. About not getting old, I mean.' Sterling grinned and smoothed the front of his shirt.

Channon looked at him for a moment. You never quite knew what Channon was thinking or feeling, because his face moved much less than other people's. This was a definite advantage in their business, though surprisingly few of them had it. There was often a hint of a smile at the corners of his mouth, but that didn't necessarily mean he was going to be nice.

Channon sighed. 'You're right, son. I mean, life and death is all one, right? But you may as well stick around if you have the option. Easier to get stuff done when you're alive.'

Sterling wasn't sure whether or not to laugh at this, so he did a sort of rueful half-smile, to cover all bases.

Channon took a sip of tea, then shook out his steel-grey ponytail and retied it. There weren't too many ponytails, sandals and linen shirts in the Agency, but the older covert-ops guys like Channon often cultivated their eccentricities.

'Newman's sat-phone turned back on?' asked Channon.

'No, sir. We'll be notified if it does.'

'I don't trust these automated systems. Check for me, will you?'

Sterling went and checked, then returned to tell Channon that the phone hadn't turned back on.

'Okay,' said Channon. 'But while you're in the office, you check every half-hour or so, will you?'

'Sir.'

'And no one's been to the apartment?'

'No, sir.'

'I just don't understand it. There's something off.'

11

They emerged from Karen's building and the man looked around, totally disoriented. He was wearing Boris's spare incongruous ski jacket, and it smelled of aggressive beards.

Karen's building was pale and grey, six storeys high, with many charming original features that had been smashed off and painted over. It stood in a street crowded full of rusty bikes, ancient boxy scooters and dilapidated vans with people living in them. On the opposite side of the road was a wall painted in lurid patterns that made the man's head swim.

'You okay, Mister?' said Karen.

The man nodded, tired just from the effort of perceiving Karen's street.

'The astronaut's this way,' she said, pointing. 'Just down Reichenberger.'

They walked around the corner, into a street even more perceptually exhausting than Karen's. It was wide and straight, flanked by tall, bare-branched trees, and every inch of every surface was covered in intricate, busy, overlapping layers of posters, graffiti, art and minor vandalism. There was a sinuous rearing dragon painted on the wall beside them, following them along the street until it terminated in a poster saying, incomprehensibly, 'Lagwago'. Over it was painted a large drippy graffiti tag that looked like it said 'Zwang'. And partly over the graffiti were pasted five identical new posters about an anti-war march. Then he realised that beneath all this was a shop, so covered by stuff that it was impossible to tell its name, what it sold, or whether it was open. The whole street was like a huge exercise book doodled over by a giant bored child.

The people around him seemed immune to all this. A woman in a headscarf pulled a shopping trolley, a man with a big white moustache slouched smoking by a lamp post, an ill-looking couple in black leather jackets slumped along, and all around them trudged anoraks, rucksacks, headscarves, cigarettes. It was a vast, swirling kaleidoscope of hallucinatory ordinariness.

'Hey, what's the matter?' asked Karen.

'Does this street not make your head feel like it's going to explode?' he asked.

She looked around and laughed. 'No,' she said. 'But I guess maybe it kind of did when I first came to Berlin. You'll get used to it. Or your head will explode. One or the other.'

They walked on for another ten minutes, past anarchist picture-frame-making collectives and Turkish bakeries. At a junction, just across from an empty lot, Karen stopped, looking up the road.

'There it is,' she said, pointing. 'I thought it was further on. Is that the astronaut you saw?'

It was. Painted on the side of a building, the astronaut loomed over what he had remembered as a bridge, but which was actually an elevated grey metal train track running above the road that crossed this one. It was the view he had glimpsed three days ago, on that first morning of his life.

'This is the street,' he said.

'That's awesome!' said Karen. 'Now we just have to find your building ...'

'It's that one,' he said, pointing to a big yellow block of flats across the street. Painted on the side was a six-foot-tall red A with a ring around it.

'Okay,' said Karen, approvingly. 'That is a fucking unbelievably massive anarchist symbol.'

They crossed over the road.

'But where are the bins?' he asked, looking at the pavement where they had stood.

'Through there,' she said, pointing into the yellow building's courtyard at a cluster of huge metal bins on wheels. 'This is easy.'

They wandered through a wide passageway, emerging into a concrete courtyard. The bins were corralled together in a storage area against one wall. All around loomed balconies stuffed with furniture, drying racks, bikes and old microwave ovens.

'And hey, wait a minute,' she said. 'Is that a jacket and wallet I see underneath that trashcan?'

'What?' he said. 'Where?'

'Just kidding. Trying to lighten the mood here.'

He got down on his hands and knees anyway, trying to see under the bins. There was nothing there but some rubbish.

'Sorry,' he said, getting up. 'It's just weird returning to the scene of my ... well, my birth. And I suppose this is where the old me died.'

'Hey, did you get the memo about lightening the mood? You're going to get your memory back, Mister. And this could be where you live.'

'What?' said the man, surprised.

'What do you mean, "What?"'

'It's just, I didn't think of that, of living here.'

'Why did you think we were coming here?'

'Just to see if it set off any memories, or if I had left a wallet here or something.' He glanced longingly at the ground around the bins.

'Mister, you've got two leads: the astronaut and a set of keys. We followed the first lead to the spot where you woke up. So now we use the second lead. Those keys are probably for your apartment. Now, if you could try every door in the city, you'd for sure find your apartment–'

'If it's in Berlin.'

'Right. But this is the thing. Me, if all I've got is a set of keys, I am trying every fucking door in this city. And of all the places to start, this is the most likely.'

'You're right. You're right. I'm just embarrassed in case people think …'

'What? In case people think you're a nutjob with no name, who only owns a set of keys and some pants, who's sleeping on the couch of a chick whose bar he wandered into, at dire cost to the only decent long-term relationship she's ever managed to have? Yeah, that would be awful.'

'You're right,' he said. 'I'll do every building on this street.'

He took out the keys, and they left the courtyard and walked around and up a short flight of steps to the building's main entrance. He selected the largest key, took a deep breath, glanced at Karen, and tried it in the lock.

It didn't fit.

He tried the second-largest key, which slotted firmly and satisfyingly into the lock.

It wouldn't turn.

He tried the smallest key, which was obviously wrong in every way.

'Okay,' he said. 'I mean, it was never going to be the first building we tried.'

'You know, you do have one other lead,' said Karen.

'What's that?'

'The hospital,' she said.

He immediately tried the biggest key again.

'I know you've got this problem with insurance,' she said, 'but I can ask my friend Pola about–'

Click.

He had tried the second key again, this time with a bit of desperate wiggling, and the building's front door was now open.

He turned to her, smiling hugely. She looked shocked, then smiled too.

Inside was a hallway with an old tiled floor and a set of metal letterboxes bolted to one dingy yellow wall. At the far end was a huge staircase with a window that admitted a tired grey light. It smelled of cigarettes, cleaning products and perhaps rabbits. The man stepped inside and Karen followed.

'I can't believe this has happened,' he said. 'Thank you.'

'No probs. Now you've just got to try all three keys in every single apartment door in this building.'

'Or I could just try the small key in all these letterboxes. Then I'll know what number it is.'

'Hey, check out the big brains on the guy with no name.'

He moved to the first letterbox. 'Oh, wait,' he said. 'There's no number on it, only a name.'

'That's how they do it here. It's fine – there'll be a name on every apartment door too. It just means you'll find out your name before your address.'

'Okay,' he said uncertainly.

He wasn't sure he wanted to find out his name from a piece of grey metal bolted to a wall. Nonetheless, he began with the top-left letterbox. His smallest key fitted in the lock, but wouldn't turn. This was a relief, because the nameplate said 'Schittekatter-Splettstoesser'.

'You know, you probably have a non-German name. You could just try those. Here's Cavendish.'

Was he a Cavendish? He didn't feel like it. He tried the key and found it wouldn't turn.

'Or Newman? Or Beecham?'

He tried 'Newman', and the key turned.

This was it. Inside the letterbox he found a letter from the German tax authorities. It was addressed to Adam Newman.

She looked over his shoulder. 'That's you? Adam Newman?'

'I don't know. I suppose so.'

'Does it feel familiar?'

'Sort of? A bit. Not really. No. Not at all.'

'That's okay, Adam. Let's go find your apartment. That may help.'

'Don't call me Adam – not yet. Maybe it's my flatmate's name. Or my landlord's. Or something.'

'Maybe it's your boyfriend's.'

He said nothing, but he found himself hoping he wasn't going to have to sleep with a man that night: they were so much less attractive than women. Karen was right though, when he unlocked the door, he could be walking into any kind of life. Could he handle it? He rapidly flashed through the possibilities. He could probably cope with being a postman, but a fishmonger would be more challenging, as would a priest. And what if he was something he didn't remotely understand, like an actuary? Then there were hobbies, which could also range from pretty doable, like stamp-collecting, all the way up to terrifying, like ventriloquism. He was far from sure he could deal with it.

They climbed the stairs slowly, looking at the nameplates by the doors on each floor. Every time, he felt a little rush of relief that this one wasn't Adam Newman. But then, eventually, on the top floor, there it was, neatly printed in capitals: 'NEWMAN, A'.

He stood there for a long moment. In a certain way, when he walked through that door, he would die. This person he had been these last three days, the only person he could remember being, this blank canvas with no memories, slowly discovering what he could do, this person would be gone. Right now he could be anyone, but once he walked through the door he would be narrowed down again to one particular person. And for that particular person, he, the man Karen called 'Mister', would be an accident, something to recover from, something to erase. He would be just a story to tell all his actuary friends after the puppet show.

'Hey, Mister. You okay?' said Karen.

He looked at her. 'I don't think I want to be a person,' he said.

She hugged him. 'It's okay. You'll still be you. You'll just find out a little more about who you were four days ago, that's all. I get it though.'

'I could just walk away. How many of the people we passed on the way here would want to be able to just leave their lives behind and be someone new?'

'Honestly? I don't know. Maybe a lot. I mean, maybe that's what I was trying to do by coming to Berlin: start over. Be a new person in a new country. And it's kind of great, that feeling of freedom. I mean, I know I don't exactly have the dream life: that weird apartment, Boris, working in a bar. But it's a hell of a lot easier than what I had in Minneapolis. And there's just this great feeling of freedom and peace here.'

'So maybe I should not go in?'

'Yeah, maybe. But, you know, one thing I've learned: most of your problems are inside of you. You can definitely go somewhere with cheaper rent and easier jobs – or where you have no name or memories – that could help. But the big stuff follows you around. Wherever I go, I'll be uncontrollably attracted to angry drummers. Wherever I go, I will not be able to make myself do a job that pays big money. I will be kind of lazy and I'll trust too much and give too much energy to helping people who'll never help me back. So.'

Her eyes were wet and she dabbed at them with the corner of her scarf. Her mouth trembled.

He hugged her hesitantly and said, 'I'll help you back. I promise.'

'Not you,' she said. 'That wasn't aimed at you.'

He stepped back.

'So,' she said. 'We going in or going home? Just so you know: I've run out of stale bagels.'

'In,' he said, and unlocked the door.

12

The strange man from the bus had given Piper a card, one-sided. In the corner was the Foreign and Commonwealth Office logo, and across the middle was a name, 'B. Michaels, PhD'.

Piper turned the card over and over in her hand, watching the name appear and disappear, as she sat on the sofa by the window. The dog's jaw rested on her lap, as though Cess were tired of carrying her giant tongue around the whole time, and the cat nestled on the window ledge beside her. This was as comfortable as she could hope to be, some part of her reassured by the animals, even as her brain vibrated in her head because of another night of broken sleep.

She was waiting for him.

When he arrived, announcing it with a quiet fumbling with the door knocker, the dog stood close by Piper's side, making the low rumbling noise that could mean so many things. She opened the door and there he stood, short and beaky, sweat on his forehead.

'Miss Palgrave,' he said. 'Good morning.'

'Hello ...' she said. She was used to calling people by their first name, but his card just said 'B'. '... Michaels,' she concluded. 'Come in.'

As Michaels stepped in, the dog made her ambiguous deep groaning noise. Michaels flinched and stepped back.

'Sorry,' said Piper. 'Don't mind Cess. That's her special noise which means everything. I think this time it means, "Hello".'

'Well,' said Michaels, inching around Cess, who was – despite what Piper had said – not at all pleased to meet him. Piper could tell by the set of her ears.

Piper showed him into the living room, where the cat was now sitting prim and stern on the back of the sofa, like a headmaster.

'Oh, and this is ... the cat,' said Piper.

'Quite,' said Michaels. 'What's her name?'

'His. This is Hastings Banda. Jonathon said the name came into his head as soon as he saw the cat for the first time. He thought it was the name of a jazz musician. But then we found out he was actually the first president of Malawi after independence, and – while he did some pretty good things – also ran a viciously repressive totalitarian regime.'

'And yet you kept the name?' said Michaels, making a friendly gesture that sent the cat sternly scurrying under the sofa.

'The problem is, the cat really *looks* like a Hastings Banda. It just suits him. Anyway, please sit down,' she said, indicating the sofa. 'Would you like a cup of tea?'

'That would be most kind,' said Michaels, taking off the large coat which was making him sweat. She took it from him and went to the kitchen, returning with the tray that always made her feel like an elderly servant in a period drama, but which was too useful to do without.

She set it down and poured tea for Michaels. With the sun on his face he looked even worse than he had the day before: paler, older, with beads of sweat in his moustache.

He sipped the tea, said, 'Thank you, my dear,' and took out a notebook and pencil.

'I need to ask you something first,' she said.

He looked at her, clearly perturbed, but said nothing.

And now that she had stated her intention, she suddenly found that there was no way of turning all the thoughts that tumbled around inside her head into a single coherent question.

'Is he all right?' was the closest she could manage.

'We don't know,' he said. 'We hope so.'

She nodded.

'Before we start,' he said, 'I must remind you that it's best at this stage not to tell anyone else.'

She nodded again.

'In fact, I must ask you to sign an affidavit to that effect. This is a … sensitive matter for all involved. I hope you don't mind this little formality.'

He held her gaze, and she said, 'Yes, fine.'

He pulled some folded papers from his jacket pocket and handed them to her, along with an old biro.

'This is the Official Secrets Act,' she said, after seeing the first page.

'Of course, my dear. There is also a waiver of liability.'

'What happens if I don't want to sign them?'

'If you don't *want* to sign them, or if you actually don't sign them?'

'Actually don't sign them?'

'In that case, I would regretfully have to terminate our interview.'

She was surprised to find little pinpricks of tears appearing in the corners of her eyes. She couldn't bear the thought of losing this connection to Jonathon.

'I thought you said it was a formality,' she said, signing both forms.

'Alas, like many formalities, it is obligatory. And rigidly enforced. I shall arrange for you to receive copies,' he said, refolding the papers and returning them to his jacket pocket. 'Now,' he said, 'shall we begin?'

She nodded again. He picked up his notebook and pencil.

'Mr Fairfax has had jobs,' he stated, and raised his eyebrows slightly. She nodded and he continued, 'Has he ever disappeared from one of those jobs without warning?'

'No, I don't think so,' she said.

He made her recount all the jobs Jonathon had ever had, or mentioned, and asked the same thing for each of them. She answered as best she could. Some strange things had happened to Jonathon, and once or twice they had stopped him getting to work.

Michaels summarised, 'So, without the intervention of outside forces, Jonathon has never simply failed to turn up for work, or gone elsewhere.'

'No,' she said, 'he's very conscientious. Or at least he feels guilty about everything, like I do. I don't know if that's the same thing. It makes us try to do what we've said we'll do though.'

'Forgive me if this seems intrusive, but has he ever suffered from a psychological illness?'

She laughed, then felt sad and looked at the dog, who looked sad back and again parked her nose on Piper's lap.

'He suffers from *something*. I don't know what it is exactly, except that the doctor can't really help. Neither can the dog. It sort of builds up in a wave, then breaks, and then he gradually gets better again. He said–' She stopped.

'Go on,' said Michaels.

'He said being with me helped. Made him better.'

Michaels nodded, looking uncomfortable. 'But did this – *something*, as you say – ever get in the way of work, or of daily life?'

'I think it made everything harder, like I've been finding everything harder since he's been missing: getting up, shopping, cleaning, seeing people, work. But I don't think it ever stopped him from doing something he said he would do.'

Michaels scribbled this down, taking such a long time about it that she felt he was writing it word for word.

He took a sip of tea and then said, 'Moving on, suppose Jonathon had a … shock or scare of some kind. What would he do?'

'I don't know. I don't know why he wouldn't phone me,' she said. And she was embarrassed to find that her lips were twitching and her eyes were wet.

'Suppose that were impossible,' said Michaels. 'Or suppose he thought that would endanger you. Then what would he do?'

'It depends where he is. The jungle? Adis Abababa? Penge?'

'It will be useful to think of a range of places. But let's begin with something fairly straightforward. A large European city, for example.'

'Is it Paris? He speaks a bit of French.'

'It's purely hypothetical, so yes, why not? Let's say Paris.'

'Well, he would trip over a bin or walk into a lamppost, that would be the first thing he'd want to get out of the way–'

'A joke,' said Michaels, noting it down carefully in his book.

'I think the first thing he would do is find somewhere he could go and pull himself together, think things through. In Paris I suppose he'd choose a cafe, if it was the daytime, or if it was evening he'd choose a bar that's as similar as possible to an English pub. Either way, it couldn't be too posh, or he'd worry about the waiters and wouldn't be able to relax. Relatively downmarket but not too horrible.'

'Not unlike our cafe yesterday, perhaps?'

'No, that would be way too horrible for him – too small. It would make him feel self-conscious. He'd want somewhere where he felt no one would notice or bother him. It wouldn't have worked of course, because people really often do end up talking to him. That's nearly always how bad things happen to him – and good ones, come to think of it.'

13

The man stepped into Adam Newman's flat and looked around.

He was standing in a small white hallway with a closed door at the end of it. On his left was an open doorway leading into a wooden-floored kitchen with new-looking units and a cooker on one wall. In the middle of the floor stood a large old table, with a coat draped over the back of one of the chairs. On the far side was a floor-to-ceiling window with a glass door, slightly ajar, letting out onto a balcony.

The man walked out onto the empty balcony. Down below was the courtyard they'd been in just a few minutes before. On the other side of it were blue, balcony-less flats, and behind them ran the street with the elevated train track. Toylike yellow trains clanked and beeped, while on the brick-paved roads below, the wheels of cars went *buba-bubabubabub*, children squealed in unseen playgrounds, and a siren needled in the distance.

'Adam?' said Karen.

He turned. She was standing in the doorway, holding a wallet and some kind of ID card.

'So you do remember your name?' she said.

'I think I'd have turned whatever name you said. I'm the only person here.'

'I found this wallet in that jacket – your jacket. This was in it.'

She came over, and he took the wallet. The card said 'Deutscher Bundestag' and had his photograph on it, along with the name Adam Newman.

'I guess that settles it,' she said. 'Mister is Adam Newman, and this is his apartment. Nice. Possibly a little clinical – just sayin' – but nice.'

He studied the card, trying to read the expression on Adam's face, on *his* face. It was perfectly blank, as though it had been poured into a face-shaped jelly mould and left to set. He took a look through the rest of the wallet, which was black leather and looked brand new. There was seventy-five euros in notes, and a single bank card.

'How come your wallet isn't full of crap?' asked Karen. 'You should see Boris's, it's like the size of a pony. I don't even know what he keeps in there – except not money.'

'I don't know,' he said. Was this who he was? A man with a neat wallet and a nice but clinical flat? A British man who somehow worked for the German parliament?

'Hey,' said Karen. 'Look down there.'

He followed her line of sight, down from the balcony, into the courtyard. There were a couple of trees, a bench, a straggle of bikes chained to metal racks, and the bins. In short, nothing of any interest.

'What?' he said.

'The trashcans, dummy – the *bins*. They're like right under the balcony.'

'Um, right,' he said. Bin placement seemed important to her. Was that unusual? Perhaps everyone had their own favourite place for communal bins. Maybe wars had been fought over it.

'Good,' he added, to be safe.

'You don't get it, do you? If that one there was just a little to the right, and someone left the lid open … Well, the rail on this balcony is not the highest. If you leaned out just a little too far, over you go – and land in the garbage. I think a trashcan saved your life.'

He looked. She was right.

Adam Newman was a clumsy idiot with a neat wallet who had toppled off his own balcony. He strongly suspected this was the truth.

'I'll just have a look around the rest of the flat,' he said.

'Good plan,' she said. 'I'll check your fridge.'

On the other side of the hallway there was a very small bathroom with a very new and luxurious shower in it. Next to that was a bedroom with a neatly made bed and two ties lying on it, as though he'd had difficulty choosing which boring anonymous tie he wanted to wear. At the end of the hallway was a large living room containing a beige L-shaped sofa, an armchair, a TV, several minimalist metal lamps, and a desk and chair. On the desk was a laptop, beside it a shelf containing two books – *The German Constitution: an Introduction* and *Types of German Parliamentary Procedure* – as well as two CDs, both by Crowded House.

He went back into the kitchen, shaken.

'Hey, are you okay?' she said, for perhaps the twelfth time that morning.

'I don't know. I think Adam Newman might be really boring.'

'Well, I guess sometimes a bang on the head is what you need to get yourself back on track. Maybe I'll take a dive off of that balcony later.'

He tried to smile, but he couldn't.

'I have two Crowded House albums,' he said, 'and no other music.'

She closed the fridge door and looked at him seriously.

'Oh honey,' she said. 'I am so sorry.'

He slumped down at the kitchen table.

'Wait,' she said. 'That means you remember who Crowded House are, right?'

'No, not even that. I can just tell what they're like from the album covers.'

'Ooh,' she said, staring at the floor.

'And I've got an IBM laptop.'

'Hey, I'm making coffee. You want some?'

'Yes please.'

'And I'm gonna make something to eat. You look like you could use it. I feel like *I* could use it. And you have a *lot* of organic food in this refrigerator.'

'Food. That's a good idea.' He was starving, and still very tired.

The big thing that didn't make sense was the people who'd tried to kill him yesterday. It was so out of keeping with everything else that he'd almost decided he must have imagined it. It must be a side effect of whatever had made him lose his memory.

'There's something I haven't told you,' he said.

'You have a wife and several kids who you aren't supporting because you're the drummer in a small-time punk-pop band?'

'What? Why would …'

'Kidding. That's just what usually follows that line, in my experience. What were you going to say?'

He told her about what had happened yesterday, before he'd walked into her bar. After the first couple of sentences, she stopped making food and brought the coffees over, and they sat at the kitchen table.

When he'd finished, she said, 'Okay. That is wild.'

'It is, isn't it?'

'You know, this whole finding-the-apartment thing has worked out way better than I expected, but I think you need to go back to hospital. Honestly, don't worry about the health insurance. This is *Germany*, Mister, they *will* have some federal programme for dealing with amnesiacs. And it will be administered by heavy-smoking women in their fifties with dyed red hair who look at you like you're a fucking waste of space, and it will be *awesome*.'

'But it wasn't really the health insurance thing that made me not want to go back. That was just an excuse so I wouldn't have to tell you about my wife and her comfy assault rifle. The hospital must have colluded with the people who tried to kill me. How else could Amy have known where I was? How else could she have known I have amnesia? Their plan wouldn't have worked otherwise.'

'I don't know. Maybe they followed the ambulance? Maybe they knew which hospital you would go to. Maybe *they* dropped you in the trashcan and it's all part of their plan.'

'Wait a minute,' he said. 'What am I doing here? This is incredibly dangerous – I'm putting your life in danger. If they could find me in hospital, they'll know where I live. Won't they be watching this place? I haven't been thinking straight. I'm so tired and confused.'

She looked around the comically orderly kitchen. 'Well, like, nobody has abseiled through the window firing a machine gun yet, so I guess we're good. Oh, is that …?' She got up, went out onto the balcony and looked up, then came back in. 'No, thought I heard a grappling hook, but I guess it was just the wind.'

'You don't believe me, do you?'

'Mister, I don't know what to believe. But you *have* some kind of brain thing, so it's not like it's totally offensive for me to be thinking, "Maybe there wasn't a highly trained team of assassins trying to kill this guy."'

'So how did I get out of hospital?'

'Uh, you walked? Maybe? I mean, I don't see armed guards and razor wire around the hospitals here, so I think they're maybe not a major challenge to escape from.'

'But the memory's so vivid.'

Clack.

There was a sound from the direction of the hallway. They both froze. The man who was probably Adam Newman silently, carefully, moved his chair back from the table. He put his finger to his lips, and Karen raised her hands as if to say, *This is stupid but I'm going along with it for some reason.* Then he padded noiselessly towards the kitchen counter, towards the chef's knife with which Karen had been slicing organic courgettes.

The door opened.

14

Piper offered Michaels more tea and did some washing up while the kettle boiled. After a few moments, she heard the kitchen door open quietly behind her. He padded over, and she looked at him out of the corner of her eye, suddenly worrying about what he might be up to. She wouldn't have been entirely shocked to see him holding a gun. But instead it was a tea towel.

'Oh, there's no need,' she said.

'It's no trouble, my dear,' he replied, rubbing a saucer badly, the clump of fat under his jaw wobbling.

They stood there for a while, her washing things, him taking them from the rack and using the tea towel to spread the water over them more evenly.

After a while, his mobile phone rang. He put a plate under his arm and answered the call.

'Good morning, Michaels speaking.'

He listened, then said, 'Might I call you back, Ms Morden? I'm' – he glanced down – 'currently drying a plate.'

He clicked his phone off, put it back in his pocket, and resumed his drying. At length he said, 'This isn't our doing, you know.'

'What isn't whose doing?'

'This … situation, regarding your … regarding Jonathon. It's a mess, but not a *British* mess. Americans, you know.'

'How does Jonathon have anything to do with Americans?'

'He didn't tell you anything? Before he …'

'Disappeared? No.'

'It's an … unusual circumstance. I'll tell you what I can, though there's much I must leave out, you understand. The facts are murky, but there are two causes for optimism, reassurance even.'

'What are they?'

'The first is that the Americans have a tremendous amount of money. Simply unbelievable, for anyone from our side. It allows them to do things that would be impossible for anyone else. It's been something of a curse for them overall, but it may help in this case.'

'And the second?'

'They look after their own, or those they perceive as their own. "No man left behind" was always their motto – or at least has at times been among their mottoes.'

Piper washed a peeler, dried her hands and went over to the kettle.

'That's one of the least reassuring reassuring talks I've ever had,' she said. 'How could the Americans possibly come to see Jonathon as one of their own? And which Americans?'

'Which Americans? Some attached, shall we say, to the American embassy.'

'Like you're "attached" to the Foreign Office?'

He inclined his head to one side, allowing her point but not endorsing it.

'But you're really in MI5 or something, aren't you?' she persisted.

'Oh no,' he said, as though slightly offended. 'Not MI5. No.'

'MI6?'

He looked at her but said nothing.

'Or perhaps one of MIs one to four,' she suggested, 'which everyone so insensitively neglects?'

'They no longer exist,' he said gently, as though breaking bad news.

'I see,' she said. 'And these Americans are in the CIA or something then.'

'Not in the least,' he said.

She looked at him again, not believing him. And he looked back, seeming to see the disbelief in her eyes and being completely comfortable with it – as though his lie and her disbelief were the same thing as him telling the truth. She had the sudden perception that this probably felt to him like a very straightforward way to have a conversation. Perhaps this explained his hair – she imagined him in the barber's chair enigmatically parrying their questions about what kind of haircut he wanted.

'Please tell me what happened,' she said.

He looked meaningfully at the tea pot. She filled it and took it back into the other room, where the dog stood protectively by Jonathon's favourite place on the sofa. They sat down again – she in the armchair, Michaels in the other spot on the sofa – and he spoke.

'Some of these chaps attached to the American embassy spotted Jonathon as a person with a certain potential–'

'He's a semi-successful illustrator,' she said, and then said, 'Sorry Jonathon,' to his place on the sofa. 'What potential could they possibly see in him? Did they need some pen-and-ink pictures of rabbits in waistcoats to hang on the walls of their interrogation room?'

'The men attached to the American embassy have some rather *unconventional* ideas,' he said, sipping his tea, 'based on rather surprising research.'

'But what ideas? What research? What are you talking about?'

'I have already told you rather too much,' he said, 'out of consideration for your … predicament. Please believe me when I say that I am telling you all I can, and setting it out as plainly as possible.'

'I can't even imagine what you're like when you're trying to be confusing,' she said, and then added, 'Sorry. I didn't mean to say that. I'm glad to know anything. It's just that having a bit of hope again is almost worse than having no hope' – she glanced at Jonathon's place on the sofa and the dog groaned slightly – 'except that it isn't, it's definitely better having hope. Please tell me something.'

'All I can say is that we work closely with the chaps at the embassy. And we have certain ways of approaching people, like Jonathon, who might have potential. There's a certain form. It is all necessarily rather … oblique.'

'Well it would be, wouldn't it?'

'I may have spoken to Jonathon. Please allow me to consider what I can tell you.'

15

'You are back,' said a slightly hoarse, German-accented voice. 'What happened to you?'

An old man had put his head around the door and was looking at them both in a good-natured way through round spectacles. He stepped into the room.

Adam Newman – or at least the man who was fairly likely to be Adam Newman – froze in place. His hand casually rested on the counter beside the chopping board and the knife.

'Um, hello?' he said.

'Hello. Indeed. I should have said this first. And good morning to you, miss.'

'Hey. I'm Karen.'

The old man danced forward and shook her hand, saying 'My name is Otto, Otto Ruben,' then retreated to the doorway.

'Hey, Otto.'

'But tell me, how are you?' said Otto to almost-certainly-Adam. 'Where have you been?' He cocked his head.

Every single thing about Otto was round and unthreatening. His head was round and surmounted by a crown of fine yet unruly white hair. He was short but quite wide around the middle, which gave him the impression of being a ball of clothes, as though some garments had got into a fight and he was trying to break it up. A multicoloured scarf orbited his neck, above a long brown woollen coat, a yellow jumper, stripy shirt, baggy jeans and incongruous trainers.

'Um, fine, thanks,' said probably-Adam.

'Adam fell off his balcony and lost his memory,' elaborated Karen. 'He's been in hospital.'

Probably-Adam felt slightly annoyed at her for sharing these secrets with someone who had just let himself into the flat without knocking. What made her think this kindly-looking old man was not also a highly trained assassin?

Otto theatrically raised his hands.

'Is this true?' he said. 'I was worried because the balcony door was for some days not completely shut, so it blows around with the wind, making a noise like "clack". I knock but no answer. I think, "He has just gone away for some holiday." But I am not so sure. Then today I hear a woman's voice in your flat, so I think, "For sure something is not right." And I come in just to see. I apologise for sneaking up like this.'

'That's all right,' said probably-Adam, now feeling annoyed with himself for being so boring that the sound of a woman's voice in his flat would be unusual enough to alarm the neighbours.

'But is this true,' repeated Otto, 'about your memory?'

'Yes. I can't remember anything that happened before Tuesday.'

'In this case I should tell you that we are neighbours: not friends but strong acquaintances. We have invited each other for coffee some times each – perhaps five or six – and we once attempted to play chess but this was not so successful. We discuss mostly German politics.'

'Thanks,' said probably-Adam.

'But, tell me, this memory loss, it is for your own life only or for everything?'

'It seems to be anything about my experience. Factual things are kind of there but a bit vague, and I don't really know them till they come into my head. Like I know Berlin's in Germany and Germany's in Europe, but I don't know how I know about it and I don't know how much I know about it.'

'But this is fascinating, this distinction between personal memories and factual memories. And language?'

'I can speak German.'

'Then this fall has done you quite some good, as you were not able to do this before,' said Otto, and laughed uproariously.

'Hey, you want to sit down, have some coffee?' asked Karen.

Otto looked at his watch and said, 'I should almost not have coffee at this time, but in this situation I say yes, thank you, young lady – Karen.'

He took a seat at the table and held out his hands for the cup, then said, 'And tell me, how do you know Adam?'

'He walked into my bar last night in just a shirt and slacks, says he's lost his memory and has only six euros and a set of keys. So I let him sleep over at my place.'

'If I had known some years ago that this was possible,' said Otto, 'I would have been walking every Friday night into a bar and saying this.'

He laughed uproariously again, and even went so far as to slap his thigh.

'Doesn't work for guys like you,' said Karen, smiling.

Probably-Adam finally decided to abandon the vicinity of the knife and joined them at the table with his coffee.

Karen said, 'I was just telling this guy – Adam – that he needs to go back to hospital.'

'This is a matter for the hospital. What did they say when they discharged him?'

Probably-Adam, embarrassed by this, attempted to distract himself by opening a little drawer in the fine old kitchen table. Inside was a large black Bible, stamped 'English Standard Version' in gold, with a little cloth and a bottle of oil beside it. *Do bibles need oiling?* he wondered. The world was constantly baffling.

'It sounds like they didn't discharge him,' said Karen. 'I think he just walked out.'

Probably-Adam shut the drawer. This was probably not the time to be contemplating the lubrication of religious works. He could ask about it later, when he felt less tired and more sane.

'Then for sure you need to go back to the hospital,' said Otto. 'This is very dangerous, leaving the hospital on your own.'

'Except I didn't,' said the probable Adam. 'A woman came to collect me who said she was my wife, and … some things happened.'

'Or didn't,' said Karen.

'I don't understand,' said Otto. 'Please explain me what you are talking about.'

'Wait, can you tell me what I do for a job?' said probably-Adam.

'You have a job which is part of a programme for foreign people who have degrees, in which you help the members of the German parliament. More than this I do not know.'

'Would anyone have a reason to kill me … because of my job?'

'No, this is ridiculous. Though you must work long hours, you are very junior, with few responsibilities. I must tell you that in my opinion you are not the sort of person who would be mixed up in anything that would lead someone to try to kill you.'

The man – Adam – looked down at his coffee, which he'd stirred so vigorously that the faint golden brown froth on top swirled around like the event horizon around a black hole. It seemed most plausible that he was a very boring slightly religious oily low-level foreigner somehow working in the German parliament, who'd fallen off a balcony and then had a hallucination. It was, by far, the least far-fetched explanation, and also the one that involved least immediate effort. He felt very, very tired.

'Now, what were you talking about?' asked Otto.

'I thought a woman came to collect me, saying she was my wife. I thought she took me to an apartment and then she and a small team of others tried to assassinate me. It was really vivid. But I escaped, then I found myself walking along the street outside a bar and went in for a beer.'

'So, alcohol is involved in this experience. How much did you drink?'

'Four beers?' He looked at Karen, who raised her eyebrows and waggled her head as though to say this was approximately right. She looked embarrassed.

'Over what time?' asked Otto. 'With how much food?'

'A couple of hours? With a bretzel. Oh, and currywurst on the way home. I remember that now. It was amazing.'

'This is a lot to drink without eating so much, especially when you have been in hospital for two days. And the hospital suspects brain problems?'

Probably-Adam nodded, and Otto shook his head and glanced at Karen, as though he were thinking she had been irresponsible giving him so many beers.

'Have you had any other odd experiences?' asked Otto.

'I've had nothing but odd experiences.'

'But any other hallucinations?'

'Wait,' said Karen, 'didn't you say that the guy who found you tried to give you some fingers?'

'Yes, that's true. And the men who took me to hospital were firemen, not ambulance workers. I thought that seemed weird but I just accepted it at the time.'

'No, this is true. The ambulances here are operated by the *Feuerwehr*, the "fire brigade". Is this not the case in England?'

'I don't think so. Otherwise it wouldn't surprise me.'

'It's not like that in the US,' said Karen. 'Why would you mix those things together? That's messed up.'

'But I think there are not so many fires to put out. What do the fire brigade does when there are no fires?'

'They, like, wait for a fire,' said Karen. And then, 'Right, I see what you mean.'

'But this matter of the fingers, this confirms it.' Otto stood up. 'Come, this is dangerous. I take you to hospital now in my car.'

There was something about Otto's tone that made probably-Adam stand up immediately. Of course he should be in a hospital. How could anyone feel the way he felt, as well as suffering from amnesia and delusions, and not be in a hospital? He should also drop this 'probably' thing. His name was definitely Adam: Adam Newman. Oily, boring Adam Newman.

Definitely-Adam handed the ski jacket back to Karen and put on the jacket and coat that hung over the back of his chair.

Karen stood too, saying, 'This is good. I mean we could wait a little while and eat the delicious organic food I'm making. But no, let's forget the delicious organic food.'

'Would you like to take it?' asked Adam. 'It'll only go off otherwise.'

'But it'll go off if I take it with us,' she said. 'I don't know how long I'll be at the hospital.'

'Young lady,' said Otto, 'you have done more than enough already. I take over now. You must have other things to do, I think.'

'Well, I do have a shift at the bar later on. But I could totally get someone to cover that.'

'I couldn't ask you to do that,' said Adam.

'I don't mind,' said Karen. 'I want to make sure you're okay.'

'No, you go to your bar,' said Otto. 'You take his food. We get in touch in some hours to tell you what happens at the hospital.'

She asked for a pen and paper and scribbled down her address and phone number, which she gave to Adam.

'Thank you,' he said, suddenly full of gratitude.

Karen turned from the emotional moment and began filling an Edeka bag with the food she'd been preparing on the counter.

'You live nearby?' asked Otto.

She turned and nodded. 'Fifteen minutes' walk. I'm just off the end of Reichenberger, so I can come over any time.'

'This is very good,' said Otto. 'And this door is closed now?' He crossed to the balcony entrance. 'It will not make the noise like "clack, clack" all through the night?' He tested it, then said, 'Okay. Right, we go.'

And so they descended the long staircase, their hands on its old and elaborately carved wooden handrail, their feet on its new, dowdy green lino floor, their steps echoing the height of the building.

Out on the street, Karen turned to Adam.

'Okay, Mister – I mean Adam. It's been great meeting you. You come visit me when you get out of hospital, okay? Or call me if you're gonna be there a couple of days and I'll come visit.'

'I have phones,' he said, patting his pockets. There was a phone in each. 'I'll call. Thanks for all your help. I'd probably have pneumonia if it wasn't for you.'

She brushed a tear from her eye with a sleeve. 'God, I am the *worst*. I cry at everything.'

They hugged and she said, 'Be well.'

And then she walked away, down the road, while Adam and Otto crossed to his car, which sat beneath a nearby tree.

16

Michaels replayed the scene in his mind. Which details could he possibly pass on to Piper?

He had been sitting in the Green Room at the Foreign and Commonwealth Office, the one they were only allowed to book for these interviews. It was very different from the tiny, dark, overheated place where he usually worked. The Green Room had high ceilings with elaborate plasterwork, a great lake of plush green carpet, and a mahogany desk moored like a ceremonial barge by the window overlooking the courtyard.

The woman pretending to be his secretary opened the door and gestured for the interviewee to enter. As he came in, the interviewee – Fairfax – somehow managed to walk into the secretary's welcoming gesture, colliding with her hand. He apologised and stepped out of her way, but the secretary had already stepped out of his way in the same direction. They tried to disentangle themselves, but again, in trying to step out of each other's way, ended up stepping into the same space. Then it happened again, seeming to lock them together in a dance from which neither could escape. Fairfax eventually managed to extricate himself only by leaping away from the secretary, into the empty expanse of green carpet, apologising as went, his face flushed.

From the doorway, the perspiring secretary asked, 'Would you like a drink? Tea? Coffee?'

'Oh, tea?' Fairfax smiled and nodded, embarrassed. 'Thanks. Um, no. Thanks.'

'Right,' said the secretary, looking confused. She backed out of the door, closing it behind her and catching her foot. She seemed to have caught his awkwardness.

Michaels began, for the first time, to wonder whether the Americans were not mad, as he had assumed, but onto something.

'Mr Fairfax,' he said, rising and holding out his hand. 'Welcome. Please take a seat.'

Fairfax walked the length of the room, catching himself a blow on the shin with his portfolio case. He sat, then held out his hand, but was too far away for Michaels to shake it. Michaels dropped his own hand and took a seat, but Fairfax was now standing, hand outstretched. They did a little dance, like the one by the doorway, alternately sitting down and standing with hand outstretched, until they finally managed a handshake.

Fairfax was tastefully dressed, but there was about him the faint suggestion that these were someone else's clothes. He wore a soft cotton shirt, an unstructured jacket, petrol blue trousers and tan shoes, all fairly new. His hair looked like it had been neat about an hour ago, but had since cut loose and decided to do its own thing.

'Tell me a little about yourself,' said Michaels.

'I'm, um, Jonathon Fairfax and I, er, I'm' – the man paused for an uncomfortable amount of time, apparently wrestling with something inside himself – 'an illustrator. Yes. I'm an illustrator. I mean, I've been doing it as my job for about a year. I've brought some things from my portfolio, if you'd like to see them. They're here in, um … my portfolio.'

Michaels nodded, rather surprised, but politely indicated his interest. Fairfax stood, wrestled his portfolio case onto the desk as though subduing a gazelle, and managed to unzip it. He opened it and pushed it over to Michaels, who began to leaf through. There was something about Fairfax's manner that made Michaels feel confident, fluent, powerful. Of course, Michaels was, in his way, powerful. But he didn't often feel it.

He flipped through the illustrations. They were not quite his thing. Michaels, before being called to the service, had studied art history, specialising in the Dutch renaissance. Fairfax's illustrations were very English, very Edwardian, with precise penmanship and deft characterisation, but they weren't to Michaels' taste. There were several rabbits in waistcoats, a family of geese who seemed to be on holiday in the 1950s, and some panels from a graphic novel in which the characters from *The Wind in the Willows* had been conscripted to fight in the First World War.

'There are some people in there as well,' said Fairfax. 'It's just I started out doing the animals, and once people have seen you do animals in old-fashioned clothes, that's what they want.'

'And what made you start drawing animals in old-fashioned clothes?' asked Michaels.

'When I was a kid I was taken to the library once a week, and they had Lewis Carrol's books, with the illustrations by John Tenniel. I really liked them. And they kind of stayed with me as I got older. I find them very comforting.'

'I see. You need comforting?'

Fairfax blushed. 'Um,' he said, 'yes, I suppose I do. Doesn't everyone? The world is a strange and disconcerting place. It's good to see that people in the past thought it was too, and that they dealt with it by drawing really solid and beautiful otters wearing trousers.'

'I see,' said Michaels again. 'And what was it about the world that struck you as strange and disconcerting when you were a child?'

'Oh, you know,' said Fairfax, looking uncomfortable, 'just the way people are. We moved around quite a lot when I was growing up, so I changed schools a fair bit. That probably makes everything seem more disconcerting.'

What Michaels had heard so far made him see another reason – apart from the Americans' mad idea – why Fairfax would be a candidate for working in the service. This sense that the world was strange and disconcerting, this difficult childhood, these were things they all shared, the people in his world. Not the Americans of course. But the British saw these as useful qualities. They made a person watchful from a young age, turned a person into a keen spotter of detail.

There was the awkwardness too. They all had it. It was a consequence of taking in too much information, being so watchful that they were always flooded with detail. And, of course, it is far harder to tell when an awkward person is lying to you. With a confident extravert, one simply watches for what disconcerts him. With an awkward fellow, everything disconcerts him, and so the signal is drowned in noise. At the Fairground, their headquarters in Battersea, one couldn't move for fellows getting their jackets caught on doorhandles, tripping over their feet, blushing at nothing.

'Tell me,' said Michaels, 'how do you feel about serving your country?'

'Um, well, I'd like to. I always feel guilty that's it's taken all my effort just to keep myself going. I'd like to do something for other people, for the country.'

'I see,' said Michaels. 'And how do you feel about the royal family?'

'Um,' said Fairfax. 'I have two opinions about the royal family.'

'And they are?'

'Well, the first is that they're all idiots, and it's insane for us to give them millions of pounds when they already own quite a lot of the country, and it's really terrible to make people wealthy, famous and powerful just because of who their parents are – it's bad for everyone, and seems to make them unhappy too.'

'And what's the second opinion?'

'That the queen opens schools and cuts ribbons and meets presidents, and does it all mostly without upsetting anyone. If we didn't have her, then we'd have to elect a president, and when I try to imagine what sort of person that would be, it's horrible. Well, it's Noel Edmonds. Also, I think it's in keeping with our national character that we have such a ludicrous system. It shows we have a sense of humour about ourselves.'

'I see,' said Michaels again, surprised to find he completely agreed with Fairfax. 'And – you may find this question unusual, given the circumstances – what are your opinions about America?'

'Oh, um. Well, most Americans I've met – with a couple of exceptions – have been clever and funny and friendly and *at ease*, and they're really good at films and TV and writing books. And there's democracy and freedom of speech. But then somehow there's also the racism and mass shootings and Garth Brooks and letting people die because they can't afford health insurance. I don't really know how to put the two sides together.'

'I see,' said Michaels, nodding and finding that once again he largely agreed. 'But you feel that democracy and freedom of speech are good things? Worth defending?'

'Um, yes. Definitely.'

'Have a look at this,' said Michaels, sliding a slim leather-bound volume across the desk, 'and tell me what you think. I remind you that you have signed the Official Secrets Act.'

Not every interview involved sliding this leather folder across the desk, but nevertheless Michaels had done so many times over the years.

The first line of the first page said, 'You are being assessed for recruitment into Her Majesty's Secret Intelligence Service (SIS). If you would not like to take this assessment further, please leave the interview room now. The following pages provide some information to help you make your decision.'

It then set out pay scales, working conditions, and generally tried to describe what the job was like, in positive but reasonably realistic terms.

Fairfax picked up the folder, already frowning and flushing, as though he knew what it contained. Then he flicked through it, occasionally staring at a page for a few seconds.

After a short time, he looked up and said, 'That thing I said about the royal family. I hope I didn't … I mean, I don't know what you think … I didn't mean to offend you.'

'Not at all,' said Michaels. Fairfax was presumably reacting to that first line, *Her Majesty's* Secret Intelligence Service.

'Good. Sorry. I'm always worried about offending people.'

'I took no offence at all. I thought it a good summary of what must surely be the prevailing view.'

'Oh, thanks.'

'And your reaction to our booklet?'

'Oh, yes. It's very good. Maybe an illustration at the beginning of each section. Like the bit about foreign service could be someone next to a well known landmark, like the pyramids, maybe holding a magnifying glass. I was thinking maybe the people could be done as friendly and intelligent-looking dogs, like maybe beagles, or labradors.'

'I see. And the words?'

'Yes, very good. No problem.'

'So, you're content to continue?' asked Michaels.

'Yes. Yes, absolutely,' said Fairfax.

'You'll have questions, of course,' said Michaels, and Fairfax nodded, 'but we usually keep those for the next stage of the process.'

'Oh, I'm used to that. Gives me a chance to get my thoughts together.'

'Good. Well, we'll be in touch to arrange that next stage.'

And so Michaels had stood, and they had once again performed the shaking-hands dance. Fairfax had effortfully packed up his portfolio as though resuscitating the gazelle, given himself a nasty crack on the shin with it, and stumbled back across the carpet and into the secretary as she came through the door. Then Fairfax and the secretary had intricately shuffled out, colliding and apologising all the way.

17

Adam collided with Otto and apologised to him.

'Sorry,' he said, 'I always go to the wrong door.'

'This shows you are accustomed to driving, I think.'

It was an old purple-red Peugeot, heavily encrusted with bird poo, the bodywork beneath looking like it had been lightly sanded.

Otto got into the car and reached across to pull up the peg lock for the passenger door. Adam couldn't stop himself glancing into the back footwell, just in case there was an assassin with a garrotte hiding there. It was empty and, even in the privacy of his own mind, Adam was embarrassed about checking.

They put their seat belts on and Otto said, 'I just call my wife. I forget to tell her where I go.'

He pressed a couple of buttons on his phone.

'Hello darling,' he said. 'I am just in Mariannen Strasse and will drive our friend Adam Newman to Vivantes Neukölln hospital, going via Kottbusser Tor, Moritzplatz and Oranienburger Strasse. He fell on Tuesday from his balcony and has contracted amnesia. By the way, he was helped very much by a young woman called Karen, who is walking back now to her apartment at the end of Reichenberger Strasse. She has dark skin and wears a green coat. Would you please buy some flowers for her? Thank you.'

'You speak to your wife in English?' Adam asked, after Otto had ended the call.

'Na, of course,' said Otto. 'My wife is American. This is how I speak so good English.'

Otto pulled away with a surprising smoothness and sureness of touch. *Bubabubabubabub* went the wheels over the brick-paved road. Adam sat back. On either side of the street, the tall, bare trees reached their nude limbs into the grey sky. Otto accelerated. Ahead, beneath the overhead train line, was a giant roundabout. In its centre, on colossal metal legs, crouched an old train station made of glass and iron. As they approached the roundabout, Otto didn't hesitate and barely slowed, slinging the elderly Peugeot into its orbit.

'You're very good at driving,' said Adam.

'Thanks,' said Otto. 'I am retired, and I enjoy taking the car for a spin.' He said this with a trace of pride in knowing this idiom.

'What did you do, before you retired?'

'I was a professor at the Humboldt. You remember the Humboldt, it is the oldest of Berlin's four universities, offering degree-level programmes in almost two hundred disciplines, focusing on the sciences?'

'No, it doesn't ring a bell. Sorry. What did you teach?'

'Politics,' said Otto, veering to the right.

Adam continued to marvel at Otto's driving. He seemed to be constantly at the maximum safe speed, speeding up and slowing down smoothly, but so that Adam could feel the acceleration press his body against the seat.

It was a big contrast with the assassin who had pretended to be his wife in the delusion yesterday. She had driven in a much more languid way, despite being in a more powerful car. He remembered her switching on the Blaupunkt stereo and nodding along to the music.

Wait, he thought, as Otto cannoned down a canyon of grey blocks of flats, what kind of delusion leaves you with clear memories of an imaginary woman's driving style and her brand of car stereo?

He tried to unthink this thought. What happened yesterday had been a delusion. That was the most rational explanation, as well as being the most convenient and least effort. He was so tired and confused, and he wanted to be in the version of the world in which a kindly old man was driving him to hospital and his friend Karen was going to come and visit him.

And Otto clearly was a kindly old man: he had even called his wife to … Oh. He ran through that conversation again in his head. It seemed much less reassuring now.

Had yesterday been a delusion? The drive in the Audi to the beautiful flat – and what had happened there – certainly did have a dreamlike quality. But it also had quite a lot of details, including the red stitching on the steering wheel. Could he really have imagined that?

They were approaching another roundabout, beside a huge vacant lot overgrown with weeds, its wire fence pasted over with anti-war posters. The traffic lights turned red, and Otto smoothly slowed down.

The man needed to make a decision. He glanced around, noting that the peg was still in the 'up' position, showing that the door wasn't locked. It all hinged on whether you could send flowers to someone based on a description of them and their route home, and how detailed delusions could be. He wished he could quickly look these things up on the internet. If delusions could include driving styles, brands of car stereo and details of steering-wheel trim, then making a break for it was the wrong choice. If not, he was probably being taken somewhere to be assassinated. He wondered if Otto was supposed to do it himself, or if he would drive to a quiet spot where someone younger and with a much less reassuring manner would take over.

It struck Adam that, if he ran away and it turned out to be the wrong thing to do, then he could explain to Otto about the problem of the unexpectedly detailed steering wheels they had in delusions nowadays and just go to the hospital another time. Whereas if staying in the car turned out to be the wrong thing to do then he would die. He really didn't want to be assassinated, especially by a twinkly silver-haired old man with kind eyes.

The car came to a halt at the traffic light, beside the kerb. Adam simultaneously pressed the seatbelt-release button, yanked on the door handle and made a break for it. It took him a second to realise that he was not out and running along the pavement but still sitting, immobile, in the car. The seatbelt had locked taut and the door stayed closed.

'What are you doing?' asked Otto.

'Um, I've decided to get out. Why is the door locked? Why won't the seatbelt release?'

'It is an old car,' said Otto. 'Relax.' And then, more gently, 'This is a panic attack? Don't worry, you suck on a sweet and this is a good way to make the panic attack go away. I have some in my door pocket.'

'No. I want to get out here, please,' said the man, trying to spool out some more seatbelt. It remained locked in place.

The traffic lights changed. Otto looked in his rear-view mirror and pulled smoothly away, around the roundabout.

'Don't worry, I drive you around the corner. We talk, and if you want you can for sure get out.'

Otto took the third exit off the roundabout and immediately turned right into a narrow one-way road that ran between a big faceless apartment block and a little secluded park. He pulled into an empty parking space behind a VW Passat and engaged the hand brake with a creak.

'Could you unlock this seatbelt, please?' said Adam politely.

'I do not understand the problem with this seat belt,' said Otto. 'You have just to press the button with some force.'

Could this be the problem? Was he just weak from his stay in hospital? Or maybe he was just generally a weaker man than he expected to be. He pushed again on the button, but kept his eyes on Otto the whole time – except for a glance around to check whether anyone was approaching the car. It was clear outside.

Otto said, 'Okay, the first is to recover from the panic attack. I have some sweets – English ones, *Werther's Originals*. You remember them?' They did sound vaguely familiar. 'You suck on one of these and it makes you to breathe through your nose. This calms you down.'

Otto bent to the little storage compartment at the bottom of the driver's door and took out a crackly plastic package, offering it in his right hand. But what was in his left? Something glinted and Adam whipped out his hand, grabbing the object – a silver canister. Adam pushed it upwards, directing it at the car's ceiling.

Otto's grip was surprisingly firm, despite his age. Adam twisted the canister, making sure the nozzle was directed upwards, and tried to use it to hit Otto's hand against the small handle above the door. He couldn't reach quite far enough – the seatbelt prevented him from moving. He was also hampered by the lingering suspicion that this was all a mistake – that the seatbelt and door were just old and stiff, the Werther's Originals a genuine attempt to help, and the metal canister something to clean the windscreen.

But Otto did not seem shocked or offended by Adam's behaviour, only steely and determined. He reached into his breast pocket with his right hand and Adam grabbed the wrist with his left, preventing Otto removing whatever was there. Then Adam braced his leg against the door, extending his reach enough to hit Otto's canister hand against the small handle above the door.

Otto released his grip. Adam snatched the canister away from him, put his finger on the nozzle and pressed, spraying Otto's face. Otto grabbed Adam's wrist, smashing his hand up against the rearview mirror. Then the mirror, the canister and Otto's arm dropped limply to the floor, all at the same time. Otto's other hand flopped from his pocket to his lap as his head slumped forward, mouth open.

Adam tried to wind down the window, but the handle was stuck. He held his breath and reached into Otto's pocket, pulling out a black, silenced pistol which he carefully put in the glove compartment. Then, still holding his breath, he fumbled under his own seat and pulled the lever there, sliding the seat backwards. There was now enough space for the man to wriggle down under the waist part of his seatbelt, inelegantly spooling his limbs and body onto the floor. He covered his face with his handkerchief as he reached across Otto, opened the driver's door, and climbed out over the unconscious old man.

It was then that he saw the large grey Audi bearing down on him.

18

'So,' said Piper, putting down her teacup, 'on considering it, all you can tell me is that you spoke to Jonathon in a room with a blue carpet?'

'As I said, my dear, I have already told you rather more than I should, strictly speaking. Perhaps I could say more if you were to tell me something about the days immediately before he ...'

'Disappeared?' she said.

He nodded.

'I don't know where to start,' she said. 'I told the police about this lots of times. Have you read their reports?'

'Imagine I know nothing,' he said. 'We are aware that he was added to the Missing Persons Register the year before last, on April the twentieth. Tell me about the period before that.'

'The eleventh was the day he didn't come home. It had been a slow time for work and he'd been getting a bit worried about it. He'd taken the dog for so many walks she was starting to look a bit thin and tired. But then there had been a ... Wait a minute, I've been an idiot.'

'My dear?'

'He went for a meeting at the Foreign Office about some work – illustrating a recruitment brochure. That was you, wasn't it? The room with the blue carpet.'

'It may have been,' conceded Michaels.

'I was really busy,' she said, 'restoring some Georgian textiles. I should have paid more attention. About a week after that meeting he went to another one, somewhere different, and I didn't know whether it was about the same thing or not. That was the day he didn't come back.'

'He told you after the first meeting that it was about illustrating a brochure?' Michaels frowned.

'Yes.'

'Nothing more?'

'No. He was relieved to have a bit of work again, though I don't think all the details had been sorted out. I think I thought that was what the other meeting was for – or maybe I wasn't thinking about it at all. I was really busy. I feel guilty about that now.'

'My dear, I'd like you to think very carefully. Did he ever mention the word "Knife-fish" to you?'

'Knife-fish?'

He nodded.

'You don't mean "fish-knife"?'

'No. Did he mention a fish-knife?'

'Of course not. We aren't the royal family. Anyway, he doesn't like fish – he says they remind him of Andrew Lloyd-Webber.'

'I see,' said Michaels, making another note in his pad.

'What?' said Piper.

'My dear, you mustn't feel slighted: many people in the service choose not to tell their loved ones. And I believe the Americans discourage disclosure even more than we do. Knowledge can be dangerous.'

'He would have told me. I know he would.'

'I'm sure he was only trying to protect you.'

'And why do you keep mentioning the Americans?'

'When I spoke to him, he indicated a willingness to proceed to the next phase of recruitment to the intelligence services. That next phase was handled by the Americans. It is not standard for them to recruit foreign nationals as officers, but – as I said – they had identified in him a … certain potential. If he left without saying anything, it can only have been that they had something important for him to do, something urgent.'

'Oh God,' she said, burying her face in her hands.

'I understand this must be distressing,' he said. 'I had thought that perhaps you had some inkling of this.'

'Oh God,' she repeated. 'You're all idiots. You've accidentally recruited Jonathon into the CIA.'

19

The man who had, until a few seconds earlier, definitely been Adam Newman flattened himself against the side of the battered old Peugeot, slamming its door. The big grey Audi thundered past and rocked to a halt further up the road.

The man who was no longer at all confident of being Adam Newman yanked the Peugeot's door open again. There was no time to remove Otto, so he climbed in on top of the unconscious old fellow, his thighs pressing painfully against the bottom of the dashboard, the top of his head rubbing on the ceiling. Where was the handbrake?

Someone had leapt from the Audi: a woman in a fluffy jumper, reaching for something in the small of her back as she strode towards him. It was Amy, who was, by the second, becoming less likely to be his wife. She took out a gun. He found the handbrake beneath Otto's limp hand, released it, and fumbled the car into reverse. Amy levelled the gun, using both hands to steady her aim, moving smoothly. The man stared helplessly at her, then forced himself to look in the opposite direction.

The Peugeot leapt backwards, around the bend in the road. He hoped this had deprived Amy of a clean shot. But he was now reversing fast towards an oncoming car. The brake he was stamping on turned out to be the old man's foot. Frantically working the steering wheel with hands that were jammed up against his chest, he swerved up onto the grass, running over a sapling, turning tightly so he was now facing the opposite direction, towards the busy road from which Otto had turned.

Spoff!

An oddly unimpressive sound. The Peugeot's back windscreen instantly webbed over with cracks and a neat hole appeared in the front windscreen to his right. A few inches the other way and she would have got him: thanks to his awkward position, there was no part of the left side of the vehicle that didn't have an important part of him in it. He scrabbled again with Otto's hand, selected first gear, then lurched out into the traffic, swerving to avoid a tiny smoking woman on a bike, and accelerated into the flow of cars sounding their horns.

'Sorry,' he said aloud, his face burning with shame.

Otto groaned very softly but didn't move. Shit. The man who probably wasn't Adam hoped desperately that none of the surrounding cars would notice that he was sitting on top of an elderly German with a kind face. He tried to push Otto a bit further down into the seat, and kicked the old man's feet away from the pedals.

He needed to drive as unobtrusively as possible, but also fast enough to outrun the Audi which must now be somewhere behind. How long would it take Amy to get back in and turn it around? He had no idea. He also had no rear-view mirror and a back windscreen that he couldn't see through. Nor were the wing mirrors adjusted for someone sitting on top of an old man – they showed him only the road surface and the Peugeot's sides.

The street was wide but flanked with parked cars, leaving only one lane running in each direction. There was a steady stream of traffic coming towards him, so the Audi – if it was behind him – would not be able to overtake. He wondered where he could turn off. On one side were tall blocks of flats with little brick balconies, on the other an incongruous Italianate church.

There on the right: a sudden open patch of grass. He took the turning – again, frantically working the steering wheel with his cramped tyrannosaurus arms – then immediately noticed the entrance to a little park just beside it, running parallel to the road. It was not meant for cars, but he took it anyway, his nose now pressed almost to the windscreen, alert for walkers. Trees to his left screened him from the road. On his right were sports courts and a monolithic concrete ping-pong table.

He pulled to a halt. Walking heavily towards him was a woman in a headscarf and a long coat. He stared at her, paralysed. Was that a gun under her coat? Or was she … just a tiny bit fat? Her eyes were fixed on his, her face set. Then she shook her head disbelievingly, and he realised that she was, quite naturally, annoyed with him for driving his car through a park. She gave him a disapproving glare and was gone. The park was empty, and it suddenly struck him that this was the perfect place for getting rid of Otto.

The man opened the door and got out. He fished hurriedly through Otto's pockets, taking his mobile phone. What else could he do to stop Otto coming after him once he came round? Ah. This was not a thing he wanted to be caught in the act of doing. But he had already driven through a park, so he used that residual shame to tide him over as he pulled off Otto's shoes and hastily stole his trousers. Then he dragged the old man over to a little square fountain, shaded picturesquely by trees, and propped him against it. If anything would discourage people from helping a kindly looking old man, it would be a lack of trousers.

'Hnf,' said Otto, indistinctly.

Then from behind came a voice. '*Hey!*'

The man whirled around. Standing there was a grey-haired dog-walker in a green quilted jacket, a small basset hound at his heel.

'*You can not this old man here leave,*' said the dog-walker angrily. '*That goes completely not!*'

'*He sleeps with alcohol,*' replied the man, unable to remember the word for 'drunk'. '*I know him not. I try–*' He wanted to say that he was checking Otto was all right.

'*And that is your car, or?*' said the dog-walker, interrupting him.

'*That goes also completely not! You spin, or?*'

'*Excuse you please,*' said the man, blushing and flustered. '*I drive it now away.*'

He got back into the car, slammed the door and drove off, thankfully unable to see how bitterly the dog-walker was disapproving. The path continued a short distance, then turned left to rejoin the main road, emerging at a pedestrian crossing. He waited for the light to turn green, then drove over the crossing and down a street beside a beautiful curved brick building.

Then he remembered Karen. Shit.

Otto had mentioned Karen to someone, had described her and her route home. The person he'd told almost certainly wasn't his wife, and would almost certainly not be buying Karen some flowers. He had to get to her.

He turned left, onto a street running parallel to the larger one, going back in the direction from which he'd come. The road was brick-paved again, and the tyres now went *ru-bu-bu-bu-bub* over the surface as he drove as fast as he dared. It was a huge relief to be the only person in the driver's seat.

He was near the vacant lot where he had tried to get out of the car, heading for the grey canyon of flats. Here the city seemed to turn suddenly into a different country, with crowds of Turkish men and, beneath the elevated train station, a little settlement of rough sleepers with beds on pallets, drying their clothes on the metal fences.

Now he was on the big roundabout, sneaking through just as the light turned red, and again on the next red light, his face burning with embarrassment at this little transgression. How could he be so instinctively law-abiding and yet have people persistently trying to kill him? Here it was, Reichenberger Strasse. There was no time to think.

Past the Sparkasse bank, the tyres again *rububb*ing on the brick surface. Up to the left was the astronaut and the site of his birth. He kept on, down the street which had threatened to explode his head that morning. He passed the sinuous dragon, slowing, looking out for Karen, afraid he would miss her, even more afraid she was no longer there to be missed.

It's difficult to scan both pavements when they're right below some of the world's most distracting walls, especially when you're driving as fast as possible and still burning with shame at having recently debagged a senior citizen.

There she was! But no, it was a woman with a headscarf the same colour as Karen's coat. There! No, a bag in a tree. He asked his brain not to supply so many false positives and drove on. Across an inter-section, past a desolate playground. And there, that actually was her: wearing not only the right coat and hat, but the correct human form. She was ambling, looking down at the pavement, swinging the Edeka bag. Nearby was a drunk, finding his way home by dragging one side of himself along the wall.

He pulled over to her side of the street, the left, and stopped in front of a parked Citroën van. He wound his window down and called to her.

'Karen!'

She looked up, saw him, and then a sequence of reactions chased each other across her face, erupting over each other like a firework display. There was surprise, confusion, recognition, and then the first half of a large smile, which was immediately overtaken by horror as she registered that he was driving Otto's Peugeot. The drunk, as if in sympathy with her, rolled his back against the wall and seemed about to topple face-forward into the street.

'Where's Otto?' she said. 'Please don't tell me you …'

'He's an … an agent or whatever – he's one of them.'

'Oh god, what did you do to that poor old guy? He was trying to help you.'

'No, listen. He tried to give me a Werther's Original–'

'What did you do? What did you do?' she moaned, clutching the Edeka bag to her chest. The drunk, again as though he were a one-man chorus in their opera, clutched his hands to his temples and started muttering something to himself.

'But it was only to distract me,' continued the man, 'while he sprayed something in my face. I managed to grab it – a metal canister – and spray it in his face, and it knocked him out. He had a gun too. And then the people from the hospital yesterday turned up in a big grey Audi and–'

At this point, right on cue, a big grey Audi roared around the cor-ner. The drunk stood up straight, made a precise gesture towards the man's Peugeot, and drew a gun.

The man called, 'Look out behind you!' just as the ex-drunk lunged forward.

Karen turned, and with reflexes honed on the streets of Minneapo-lis, hit her attacker smartly in the face with a bag of delicious organic food, knocking him down and sending his gun flying.

Behind them, the Audi's doors opened and Amy jumped out, gun in hand.

'Get in the back, please!' the man shouted at Karen.

She wrenched open the back door and threw herself inside.

The man scrabbled with pedals and gears. There was – perhaps – just enough room to pull out forwards without hitting the Citroën in front. He engaged gear, put his foot down, wrenched the steering wheel. The Peugeot leapt into action, backwards – he must have missed first gear – and was now reversing at speed towards Amy, who jumped out of the way. He found first gear, stepped too hard on the accelerator, making the engine roar, and then sprang forward and drove off as fast as he could, remembering just in time to move into the right-hand lane.

'Left! Left!' shouted Karen, and he swung the car around the corner, the tyres blubbering furiously over the cobbles. At the end of the street was a high brick wall with a wider road running in front of it.

'Left again!' she said.

There was a red light ahead but he blared the horn, cheeks burning, cutting across the edge of the pavement, fitting into the space between an ancient green Mercedes and a rapidly braking black VW. They sped past Travolta and hit the big street with the railway running above it.

Karen sat in the back seat, leaning forward, hands on the corners of the front seats. The man had switched onto quieter streets for a while, then hit Karl Marx Strasse and followed it out of the city. They were now on the motorway, driving as sensibly and unobtrusively as he could possibly manage.

'Where are we going?' she asked.

'I don't know,' he said.

'Well that's great!' she said with facetious enthusiasm.

'I'm just trying to make sure we don't give the people in the Audi a chance to catch up with us.'

'Gotcha.'

They drove in silence for a while.

'Shouldn't you wear a seatbelt?' he said.

'Is it a bullet-proof seatbelt?' she asked.

'I don't think so.'

'Then I'm good, thanks.'

There was more silence. They passed a herring truck and a beer tanker.

'I can't believe Otto was a bad guy,' she said.

'I know. But you can check up here in the front. There's a spray can full of knockout gas in the footwell, a gun in the glovebox and a packet of Werther's Originals in the door pocket. I should stop mentioning the Werther's Originals: there's really nothing sinister about them.'

'I know Werther's Originals – my dad used to bring them back from trips to Ireland. Hey, can I have one?'

'What if they're drugged or something?'

She sighed. 'I guess you're right.'

'So,' she said, as they passed a sign telling them it was ninety kilometres to Poland, 'what did you do to make all these people want to kill you?'

'I don't know. I just don't know. I'm sorry I've got you mixed up in all this.'

'It's okay. I guess. I mean, no, it's totally not okay. But I guess you didn't mean to, did you?'

'No. I was just confused. It was cold and I really wanted to go into a warm pub and have a beer. And then you were nice to me and let me sleep on your sofa. I should have told you that some people had tried to kill me before I slept on your sofa. No, I should have told you and then not slept on your sofa. Or not told you and not slept on your sofa. I was being selfish.'

'It's not selfish. You can't sleep on the street in Berlin in March. You'd die. I can't even think what I would have done in that situation.'

There was a brief silence.

'So what happened back there?' she asked.

'I'm not completely sure,' he admitted. 'Otto called someone and basically told them you'd be walking back along Reichenberger. The drunk man who suddenly pulled out a gun must have been an agent or assassin or whatever – he was following you. And then I suppose the people in the Audi were already on their way to get you after losing me in a small park. I think.'

'And why was the drunk guy who was really an agent following me?'

'You probably know too much. I mean you know about me and you've met Otto. And maybe they planned to use you to get me.'

'So you saved my life?'

'Having first endangered it. It's a bit complicated, but I'm definitely a very, very bad element in your life. I'm sorry you met me.'

'You know what?' she said. 'Even with all this, you're still not even close to being the guy who's had the worst effect on my life.'

'Wow,' said the man. 'Sorry about … um … guys.'

'It's okay. You know, I think I'm going to take a chance on one of those Werther's Originals.'

And so they sped on, towards Poland, each sucking a possibly lethal boiled sweet.

Part Two

The Night
Mismanager

Saturday

20

'Buy you a drink?' said the woman on the next barstool.

'I'm married,' he said, without looking up from his phone.

He was a strikingly handsome man, with the kind of sculpted face that makes you instantly feel bad about yourself if you're looking at it from inside a normal face. And he was wearing a suit, but not in the way that someone who works in an office wears a suit, so that it seems like a shiny disguise or a slightly cleaner alternative to a prison uniform. He was wearing it the way, say, Frank Sinatra wore a suit, so that it seemed entirely natural and not remotely conformist. He was also poised and perfectly at ease simultaneously, which is why he was in the unusual position of constantly having women bother him. But all of this is just a long-winded way of saying that he was Lance Ferman.

'Buy you a drink anyway?' she persisted.

'I'm good, thanks.' He was English, but he'd been living here in New York long enough to have picked up some American expressions, despite his best efforts.

'It's on the CIA,' she said. 'And the Agency is not trying to sleep with you.'

'I'll have a gimlet, please,' he said, swinging around on his stool and putting his phone away. This, he thought, had to be worth hearing. He looked at her for the first time.

She was a big woman in a tan trouser suit worn with chunky white trainers, and her hair was such a fiery copper-red it made Lance want to reach for the brightness control on his eyes. She had a delicate pointed nose, like a good-humoured hedgehog, and her white skin was flushed pink.

She ordered his gimlet and an old-fashioned for herself, leaving a small pile of notes on the bar.

As Lance took his drink, he glanced at the woman and said, 'Can

I see your badge?'

'We don't have badges. That's the FBI.'

'That was a test,' he said. 'And you passed.'

'Great,' she said, drily. 'I feel special.'

'So,' he said, 'why is the CIA hitting on me?'

'The CIA has seen you around and thinks you're kind of interesting. But it really has the hots for a friend of yours.'

'Sometimes it seems like all the nice intelligence agencies prefer my friends to me.'

'Be patient. There's an intelligence agency out there for everyone.'

'So who's my friend?'

'Jonathon Fairfax.'

Lance's stomach lurched and there was a sensation in his head as though his ears were about to pop. He gave her a hard look. She looked back at him, her eyes quick and alive.

He said, 'I was about to say, "That's not funny – he disappeared two years ago." But then I thought you probably know that, and it's probably the point.'

Jonathon's disappearance had upset Lance to such a degree that he had gone beyond congratulating himself for his emotional range and instead begun to worry that he had fatally overextended his capacity for feeling. He had even cried, and his wife had, for a whole two months, switched to calling him 'honey' instead of 'jerk'.

'Not just a pretty face,' said the woman. 'Listen, I'm Lizzie Morden, and I'd like your help to find Jonathon.'

She handed him a card. It said, 'Elizabeth Morden, Director, Global Institute for Policy Studies,' giving an address in McLean, Virginia.

Lance presented a programme called *MTV Undercover*, in which he did pieces to camera shot in black and white, with his collar turned up, and then played music videos that tangentially related to spying. This meant he knew that most CIA institutions which weren't in Langley, Virginia, were instead in McLean, just down the road.

'How come you're interested in Jonathon?' he said. 'I mean, I know that for an unassuming guy he gets in a lot of trouble, but even so. From what I've heard, the CIA doesn't concern itself with finding missing persons. Or indeed doing anything good.'

'Except for protecting American interests around the world, which pretty much equates to defending Western civilisation. *You're welcome.* But, to answer your question, Fairfax was working for us.'

'Well that's the least likely thing I've ever heard. What?'

'I'm going to tell you some stuff, Mr Ferman. Now you understand that this goes no further, don't you? We don't want to raise the hopes of anyone who knows Jonathon. Nor do we want to risk information reaching anyone who may not have his best interests at heart.'

'I understand,' said Lance.

'Could I get that in writing?' she said, taking a contract from her pocket and pushing it along the bar.

He scanned it quickly, knowing that he was now too curious to refuse to sign. It looked like it just prevented him from legally telling anyone about anything ever again.

As he was signing, he said, 'I'm not sure why you bother with these. We all know that if I upset you, you'll do more than just dig up my old library fines.'

'I wish,' she said. 'The paperwork I'd have to go through to do even that in the States these days.'

'And outside America?'

'That's a different story. Outside of the US I could infect you with the ebola virus and fire you into the moon if I wanted.'

She smiled at him pleasantly. He smiled back warily and clinked glasses.

'I'll just have to make sure I stay in the US then,' he said.

'Relax,' she said. 'I'm kidding.'

'I hope so. So what's this stuff you're going to tell me? Why would Jonathon agree to work for the CIA? Is he okay? Why did he disappear? Why has he reappeared? Does Piper know? I'm worried about her. How can I help?'

'Okay, slow down. I don't know all of this, and I can't tell you everything I do know right now. Also, please understand that I don't necessarily approve of every single thing the Agency does. Our remit is to gather intelligence around the world, and as far as I'm concerned that's what we should stick to. But the whole world knows that's not always the case.'

'That's very broad-minded of you.'

'Thanks. Now there are people in the CIA – including some of its senior leadership – who have some pretty out-there, woo-woo beliefs. You've probably heard of experiments with psychic powers, psychedelic drugs, UFOs, squirrels, etcetera, etcetera. And some of that stuff is true. And there's also stuff you've never heard of, some of which is even weirder.'

'Like what?'

'Like never you mind. But also like a programme run by a guy named Doug Channon, based in Europe. Everyone at Langley's whispering about it being this new weapon that'll solve all our problems.'

'So what is it?'

'No one knows, exactly. Channon's keeping it pretty close to his chest. Apparently it's still in development, and he doesn't want to unveil it till he can prove its utility.'

'But what's this got to do with Jonathon?'

'We believe he's part of this programme. Or at least he was.'

'Was?'

'He disappeared recently.'

'Wait, so he disappeared two years ago and now he's disappeared from his disappearance?'

She nodded.

'Any idea why?' he asked.

'Some idea. Nothing I can tell you right now.'

'None of this makes any sense at all. Why would the CIA even want to recruit Jonathon? Do you need secret illustrators?'

'Maybe? I don't know what qualities they were looking for in Channon's secret programme.'

'And how did you get him to agree to join anyway?'

'He believes in freedom and democracy, doesn't he?'

'I'm pretty sure he has at least two opinions on those things, but broadly, yes. Not enough to suddenly vanish from Piper's life though.'

'Well, maybe that was never part of the plan.'

'I still can't ever imagine him getting involved in the CIA. It's just a weird, weird mismatch. It's like a giant squid joining the Boston Symphony Orchestra.'

'I'd watch that movie,' she said.

He shook his head and took a large sip of gimlet.

'And how did you know about me?' he asked.

'From Fairfax's file.'

'I'm in a CIA file?' He felt shaken and oddly flattered at the same time, and wondered if that was how his wife felt when construction workers wolf-whistled her.

'Relax. I've … redacted your details. You won't need to deal with anyone else from the CIA.'

'And how do I know I can trust you?'

'In your phone you have a number for Douglas Rushkoff, the media theorist, correct? You met him a couple of times at conferences.'

'Yes,' Lance admitted.

'Call him. Ask about me.'

'Okay.'

Lance took out his phone and scrolled through his contacts list. He pressed a button. The phone range twice and then a voice said, 'This is Rushkoff.'

'Hi, this is Lance Ferman. I'm here with Lizzie Morden. She said to ask you about her.'

'Oh, right, right. This is that thing. Hold on a second.' *Thud. Shuffle. Thud.* 'Okay. All yours. You're … Linus Thurman, right?'

'Lance Ferman.'

'Yeah. Sure, I remember you from the *Digital Futures* conference. Mr Handsome. So, Lizzie? She's the good guys. And she's smart. You can trust her.'

'Okay. And how do I know this is actually you?'

'It's a paradigmatic modern problem. I mean, what am I going to do? Give you Naomi Klein's number so you can check it's me? Then how do you know it's her? Pretty soon we've got ourselves into an infinite regress.'

'Okay, it's you. Thanks.'

Lance clicked to end the call, and looked expectantly at Lizzie.

'So anyway,' she said, 'I think I've answered all of your questions as much as I can – for now. There's just two left over. Does Piper know? No, she does not. Our ethics are not always spot-on, but we did not want to put her through any more stress or uncertainty. She won't discover Fairfax has been found until we're in a position to send him right on home to her. And you need to respect that too.'

'Okay.'

'Finally, how can you help? We're not totally sure yet. Probably just answer some questions about what he'd do in this or that situation. Maybe a little more. I appreciate that is a lot to lay on you out of the blue. Will you help us? This is pretty urgent so we need an answer in like an hour.'

Lance turned to the barman. 'Same again,' he said. And then to Lizzie, 'Yes, I'll help you.'

21

The man was sitting on a hard bench seat beside Karen in Boris's van. He glanced nervously at Boris, who gripped the steering wheel and stared furiously ahead, past the windscreen wipers. It was raining, a grey day made of dishwater and grit, spitting and slobbering disgustingly against the van's front window. The landscape was perfectly flat and bleak, the crops growing in what looked more like open-air food prisons than farms.

No one had said anything in a long time.

The day before, Karen and the man had driven for an hour in Otto's car, trying to put as much distance as they could between them and the assassins' large grey Audi. The man had taken turnings at random, heading broadly east, reasoning that if he and Karen didn't know where they were then their pursuers probably wouldn't know either.

At a certain point they had looked at each other and Karen had said, 'Are you starting to feel like it's maybe not ...'

She trailed off and he finished her sentence: '... a good idea to be driving towards an international border in a stolen car with a gun in the glove compartment?'

'Yeah. That.'

'Yes, I'm starting to feel that. And I'm worried that they might have some kind of tracking device in it.'

'Oh my god, I hadn't thought of that.'

'We should probably abandon it. Let's stop off and get some money first though. If I work for the government I must have enough for a cheap car and a few nights in an obscure hotel.'

'Yeah. I mean, look at your coat, look at your shoes. They're good quality. You've got money. I can't help much. I get paid cash, and I'm meant to pick it up back in the city where they're trying to kill us. But I think I've got maybe seventy euro in my account, plus nearly twenty on me.'

'No, you shouldn't have to pay anything. This is my fault. Or Adam Newman's fault. Or someone's fault, but definitely not yours. I'll go to the bank.'

And so they'd stopped at a bank in suburban Brandenburg. Karen went to a cafe where she nervously watched the car, while the man went inside.

'*Hello,*' he said, '*I have my PIN-number forgotten. May I it change?*'

The assistant behind the counter – a meaty man with chunky white glasses – gave him a look which clearly said, 'You are not fooling anyone with this pathetic attempt at German.' But with his voice he replied, in English, 'Of course.'

'Great, thanks,' said the man.

The assistant tapped something on his computer and then looked up with irritation. 'I will need your card and identification.'

'Oh, sorry,' said the man, confused at being told off. He took out his wallet and handed over his cashcard and the other card that proved he worked for the Bundestag.

The assistant took them, frowned, and tapped on his computer keyboard for a while. Then he handed the two cards back and stared at the man.

'Oh, is that done?' said the man.

'Of course.'

'That's great. Thanks very much.'

'Hm,' said the assistant. It was a noise that seemed to mean, 'I'm aware that a response is required, but I refuse to invest it with any meaning.'

'So,' said the man, 'I can just choose a new PIN, can I?'

The assistant nodded fractionally, not moving his facial muscles in any way. He looked like he might have never moved his face in his life.

'Right,' said the man. 'Good. Do I just put my card in the cash machine then?' He pointed at the cash machine a few steps away.

'You must just to fill in the form that has been sent to your address and then post it.'

A wave of horror crashed over the man. 'But I can't get to my address. I'm a hundred miles away from it and, um, I can't go back.'

The assistant shrugged.

'Is there any way I can change my PIN now?' said the man. 'Can I just fill in the form here?'

'The form has been sent to your address, as I have said.'

'But can you cancel that and just give me the form?'

'This is not possible.'

'But why did you send the form to my address?'

The assistant looked at him as though the man had asked, 'But why is your head above your torso?'

'Can I change the address you have for me?' asked the man.

'Of course.'

'Okay. How do I do that?'

The assistant clacked a few buttons on his keyboard. 'I have sent a form to your address. You must just to fill in this form and to post it.'

'But I've told you I can't go to that address.'

The assistant shrugged.

'Can I use this card to withdraw money from you, over the counter?'

'Of course.'

'Great. How do I do that?'

'Insert your card in the machine to your right,' he said, indicating a small grey device.

The man put his card in the machine. 'Okay.'

'And enter your PIN number, as requested by the machine.'

'But I've told you I've forgotten my PIN number.'

The assistant shrugged.

Back out in the car, the man told Karen what had happened. 'What did I do wrong?' he asked.

'Nothing,' she said. 'I guess you've forgotten that all Germans who have jobs where they deal with the public totally *hate* people.'

'Oh, that's weird.'

'Yeah,' she said.

'Do you get used to it?'

'Not really.'

After that, afraid that the transaction in the bank might have been traced, they found a motorway and drove fast until they reached a service station. There they left the little purple-red Peugeot at the remotest corner of a huge car park, and Karen called Boris. Perhaps unsurprisingly, he was very angry, but he agreed to drive to them in his van – after finishing his shift in the bar and performing a gig.

They had spent the rest of the day waiting for Boris. They sat in a very large Burger King at the service station, anxiously watching the purple-red Peugeot far away in the parking lot, wondering at every moment if they would see a grey Audi pull up and disgorge a crew of assassins.

'So,' Karen had said, 'any idea who these assassins are?'

'No, but I'm worried I have something to do with them.'

'Really? Why? You don't seem the type.'

'When I first woke up I had this instinct to fight the people taking me to hospital. I was too weak to actually do it, but it felt like I'd been trained how to. And then that training came out the first time they tried to kill me.'

Karen took a sip of her coffee. 'Wow,' she said.

'I can tell you that there are two exits from this place, and that the left one isn't overlooked by anything that would provide cover for a sniper. I can tell you that the man at the next table weighs two hundred and fifteen pounds and has spilled ketchup on his trousers. And I know that at this altitude I can run flat out for half a mile before I trip over something. Why would I know that? How can I know that and not know who I am?'

'I don't think the ketchup on the trousers means anything,' said Karen, 'but the rest might.'

'And the guns the assassins had felt familiar. The one I threw away, I can picture how to take it apart. I know there's an annoying little spring that flips out when you're cleaning it. How would I know that?'

'You're in a gun club? Do they have those in England?'

'I don't know. And I don't know why I know about the annoying little spring but not about gun clubs.'

'Can you remember anything else about the people who tried to kill you?'

'There was a tall bald man, the policeman with the big jaw, and the woman in the fluffy jumper. I only heard the woman speak, and she had an American accent, like you.'

'Have you heard of the CIA?'

'Yes, I remember about that. The Central Intelligence Agency, created in 1947 by order of President Harry S Truman to collect intelligence and conduct covert operations overseas.'

'That sounds like some kind of dictionary definition, like you've been taught it. You think you have something to do with the CIA?'

'I don't know. I don't know how my memory works. Sometimes a fact just pops into my head. And I don't know if it's just random, or if there's some pattern to it. Like, I know that in 1878 Charles Wollaston became the first football player to win five FA cups.'

'Wow, that's boring.'

'Yes, I don't even know what it means.'

She sighed. 'I guess right now, our best chance is to hope enough of your memory comes back for us to know what to do. Till then, we just need to keep a low profile and stay alive.'

The grey Audi did not arrive but Boris eventually did, driving his old East German van. It was bulbous and massive, like a cartoon cloud built in a tank factory. In the back was a drum kit, two bench seats, some boxes, and the old and odd-smelling sleeping bags in which they passed the night, parked in a side road.

The amber glow of streetlights had crept in through the thin, stained curtains. The night had been very cold and the man had slept on the floor, waking often to worry about his extremities falling off, and whether the van was surrounded by assassins.

And that was why they were now, the next day, in Boris's van, driving through the rain.

'I still think you two should go to the police,' said the man.

'We can't,' said Karen. 'My visa expired over a year ago. I'm not allowed to be here or have a job, so I'd be deported and then I wouldn't have the constant bliss of this amazing supportive relationship with Boris.'

Boris gave her a sidelong glance. But if he understood that she was being sarcastic, he didn't show it.

'We do not go to police,' said Boris. 'Never. We are anarchists.'

The man said, 'But doesn't that just mean you want a society where there's no need for police? In this society there already are police, so there's no reason not to use them.'

Boris said, 'This like vegetarian saying, "But chicken is already dead, is fine for me to eat."'

'Especially,' said Karen, 'if eating the chicken meant the vegetarian was going to be deported.'

'But wouldn't it be better to be deported than run the risk of being …?' The man didn't finish his sentence. 'I mean, after all, you could always marry Boris so he'd get a green card to live in America.'

'We do not marry,' said Boris. 'Never. We are anarchists.'

Karen turned to the man and said, 'But why don't *you* go to the police?'

'Because one of the people who tried to kill me was a policeman,' said the man. 'I'm scared of them.'

'Could he just have been dressed up as a policeman?'

'Yes, I've thought of that. But then when I got away from him, other police were chasing me.'

'But maybe someone called the real police, and when you ran away from them, they thought you were a criminal and chased you.'

'It's possible. But if the assassins are in the CIA, the police might just hand me over to them.'

'That wouldn't happen. This is Germany.'

'But then this feels like the conversation where you convinced me this was all a delusion and I should go back to hospital, and then the kindly old man tried to kill me.'

'All of this is delusion,' said Boris angrily. 'No one is trying to kill you. You are sick in head. And I am wasting my time sleeping in van and driving you to Hamburg just because you are Karen's friend since five minutes ago. You should go to hospital.'

This hit the man like a punch in the stomach. Maybe he really was just a mad person who kept having really, really detailed delusions. But if that was the case, how did he know this wasn't a delusion too? Maybe it was and he was actually still in hospital.

'But wait a minute,' he said, 'you're an anarchist. Surely you don't go to hospital.'

Boris looked at him with irritation. 'Of course we go to hospital when we are sick. We are anarchists, not idiots.'

'But then you saw that the drunk guy had a gun, didn't you Karen? And that the people in the grey Audi had guns?'

'Yes,' she said. 'I saw all that.'

Boris glanced at her and said nothing.

'Anyway,' said the man, 'whatever's happening, I've lost my memory, I hurt all over, and I've barely slept for four nights. I'm not going to make good decisions like this. If I can just get a bit of space and sleep then maybe my memory will start to come back and I'll be able to work out what's going on and what I should do.'

'Plus there's your phones,' said Karen.

'Yes. I've got two phones in my coat pockets that won't turn on. If I can charge them up, then I might be able to get in touch with someone who can tell me who I am and what's happening.'

'Why you don't mention phones before?' said Boris. 'This is first thing you have said that makes sense.'

'Hey!' said Karen.

'This is load of fucking bullshit,' said Boris. 'I drive to you in middle of fucking night–'

'It didn't have to be the middle of the night! I called you at like five thirty to tell you I'm in danger and you decided to *play a gig* first before coming to pick me up. I can't believe you.'

'What? I am in band. I have responsibilities. Drummer is *engine* of band. No drummer, no band.'

'I thought you had a responsibility to me. My life's in danger.'

'I AM FUCKING HERE!' he yelled, yanking the steering wheel so they skipped in their lane. He hit the steering wheel hard and sounded the horn, which was too quiet and cute to express his rage. Then he stared out of the window, eyes wide and shining, breathing hard.

There was a long silence in which they all stared out into the rain-lashed gloom.

'So now we go to Hamburg?' said Boris, at length. He said it roughly forty percent sarcastically, but evidently with enough of a question mark for Karen to answer.

'We're going *past* Hamburg. We're headed for a place called Norder-stapel – it's a little village and we should be there at like three o'clock. I called a friend while we were waiting in Burger King *for six fucking hours* watching the car park in case fucking killers turned up. Pola's parents live there and she said we could stay. She's coming up from Berlin to join us.'

'I can't believe she would do that,' said the man.

'Pola's the best,' said Karen. 'You know what, Germans are great in a crisis.' She looked pointedly at Boris. 'They really take it seriously and they are there for you.'

'I should pull over and leave you here,' said Boris, jaw thrust out. 'Go back to Berlin and live my life.'

'Yeah, right,' said Karen, 'till the CIA come to the apartment and kill you.'

'Why CIA would kill me?'

'Because you know me.'

'And why they would kill you?' said Boris.

'Because I know him,' said Karen.

'Sorry,' said the man. 'This is all my fault.'

'It's all the CIA's fault,' said Karen.

'We don't even know that it's the CIA,' said the man. 'I only thought that because the woman who said she was my wife had an American accent, and because I know how to clean her gun.'

'Maybe it's the KGB,' said Karen.

'KGB does no longer exist,' said Boris.

'Well there must be something instead of it,' said Karen.

'Is SVR,' said Boris. '*Sluzhba vneshney razvedki.*'

'So maybe Mister's in the SVR.'

'I have no way of knowing,' said the man.

They headed on, through the dismal grey world, through the dirty beating rain, trying to get to a place where no one was trying to kill them.

22

'So I told him they were all idiots,' said Piper.

She was sitting with her father, Gus, at his battle-scarred kitchen table, drinking tea.

'I see,' he said. He took her nearly empty tea cup and gazed into it as he swirled the dregs around.

'Are you learning to read tea leaves?' she asked, distracted.

'I'm interested in the patterns they make.'

Gus, her father, was a man who had never been known to use teabags. He always made a pot of tea with good-quality loose leaves and an old tea strainer. Though Hungarian by birth, he constantly behaved as though he were in a hard-fought contest to be the most English man alive.

He swirled the cup three times and then held it upside-down over her saucer, so that the last of the tea drained out. When it had stopped dripping, he held it in front of her.

'This is your fortune,' he said.

'What does it say?' she asked, excited in spite of herself.

'It says you will make a journey, and there's good luck in the offing,' he revealed.

'How do you know that?'

'These tea leaves here are in a straight line, which represents a journey, and it goes to the handle, which represents you, and then these curly bits coming off it look like little palm trees, which indicate good luck.'

'Well that's good. Do yours.'

'I've already done mine.'

'What did it say?'

'It said I would make a journey, and that there's good luck in the offing.'

She gasped very slightly. 'Perhaps it's the same journey: we'll make it together.'

'Perhaps,' he said. 'But I've been doing this for about a month now, and it's always the same. I think it's just in the nature of tea leaves to form lines to the handle of the tea cup and shapes that one can see as palm trees.'

Piper said, 'If there's even a single thing promising me good luck

– no matter how stupid or totally discredited – I'll take it. Otherwise I have to rely on looking at what's actually happening, and that's a nightmare.'

'I have a wise daughter,' Gus said, patting her hand.

She smiled.

'I keep her locked in the attic,' he continued mischievously, 'so that she won't make you feel bad about yourself.'

Piper suddenly, from nowhere, began to cry – as though somewhere in her head a tap had been left running and the water was leaking out through her eyes.

'I'm sorry,' said Gus. 'I don't really have another daughter whom I keep locked in the attic. I mean, I don't even have an attic.' He hunted through his pockets and handed her a handkerchief.

'I know,' she said, holding it to her eyes. 'I'm not stupid. I'm not crying because of that. I don't know why I am crying. Except that you've finally moved on from saying that Jonathon will come back when he's ready – as though you think he's an unusually tall cat – and now you're just saying "I see" and reading my tea leaves.'

'Oh dear. I'm sorry, Piper. You know I'm not very good at … well, at saying anything that even lightly touches on uncomfortable emotions. I've always found it easier to "keep the noiseless tenour of my way."'

'That's why mum left,' she said.

They looked at each other, perhaps equally shocked that she'd said it.

'Yes. I suppose it is,' he said, 'partly. When Jonathon disappeared I thought of something he'd told me about a girlfriend of his, who also suddenly disappeared. She went to France and married a farmer.'

'Rachel.'

'Was that her name? Yes. When people get together, it's not uncommon for one of them to suddenly – well, I don't like the term but no other seems to be suggesting itself – so, *freak out*' – Piper couldn't help laugh at hearing her father use a phrase coined in the last forty years – 'and need to get away for a bit. I assumed that was what had happened, and that he would be back soon.'

'We were happy,' she said. 'Mostly happy. I would have known.'

'Yes. I was … well, does "wrong" about cover it? I think it does. Yes, I was wrong. Forgive me.'

'Can you please say something about what I told you before you started reading my tea leaves?'

'I … I don't know what to say. It all seems so unlikely. I mean, the idea that Jonathon was accidentally recruited into the CIA, then went missing mysteriously and now a preposterous little man who says he's attached to the Foreign Office needs your help to find him.'

'I know it's unlikely,' she said. 'But if anyone was going to get inadvertently recruited by the CIA, who would it be?'

'Jonathon would be high up my list of candidates to suffer from any kind of misunderstanding, it's true – and the less likely the circumstance, the more likely it would be him.'

'Well then.'

'Then there are just two things I'd like to say. The first is this, and please don't be upset by it. Are you absolutely sure this little man exists? Grief can play tricks on the mind, and Jonathon's disappearance hit you with some force.'

'He exists. I thought of that. I saved the tea cup and the little plate he used. There's a tiny silver moustache hair on it. My imagination couldn't have grown that, could it?'

'Very well. Even your imagination is not so well developed that it needs to shave. And that brings me to the second thing: are you sure this man is who he says he is, and not a confidence trickster of some kind?'

'No, I'm not sure at all. He barely says who he is. He seemed almost offended when I asked if he was in MI5. But he says he's only "attached" to the Foreign Office, and I don't know what that means. And he's given me no proof of who he is or what he does, except an uninformative business card and a very heavily redacted account of an interview with Jonathon, which I've already told you about. That's when I told him they were all idiots.'

'I see. Then please allow me to accompany you next time you meet this man.'

'I'd like to. But I signed the Official Secrets Act. I'm not meant to have told you any of this.'

'I think he's unlikely to prosecute you for telling your own father. And there's no reason why I shouldn't also sign the Official Secrets Act. Perhaps if I just happened to be there the next time you meet him ...'

'Really?'

'Yes. I may be no use at all with uncomfortable emotions, but I'm on home ground when it comes to practical help dealing with odd men.'

'Thank you,' she said.

'Besides,' he said, 'I think if he is part of British intelligence, their involvement in this affair bodes very well.'

'Why?' she asked sceptically, thinking of the little sweating man who had sat in her living room.

'Because the British have always made exceptionally good spies. It seems to me that the elements of the British national character that most handicap us in other spheres are the ones that ideally suit us to being spies.'

'What do you mean?'

'I mean our culture encourages emotional reticence and politeness, which means avoiding saying what we really mean. In consequence, even the dimmest of us is expert in maintaining several different complex fictions. In short, we are a nation of excellent liars.'

'Does that really bode well?' she asked. 'That my only link to Jonathon is probably an excellent liar?'

'I should say so, especially since the Americans – despite what Hollywood tells us – are terrible spies. America is fundamentally an emotionally open culture. What makes Americans good at so many things is what makes them bad at espionage.'

'Well, that's a comfort then, that I have the liar to help me with the incompetent spies.'

23

At his desk, Sterling busied himself with the paperwork for surveillance of a German politician – Martin Baumberg of the Democratic Socialist Union. The problem with Germany was that the scruffy radicals you expected to be in opposition were actually in government. And the slick capitalists you expected to be running things were actually a small fringe element of the opposition. Yet, despite that, they had a great economy and the whole world wanted to buy all the expensive cars they made. This made it difficult to keep things straight in his head.

So did what was going on in Channon's glass-walled office behind him. Twenty minutes ago, someone had entered Channon's office and was now being given a hard time. He could tell because Channon's voice was completely inaudible, but his visitor's had been getting steadily louder and more defensive. This was also distracting because the visitor was, by most ways of reckoning, higher in the Agency's hierarchy than Channon.

Finally, he heard the door open behind him.

'Well, thanks,' said Channon from the doorway, with a quietness and lack of expression that indicated he must be furious. 'So long.'

'Hey, don't shoot the messenger, Doug. You needed to know,' said his visitor.

Sterling looked up involuntarily, and the visitor – a suited, greasy-looking man of about fifty – caught his eye. The greasy man tensed his mouth, straightened his tie and headed for the lift. Behind him, the door to Channon's office clicked shut.

A few seconds later there was a loud crash, as though something heavy had fallen to the floor. Sterling instinctively jumped, turned, and was at Channon's door before he knew it. Through the glass wall, he could see that the heavy computer that usually sat on Channon's desk was lying in the middle of carpet. Now was clearly an exceptionally bad time to go in. But Channon had seen him, so there was no going back.

He knocked on the door and put his head inside.

'Everything all right, sir?' he asked.

Channon was standing with his hands in the pockets of his baggy yellow trousers. The computer had dragged its keyboard and mouse with it to the floor, but the flat-screen monitor stood poised, miraculously, at the very edge of the desk.

'You ever observe the half-life of anger, son?' asked Channon.

'The half-life? Like radiation?'

'The time it takes for half of it to decay, yes.'

'I can't say I have, sir.'

'Well, when you do, you'll see the half-life is very short: a minute, tops. The only way to make anger last longer than that is to keep feeding it with angry thoughts. If you just look at your anger, you'll find it unwinds and drifts away.'

'Right. Yes, sir. Is that what happened here?' Sterling looked at the undesked computer.

'Yeah. That was right before the anger unwound. Give me a hand with it, will you?'

Sterling helped Channon pick up the heavy piece of beige metal and replace it on the desk. Its casing had come adrift at one side, but it looked okay otherwise.

While they were waiting for it to boot up, Channon said, 'You should have seen me before I took up meditation. It's helped a lot, but I'm cranky these days, cooped up here.' He gestured to the folded camp bed in the corner of his office. 'And then Hasselblad comes over from MK-Ultra–'

'I thought they shut that down.'

'Well, that's an understandable mistake, son, since we announced we'd shut it down in 1973. But ... well, we lied. Anyways, he gave me some pretty bad news about the propensity of MK-Ultra personnel for reverting to an amnesiac state: much greater than I was led to believe.'

'There are MK-Ultra guys here?' asked Sterling, looking through the glass wall. He bet Kerr was one, with those neatly pressed cargo pants he always wore. Kerr was definitely *something*.

'No, not here,' said Channon. 'But we've got one in the Knife-fish programme, or we did.'

'Knife-fish?'

'Never you mind. Let's just say we're relying on it to disrupt the German government's anti-war tendency. I guess you've heard about the debate Tuesday on this motion to oppose the war?'

'Uh, yes. I've seen the posters everywhere about the march. I guess people want to make sure the deputies know which way to vote.'

'Yeah, well that vote can't happen. Or at least it can't go against us. The president doesn't mind invading on our own – he's already set the date for it – as long as it doesn't look like every other country is lining up to stop us.'

24

The house was not quite as inconspicuous as the man could have wanted. It had a vast thatched roof, so neat it seemed it must have been poured on, left to set, then held up like a pie and had the edges trimmed off. Beneath, tidy walls of little bricks were inset with rounded windows and doorways.

They parked the van beside an old Saab and walked the yellow path through an emerald garden to a dark-green front door. The man felt he was stepping into a fairytale – which was welcome, after the kind of story he'd just stepped out of. But then he began to dimly remember what fairytales were like: domestic abuse, rural poverty and grisly child murders. Wasn't there one about a very long sleep? That sounded good, even if it ended with being baked in a pie or turned into a swan.

Karen looked up from her phone. 'Okay, Pola's gonna be here in like an hour. Guys, why are you not knocking on the door?'

Boris was stretching, scratching his vest and bristling his beard at the trees. Beside him, the man was staring at the door knocker and thinking about how he would cope with being a swan. He had been in a car-sleep for the last hour, which seemed to provide all the downsides of real sleep but with none of the advantages. His mind felt raw and tender, as though it had been used to scour pans.

Just as he reached for the knocker, the door opened.

Standing there was a person with a fanfare of dramatic white hair and a large frank face, like a poet on a monument. He wore a very large white cardigan, an old patterned neckerchief and faded red trousers. From behind him, a big black dog darted out and trotted in a neat semicircle around them, benignly herding these exciting tall sheep who had arrived.

The monumental poet looked at them for a second, and then said, 'Hello. You must be the friends of Pola. Yes?'

'Yes!' said Karen. 'Hi. Great to meet you. Sorry, these guys are like half-asleep.'

The monumental poet said, 'You have had a long jour–'

'Do not leave them standing outside,' said a woman who appeared next to him, wearing jeans and a hoody. She had a squarish face, its lower part occupied almost entirely by a smile, and its upper part by a large pair of glasses. 'Come in, come in,' she said, pushing the monumental poet out of the way and opening the door wide. 'Welcome in our home.'

'Yes, come in,' agreed the poet, and then said, 'Emil!' sternly to the dog, who was eating something unsavoury from the lawn.

She led them past the edge of a vast dim room filled with antique machinery and old furniture, and up a step into a small, cosy kitchen. There was a table beside the window. There were open shelves lined with crockery, tins and jars. And, in the corner, there was an old metal range, pumping out a comforting glow. She waved them to sit down and began making coffee.

'I am Gabi, and my husband is Hanno. You take milk in your coffee?'

They replied with their names and their disavowal of milk, and she nodded at each of them, her broad smile seeming to be as permanent a part of her facial furniture as the glasses.

'So, Pola says you are in danger, or?' she said, sitting down and pouring coffee for them.

'Yes,' said the man.

He exchanged glances with Karen, who said, 'Some people are

trying to kill us.'

'Sorry,' added the man. 'We thought it was best to tell you.'

'Now is wasted, seven hours driving,' said Boris angrily.

'Is there a hotel or something nearby?' asked the man.

'Yes. But you stay here, of course. No one will find you here.'

'You're sure …?'

'We stand up to the Stasi, and we stick up for you,' said Gabi.

'Of course, this area was always in West Germany,' said Hanno.

'Yes, but it is the principle. It is good that we have this chance. Remember, we once host Dieter Ernst? He is a defector from the East,' she explained. 'A writer.'

'Yes, this is true,' said Hanno. 'Not here, of course. We buy this place eleven years ago. This hosting of Dieter Ernst was in our previous flat in Hamburg, while he makes an application for asylum.'

'Which was accepted,' said Gabi. 'He lived in Bielefeld for some years. I forget where he lives now.'

'He was abducted' – Hanno paused for a tiny proud smile at remembering the word – 'and taken back to East Germany. He is executed.'

'Are you sure?' asked Gabi.

'Of course. It was on the news.'

'No, you are thinking of this other one. What is his name?'

'It was Dieter Ernst,' said Hanno.

'No it was not,' said Gabi. 'I know you are completely *wrong* about this. But this is very boring for our guests,' she said, turning back to them.

Hanno threw his hands up and shook his head. 'Emil!' he warned the dog, who was sniffing busily at the man's groin.

'So. But please,' Gabi said. 'Tell me who is trying to kill you.'

'We don't know,' said Karen. 'The CIA?'

'All we know,' said the man, 'is that it's a group of people including a woman with an American accent, an older German man, a German policeman, and a couple of others.'

He explained to Gabi and Hanno about waking up in a bin with amnesia, how someone at the hospital must have tipped off the assassins that he was there, the arrival of his fake wife and the first attempt to kill him, meeting Karen, finding his flat, the business with Otto and then their escape from Berlin.

Gabi and Hanno listened with open mouths, forgetting to drink their coffees.

After a while, Gabi said, 'But one thing I do not understand at all.

Why did you get in the car with this German man–'

'Otto,' supplied Hanno.

'–if you knew there are people trying to kill you?'

'I was just really tired and confused. I couldn't sleep properly in hospital and … well, and Karen thought I must have imagined it–'

'Can you blame me?' said Karen. 'It makes, like, no sense at all. I mean, it's basically the plot of that movie with the name I still can't remember – except dumb.'

'I think I understand this,' said Hanno. 'I was in hospital two years before, and it is very confusing. I would have entered the car of anyone afterwards.'

'So,' said Gabi. 'Me myself, I think it is best to make all this very public and then to go to the police. But yes, you are now tired and confused, and the best is just to eat some food, drink some wine – not too much – and sleep. There are two guest bedrooms through the farm room.' She gestured off, beyond the room full of machinery and furniture. 'This is not deluxe accommodation, but you will sleep well, I think.'

Hanno's phone beeped. He glanced at it and stood up. 'I must drive to the station. Pola's train is here.'

When Hanno returned with Pola, they were all standing around the kitchen table, chopping vegetables for a stew.

'Na, so, it is not that we are lazy,' Gabi was saying. 'But this front part of the house, this we have decorated and made nice. This is where the humans lived. Because this is a farmhouse from the sixteenth century, so this other big part through there is where in the past they keep the animals when it is cold, and they keep the tools and the preserved food. So, we have plans to make this also nice, but there are laws about what we can do. It takes a long time. And then we inherit some furniture and things, both of us, and Hanno cannot see something that is old and completely useless without buying it and also putting it with all this stuff. So, this explains this large zone of junk that you have seen.'

'I know she is saying these mean lies about me when I am not here,' said Hanno, good-naturedly, opening the kitchen door. He put a bottle of wine on the table.

'Not there,' said Gabi, moving it to a shelf in the larder.

'No, Emil,' said Hanno to the dog, who was eyeing a sausage with wounded longing.

'Hallo!' called a musical voice from outside, and in stepped a woman a bit younger than Karen, with bushy golden-brown hair and a face that combined Hanno's frankness with her mother's large smile.

'Hallo Pola!' said Gabi, hugging her briefly, then standing aside so her daughter could fold Karen up in a large embrace.

'Karen, how are you?' said Pola. 'This is completely crazy what you have told me on the phone yesterday. You are all right?'

'Oh my god, you are so sweet, Pola. Thank you so much for inviting us here, and for coming up from Berlin.' And then Karen's eyes were full of tears. She put down her chopping knife and felt for a tissue. 'What, crying *again*? I am the worst.'

Karen wiped her tears away and resumed her chopping, while Pola said a restrained hello to Boris and was introduced to the man who didn't know who he was.

'So, this is … well, I basically just call him Mister,' said Karen. 'His name might be Adam, but we don't really know.'

'Mister,' said Hanno. 'This has a ring to it. I can say that? "It has a ring to it?" It's correct?'

The two native English speakers assured Hanno this was correct and Pola gave the man a welcoming hug.

Later, when they were all sitting together eating, Pola turned to the man.

'How does this feel, that you don't know your name? That you have no memories?'

'I don't know,' said the man. 'I don't think I'll know till I have something to compare it to.'

'But you can maybe compare it to how you think other people feel, no?'

'I suppose so,' he said. 'Yes. In that case I feel a bit like a child when everyone else is an adult. Or like some airline ham when everyone else is a delicious traditionally made sausage. These are really nice sausages, by the way.'

'Thank you,' said Gabi. 'I get them from the local market.'

'This is very interesting,' said Pola, her eyes serious, 'about the airline ham. Do you mean you don't think you're as real as everyone else?'

'Do I? Yes, probably. But then I must have some sort of memory inside, because there are some things I expect and kind of recognise, and some things I don't. But then I don't know what sort of person I was, so I don't know how accurate my reactions are.'

'But this tells you what sort of person you were. You are someone who thinks too much and doubts a lot.'

'Was I? I'm not sure. I should … Oh, right. I see what you mean.'

'So, and how does this feel now, this sitting down and eating a meal? Do you recognise and expect this?'

'Sort of. But this … talking about my emotions … this feels a bit strange.'

'This sounds like you are English. My boyfriend is English. He also finds this very strange.'

'Make him say "cup of tea,"' said Karen.

'But why do you think you might have done something bad?' asked Pola.

'Mainly because people are trying to kill me.'

'But maybe they're trying to kill you because you did something good,' said Pola.

'Maybe,' said the man, 'but I also feel really guilty about something and I don't know what.'

'Everyone has that,' said Karen. 'That's just because we're filling the sea with plastic and not eating enough vegetables.'

'We're filling the sea with plastic? Why?'

'We're dicks,' said Karen.

'This is very interesting,' said Pola again. 'For me, if I didn't have my memories, I would definitely still be myself.'

'Maybe you're right,' said the man, feeling a bit better. 'I was worried that if I find out that I'm … I don't know, a murderer, then I'll suddenly have to start murdering again, even though I don't want to. But maybe the fact that I don't want to shows that I'm not.'

'This must be true,' said Pola.

'Oh. I feel better,' said the man, suddenly noticing that he did. He felt fine, almost like a person.

'And are there any clues about who you are?' asked Pola.

'Your phones!' said Karen. 'We forgot about your phones.'

'Yes,' said the man, 'I've got two phones in my coat pocket. They're out of battery, but if I can go somewhere tomorrow and buy chargers for them, I might find out a lot about who I was. That doesn't seem quite as scary now, somehow.'

Hanno jumped up. 'Can I see them?' he said. 'I have a workshop upstairs.' He gave the man a conspiratorial look and added, 'I have a lot of electrical things, so maybe we find something that fits your phones.'

'Let him finish his dinner,' said Gabi.

Hanno sat down, looking a little deflated, but still eager to help. 'Down, Emil,' he said to the dog, who was once again ogling a sausage.

25

They were in a corner of the deserted canteen, sitting around a small table. Four of them, nursing coffees and danishes. Overhead ran pale strip lights. Windows high up showed slices of the grey Berlin sky. In the far corner lurked a food counter, opposite the racks for depositing empty trays.

'So, I talked to Grey Owl last night,' said a woman, flicking a crumb from her fluffy pink jumper.

'And?' said a tall, bald man.

'Apparently, our plan was the problem.'

'That is bullshit,' said a man with a square jaw.

'That's what I said,' said the woman in the fluffy jumper. 'I mean, what better plan was there? Who wants to kill someone in hospital where there'll be a giant investigation, or on the street where anything can happen, anyone can get involved? How many hits have been blown and ended up all over the evening news because of that sort of shit? We take him to an apartment and do the hit there. This is planned, clinical, an expert sniper at short range with the target all lit up right in front of him.'

Heads nodded. There were murmurs of assent. The woman in the fluffy jumper, clearly annoyed, continued, 'I said, that operation was *perfectly* planned, with *multiple* levels of redundancy. I mean, as soon as we'd worked out he'd survived the balcony hit–'

An old man with white hair and a German accent interrupted, 'And I have said, "Sorry, this is my bad work not to check after I push him from his balcony." I have said this. And Grey Owl says, "I do not blame you, Tide Pool", but I feel blamed. I feel this.'

'That's what Grey Owl's like,' said the man with the square jaw. 'You do one thing wrong … or not even *wrong* exactly, just–'

'This is absolutely not exactly wrong,' said the old man. 'In my previous service this is what we specialise in, these accident-looking hits. And we are always told, don't go back and check, because this is where ninety percent of detections happen. Just make sure you are not seen, and make sure the "accident" is right–'

'The accident was perfect,' said the man with the square jaw.

'Yes, I wait a long time on that roof for him to come out, and then he comes out and is staring down at the ground. And I strike. I am not seen, and who can survive a fall from more than twenty metres? To be certain of death, fourteen metres is enough. But I understand the protocol is different here and that technically I should have checked he was dead–'

'It's not even like the protocol's set in stone or whatever,' said the man with the square jaw. 'It's like, use your judgement–'

'But this is precisely my problem with Grey Owl,' said the old man. 'It is not okay to use one's judgement.'

'What Grey Owl says and what Grey Owl means – they are two totally different things,' said the woman in the fluffy jumper.

'But excuse me,' said the old man. 'I interrupt you.'

'That's okay,' said the woman in the fluffy jumper. 'What was I saying? Oh yeah, perfectly planned. So next morning Tide Pool here's on top of the police, emergency services, morgues – he spots something's gone wrong because no dead body's been found. And he finds out which hospital the target's in. And our source in the hospital tips us off that he's lost his memory–'

'Did Grey Owl say anything about that?' asked the man with the square jaw. 'That we knew about the memory thing?'

'Uh, no, because that would have been *nice*,' said the woman in the fluffy jumper. 'And I said all this. I said, yes, we'd like to have been in there within twenty-four hours, but we all have our day jobs. So I think forty-eight hours – maybe a little more – but with a rock-solid plan is pretty good.'

'But is Grey Owl seriously saying the plan wasn't rock-solid?' said the man with the square jaw. 'I mean, we rent a premium holiday apartment, you turn up *in the Audi* – I mean, that is a sweet-ass SUV – and it's *you*. Who doesn't want to be married to you? Who isn't going to do whatever you tell them?'

'Uh, Great Lakes?' said the bald man. 'I think you're revealing that you're in love with Two Rivers.'

Great Lakes, the man with the square jaw, said, 'So? Two Rivers knows I think she's hot.'

'Hey, come on guys,' said the woman in the fluffy jumper. 'The target's lost his memory and he's just spent two days in hospital. He'd have gone home with Great Lakes if we'd put a little lipstick on him.'

The bald man said, 'But the proof of the plan is that it worked. He sits right down in the chair, he's all lit up, I'm in the apartment across the way. I've got a perfect shot lined up. I'm squeezing the trigger. And at *that exact instant* he's suddenly up and on the other side of the room. It's like he knew. I take a second shot, but he's already hit the deck. And then Two Rivers comes in to confirm the kill and start the tear-down. Second level of redundancy: she has an assault rifle, in case he's not dead. But he gets past her – somehow.'

'I don't know how he did it,' said the woman in the fluffy jumper. 'It's like he moved so *awkwardly* … I didn't know where he was. I don't understand it. I mean, I've taken down professional wrestlers. Remember that Bulgarian guy?'

'Czech,' said the bald man. 'You always say Bulgarian. He was Czech.'

'Seriously?'

'Yeah. Sedlak? We've had this exact same conversation like two or three times already. Anyway, whatever, he gets past you but this is also fine. We've got this covered because Grass Green's also in the apartment–'

'Where is Grass Green, by the way?' asked the man with the square jaw.

'Rixdorf,' said said the woman in the fluffy jumper. 'He should be here in like twenty minutes.'

'But he gets past Grass Green too,' said the bald man. 'So, fourth level of redundancy: Great Lakes is waiting outside the front door. But the target gets past him too–'

'Like Two Rivers said, it's that awkwardness, man.'

'And he totally disappears. I don't want to say it, but it looks like he's exactly what they say he is.'

'Yes, I must agree strongly with this theory,' said the old man. 'I am doing my turn, watching the flat, assuming that if he is back, he has regained his memory. But no. He found the apartment without getting back his memory. How?'

'Yeah, it's a mystery,' said the woman in the fluffy jumper.

'I call you, then I go in to the flat, and I must to improvise. Maybe I should have tried to shoot them both. But he is standing by a knife on the chopping block. I manage to split them up. I get him in the car, and I know I have just to get him to a quiet place, because you and Grass Green have answered my call. I know you will be with me soon. But he seemed to know. Suddenly. One second he believed me that I was his neighbour; the next second, not.'

'And before you know it, you're unconscious, lying under a tree in Waldeck park with no pants,' said the bald man.

The old man looked down at his new jeans, took a sip of coffee and shook his head.

'Feels like we're all kind of lying under a tree with no pants right now,' said the woman in the fluffy jumper. 'I mean, me and Grass Green lost him. We just flat lost him. That does not happen.'

'Yeah,' said the man with the square jaw. 'And I'm trailing this girl – who knows where *she* comes from, by the way? – back to her apartment. And this'll be the one good source of information we have. If we snatch her, we'll start to know what we're dealing with. But suddenly he turns up. And again, we're running around the streets in broad daylight with guns. We cannot keep getting manoeuvred into doing this. And now he's gone, and we have to work out how to account for Tide Pool's missing car. I mean, I thought Knife-fish must be bullshit, but I have to agree: maybe this guy's the real thing.'

'And I said that to Grey Owl,' said the woman in the fluffy jumper. 'I said that.'

'And? Reaction?'

'That we're using it as an excuse. Apparently Knife-fish doesn't work like that.'

'But–'

'I know. So, Grey Owl's disappointed in us. I mean, really pissed. The target's out there somewhere, he's seen us clearly, and sooner or later he'll get his memory back. It's a ticking time bomb for all of us. Grey Owl has a plan, says there's a slim chance of turning things around, but our part of this plan is basically hit pause, keep quiet, and wait for a call.'

There was a stunned silence.

'After everything we've done,' said the bald man, 'Grey Owl's going to let this one setback mean total failure?'

'Why are we not having this conversation in a bar?' said the man with the square jaw. 'I feel like we need to get shitfaced.'

26

The moment dinner was over, Hanno excitedly jumped up and took the man and his two dead phones upstairs to his workshop. It was in the human part of the house, and looked recently renovated, with wooden panelling and a window at one end. It was crammed full of equipment and technology of all kinds. There were two computers on a crowded desk, and several shelves full of equipment cases, all surrounded by cables and baskets of oddments.

'This is my room of new things,' Hanno said, with that same conspiratorial glee he had shown earlier. 'So, let me see these two telephones.'

The man handed the phones over to Hanno, who prowled around, trying many different plugs, opening drawers and being struck by brainwaves. He produced a charger for the smaller, more standard-looking phone first. They plugged it in. A few seconds later it turned on and its screen told them in German that it had five new messages. The man listened to them, and found they were all from a German named Stefan, asking him why he wasn't at work.

By this time, Hanno had managed to splice together an adapter and a plug from two separate devices, stripping the wires and taping them together. He plugged this phone in and smiled delightedly when its screen lit up.

He was animatedly explaining the way he had combined the two cables when the phone began to vibrate, displaying 'Number withheld' on its screen – in English. Hanno picked it up, pressed the large green answer button and handed it to the man.

Oh, this is happening now, he thought. He held it to his ear.

'Hello?' he said.

'Is this Newman?' said a measured official voice with an American accent.

'I don't know,' said the man. 'Maybe.'

'Uh, please state your call sign.'

'I don't know anything about call signs. I've lost my memory.'

'I suggest you find your memory and state your call sign.'

'I told you, I don't know my call sign. I don't know what's going on. Are you trying to kill me?'

'Uh, please repeat.'

'I said, are you trying to kill me?'

'Uh, please hold.'

The line went quiet, presumably while the official-sounding voice went off to find out whether they were trying to kill him. The man looked at the device, then put it back to his ear. Hanno raised his eyebrows theatrically, his eyes asking a silent question. The man made an 'I don't know what's going on' face. It didn't feel much different from his normal face.

'… over. Yeah, I got it,' said the official-sounding voice, as though he were talking to someone else. 'Transferring.'

After a few seconds a new voice came on the line.

'Channon here.' This voice was older, wearier, less official, but still American. 'So, what's going on?'

'Um, I've lost my memory and people are trying to kill me.'

'Okay, son. Don't worry. Where are you now?'

'I can't tell you.'

'You don't know?'

'I know, but I think if I tell you you'll come here and try to kill me again.'

'Son, we aren't trying to kill you. We're on the same side. I'm your boss, remember?'

'No, I've lost my memory.'

'Well, that figures.'

'What do you mean?'

The voice who had identified itself as Channon didn't answer, but instead asked, 'Who are you with?'

'No one.'

'Listen, I've got to wonder whether you've been compromised, son. If someone's got you, I'm saying to them now, if they're listening: state your demands and we can talk.'

'Um, no one's got me. But I've got some demands – well, requests really.'

'Okay, shoot. What do you want?'

'Well, the first one's the most important, really: could you please stop trying to kill me?'

'We aren't trying to kill you, son. What's next?'

'Well, if you aren't trying to kill me – and I have to bear in mind that you'd probably say that even if you were trying to kill me – I'd like to know who is trying to kill me and how to stop them.'

'Son, if someone's trying to kill you, we want to stop them just as bad as you do. Anything else?'

'Yes, I'd like to know who I am. Oh, and also what my bank details are. Do you know? I've got a card but no PIN, and I've only got twenty euros left.'

'You need money?'

'Um, yes.'

'Listen, if someone has got you and they want money, they need to say that. Strange as it may seem, the way our budgets work, it's actually easier for us to get money to pay a ransom than it is to make an emergency field payment. So, again, they need to let us know.'

'No one's got me, yet.'

'Okay, and I know you may not be at liberty to say if they have.'

'They haven't.'

'If they have, signal it now by saying, "I'm fine."'

'They haven't.'

'Still not conclusive, but okay, let's go with that for the moment. So, here's what we're going to do. I'll send some guys out to pick you up. They'll bring you here to Berlin station, and we'll straighten everything out – get your memory back, and reunite you with your bank account.'

'I can't do that because I still think you might kill me – sorry.'

'Okay. Well, do you have a proposal?'

'Not yet. I'm really tired, and it was you who phoned me, remember?'

'Yeah, right. Well, that was technically not me but Kerr, who was following protocol, though I had asked–'

'Okay. I was only saying.'

'Can I ask you a couple of questions?' said the voice.

'Um, yes. All right.'

'Have you survived an assassination attempt?'

'Yes. Two attempts.'

'Did you get a good look at the assassins? Could you describe what they did?'

'Yes.'

'Great. Are you currently armed?'

'You mean with a gun?' asked the man.

'Yes.'

'I don't want to answer that. It might influence whether you try to kill me, if it is you who's trying to.'

'Fair enough. One more question: you have any memories at all?'

'Not really.' He decided not to mention the cockneys.

'Okay. And have you been in touch with anyone else?'

'I don't want to answer any more questions tonight. Sorry.'

'So, what do you want to do?'

'I'm going to finally get some sleep, and then I'll call you tomorrow afternoon.'

'You remember how?'

'No.'

'Then I'll call you. Noon. Meanwhile I'll start in on the paperwork for a field payment. And if someone is holding you, make sure they understand about our ransom budgets. It's so much easier if they declare it.'

'Right.'

'Just one final thing. You need to come in, for the sake of your own health. We understand this amnesia, and we can treat it, help you remember who you are. Now we can talk tomorrow about how you do that, and give you any guarantees you need. In the meantime, whatever you do, don't go to the cops. You won't be safe if you do.'

27

———

It was late afternoon and the shadows were long and grey, diluted by the fuzz of fine rain. Michaels pulled his battered Rover into the driveway of a grand old Victorian house, and came to a stop behind a large, quietly new Volvo. He sat for a moment, listening to the creak and rub of the windscreen wipers. Then he turned off the ignition and took his old leather folio case from the passenger's seat.

Shoulders rounded against the rain, Michaels crunched up the damp gravel path. He gazed at the old rocking horse in the bay window – far too beautiful a thing, with its carefully painted saddle and horsehair mane, to be used by real children – and then climbed the steps to the front door and rang the bell-pull.

A click. The coloured glass in the fanlight above the door lit up. Forthright steps sounded on a stout wooden floor. The door opened.

'Michaels,' she said. 'Do come in.'

She was imposing, like a human cathedral, with her bobbed white hair and imperious nose.

'Dame Margery,' he said. 'Thank you.'

She stood aside and closed the door behind him, then held out her arms. For a horrified second, he thought she was waiting for him to embrace her. But then he realised she intended to help him off with his overcoat, which had absorbed a really surprising amount of moisture during his brief walk up the drive.

'So glad you could come,' she said, putting his coat on a hanger. 'I do prefer to be here at the weekends if I possibly can. Monday to Thursday is quite enough time at the Fairground.'

The Fairground. That was what they called it. A large, leaky interwar building standing near what had been Battersea Park's funfair. The park's real fairground, drab and regrettably lethal, had been closed in 1972. But the name had stuck. Dame Margery was comptroller of Michaels' section.

'Thank you very much for your kind invitation, Dame Margery,' he said.

'Fiddlesticks,' she said, in her direct way. 'You would have preferred not to have driven two hours in the rain to talk to me.'

He opened his mouth to deny it, but she had already turned her back and was marching towards the kitchen. Michaels followed. Stepping inside, he was hit by a wave of cosiness that steamed up his glasses. A large blue Aga dominated one wall, while the others were taken up by old Welsh dressers and cast-iron cookware.

Dame Margery indicated that he should sit at a vast, dark Georgian table, while she busied herself making Bovril for them. No one could persuade her not to, especially on a rainy day.

During the week she wore rather severe suits, but today she had on an asymmetrical jacket of plum-coloured velvet, a man's checked shirt, a cravat, and brown corduroy trousers which she had tucked into her socks.

Michaels cleared his throat, wondering how to begin.

'So,' she said, 'what has upset you?'

'Upset me?' asked Michaels.

'Yes. Why are you here?'

'I have been party to three rather unusual conversations in the last two days. I was curious as to your thoughts.'

'Tell me,' she said, stirring a small cast-iron saucepan with unusual force.

'Well, as I think you know, Mr Channon asked, as a matter of form, that I liaise with the co-habitee of a British citizen he recruited, and who has gone missing.'

'I was aware he had been in touch, yes.'

'Mr Channon wanted me to find out whether that citizen had been in touch with the co-habitee. He also asked me to see what I could find out from her, in a rather vague way. He said I should gain her trust, which I endeavoured to do by asking about the cat and helping with the washing up.'

'Names,' said Dame Margery, 'are a great help in distinguishing between people, I've always found.'

'Forgive me. The British citizen is a Jonathon Fairfax – spelled, rather against convention, with a penultimate "o". His former co-habitee is Miss Piper Palgrave.'

'And?'

'He had not – not been in touch with her, I mean. But one or two things she said awakened a doubt in me as to whether Fairfax joined the Americans entirely voluntarily.'

'One or two things she said?'

You're all idiots had been one. And of course *You've accidentally recruited Jonathon into the CIA.* He decided not to repeat them verbatim.

'Subtle things,' he summarised. 'And the fact that, following his disappearance, the Americans are worried that Fairfax might have got in touch with her. It's …' He couldn't quite find the word for what it was, so he let the sentence hang in the air above the Georgian table.

'I see,' said Dame Margery. She set two earthenware mugs on the table and shared the Bovril between them. Then she took a small bottle of brandy from the shelf and sloshed a measure into each.

Michaels looked unhappily at his Bovril and brandy, wishing there were something he could do to avoid it. But it was just what happened here. He took a horrid, scalding sip and continued.

'He hadn't been in touch with her before, you see, ever since being recruited. He had just vanished.'

'Well, that is the way some men like to play it.'

'It seemed out of keeping in this case.'

'Well,' said Dame Margery, 'if what you suspect is true – a British citizen has been forcibly recruited to the CIA, leaving his co-habitee …' She searched for a word.

'Distraught?' he suggested. 'Bereft?'

'Distraught. *If* all that's true, I would put it under the heading of "Unfortunate but, in the wider scheme of things, unimportant." Wouldn't you agree?'

'Not necessarily.'

'I see.'

'I have a source who has reason to believe that Mr Channon is not necessarily extraordinarily reliable.'

'Meaning?'

'He's working for someone else, another intelligence service.'

'Channon's a mole?' Dame Margery asked.

Michaels nodded.

'Working for whom?' she asked.

'My source didn't say.'

28

When Channon put the phone down, Sterling saw him smile properly for the first time. This was not his usual slight upward tension at the edges of his mouth, but a full grin, exposing a set of bright Californian teeth. Channon, sitting at Sterling's desk, leaned back, looked at the ceiling and let out a long breath.

'I'm glad you spotted that call, son.'

'No problem, sir. I've been looking out for the system flag to say his sat-phone's turned back on.'

'Good job, son. And now we know Newman's still alive. In fact, a lot of mysteries have just been cleared up. He's alive, he's lost his memory – like the MK-Ultra guys said – and he survived an attempt to kill him, which means he's the first lead we have for identifying who's behind these killings.'

'That's great, sir.'

'Of course, we still have to bring him in.'

'You think he's being held?'

'I don't know. But we know where he is now his sat-phone's back on, so the first step is to get eyes on him.'

'Anything I can do to help, sir? I can stay here as long as it takes.'

'Actually, yes. Tell Lake that you've been transferred off surveillance accounting. Tell him you're working on Newman, for me.'

'Yes, sir. Thank you. How do you want to handle this?'

'First thing I want you to do is get a spyplane up there – a U2, if you can find one. Patch it through to my workstation. I want eyes on Newman ASAP. Second thing is, get a team up there – reliable guys, discreet. From Berlin if possible, Hamburg if not. Get them up there ASAP too, but quietly.'

'Sir. Anything else?'

'Yes. After that, go home, get some rest. Nothing's going to happen till tomorrow.'

Sunday

29

RURR-RURR RURR
   RURR-RURR RURR
The man was deeply submerged in sleep – the sort of sleep where your mind and body fully shut down, giving you a lovely little jaunt into nonexistence – and he had to swim long and hard for the surface, for consciousness. He emerged in a small room, dark but for the moonlight shining through the thin cotton curtains – and the screen of the phone vibrating beside his bed.

The bed was incredible. His body had never been so warm and comfortable as in this lumpy bed in this unheated room. Compared with the hospitals, sofas and vans he was used to, it was like lying in a large toasted marshmallow.

RURR-RURR RURR
   RURR-RURR RURR
The phone. He'd been drifting off again. His arms still ached and his hands, stupid with sleep, had forgotten how to hold things. He fumbled the phone onto the bed, briefly lost it, and at last had it in his hands. 'Number withheld,' said the screen. He untangled himself from the charging cable and coaxed his blurred thumb into pressing the large green answer button.

'Hu-muh?' he said with his vague mouth.

'Do not talk,' said a voice. 'Remain silent. You are in danger. But I am going to guide you through it. This is Channon again. If you have heard and understood, tap the microphone: that's the small hole near your mouth.'

The man looked at the phone and tapped a small hole near the bottom.

'Son, you need to work on your tap,' said Channon. 'Try again.'

The man did it again, this time with his fingernail, and with a finger that didn't feel quite so much like it was made of spongecake. He was rapidly waking up.

'The house you are in is surrounded by a team of at least four hostiles. I can't see much detail from my pictures. But it looks like two are taking up covering positions, one on the southeast corner, the other on the northwest. Then there are two more together at a point on the south side, close to the house, probably working to open a window or a door. You have seconds to react. Staying in your current room, move silently to position yourself against the outer wall. Then tap.'

The man got out of bed as quietly as he could, disconnecting the phone from the charger cable. He stood in the narrow space between the end of the bed and the outside wall, his feet ice cold on the tiled floor. He tapped his fingernail on the phone.

'Are you in a room with a window?' said Channon. 'Tap once for yes, twice for no.'

The man tapped once.

'Turn your head to the window and inch toward it. Stop before your eye is level with the vertical edge of the window frame.'

The man frowned, finding the language too technical to immediately grasp. Which one was vertical? Was he meant to be upside-down? While he was trying to work it out, he stayed hidden beside the wall and glanced out of the window, which – he suddenly realised – was what Channon had meant him to do.

'Tap once if it's clear,' said Channon, 'twice if you can see anyone outside the window.'

The man tapped once.

'German windows are typically hinged on the side and open inwards. Is that the case here? You know the drill: tap once for yes, twice for no.'

This window was old, with many small rectangular panes, and a large cast-iron handle, but it opened the way Channon was suggesting. The Germans must have started thinking about the best way to open windows a long time ago. He tapped once.

'Okay. Do you know which way is north?'

The man was surprised to find he did. The sun had been setting behind them when they had parked. That meant the dark-green door where they'd been welcomed was on the south side of the house – which must be where the people Channon called hostiles were trying to get in. This room was on the opposite side, just off the huge space full of the old and completely useless things that Hanno had inherited or bought. He tapped once.

'That's good, son. Now which wall are you up against? Tap when I say the correct compass bearing.'

When Channon said 'north', the man tapped.

'Okay. That's good. Now, can you hear anything?'

The man took the phone away from his ear, listening. There was no noise from anywhere in the house. It struck him that, last time they had spoken, he had assumed Channon was trying to kill him. Why was he now doing what he was saying? He didn't really know. The world was really confusing and he could never get enough sleep to think straight.

He tapped twice. *No.*

'That's good,' said Channon. 'Look at the window. You think you can open the catch without making a noise?'

The cast-iron handle looked old but well used: the paint was all worn off on the surface that kept the window shut. The man tapped once.

'On my monitor, it looks like there's a patch of vegetation directly in front of you. It appears to be a dividing line between properties. Is there an obstacle behind or within it?'

Beyond the window was a narrow strip of straggly grass and then a slightly wider border, crowded with leafy plants and bushes. Behind that was an old wall of about head height. The man tapped once.

'If you got out of the window, could you run to the patch of vegetation?'

Tap.

'Could you climb over the obstacle?'

'It's a wall,' whispered the man.

'Do not speak,' said Channon. 'Could you climb over it?'

Channon sounded annoyed, and there was no tap option for 'maybe', so the man single-tapped for yes. He could definitely climb over it. He just didn't know how.

'Okay,' said Channon, sounding slightly mollified. 'Is there something in the room that's small enough to pick up and throw easily, but big enough to be seen from a distance? Like a pillow or a cushion?'

Tap. There was the pillow he'd slept on. It was a bit baggy, but throwable. He made a mental note to buy Gabi and Hanno a new pillow, if he didn't die.

'Pick it up and get ready to go. As soon as I see those hostiles enter the house, you need to open the window, throw out the cushion and then run for that cover.'

Tap.

'Two things you need to remember. One. Don't believe the movies: it's hard to hit a moving target, especially at night, even if with night-vision equipment and a lot of training. So move. Two. If you're running, run fast in a straight line. Don't get clever with zig-zagging and all that shit. I hope some of the rest is in your muscle memory. But keep those two things in mind. You got that?'

Tap.

'Unless the hostile in cover to the northwest has his gun on your window already, it'll take him longer to adjust his aim, pick up a moving target and fire, than it will for you to run to those bushes and hit the deck. Most likely, he'll wonder what you dropped, and that will encourage him to keep back. He'll radio to the two mobile hostiles, but they'll be slowed down by having to get back out of the house. You need to throw yourself over that wall. Then you're in a garden with a house in front of you. You put yourself on the other side of that house and run faster than you ever ran in your life. You need to do all that in the time it takes them to get out of the house, run around it and reach that wall. You got that?'

Tap. Jesus, it sounded awful. He'd better put on some trousers and shoes first. He was wearing only his hospital-laundered boxer shorts and a mystifying old mauve band T-shirt Hanno had lent him, bearing a picture of some bearded men and the words 'Agitation Free'.

But at that moment Channon said, 'They're in. Three, two, one. Go!'

The man grabbed the handle, pulled the window open, bundled the pillow clumsily out, and then leapt out himself, rolling instinctively and unexpectedly as he hit the grass, then flopping under a bush beside the wall.

Zoop!

That sound, the same sound he remembered from the night his pretend wife had tried to kill him.

He pressed himself desperately into the damp soil.

Zoop! Zoop!

'Get over that fucking wall, son!' screamed the phone in his hand.

30

RURR-RURR RURR
  RURR-RURR RURR
Piper was suspended between sleep and waking. She was a dim disembodied consciousness that lived in a warm void where there was only an insistent regular buzzing and nothing else.

Then other elements joined the void. There was a weight on her legs, the almost theatrical overbreathing of the dog, the swish of distant traffic, the discomfort in her hand which she had again trapped under her pillow.

She had shared her bed with a cat and a dog for so long that she was now able to sleep through a huge variety of odd noises. Before he had disappeared, Jonathon had helped her improve this skill by regularly talking in his sleep, mostly explaining defensively the extreme difficulties involved in drawing hands.

By now, enough of Piper had arrived back in the world that she was able to realise that the buzzing was her phone, in her bag over by the door. It stopped. Who could it have been?

RURR-RURR RURR
There it was again. Piper shifted her legs and the cat huffily got off them and went to sit on the far side of the bed. Cess was lying against Piper's back. The dog gave one of her deep groans and rolled onto her side.

RURR-RURR RURR
Piper got out of bed and rooted through her bag in the gold streetlight that seeped in around the curtains. Her hand was faint and fizzy from being trapped under the pillow by the weight of her head. She fumbled with the phone, finally getting a good grip. It stopped vibrating.

'Missed call(s): 4,' the screen told her.

Who were they from? She pressed the 'menu' button and immediately the vibrating began again. She dropped the phone, scrambled in her bag, pressed the button.

'Hello?' she said.

'Good morning, my dear. I do hope I didn't wake you.'

'Of course you woke me. You rang me five times in the middle of the night.'

'Ah, yes. Of course. I should have said that I'm sorry to have woken you. It's early and I'm not thinking as clearly as I should like.'

'That's all right, um, Michaels – if you're sure you want me to call you that. What is it?'

'The Americans have made a breakthrough in finding Mr Fairfax. They've asked for your presence in Berlin, to help them.'

'But that … that's great. Isn't it? When do they want me to go?'

'Immediately, I'm afraid. They have booked you a seat on a rather optimistically early aeroplane. I'll accompany you.'

'Oh, thank you. What do you mean by immediately? And where are you?'

'By "immediately", I mean ten minutes' time at the very most. I am standing outside your front door.'

31

'I said get over that fucking wall!' shrieked Channon again.

The man heard him even though the phone was a fair distance from his ear, which was pressed to the ground behind a leafy bush. It seemed unfair of Channon to be so insistent on silence if he was going to shout so loudly through a phone.

Nonetheless, the man did as Channon said. He leapt to his feet, grabbed the wall with his left hand and right wrist, threw himself at it, getting a painful hold on the ancient mortar with his ankle and little toe, throwing an elbow over, holding on with his chin, slithering his chest sharply over the wet bricks on top, balancing weirdly on his stomach, kicking his legs, dropping hard down the other side, landing on the top of his head, collapsing flat on his back, scrabbling for the phone, then running, running.

There was absolutely no way they hadn't shot him: getting over the wall had been the slowest, clumsiest and loudest physical action ever performed by a human being. He hadn't heard them, but surely they must have got out of the house and started firing before he was even halfway over the wall. He must be bleeding to death as he ran. Perhaps it was cheating to keep on running anyway, but he did.

He ran around the side of the house, just as Channon had told him to. The grass was cold and wet, and his feet were telling him in detail about all the sticks, crunching snails and animal poo they were running over. At any other time he would have stopped immediately, but right now all those things – painful though they were – were of purely academic interest.

He ran through the front garden, across a narrow road that slapped sharp and cold against the tender soles of his feet, and on towards a large metal barn with the name 'Hartmut Börm' painted on it.

A dog started barking, and then cows began to moo – a vast bellow reverberating from the barn, as though a lot of very fat and unhappy Yorkshiremen were all saying 'ooh' at once. He ran beside it, dodged right, crossed a courtyard, tripped over a piece of wood and fell, lying there as he adjusted to the shock of it, and to the shock of there being no blood pooling around him, the shock of not having been shot. And then he was up again and running, hearing now the feet of his pursuers on the road. He ran through the courtyard, between two outbuildings, and out into a wide street. He saw the street sign – *Wide Street*, it was called – and he couldn't help thinking that the Germans just never, ever stopped being German, even for a second.

'What now?' he said into the phone.

'Turn right. Left is open country.'

The man turned right, running south down Wide Street.

'Look out for opportunities to run left, through gardens. I don't have the detail on this monitor.'

There! He charged off left beside a white house, down a driveway that led to a garden. His feet were hurting so much that they had almost stopped bothering to tell him about it.

Zoop!

The noise came from behind, from Wide Street, and was instantly followed by the snare drum of a breaking windscreen.

The man was in a dark garden enclosed by wooden fences. Trapped. He ran for the south fence, getting a toehold on one of its vertical wooden slats, flinging both arms over the top, so that he was clinging to it by the armpits. He threw one shoulder forward and somehow got his heel up to the top. As he did this, his penis flopped out of his boxer shorts and – even in the dark and running for his life – he felt a flush of embarrassment on his cheeks. Then he fell down the other side, through a scratchy bush. He could hear pounding footsteps.

The man was in another garden, again enclosed by fences. He had the impression that his pursuers had reached the garden behind him. If he tried to get over the next fence they'd surely see and shoot him.

119

It felt too much of a risk. He looked around desperately. Could he get into the house?

An instinct in him ignored this thought – as though his conscious brain was now irrelevant – and hurled his body at the fence to his left, running his shoulder into it at full speed. There was a crunch as the slats splintered, folding inward but remaining in place. His whole body was jarred. He ran again. This time there was no resistance in the slats; they burst and he toppled into the next garden, tripping over the unbroken lower slats, hitting his ear on the upper slats and jarring his neck as he went.

Zoop!

Behind him there was the heavy rattling of someone with boots climbing a fence. He ran down the garden, around a greenhouse, beside a bungalow, turned right into another street. From behind he heard the cymbal roll of smashing plate glass.

He had only a tiny sliver of time before they would be out onto the street behind him. He wanted to turn right, get further up in the nest of gardens and fences he'd just left. Again, his body ignored him. He felt himself turning left instead, running across the narrow street, beside a large house with a pond. He sheltered behind the house, near the pond, looking back into the narrow street he'd just left, thinly illuminated by the sparse streetlights.

An angry male voice called from a window somewhere in the street, '*What make you there?*'

There was the sound of running footsteps. A dark figure with an assault rifle appeared in the street, wearing combat boots, a bullet-proof vest and a fluffy jumper. Amy.

The window slammed shut. Whoever had shouted at Amy had evidently thought again once he saw how heavily armed she was. Amy said something quietly into a microphone. She was joined by another dark figure, bigger and with a square jaw, emerging from the same garden. Amy signalled, and this second figure ran on, up the street, looking left and right.

His pursuers didn't know which way he'd gone.

Amy stood there, looking around with her night-vision goggles. The man, still hidden behind the house, froze. He drew back into the darkness.

Now he could see nothing, only hear. He worked hard to quieten his breathing. His body wanted to take in big, noisy lungfuls of air, but he was forcing it to take in less, slower. Each breath was a fight to prevent himself taking a bigger breath. He needed oxygen: he'd been running, climbing and shoulder-barging fences for quite some time now. But he was terrified Amy would hear.

He tensed his stomach and chest, let out a long, controlled exhalation and allowed himself to breathe in. Then he put one eye around the wall. The street looked empty. Had Amy moved on? Or was she walking stealthily along the other side of the house, about to come around the corner and see him?

He moved off, at a crouch, making for the front of the house. Reaching it, he put one eye around the corner, looking down the little street.

Neither Amy nor the other armed figure was anywhere to be seen. In the house across the street, the lights were on and someone in an upstairs room was talking anxiously into a phone.

The man turned right and ran up the street, heading north, then ducked behind the first house on his right. Looking around the corner, he saw the street was still empty. He was terribly tense and afraid. Had his pursuers gone?

He took stock. He was a very cold and confused man hiding behind a house. He had badly damaged feet, a weird T-shirt and fourth-day boxer shorts. Oh, and the phone in his hand.

'Hello?' he whispered into it.

'You hit?' said Channon.

'Um, I don't think so. No.'

'Good job, son,' said Channon. 'The two mobile hostiles are heading back in the direction of the house. The other two are still covering it.'

'Is everyone all right?'

'The hostiles?'

'No, the people in the house.'

'I guess so. The hostiles haven't been back into the house. But you can't afford to focus on that. You are the priority. You ... Wait. They've turned around. Looks like they're headed back your way. You're gonna need to ditch this sat-phone.'

'But I need to stop anything bad happening to the others. And why do I have to, um, throw away the satellite phone?'

'The two mobile hostiles are heading back in your direction. I can see the approximate location of the sat-phone – within around three hundred metres. They must be able to as well. What can I tell you? It looks like we've got security problems. My advice, leave the phone hidden where you are and head southeast, towards what look like shops or commercial lots of some kind. There's plenty of cover in that direction.'

'Have you, er, called the police?'

'No. The police are after you, son. And–'

'But what for? What did I do?'

'There's no time to go into that right now. The cops are not your friends, and I don't think you'll be safe in a cell. Listen, I have a team headed out there. They should be with you in forty-one minutes. You have around thirty minutes till daybreak. My guess is that the hostiles won't keep up the pursuit in broad daylight. But if they do, my guys should be able to deal with them. They'll be in blue Audi SUVs. If the hostiles are still there, they'll engage. If not, they'll wait for you in front of Holger Kähler's car dealership. Stay alive and hidden till then. If something goes wrong and you need to get in touch, find the number for Berlin Surf Shack and ask to speak to Ronald. You got that?'

'Surf Shack Berlin, Ronald, hide the phone. Blue Audis, car dealership. Daylight.'

'Good job, son. Godspeed.'

The man pushed the satellite phone neatly into the soft earth behind a large petunia. Then he looked around the side of the house, up the narrow street. It was still clear.

He didn't run southeast, as Channon had told him to, but northwest, back the way he'd come.

He soon reached Wide Street, turned off it beside where Hartmut Börm's cows were now bellowing more softly, and cut left, around the first house he'd come to, back to the wall. He crouched behind it, breathing hard.

He was so cold, so battered, and so offended by these repeated and very personal attempts to kill him that he found he was silently weeping.

If he climbed over the wall, someone would almost certainly try to shoot him. And after that, several more people would energetically try to kill him in other ways. It seemed likely they would keep on trying until he eventually obliged them by dying.

If he didn't climb over the wall, he could probably run away and stay hidden till Channon's people arrived. He would then have the protection of one of the most powerful organisations in the world, and would presumably get answers to all the questions that had tormented him.

But all the people he had known in his five-day life were on the other side of the wall: everyone who had been kind to him for, as far as he could calculate, no reason at all. And if the assassins had tried to grab Karen before, why wouldn't they do it again?

At this moment, the only thing capable of offering any resistance at all was himself: a thin man in a stranger's T-shirt and four-day-old boxer shorts, full of fear and yearning, shivering in the night in a stranger's floral border.

Was he really going to do this?

32

Piper's suitcase was on the bed, her bag open beside it. She was in the little en-suite bathroom, gathering things, filling a spongebag, ready to compose herself in the airport toilets. As she turned back to her spongebag, she made the mistake of glancing in the mirror.

She was a monster.

Her hair and face had twisted themselves into weird shapes during the night. Or perhaps it wasn't just during the night: it was the effect of all these months of grief and worry. She imagined Jonathon looking at her and saying, 'Um, do you ... have you seen Piper?'

Her brain helpfully conjured another scenario: them together in a room and him saying, 'I'll just, um ...' and then the sound of the door slamming and feet running as he escaped down the road. But of course they wouldn't be reunited because he was missing, gone, dead. And all these thoughts flashed through her head in a second as she saw herself in the mirror, a tube of moisturiser in one hand and her spongebag in the other. And there was her oversensitive white dog sitting in the doorway, viewing her with sympathy and grave concern. Piper began to cry and instantly stopped.

She could hear Michaels in the kitchen, incompetently making a cup of tea. Soon he would say, 'Are you ready?' or something like that, and she would say, 'If I were ready I would be standing by the door fully dressed and holding a suitcase.' And then she would cry again or start laughing in an unhinged way, or both. And anyway, why had they woken her up in the middle of the night and given her ten minutes to leave? Jonathon had been gone nearly two years, so how could a few minutes more make any difference?

She sat on the laundry basket, straightened her dressing gown and took a deep breath. You're not a monster, she told herself, just a woman woken in the middle of the night whose legs need shaving. Or a woman woken in the middle of the night who was being oppressed by an unrealistic beauty standard. Or something.

Cess padded over and Piper ruffled the dog's ears and the top of her head, and instantly felt much better. Then Michaels appeared on the landing, holding a cup of tea and averting his eyes.

'Are you ready yet, my dear?' he asked.

'Nearly,' she said. 'The only things left to do are packing and dressing.'

He seemed on the point of saying something, but changed his mind and instead put the tea down beside the bedroom door.

'I'll leave your tea here,' he said. 'We must leave in four minutes, so you have time for three sips.'

'Thanks,' said Piper. And then she put on yesterday's clothes and piled objects in her suitcase until it was full.

33

The man threw his hands up, grabbed the top of the wall, dug his big toes into the mortar, pulled himself up and over in a single motion, dropped into the shrubbery, rolled onto the grass and dived through the little bedroom window.

Zoop! Zoop! Zoop!

He landed with his face in his own shoes, scrambled around and banged the window shut, turning the handle. Shivering, he grabbed his coat, felt to check the wallet was inside, pulled it on, then ran out through the bedroom door, slamming it behind him.

He heard the glass in the bedroom window smash. He worked fast, desperately. He had only the length of time it would take the hostile outside to put his hand through one of the panes, open the catch and climb in through the window. Grabbing a heavy, petrol-driven lawnmower, he wheeled it so it stood sideways-on to the thick and ancient bedroom door, keeping it closed.

Where was everyone? Oh, god. Were they dead? Or ... Surely they couldn't have just *slept through* everything that had happened in the years since he'd been woken by the vibrating satellite phone – the low-ing of the cattle, the shouting German, the *zoop* of suppressed gunshots.

He hammered on the door of the bedroom next to his, where Karen and Boris had retired the night before.

'Um, Karen!' he yelled. 'Wake up please! Are you alive? Sorry to disturb you!'

She pushed the door open, nearly hitting him in the face with it. He skipped backwards. She was wearing an old pink 'Hello Kitty' T-shirt and an expression of annoyance.

'What the fuck …?' she began, and then, her eyes widening, 'What happened to you?'

He pulled her out of the room, pushing her against the wall, afraid the hostile outside might fire through the window. But a kicking noise from behind his own bedroom door told him that the hostile was now there. Luckily that door looked like it was about two hundred years old, and made from the best part of a whole tree, as well as a prodigious quantity of wrought-iron fittings and nails. The lawnmower hadn't budged yet, but he felt it was only a matter of time.

'Sorry,' he said. 'We're under attack. There are four, um, hostiles with guns. You and Boris–'

At this moment Boris appeared in the doorway, wearing only a pair of jeans, some terrifying upper-body tattoos and an expression of rage that could have melted your face off.

'What the fuck …?' he began, and then, eyes widening as he saw the state of the man, 'What happens to you?'

Karen said, 'We're under attack from some guys with guns.'

'Hostiles,' said the man. 'Sorry. Four of them. We need to pile heavy stuff against the doors, so they can't get in. It's a really tricky situation.'

The bedroom door strained against the huge old lawnmower. Boris slammed his own bedroom door shut and, looking around, grabbed a crate of old bowling equipment and began to stack.

'Fuck sake,' he said as he stacked, shaking his head in just the same way as he had the first time he'd met the man.

Meanwhile, the man looked over at the front door, and saw that it stood open. He ran and closed it, then began frantically stacking stuff against it, with Boris and Karen doing the same for the two bedroom doors. Luckily, there was an immense amount of stuff that could be stacked: a big wooden table, a kitchen cabinet, a large bowl in the shape of a tomato, a linen press, a chandelier, an old beach chair, logs, an ancient metal vacuum cleaner. All of it went against the doors, and there was still more to come.

The man recognised that this was mainly a way of filling in time till his inevitable death. He saw how stupid it had been to come back to the house instead of running off southeast through the back streets, as Channon had told him to. Not only did it mean that he was definitely going to die, but also that he'd given the hostiles even more reason to kill Karen – and perhaps the others too. Still, moving heavy items in front of doors really did help to keep his mind off it. He'd have to remember this tactic for the next time he was killed.

Boris was angrily helping the man to stack a moth-eaten green sofa against the front door when Gabi and Hanno appeared at the top of the stairs, both wearing long white nightshirts. Emil, their German shepherd, appeared from behind their legs and padded halfway downstairs, looking keenly around.

'What are you doing?' asked Gabi, reasonably.

'I'm really sorry,' said the man, 'but there are some hostiles trying to, um, kill us. There's one in the bedroom over there, and they managed to break the lock on the front door, so we're piling stuff up to stop them getting in.'

'There are some what?' asked Hanno.

'Um, hostiles? You know, people with guns. It's my fault. Sorry.'

There was the sound of breaking glass from Karen's room.

'Shit,' said the man. 'He must have got into the other bedroom. Is there enough stuff piled against the door?'

Boris was already lugging a mysterious antique made of wood and porcelain over to the door. The man rushed to help him.

'I get something,' said Hanno, heading back to his bedroom.

Gabi looked at the old wood and porcelain object. 'I forget we have this,' she said to herself. 'We have it from Hanno's grandmother in Buxtehude.'

There was a loud bang from behind one of the bedroom doors, then the other. As they looked over, smoke began to drift up from among the objects piled against it.

'Upstairs!' shouted the man, forgetting to say please. 'They're using gas grenades.'

All of them charged upstairs, making for the bedroom furthest from the fumes.

As they charged into her room, Pola sat up in bed, staring at them dumbly. Emil bounded over and jumped onto her duvet, barking excitedly. Gabi was beside her, now wearing her hoodie, and Hanno appeared in the doorway, still wearing his nightshirt though now holding an old but pristine cricket bat.

'It is a present,' he explained to no one in particular as he made his way around the bed to the far window, 'from an Englishman I work with some years ago who is from Uppingham. You know Uppingham?'

Once Karen and Boris were in, the man shut the door behind them. It had a lock, but he couldn't get the old key to turn.

'It's probably best to stay away from the windows,' he said, glancing at Hanno.

'What are you all doing in my bedroom?' asked Pola.

'There are some hostiles,' said Gabi.

'I don't know Uppingham,' said Karen. 'Is it in the UK?'

At that moment, as though Karen's words had offended the gods of Uppingham, all the windows smashed at once. Behind the sudden sharp noise was a swarm of *zoops*. Then there was a hollow thud. Off in the distance was the high wail of sirens, and from somewhere nearby a cockerel crowed.

Uck-a-ah-aaaaaah!

They were all lying on the floor, except for Pola, who was lying on the dog, Emil, holding him tightly. There was smashed glass everywhere, in sheets and shards and slivers. And on the neatly polished floorboards at the foot of Pola's bed sat a grenade: small, neat and green, with a gridded surface.

The man rushed to it, across the glass, picked it up, fumbled and almost dropped it, but managed to push it out of the open window. He fell to the floor. There was a loud noise from outside, like a giant clearing its throat.

The dog began to bark again, echoed by barks from surrounding houses. The cows were still lowing, the crying of the sirens was louder, closer.

The man got up and crawled as carefully as he could across the broken glass. He peeked out of the window, using the wall as cover. Outside, there was no grey Audi, no figures in helmets and bullet-proof vests. No fluffy jumper. The sky was light, the shadows were weaker, the ink of night draining away; colours and shapes were returning.

A police car, an old BMW in green and white, had pulled up outside, blue lights flashing, and a policeman jumped out of the passenger side. He was holding a pistol and he took cover behind the car's bonnet, squinting through the cloud of smoke that drifted across the garden. As the smoke wafted gently towards the police car, it began to reverse, so that the policeman with the gun had to awkwardly step backwards, still crouching, to keep his cover. Another police car arrived behind them and also began slowly reversing away from the tendrils of gas and the explosion on the lawn.

'The hostiles have gone,' said the man, 'but the police are here.'

'*God be thanks*,' said Gabi.

'Channon told me that the police want to arrest me, and that I won't be safe if they do,' he said. 'I don't know what to do.'

'Who is Channon?' asked Gabi.

'He's a kind of disembodied authoritarian voice on the satellite phone,' said the man. 'He says I work for him, and that he'll tell me who I really am.'

'And you believe him?' asked Gabi.

'I don't know. He did wake me up to warn me about the hostiles, and then he told me how to get away from them.'

Gabi sighed.

'Go out of the back,' she said. 'Take our car.'

'Are you sure? Thank you very much. I'll have to go through the CS gas,' he said. 'Does anyone have …?' he mimed holding something over his face.

'I have a scarf,' said Pola, rummaging in a bag by the bed.

'Hanno?' said Gabi. '*Loveling, what is loose …?*'

Hanno was sitting against the wall, his face almost whiter than his hair. He had his hand to his shoulder, and there was dark red blood all over his fingers and his nightshirt.

'They have shot me,' Hanno said weakly. 'This is correct, "shot"? Or "shooted"?'

The man assured him he'd got it right first time, took a shard of glass and used it to cut Hanno's nightshirt away. Then he took the T-shirt from Pola's frozen hand, wiping away blood, and saw that it was a single neat bullet wound near the shoulder. He balled up the fabric and got Gabi to press it to the wound, stanching the flow of blood.

'Um, Pola,' he said, 'could you call an ambulance on your mobile phone? The blood isn't bright red, so he'll be fine as long as you keep something pressed to the wound till the, um, firemen arrive.' Then, turning to Gabi, he asked, 'Do you trust the police?'

She nodded. 'These are our police. They do not do anything to us.'

'Do you mind if I head off? I might be wrong, but I am a bit worried that they'll also try to kill me.'

'I think you are safe, but I agree the situation is completely confusing. Really, take our car – it is faster than your big vehicle. The keys are on a hook by the door.'

He nodded. 'Thank you very much. I'll pay you back. Sorry about …'

He glanced at Hanno, and then around the room, indicating the awful destruction he had brought in his wake.

She waved aside the wreckage as though he were apologising for having dropped an old plate.

'It makes nothing,' she said. Then, to Pola, who was calling an ambulance, she said, 'Pola, call an ambulance.' Turning back to the man, she said, 'Go.'

Karen exchanged a look with Boris and said, 'We're coming too.'

'But ...' said the man.

'If you're not safe with the police then neither are we.'

This was possibly and maybe probably true. But in any case there was no time to think about it. He nodded, and gave them the scarf from Pola's suitcase. They each held an end over their noses and mouths. The man pulled the collar of his coat up over his own mouth, and opened the bedroom door.

They ran downstairs, collecting the car keys from the hook by the front door, holding their breath as they wheeled the old lawnmower away from the door to the man's bedroom. Then they clambered out of the window, ran along the house's back wall and jumped into the elderly black Saab, tears running down their faces from the gas.

The man put the key into the large central console. Even in this situation he was pleased by the impression it gave that the car was, in some important respect, a road-going aeroplane. He adjusted the seat, *bammed* the engine to life, and reversed out of the driveway.

34

They had been driving for half an hour, Piper staring distractedly through the window into the blackness, when a thought struck her.

'Oh god, I haven't fed Cess or Hastings Banda!' she said.

'Call your father and ask him to do it,' said Michaels.

'Oh god,' she said again, clutching her head, 'he was meant to be coming with me!'

'I'm afraid that will be impossible, my dear.'

'I can call him though, can't I?'

'Call him from the airport and ask him to feed the animals, but don't call him after that.'

'Why not?' she asked.

'You'll be put up in a hotel room, which will be bugged. You should also assume that anything you say on your mobile phone will be overheard – by the Americans, at the very least.'

'But they're meant to be on our side, aren't they?'

'It may be best for you to discard the notion of "sides", my dear. I would also not get too attached to any particular idea about what's going on. Try to hold several hypotheses in mind at any time, and look for evidence both for and against each of them.'

She was silent awhile, watching the street lamps swish overhead, staring at the headlights of cars coming the other way.

'What are your hypotheses?' she asked.

'I'm afraid I can't tell you. And that brings me to a final word of counsel: don't tell anyone else what you think.'

'If I try to do that my head will explode,' she said.

He glanced at her with alarm.

'Metaphorically, obviously,' she added.

'Then try at least not to share what you think with people you haven't known long. And if you must say what you think, do so only in public places that you have selected yourself – and in a soft voice.'

'Is this …? This is dangerous, isn't it?'

'I would certainly entertain that as a hypothesis,' said Michaels seriously, glancing at her and then pulling in to allow a speeding car to overtake them. She looked over at the dashboard and saw that he was driving at precisely the speed limit.

She sat and stared out of the window while a question grew in her mind.

'Michaels,' she said, at length, 'again, if that really is what you prefer to be called–'

'Yes, my dear?'

'Don't you find all this … all this not telling anyone what you think, entertaining hypotheses and all that – don't you find it lonely?'

'Oh, unbearably so,' he said in an offhand way. 'Nevertheless, it is important not to tell anyone what you think.'

She watched the grain of the road rush past in the ghost of his headlights. Some rain added texture to the blue-black sky.

'What's going to happen when we get to the airport?' she asked.

'A gentleman will meet you there, the cultural attaché of the United States embassy in Berlin. He will have plane tickets for both of you, as well as a hotel reservation in Berlin.'

'Am I going to have to pretend to be married to him?'

Michaels did his serious glance again. 'The reservation will just be for yourself.'

'And does this mean you won't be coming?'

'My role is to drive you to the airport. It is etiquette that all first-country nationals are liaised with by their home service.'

'You mean the Americans have to work through your lot – whoever they are – while I'm still in Britain?'

'That would be an alternative way of putting it.'

'So what will you be doing once you hand me over to the gentleman from the embassy?'

'I have decided to put the early morning and the trip to the airport to good use, by taking a short international holiday.'

'Oh,' she said. 'Where will you be going?'

'Berlin,' he said. 'I'm told it is very pleasant at this time of year, immediately before the spring.'

35

'Buffalo gals can't you come out tonight, can't you come out tonight, can't you come out tonight.'

They were less than a block from their Chelsea apartment, walking home hand-in-hand, singing Buffalo Gals, like two people who are in love with each other, which they were.

'Buffalo gals can't you come out tonight' – she hit the note, which he missed by a wide margin – 'and dance by the light of the moon.'

They walked on, past the enormous yet somehow poetic metal fire escapes in this part of New York. He held her hand as she jumped a puddle.

'Did you ever hear back from the buffalo gals?' he asked, expertly jiggling the key in the building's front door.

'Nothing,' she said. 'I think we should make other plans.'

'Well, this is our building. We could just go in here.'

'I like that idea. And it is one in the morning.'

A car door clacked open.

'You guys are so cute,' said a woman's voice.

Lance stopped and turned, drawing his wife back. Someone emerged from the car's dark interior and stepped into the glow of the street lamp.

'Lizzie,' said Lance.

'That's me,' she said. 'Let me guess: you guys have just seen *It's a Wonderful Life*. Probably over at the West.'

'Right-amundo. Have you been following us?'

'No, I just like movies.'

His wife said, in her absurd burlesque imitation of Lance's voice, 'Hey, uh, Lizzie, this is my darling wife Arlene. Hi Lizzie! My darling wife Arlene, this is Lizzie, who I know from …'

'A bar,' said Lizzie. 'Hi Arlene!'

'Hey,' said Arlene. She was petite, with the kind of cheekbones you could use to cut wafer-thin slices of Serrano ham, but there was a kind of playful fierceness in her. Lance particularly noticed this when she met other women in his company.

There was a half-second's silence, and then Lizzie said, 'Listen, I know this is kind of weird, turning up at your apartment so late, and when you're having a nice night. But could I come up and talk to you? It's kind of urgent.'

There was another half-second's silence in which Lance and Arlene exchanged a glance.

'Sure,' said Arlene.

'Come on up,' said Lance. 'By the way, you want the moon?' he asked, slipping into his Jimmy Stewart impression. 'I could lasso it for you.'

'I'm good, thanks,' said Lizzie.

Up in their apartment, Lance offered Lizzie a seat on the sofa and asked if she wanted a bourbon.

'This is more of a "your-breakfast-bar-and-a-coffee" kind of conversation,' she said. 'Also, I need you, Arlene, to sign a confidentiality agreement before we even have it.'

'Sounds serious,' said Lance. 'Our coffee machine isn't great. I used to have an amazing one but it was taken away by some polite men with moustaches the day I met Arlene.'

'Which is maybe not strictly relevant at this moment,' said Arlene.

'I'd like to hear that story,' said Lizzie. 'On the plane.'

'What plane?' said Lance, stopping in the act of spooning some coffee into one of those metal things with a handle.

'The plane to Schoenefeld airport, Berlin, that I want you to take tonight.'

'Oh, that plane,' said Lance casually – adding a second later, as though he were in a sitcom, 'Say whaaaaat?'

'Whatchoo talkin' 'bout, Lizzie?' added Arlene.

Lizzie looked at them both, sat down, and switched on a face that said, 'This is very serious.'

Lance tried hard to move into serious mode, but he'd had a wonderful night celebrating Jonathon's foundness. He decided a coffee would help him, and by a curious coincidence found he had a level measure of fresh ground coffee in one hand and a small cup in the other.

When he'd prepared their coffees and Arlene had signed a confidentiality agreement, they all sat at the breakfast bar and Lizzie spoke.

'Okay, my name is Lizzie Morden,' she said to Arlene, 'and I spoke with your husband earlier today – or yesterday now – in my capacity as an officer with the Central Intelligence Agency.'

'I know,' said Arlene. 'He told me. You think you've found Jonathon Fairfax.'

'Yes. Strictly speaking, Lance shouldn't have said anything to you, but let's ignore that. The situation has become critical a little sooner than we thought. We're gonna need help to liaise with Jonathon and bring him in, so we can give him the care he needs.'

'What care does he need?' asked Lance, suddenly worried.

'He has amnesia. We don't know exactly how severe, but it's made him very wary, as you can imagine.'

'I can imagine,' said Lance. 'He was always terrified of everything anyway – except actual danger, of course.'

'But if he has amnesia,' said Arlene, 'how will he remember Lance?'

'There's a good chance he won't – consciously, at least. Amnesia, of the type we believe he has, disrupts episodic memory. So he might not be able to consciously recall any of the times he's met Lance. But memory is complex. It relies on many different systems in the brain and body. So he might not remember who Lance is, but he might well experience feelings of familiarity and trust. And to begin with we'll mainly need help predicting what he might do, where he might go, which approaches could be most effective.'

Lance felt something which, with an involuntary glow of pride, he recognised as guilt. For a long time he had been working to counter his lack of emotional depth, which was an unfair product of his tremendous confidence and good looks. Guilt was the one he'd always found hardest to get – like that rare football card that's never in the pack, no matter how many you buy.

'Are you okay?' asked Lizzie.

'Yes. Just thinking about Jonathon,' said Lance. He was actually thinking of all the times he'd recklessly endangered Jonathon's life and all the other times he'd prioritised sordid sexual gratification over their friendship. He wondered whether the memory of that might have been retained by any of the complex systems in Jonathon's brain and body.

'You said the situation was critical,' said Arlene. 'What does that mean?'

'I'm afraid it means his life may be in danger. He's with people who may intend to do him harm.'

'Who are they?'

'I'm afraid I can't tell you that. Not right now. Believe me, I will tell you as much as I can as soon as I can.'

'So you want Lance to fly to Europe with you tonight without telling him more than some vague bullshit about amnesia?'

Lizzie looked at her solemnly. 'Yes,' she said.

Lance looked at Arlene, who said impatiently, 'Well what are you waiting for? Go pack.'

'You don't mind that I'm taking a plane in the middle of the night with a strange woman?'

'What? No, I like her.'

36

The cultural attaché was waiting for them near the flexible barrier that wound its way to the check-in desk. He was younger than Piper had expected – younger than her, perhaps – with sleek hair down to his collar, polished shoes, light trousers and a subtly expensive checked jacket. He stood with his thumbs in his belt and his chin up – almost offensively at ease in a way that only a certain type of rich American can manage.

'Hey Michaels,' he said. Then to Piper, 'Hey, I'm Nick Ellis. You must be Piper Palgrave.'

'Yes, I am,' said Piper, balancing her wheeled suitcase and putting out her hand.

He took her hand and kissed her once on each cheek, as though this were a thing that absolutely everyone did.

'Oh, suitcase,' he said.

'Oh,' said Piper. 'I thought …'

'Hey, no. Not a problem,' said Ellis, tapping his jacket in the place where either a wallet or a gun would be.

'I can pay–' began Piper.

'*Not* a problem,' said Ellis. 'It's included.'

'She will be there at least one night,' added Michaels, a touch defensively.

'It's not a problem, Michaels,' said Ellis, looking down at him.

Standing beside Ellis did not do Michaels any favours. He was wearing a slightly silly light-grey brimmed hat, his upper lip was sweating through his moustache, his face was pale and his either-cheap-or-expensive overcoat was bunched at the shoulders. He was a head shorter than Ellis and a head fatter, if stomachs could be measured in heads.

'Okay, so …' said Ellis, gesturing towards the check-in desk.

Piper wheeled her suitcase into the snaking path marked out by the flexible barriers.

'Uh, business class,' he said, and smiled.

'Oh,' she said again, changing direction.

They walked over to the check-in desk, and Ellis took two tickets from his pocket.

'I'd like to add a suitcase to this. It's not pre-booked – my mistake.'

The woman behind the counter – uniformed, with a tight, shiny face – checked the tickets and passports.

'Certainly, sir. Could I just ask you to put the suitcase up here for me?' she asked, indicating the conveyor belt beside her.

Ellis grabbed the suitcase with one hand and lifted it on, as though he had been waiting for an opportunity to demonstrate his lifting technique.

'That's absolutely fine, sir,' said the woman behind the check-in desk, and attached a printed tag to the suitcase.

'Thanks,' said Ellis. Piper, who'd nervously got out her purse, put it away again.

Michaels cleared his throat.

'Okay, so … Michaels,' said Ellis, dismissing him with a nod of the head.

'I have decided to take a short holiday in Berlin,' said Michaels, but he got the timing of it wrong, starting a little too soon and speaking a little too fast.

'That's great for you,' said Ellis, doing that trick, which only Americans can pull off, of subtracting just a quantum of energy and sincerity, so that a pleasantry becomes devastatingly humiliating. This tiny vocal trick was somehow easily as belittling as pulling down Michaels' trousers and kicking him onto his face.

Michaels coloured, not managing to find anything to say to this.

'Could I buy a single ticket on this flight to Berlin, please?' he asked the woman behind the check-in desk.

'Business class?' she asked.

Michaels nodded.

'That will be seven hundred and eighty-eight pounds, sir,' she said, a little coldly, as though colluding with Ellis in humiliating Michaels.

He reached into his breast pocket, his hand clutching his wallet, but seemed unable to take it out. He swallowed.

'Do you have any … economy class tickets remaining?' he asked.

She sighed and clicked her keyboard with long-nailed fingers.

'Hey, ah, maybe catch you onboard, Michaels,' said Ellis, turning and walking off with a glance to Piper to follow him.

'I'm waiting for Michaels,' said Piper.

37

They reached a service station on the outskirts of Hamburg, and climbed out of the battered old Saab.

The man looked at his companions, both dirty from the night's work. Karen was wearing just an outsize pink T-shirt with a picture of a cartoon kitten on it. At odds with this breezy innocence was her face, which wore the horrified expression of someone who has not only nearly died but also moved a lot of furniture. Boris, still wearing only his baggy, ripped jeans, looked merely quite cross. He was heavily tattooed, with a huge yellow skull across his chest. From one of its eye sockets emerged something that was perhaps supposed to be a snake, but in this light looked more like a sinister courgette.

Boris and Karen looked at the man and said, in unison, 'Fuck'.

He looked down at his bare feet, covered in mud, blood and animal poo; their smell reached up through his nose and jabbed him in the brain. Then he caught sight of himself in the service station's window. His legs were bare and covered with dried blood from the cuts he'd got by crawling over broken glass. His boxer shorts and mauve 'Anxiety

Free' T-shirt were also covered in blood and mud. There were pale tide-marks over the bearded men's faces, which were ripped brutally in half. The T-shirt had torn across the chest, revealing another bleeding scrape beneath.

His smart black overcoat somehow made the rest of him look worse. His hair was pointing desperately at something above him and to his left. His face was white as a van, and just as covered with filth. His eyes were wide and bloodshot. And then there was the fact that he was shaking violently all over and seemed unable to stop.

That was why they had pulled into this service station. It seemed foolish and dangerous to stop, but he'd been shaking too violently to carry on. They had no idea whether or not they had escaped. In a way it would be a relief to finally be shot dead by his fake ex-wife, just so that he could stop worrying about the constant danger of being shot dead by his fake ex-wife.

The man had twenty euros in his wallet, and Boris said he had ten in his pocket. But it suddenly seemed dubious that they'd be allowed in. He suddenly remembered the phrase, 'No shirt, no shoes, no service', and wondered if they had the policy in Germany. Even if they didn't, there might be an informal prohibition on semi-naked bloodstained shaking people reeking of animal faeces.

But what else could they do? He had already driven a hundred and fifty kilometres with bare feet slathered in excrement. And one of the few things he knew was that he could not go on unless he ate something.

Karen put her arm around him and steered him towards the service station's cafeteria. Then he felt, with some surprise, Boris's hand on his shoulder.

'It is okay, Mister,' said Boris.

They pushed open the doors for him, and led him to the counter. Behind the glass he saw exactly the thing he'd been given to eat in hospital: a bread roll with artificial-looking cheese and ham in it. It seemed suddenly heartbreakingly comforting, reminding him of the long-lost halcyon days of his youth, when he had lain innocently in a room full of machines going beep, being asked what a pen was while absolutely no one tried to kill him. He desperately wanted it.

The woman behind the counter stared at him impassively.

'Ja?' she said.

He replied, '*I'd have gladly a ham-bread, please.*'

She sputted it onto a plate and plonked it on the counter.

They were being served. Just exactly as though they were normal-looking people whom nobody wanted to murder. Karen and Boris whispered their orders to the man, and he passed them on, the breakfast accumulating on the counter. He paid and they went and sat down, the man finding that he couldn't carry anything because he was still shaking too much.

After they'd eaten twenty euros' worth of ham rolls and coffee, they all felt a bit better. They then took turns to slip to the toilets and wipe from themselves whatever was most offensive, which in the man's case required nearly a whole toilet roll.

'You look like new man,' said Boris when the man returned, sounding like he didn't quite know what tone of voice to use for being nice to people.

'Thanks,' said the man, sitting down and shaking a little less strenuously.

'So what's the plan, Mister?' asked Karen.

'Um, I need to look up the phone number for Berlin Surf Shack and ask for Ronald. Then a man with a mysterious authoritarian voice will tell me who I am and how to get some money. Unless it's a trap, in which case I'll be shot by a woman I was never even married to.'

He went to the counter and asked the young woman there for the directory enquiries number. Again, she looked at him neutrally, impassively, and reeled off the number, not seeming to register how much blood and earth his face had lost. He borrowed a pen and paper and got some change for the payphone. Berlin Surf Shack existed, which surprised him as he took down its number. He called.

'Yo, Surf Shack,' said a woman carelessly.

'Er, hello. Can I speak to Ronald, please?'

'Okay. Do you want to speak to actual Ronald? Because he's only in Thursdays. Or did someone say "call this number and ask for Ronald"?'

'Um, the second one.'

'Kay. Putting you through.'

There was a click, a silence, another click.

'Well that was dumb,' said Channon.

'Yes,' said the man.

'Is anyone else still alive?' asked Channon.

'Yes. Um, everyone. Hanno got shot in the shoulder, but everyone's alive.'

'Are you safe?'

'Sort of. We're in a service station with ten euros, no shoes and only one pair of trousers between us, eating food like I had in hospital.'

'You were in hospital?'

'Yes. I thought you knew.'

'I should have known. After you went missing, we should have automatically looked at hospital admissions matching your description. I don't know why that didn't happen.'

'Oh,' said the man, not knowing what to say. 'Sorry.'

'Okay. So, where are you?'

'Don't you know?'

'Son, one day you may try using cameras mounted on an aircraft flying at fifty thousand feet to follow a black car at dawn on German autobahns, and then you'll see that it ain't easy.'

'Right.'

'Okay, so I guess I have to say "good job".'

'Thanks.'

'Are you ready to come in?'

'Are, um, are you ready to tell me who I am?'

'Sure, I'll tell you who you are – when you come in. My organisation has a station in Hamburg.'

'What, Surf Shack?'

'No, my other organisation.'

'Wait, I thought you said you didn't know where I am.'

'I didn't, but I do now. I just got the trace for the payphone you're using.'

'Oh god. Does that mean some people are going to come here and kill me?'

'I hope not. Like I said, it looks like our security problems are worse than I thought – and this hospital thing only adds to that. I guess we have a mole, so as of last night I'm no longer recording or sharing any information relating to you. I haven't logged your number or location on our system.'

'Um,' said the man, who was very tired, 'what?'

'I said, I don't think anyone's coming to kill you. So come in. You'll be safe here, and we'll tell you who you are. And the memory problem – we understand how that works. Unless you come to us for treatment, your brain will kind of break down before too long. If you get treatment elsewhere, it won't work.'

'Sorry, I can't really trust anyone. It's nothing personal.' The man said this, but he also suspected it was something personal, because Channon had apparently just saved his life.

'Okay, I get it,' said Channon. 'There something I can do to make you trust me?'

'Can you find out the PIN for my German bank card?'

'Son, we are an intelligence agency, not wizards.'

'I tried to change it but they just sent some forms to Adam Newman's flat in Berlin.'

'We cannot solve any problem relating to bureaucracy within the German banking system. No one can. I can get you money though.'

'Without me having to trust anyone?'

'Almost. I guess you'd have to trust that bureaucracy within the German banking system is such that a bank will hand over the contents of a safety deposit box if I give you the code for it.'

'But why would you do that?'

'To prove to you that I'm on your side and that I trust you, even though you lost your memory. Besides, although leaving you out on a limb with no pants and only ten euros in your pocket would put some extra pressure on you to come in, it also keeps you out in the wild where you can be killed by whoever the fuck is trying to kill you. You're not the only one, you know. We've lost a lot of guys recently, and you're the only lead we've got to help us identify who's behind all this.'

'Sorry to be suspicious, but how do I know it's not a trap again?'

'Just ask your friends if they think anyone could get a branch of Haspa bank to kill someone. These places are unionised up the ass in Germany; there's no way the staff would put up with that shit.'

38

'Hey Sterling!' Channon's voice was sudden, jerking Sterling out of his daydream. 'Get in here, would you?'

Channon was standing in his office doorway, the collar of his shirt half sticking up, wisps of hair escaping his ponytail.

Sterling walked in and Channon shut the door behind him. Channon gestured to a chair and Sterling sat. Then Channon walked slowly around the desk and eased himself into his own chair. Channon steepled his fingers. His breath was even, his gaze unnervingly direct.

'You a mole, Sterling?' he asked.

Sterling froze. His heart began lightly refrigerating his blood, so that a cold current passed through him. Why would Channon think that?

'No, sir,' he said.

'You would tell me now, wouldn't you?'

'Yes, sir,' said Sterling. 'I mean, no, sir. If I was a mole I would not tell you. That would be dumb. But I'm not a mole, sir.'

'Okay. Well, I'm glad we got that straightened out,' said Channon, and continued to look at him, his face expressionless. There were grey bags under his eyes.

'Is this why I can't get into the working files on Newman, sir?'

Channon nodded. 'You're off the case.'

Sterling bowed his head. 'Okay, sir. I understand.'

'I'm just wondering. How come you wanted to stay late last night? How come you came in at eight this morning? Your shift doesn't start till twelve.'

'You want to know?'

'I want to know.'

'Sir, I worked hard to get into the Agency. I don't know if you noticed, but unlike everyone else here I am not the whitest person.'

'I spotted that.'

'I grew up in Missouri and I got two degrees, which is not the easiest thing to do if you look like me. And then I got into the Agency, just like I wanted, I got into ops, just like I wanted, I'm posted out to Europe, like I wanted. And none of this is simple to achieve. And then here I am, after all that work, and I'm doing surveillance accounting and making really excellent cups of green tea.'

'It's all about the water temperature.'

'So if you ask me to work on something that makes a difference, that is a big deal to me. I'm going to be the last man out and the first man in. I am going to be indispensable. So, yeah. That's why.'

Channon looked at him a long moment, his face still unmoving.

'Okay,' he said eventually.

'Okay?' said Sterling.

'Okay,' confirmed Channon. 'Last night, about four in the morning, a team took up positions around the house where Newman was sleeping. They went in and tried to kill him.'

'Seriously?'

'No, it's material I'm trying out for a stand-up comedy routine. I guess it needs work.'

'The feed line's okay, sir. It's the payoff I'm having trouble with. You don't mean the team I put together, from Hamburg?'

'No, they turned up a couple hours later. So the timings make it look like the hostiles knew they had a window of opportunity.'

'Maybe, sir. Also four would be pretty close to the darkest part of the night. Best time to mount an assault.'

'But the way they behaved, it was pretty obvious someone in the team could see the location of Newman's sat-phone.'

'They knew which room he was in?'

'No. The location data isn't exact enough for that. But when he got out of the house, after he evaded them, they went back to their vehicle and someone in it knew which way they needed to go to find him.'

'How did he get out of the house, sir?'

'I woke him up and guided him.'

'How did you get over there?'

'I called. I couldn't sleep. I was trying to read' – he held up a book: *Natural Disruptors* by Nicholas Emir Brunsengett – 'but then I got to thinking how Newman's the key to everything right now. So I was just watching the pictures from the U2. Just watching that house, for hours. Watching and thinking. And then a vehicle draws up and these cats get out and deploy for an assault. At first I think it's our team, covering the house. But then I look on the system and find our team hasn't left Hamburg yet. So I called him.'

'You managed to guide him past the hostiles over the phone?'

'Yeah. A lot of the training is still there inside him somewhere. Like I said, he doesn't know what he knows. He could probably still do shorthand pretty well if he only knew he'd learned it.'

'So, you saved his life? He's got to trust you now, right?'

'He trusts me a lot more than he did. Whether it's enough, I don't know.'

'Wait, did you … set this whole thing up to win his trust?'

'That would have been a pretty good plan, wouldn't it?' Channon again looked inscrutable.

'Yes, sir.'

'Unfortunately, that's not what happened.'

'Right. So where is he now?'

'Listen, I'm not sharing current information about Newman with anyone now. I have to assume everyone's the mole.'

'I get it, sir.'

'But basically this mole is good news.'

'*Good* news? Has a new definition of that phrase been issued, sir?'

'Same old definition, son. But yesterday I thought we didn't have a mole and I was dead wrong. Today I think we do have a mole and I'm dead right.'

'I see what you mean, sir. I guess that is better.'

'And since I'm not sharing current information or logging anything on the system with respect to this case, the mole will be working blind.'

'Moles *are* blind, sir.'

'Real moles are blind, Sterling. Metaphorical ones aren't. Till now.'

39

They flew economy, which surprised Lance. And he didn't get an upgrade, which surprised him even more. Was he losing his touch? Or was it because of Lizzie? He just didn't know. It unsettled him, as far as a man like him could be unsettled.

He filed slowly in with all the economy-class people and their resolutely normal faces, clothes and hair, and then he and Lizzie sat in their narrow seats and didn't drink the free champagne that no one offered them because it didn't exist. They watched the uniformed people tell them some ways to avoid dying, and then the plane effortfully shook itself free of the earth and sat huge and heavy in the sky, inert and trembling.

'Okay,' said Lizzie in a low voice, 'I'm going to need to get started asking you some questions about Jonathon.'

'All right,' said Lance, quietly out-lowing her in the voice stakes. 'But first I have a few questions for you.'

She held his gaze for a few seconds. Neither of them blinked.

'Okay,' she said. 'Shoot.'

'You seem nice,' he said. 'I mean, you drink old-fashioneds, you love *It's a Wonderful Life*, Arlene likes you. How come you're in the CIA?'

'Seriously?' she said. 'You're allowed to be nice and work for the CIA. There are some assholes, I'll admit, but a lot of us are just as great to be with as I am.'

'Doesn't being nice make it harder to do all the weird and stupid stuff that the CIA does? I mean, how does a nice person pay the mafia to poison Fidel Castro's ice cream? Or recruit all the surviving Nazis after the war? Or fix the Italian elections for several decades?'

'How do you know that stuff?'

'It's not difficult to find out about. A lot of the weird and stupid stuff the CIA has done is incredibly well documented. Which is another thing, really: how do you be a nice person and work for the least intelligent and most unsecret secret intelligence service that's ever existed?'

Lizzie maintained eye contact for a couple of seconds after he'd finished speaking, then looked at the ceiling and took a deep breath.

'Well,' she said, 'I can tell you, it's not easy. And people don't know half of it – even after all the books and documentaries. Why do I do it? Because I believe in America. I believe in what America can be.'

'What, even after Vietnam? The Bay of Pigs? That time you thought the Chinese embassy was a weapons factory?'

'Even with all the shitty stuff we do, we're still basically the best thing that's ever happened to the world. You think if any other country was as powerful as we are, they'd be so benign, generally? I mean, you think we're better or worse than the Soviet Union, the Mongol hordes, the Ottomans? Can you even imagine how insufferable France would be, in our position?'

'Okay, I'll admit you have a point there.'

'Right. Even with all our mistakes, we're basically a force for good–'

'Although you did fund Saddam Hussein.'

'*Okay*,' she said, with an air of finality. 'You've made your point. Listen, I agree with you. In fact, I worked on a big internal research and analysis project to quantify the effects of all the Agency's covert interventions.'

'And what did you find?' he asked.

'I can't tell you that.'

'Okay. So the public's never going to find out what this report says?'

'Lance, most people in the CIA are never going to find out what the report says.'

'Were the results that bad?'

She gave him a look that said *You know I can't answer that question*. Unless it was wind.

'And yet you're still in the CIA,' he said.

She sighed. 'I'm working to change it from the inside.'

'But how?'

'It's tough. I'm trying to get promoted while challenging anything illegal and unethical – not the easiest combination. But I console myself with this thought: at least my job's being done by someone like me, instead of by some guy who thinks the answer to every problem is to flood Florida with cocaine and launch a coup in Guatemala.'

'Well, that is a comfort,' said Lance.

Lizzie gave him a look, and he added, 'Hey, no, really. It is much braver to stay and try to change things, instead of leave and let the CIA go on doing the things it's always done.'

'Thanks,' she said, looking down, as though contemplating just how big a job she'd taken on.

'You had some questions for me,' Lance prompted. 'About Jonathon.'

'Yes, right. So, okay, you know he's suffering from amnesia. Here's a scenario: he's in Berlin and it's like he's never been there before. He's had some sort of physical or emotional shock.'

'What sort of physical or emotional shock?'

'Let's just say *some* sort, for right now. He's just wearing a shirt and slacks, and he has no wallet – only maybe some coins in his pocket. So, what would he do?'

Lance thought for a minute. Jonathon had always, in some important way, totally failed to grasp what was going on. And he'd always been reeling from shock of one sort or another. So how much difference would amnesia make to his normal modus operandi?

'I think,' he said, 'that if he found himself in a strange city, having just had a shock, he would want to collect himself. He'd almost certainly go to a cosy but slightly down-at-heel cafe, if it was the daytime, or a cosy but slightly down-at-heel pub if it was the evening.'

'Really?' said Lizzie.

Lance nodded. 'I think so.'

'How about if he'd just survived a physical attack, for example? He wouldn't try to put as much distance as possible between himself and the attackers, or attempt to arm himself?'

'I think he'd go for a long walk till he felt a bit better, and then go to a cafe or a pub, and have a cup of tea or a beer, depending on the time. Even if he didn't have much money. He'd want to calm himself down, and get out of the cold. Then he'd have a bit of a think about it all and come up with some sort of plan.'

'What kind of plan?'

'A pretty vague, general plan. I think his priority would be to get somewhere quiet where he could have a longer think about it all.'

'Somewhere in the countryside?'

'Maybe, if he could. It wouldn't have to be. How would he get there?'

'I don't know. And what about going to the authorities?'

Lance made a face. 'That depends. It's not that he isn't law-abiding, but I think he's afraid of people in authority.'

'So, if he thought he was wanted by the police …?'

'Is he?' Lance was surprised. Jonathon got into a lot of trouble for a man who mostly stayed at home drawing anthropomorphised animals.

'Just hypothetically.'

'Well, it depends on the amnesia – if he still hypothetically has amnesia?'

Lizzie nodded.

'Well,' said Lance, 'if he was wanted for something he could remember, and he felt guilty about it – which would cover pretty much any crime I can possibly imagine – then he would turn himself in. But if he didn't remember what it was, if he didn't know what it was, then I'm pretty sure that would add to his urge to just go somewhere and give it a good old think.'

'Right. So his plan is to have a think. That really is vague and general.'

'That's Jonathon. I mean, maybe I'm wrong, but that's my instinct. I could probably be more precise if you gave me a bit more information. Have you talked to him?'

'I haven't, no. His handler at the Agency has though – Doug Channon. Channon's pretty much the anti-me: he's big on CIA intervention. It's pretty much his favourite thing. He's head of covert ops for Western Europe and also runs a bunch of secret programmes. As I mentioned, Fairfax is a part of one of those. It's codenamed Knife-fish.'

'You mean Fish-knife.'

'What? No. Why would you call a programme Fish-knife?'

'I don't know. If it was designed to get under the skin of hostile governments and pick small bones out of their freshly cooked flesh?'

'What does that even mean?'

'What does knife-fish mean?'

Lizzie looked like she expected a crushing retort to come from her lips, but was surprised to find she didn't have one.

'Yeah, okay,' she said. 'I don't know. But it's not the Fish-knife Programme, okay?'

'Okay,' said Lance, though he still privately suspected that Lizzie had just read it wrong. 'Anyway, you were saying that Channon's talked to Jonathon.'

'They had one phone call, and I saw a transcript logged on the system – before it disappeared.'

'Disappeared?'

'Yes. Channon now believes – or says he believes – that there's a mole in the Agency. All records pertaining to Fairfax have disappeared.

Channon's no longer sharing anything.'

'Who does he think the mole's working for?'

'He won't say. But twelve senior Agency leadership have been assassinated in the past two weeks. Channon says the same people are trying to kill Fairfax – even though Fairfax wasn't senior at all.'

Lance said nothing. Someone gave him a small orange juice and a little plastic tray covered in silver foil. Then someone else gave him a coffee.

'So,' he said, when he'd drunk some coffee, 'I'm sitting in economy class next to someone who, I guess, must be on the assassins' hit list, and we're flying towards Jonathon, who they also want to kill.'

She nodded, then said, 'Wow. Flying economy class is right up there with assassination for you, isn't it?'

'I'm used to being upgraded,' he said, feeling suddenly very tired. 'In economy they don't give you enough legroom for your legs, and they're the main thing I want to keep in it.'

'Sorry,' she said. 'Cutbacks. We're doing more with less.'

They drank their tiny orange juices and ate strange, cramped omelettes and little bread rolls. Then Lizzie wiped her mouth and, with the air of someone trying hard to find a way of making someone else feel better, said, 'You know, I do have a contact in British intelligence. I have a feeling he will be a big help with all this.'

'Really?' said Lance, putting down his miniature butter. He was always ready to have someone make him feel better.

'Yeah. A guy named Michaels. I believe he talked to Jonathon, in the early stages of his recruitment. Anyway, this guy Michaels has a ton of experience, he's very well thought of, and he has an exceptionally sharp mind. He was at Oxford, you know – got a PhD. I would love to do a PhD. Actually, weren't you at Oxford?'

'Yeah,' said Lance, modestly omitting to mention that it had been for a stag do.

The plane hurtled on towards Schoenefeld, and all that awaited them.

40

Piper and Ellis had, of course, not sat with Michaels on the plane to Berlin. He was relegated behind the curtain which protects those in business class from seeing ordinary people – as though rich people, like babies, think things stop existing when they can't be seen.

Piper had slipped back to talk to Michaels, but he was in the middle of a bank of seats, so there was no way to have a conversation. There was also nothing to talk about: their usual mannered, high-stakes conversational style was impossible when one of them was standing in the aisle and the other was sitting next to a man wearing leather trousers and a deep V-neck T-shirt.

So she had gone back to business class, where Ellis was reading an aspirational magazine full of car reviews and photos of men in polo necks holding leather luggage in such conceited and offensive poses that they would surely have been set upon and beaten if they ever tried it in real life.

At Schoenefeld airport, they stepped out of the plane into air that was shockingly colder than London's. They walked across the concrete emptiness to a gigantic metal building where a sign said 'Wilkommen in Berlin', and they queued to show their passports to expressionless fat men in booths.

After this, they waited in the baggage hall, where Ellis seemed very slightly huffy as he stood beside the carousel, hands on hips.

'You like to ski?' he asked her.

'I've never tried,' she said.

'Right,' he said, looking around. 'Right.'

As they walked into the arrivals hall, Piper felt she'd stepped twenty years into the past. Heathrow had not seemed clean, modern or fancy while she'd been there, but it did now. Schoenefeld felt like a tiny provincial shopping centre that had been left untouched since the early eighties. Harsh square lights shone down from the ceiling tiles and strange sandwiches lurked behind perspex counters, while a single oddly clinical shop sold unfamiliar newspapers as though they were medicines in a pharmacy.

Michaels appeared before them, a newspaper under one arm and a paper cup in his hand.

'Ah, good morning,' he said. 'I wondered if we might share a taxi into the centre.'

Ellis pinched the bridge of his nose and seemed about to say something when Piper cut across him.

'Of course,' she said.

'Actually,' said Ellis, 'we kind of have an embassy car picking us up, and we can't …'

'Of course,' said Michaels. 'I understand. And which hotel are you …?'

'I can't remember,' said Ellis. 'I'll make a call in the car.'

Michaels looked rather hurt and, perhaps to distract attention from this, looked hurriedly at his watch.

'What t–' he began, but his sleeve had somehow flipped the newspaper, knocking the cup from his grasp, so that coffee splashed over Michaels' hand and caught the edge of Ellis's trousers, causing him to step back.

'Mother–' said Ellis. He stopped himself, but added, 'Jackass!'

Michaels was biting his lip in pain, his face red and his hand in his armpit.

'I am sorry, Mr Ellis,' he said, wincing. 'Please do send me the bill for the dry-cleaning.'

'What for? You won't be able to afford it,' said Ellis. 'Come on,' he said to Piper, 'we've got a car.'

Piper turned to Michaels, unwilling to abandon him.

'Please, do go on,' he said. 'I'm afraid I must go to the lavatory and run my hand under some cold water.'

He turned, but then looked back.

'Just one more thing,' he said.

'What?'

'It was green,' he said, still holding his hand and wincing. 'The carpet in the room where I interviewed Mr Fairfax. I said it was blue, but it was green.'

And then he hurried off.

41

As they drove further into Hamburg, down the long, wide road called the Reeperbahn, the man began to realise why the woman at the service station had paid their appearance so little attention: they had inadvertently adopted one of Hamburg's signature looks. All around him, people were attired for dress-down Friday during the Apocalypse. Though it was not warm, these people were missing important parts of their clothing, and had spilled things over the parts they did have. They made the people of Berlin look like they were all on their way to the opera.

The man began to feel a bit better about his impending visit to the bank. He had planned to ask Boris if he could borrow his jeans, but now he began to fear that this might make him look conspicuously dressy.

They followed the Reeperbahn to the station, which resembled an overturned boat between two grandfather clocks. Then they turned left, eventually finding a multi-storey car park, where two hours' parking cost most of their remaining ten euros. The man returned with the ticket and ducked inside the car to stick it to the windscreen.

'It is trap,' said Boris.

'Don't you think it might be a trap?' asked Karen.

'Yes,' said the man, still lightly shaking.

'So why are you going there?' asked Karen.

'Because all our other options might be traps too. We could go to the police, who might want to kill me and definitely want to arrest me, and who are very unlikely to explain who I am and what's going on. Or we can keep trying to run until we've spent our last two euros and used our last drop of petrol, some time this afternoon. At that point we'll have no option but to wait for the people in the grey Audi to come and kill us, probably also without explaining who I am and what's going on. Or we can try to accept help from a man with a mysterious authoritarian voice who has probably saved our lives and who says I work for him.'

'There must be more options than that,' said Karen.

'Join the circus?' suggested the man. 'Pray?'

'Sarcasm doesn't suit you,' said Karen.

The man decided not to tell her that he wasn't being sarcastic and had only reluctantly and at the last moment dropped these from the main list of options.

'I think,' he said, 'that you should wait somewhere other than this car, just in case they've managed to track it.'

'But where can we go?' said Karen. 'I'm only wearing a T-shirt, and he's only got a pair of jeans.'

'Ah. Yes,' said the man. 'Boris, do you think I could borrow your jeans?'

'What?' said Boris.

'I'm a bit worried that they won't let me in the bank with my damaged legs, even though they look a lot better since I wiped the poo and blood off them in the service-station toilets.'

'But I do not wear anything under them,' said Boris.

'I could swap them for my boxer shorts,' the man offered.

'For fuck sake,' said Boris, shaking his head sadly. He looked at the ceiling and, for a horrifying second, the man thought Boris was about to cry.

'It's just that this is our best chance,' said the man. 'If they let me in, I'll be able to get some money, and then we can probably afford a pair of trousers each. Maybe even shoes or a ski jacket.'

Boris frowned furiously, but the man had seen his eyes light up at the mention of a ski jacket.

'Okay. But you give back.'

'Thanks a lot,' said the man. He wrapped his coat around him as he wriggled out of his boxer shorts, passing them to Boris, who handed over his heavy jeans. The man shuffled into them and did the belt up as tightly as it would go.

Karen said, 'What do we …? I mean, you know, if …?'

'Oh,' said the man, 'yes. What should you do if I don't come back?'

She looked helplessly around, as though trying to think of a different way of saying it, but eventually settled on, 'Yes.'

'Um, I don't know. Here are the car keys. You could try selling it?'

'Who's going to buy a really old second-hand car from a naked couple?'

'I don't know. Could you call Pola?'

'I don't have her number. It's in my cellphone.'

'In that case I'll just make sure I come back from the bank,' he said.

He straightened his black overcoat, hitched up the huge jeans and handed over the last of the money. Then he hugged Karen and offered his hand to Boris, who unexpectedly hugged him.

'Right,' said the man. 'Right.'

And off he went. He made his way downstairs into the street, emerging between two sheer cliffs of square neoclassical buildings. At a nearby crossroads, he looked around. Channon had said the bank was near the town hall. Was there someone he could ask for directions?

Here in the centre, the dress code had shifted decisively away from apocalyptic-casual. People looked rich, or like tourists, or they were dressed almost aggressively normally. The man couldn't face talking to any of them. He knew he looked like the sort of person no one wants to deal with, especially since he kept looking nervously around to check whether he was being followed.

Off to the left, in the distance, he saw a tall red spire, and he decided this must be the town hall, so he headed that way. Walking slowly and painfully, he passed glass-fronted shops and bare-limbed trees.

The spire turned out to belong to a church, but beside it he found a signpost to the town hall. Two shop-filled streets later, he emerged into a vast public square surrounded by huge buildings and colonnaded walkways, full of people. Looming over it was the town hall – a mountainous riot of green roofs, gold clocks and statues of grave-looking men. Just beyond it, over a small road to its left, was the Haspa bank.

He had made it. He just needed to get across the square and he'd be in.

The man glanced about, took a deep breath, and set off, walking mimsily to spare his tattered feet, and wincing at each step. The first half of the square was full of glass awnings and trees, but then he reached an open expanse and realised this would be an ideal place for a sniper to shoot him dead.

He willed himself to walk faster, but his feet were now so painful that every step was a separate task, one he had to psych himself up for, laboriously work through and thankfully complete. He tried ducking once or twice, just in case the shot happened to come at that moment, but it made the tourists stare at him, so he gave it up.

He now regretted so blithely promising Karen and Boris that he would return from the bank unassassinated. But he had led them into a position where they were running from assassins and the law with only two euros and two articles of clothing between them. Like it or not, he did have to stay alive for them.

The man succeeded in staying alive all the way across the square. There was now only the narrow street to cross and he would be at the bank. It stood there, ancient and dignified above, with a glass front and a big red sign at street level. The traffic had stopped at the crossing, and the green man was lit up. He made a final effort, one foot in front of the other. Halfway across he looked up and saw it: the large grey Audi.

His heart gurgled down a plughole in his chest and swirled into his stomach. His feet, in no condition to run, stood rooted to the spot. He looked at the Audi, waiting for the door to open, for Amy to step out with her gun and shoot him dead. Time stood still.

And then he realised that he was staring through the Audi's tinted windscreen into the eyes of a chubby fellow with swept-back hair and a turtleneck sweater, sitting alone. The driver looked back at the man with a mild curiosity that soon turned to irritation as the lights changed and the man continued standing in the middle of the road, trembling with relief. It wasn't *the* grey Audi, just *a* grey Audi. Three of the five cars behind were also grey Audis. The man had picked the wrong city for being afraid of grey Audis.

He staggered to the pavement, and in through the revolving doors. His heart was still thudding against his stomach as he approached the customer-service desk.

'Moin,' said the assistant casually, a greeting the man had never heard before.

The man said, '*Um, good day. I have here a closing compartment with a code and password.*'

'Please wait over there,' said the assistant in English. 'My colleague will be with you shortly.'

Even after all he had been through that day, the man was still slightly offended that the assistant didn't think his German was good enough to warrant a reply in the same language.

The man stood by the desk until another assistant appeared, this time a pale young woman with pitch black hair and a raven tattoo. She asked him to step into a lift, which pulled them both down into the earth. The man took up a position in the corner, expecting that at any moment the lift would stop and the pale woman would extend a razor-sharp blade from one of her shoes and stab him through the head. But instead they continued smoothly down, and the pale woman extended nothing more deadly than a puzzled glance at this shaking barefoot man.

The doors opened. He was led past an unoccupied old wooden desk and chair, and ushered into a booth containing a computer. A curtain was drawn, and he typed in his code and password while no one at all garrotted him to death from behind. Instead, the computer rattled out a little plastic capsule containing a key with a number on its tag.

Emerging from the booth, the man was not hatcheted in the chest by the pale woman waiting outside, despite her sinister tattoo. Instead, she led him to a door, where she typed a code and laid her hand on a sensor. A metal door made a noise that sounded like a sigh of relief, and slid aside, revealing that it was nearly two feet thick. The pale woman gestured the man forward, into the vault, and the door closed behind him.

He was now sealed in a large circular room, with a thick pillar at its centre. The man's heart was doing a complex drum solo, which suddenly made him remember the existence of Phil Collins. The surface of the walls and the pillar were made of highly polished steel, divided up into rectangles of many different sizes, each with a number precisely etched into it. On the ceiling were several glass domes, each with a little camera sign beside it. And set into the walls were three curtained booths, each with a green 'vacant' sign above it.

The man patiently tracked down the steel rectangle that had the same number as his key, then inserted it and turned. There was a whisper-quiet *tick* and the outer plate emerged half an inch from the wall. The man pulled and a drawer smoothly opened, revealing a metal case.

The man took the case and carried it over to the booth. He laid it on the little table, drew the curtain behind him and pressed a button marked 'engaged'. Then he clicked the catches and opened the lid.

42

'I guess you think you and Channon are getting pretty close, huh? Good buddies?'

Sterling turned from the green tea he was making. Kerr was standing in front of the closed door of their little office kitchen.

'I don't think we're buddies,' said Sterling. 'But I respect Channon and sure as hell want to work more closely with him. Don't you?'

'Hey, I work closely with Channon. Don't worry about that. And I do it without kissing his ass.'

'Great. So there's no problem.'

'Listen, I'm trying to warn you that if Channon seems like he's interested in your opinion, he isn't. There's always something else going on with Channon.'

'Oh yeah? Like what?'

'Like anything. Like Newman from Knife-fish has disappeared and Channon's trying to find him. But it won't be that. Maybe Newman never existed. *I've* never seen him. Or maybe Channon's trying to kill him: maybe it's easier to tell the bosses that someone else is dead than that Knife-fish doesn't work. Or maybe it's all a ruse to draw someone out – this mole maybe, if the mole exists. Or maybe he needs a fall guy and he's manoeuvring you into position.'

'That's a lot of maybes.'

'Maybe that's the point, Sterling. The point is that it's not the way you think. Nothing here is the way you think.'

'Including you?'

'No. This is a straightforward friendly warning because you're new here and I can see you don't know how things work.'

And with that, Kerr turned and left the kitchen, returning only briefly to ask if he could borrow Sterling's stapler.

43

In the car, Ellis pointed out the best places for Piper to get food she didn't understand.

'That is a great place to get matzo,' he said, pointing to a shop.

'What's matzo?' she asked.

'Seriously?' he said. 'It's like this Jewish flatbread that's having a moment right now.'

'Oh, right.'

'And that place does seriously good kanpyo rolls.'

This time she nodded and smiled, as though she had been wondering where her next kanpyo roll had been coming from.

'This is the place to go for shoes,' he said next, not looking at her shoes.

'Oh, okay.'

They sat in silence for a while. She wondered whether his off-handedness was a trick to disguise an eagle-eyed scrutiny of her. Another hypothesis was that he thought this whole business of escorting her on the plane was beneath him. In any case, as Michaels had said, she needed to be on her guard.

'Hey, you play tennis?' he asked.

'Not really,' she said. 'I can't do the hitting bit of it.'

He turned to her. 'That's, like, *literally* the whole of tennis.'

'I know.'

'That is hilarious,' he said, unsmiling, and looked out of the window again.

As they got out of the car outside the Adlon, Piper thought it looked a bit like a Monopoly hotel: a big rectangle with a pitched roof on top. It stood on a large public square at the end of an enormously wide and long street. Not far from it, there stood one of those monuments with columns and a chariot on top.

'Brandenburg Gate,' said Ellis, off-handedly, as though he felt he could have done a better job of it.

'There's a forest on the other side of it,' said Piper, looking through the gate. 'That's original.'

But Ellis was ushering her towards the entrance, not listening. The doors were opened by a uniformed man wearing a little cape around his shoulders, which she found indefinably kinky.

She stepped into a vast white lobby, circular and with a glowing domed ceiling. A pianist softly tickled the keys of a fat piano, ignored by all the well-fed people and men in bright red knitwear who lounged among the lustrous armchairs, as waiters in black waistcoats scurried about. In the centre of the room stood a cluster of metal elephants blowing water at the ceiling.

Ellis trundled Piper's suitcase towards the reception desk in the corner and she followed. He checked her in with his offensive ease and passed her the keycard.

'Okay, this is you. Room 204.'

'Thanks very much.'

He looked behind her. She turned and saw a big man in a black suit.

'This is Bill Drummond,' said Ellis. 'He'll handle your security. We take that very seriously.'

'Oh, hello Bill.' She reached out to shake his hand.

Bill Drummond looked at her for a second, expression unchanging, and took her hand between his thumb and fingertips, as though afraid of breaking it.

Ellis said goodbye to her and reminded her to check out the matzo place. Then Bill Drummond took her suitcase upstairs and showed her into her room.

'I'll be right outside,' he said, closing the door.

The room had a polished parquet floor, a bed with shiny golden sheets, an armchair, a small desk, and a blue chaise longue.

Piper took off her shoes and climbed under the shiny golden bed-sheets, the only place she could be sure there were no cameras, and looked at the phone she'd found in her pocket during the car ride over.

It was a cheap phone made of grey plastic, with a green screen and spongy keys. There were no missed calls, no voicemails, no contacts. But when she looked in the drafts folder, she found a message.

The message said, *Keep hidden. Wait for call. Use only with shower running. Please delete.*

44

The man found Karen and Boris sitting, waiting, in a doorway on the street just down from the car park. She was hugging her legs to her chest, her pink 'Hello Kitty' T-shirt pulled over them, staring at the pavement. Boris was sitting beside her in just a pair of someone else's underpants.

The man stopped beside them. Karen and Boris continued to stare listlessly at the gap of unused paving that pedestrians evidently felt was too close to these semi-naked vagrants. After a few seconds, Karen – finally noticing that there was a barefoot man standing beside her – looked up.

'Oh. Hey, Mister,' she said, giving him a small, tired smile. 'No luck?'

He produced the metal briefcase that had been hidden by his large black overcoat.

'Hey, we could sell a case like that,' she said excitedly. 'Look at it, Boris!'

'Is good,' said Boris, tiredly.

The man sat down beside Karen, his feet somehow even more painful when he took the weight off them.

'I don't think we'll have to sell it,' he said, flicking the catches and giving Karen and Boris a glimpse inside.

They both looked at him, surprise having wiped all expression from their faces.

'How much is that?' said Karen quietly.

'It's fifty thousand euros,' said the man.

'What the fuck?'

'I know.'

'Is there anything else?'

'Some passports and ID cards, a torch, a compass, a wig, and a gun, which I threw in the river. I'm really starting to worry about the environmental impact of all the guns I'm throwing away.'

'Did you not think a gun might be kind of handy?'

'The only thing I'm sure of is that if we start killing people we've lost.'

Karen made a gesture that took in the man's feet and the whole of her and Boris, as if to say, 'We've already lost.'

'Well, yes,' said the man. 'But still. Anyway, we've got fifty thousand euros. And I kept the case the gun came in – it's a hollowed-out bible, with a little bottle of oil in it, like the one I saw in the kitchen drawer.'

'Great. And we have a *super*-cool case.'

'What we will do with money?' asked Boris.

'Why don't we save it?' said Karen. 'Put it in a pension fund for our old age.'

The man and Boris turned to look at her.

'Just kidding,' she said. 'I know we're all going to die. But first, let's get clothes. Let's eat.'

'I also need to see a doctor about my feet,' said the man. 'I don't think they're meant to bleed and hurt this much.'

They went and had some very expensive fresh waffles, Karen and Boris buying dressing gowns and slippers on the way, to tide them over. After the waffles and some coffee, the man got them to take him to a doctor, who explained that it wasn't really what he did, but nonetheless bandaged and treated the man's feet in exchange for some money. While the man was having his feet bound, Karen and Boris went and bought some clothes for all of them, along with suitcases to keep them in, and a pair of the most orthopaedic sandals possible.

And so it was that they repaired themselves, bought a modest car and drove back to Berlin, constructing a plan on the way.

45

The woman in the fluffy jumper slumped down into a seat, joining the three men who were already sitting around the table at the back of the smoky bar.

'I need a beer,' she said.

'We got a pitcher,' said the man with the square jaw.

'So what did Grey Owl say?' asked the bald man.

The woman in the fluffy jumper gestured at her glass, and the man with the square jaw poured her a beer. The woman immediately drank half of it.

'Grey Owl's mad at us. As per fucking usual.'

'Grey Owl's mad?' said the bald man. 'We're the ones who should be mad – at Grey Owl.'

'I know. And I explained what happened. It's clearly not our fault.'

'We had a fucking great plan,' said the man with the square jaw. 'Again. Like always.'

'I mean, it wasn't even exactly a plan,' said the woman in the fluffy jumper. 'Just standard tactics. Tried and tested.'

'Yeah,' said the man with the square jaw. 'Exactly. Great tactics, I should have said. You're right. Two guys with rifles and scopes, each covering two sides of the house. Two guys go in: silently pick the lock then locate the target. One guy's in the car, monitoring the system for intel. I mean, yeah, it's textbook. But then all of a sudden he's out. Bam.'

'And it's like he's forgotten exactly zero percent of his training,' said the bald man. 'He throws something to draw my aim, then jumps and rolls, takes cover, and he's over the wall in one movement. I mean, it's a low wall, so he practically steps over, and … What?'

The woman in the fluffy jumper was pulling a face.

'It wasn't that low of a wall,' she said. 'I mean, we were out of the house and after him in like two seconds, but that wall was high enough to slow us down.'

'Yeah, no,' said the bald man. 'I didn't mean … It was like medium high.'

The man with square jaw nodded. 'Medium high. I'd go with that. I mean, we're over it quick, but now he's out of that garden.'

Here the old man interjected. 'In any chase, one loses sight of the target. Always this happens. But when you are good you have the ability to know where he will go. You keep calm. You pick him up again.'

'Right,' said the woman in the fluffy jumper. 'And we did that. We stayed calm, we looked, and we picked him up going into this barn or farmyard or whatever.'

'But we talked about this in the car, right?' said the man with the square jaw to the woman. 'He knows where to go. It's like he knows where's going to be hardest to follow.'

'So has he still lost his memory?' said the bald man. 'Or is he getting it back? Remembering all his training?'

'You know what I think,' said the man with the square jaw. 'He's got his memory back.'

The old man said, 'I think it is not all back, but just some parts.'

'Well I'm kind of on the fence,' said the woman in the fluffy jumper, 'because Grey Owl says probably not.'

'But how would Grey Owl know?' said the bald man. 'Has Grey Owl seen him? No.'

'And we're the ones who are out there chasing him through gardens and vaulting fences,' said the woman in the fluffy jumper. 'And he just charges through this fence. It's that awkwardness again: it's like he just does this high-speed bumbling, and he's through.'

'Right,' said the man with the square jaw. 'He's not a big guy, but he has technique, or something. I was *this* close to hitting him, and then he's gone.'

'And then I get a clear shot at him, but suddenly he's dodged right,' said the woman in the fluffy jumper. 'And that's when I notice the glass thing–'

'Greenhouse.'

'Sure. And I've hit it. Massive smash.'

'Hey, Two Rivers, if you hadn't done it, I would have,' said the man with the square jaw. 'I was just about to take a shot.'

'Please, you're great at all this stuff. You never put a foot wrong. I was the one who shot up the greenhouse and woke Mr German Light Sleeper of the Year.'

'Who, of course, has to turn on his lights, open the window and start yelling.'

'But even then, we keep our heads. Calmly scan the streets, head back to Tide Pool in the car.'

The old man said, 'And I have paid good attention. I tell you the approximate location of his sat-phone.'

'So we go back …' said the woman in the fluffy jumper.

'And he's gone,' said the man with the square jaw. 'I still can't believe you spotted those bushes had been disturbed. You got his sat-phone.'

'I don't know,' said the woman in the fluffy jumper. 'My eyes are just attuned to detail or something.'

The old man said, 'But the point is this. His sat-phone stopped moving nearly as soon as I tell you the location and you go away from the car. This tells me that he knows you are coming back. But how can he know? Clearly someone is guiding him. Of course, we cannot know what happens because now all this information is removed from the system.'

'Right,' said the woman in the fluffy jumper. 'Someone's guiding him. And this is not any part of Grey Owl's briefing.'

'But Grey Owl must accept this, or?' asked the old man.

'Grey Owl must accept that the briefing missed out vital details? Please.' She took another drink. 'Anyway, you know what it's like with Grey Owl. You explain what happened, but when you hear yourself say it, suddenly it sounds like bullshit. You know?'

'I know this precisely,' said the old man. 'It is a superpower.'

'But despite all that,' said the woman in the fluffy jumper, 'despite this bullshit briefing, despite the target maybe having his memory back and definitely being guided, we still do everything right. We go back to the house – and there he is.'

'Yeah. Because I let him back in,' said the bald man. 'I hold my hands up. My bad. All I can say is that I had a pretty broad area to watch, and I'm in someone's driveway and it's getting light. So I'm a little distracted, and do I use the night vision now or not? And then he's just there and in, all in one move. He's like this ungainly blur. And I nearly get him, but …'

'Hey, don't blame yourself, Mighty Oak,' said the woman in the fluffy jumper. 'It's not an easy situation. And there we all are again, running around with guns in broad daylight.'

'And then the cops show up,' said the man with the square jaw.

'Right. And the last thing we need is a firefight with the German cops. Can you imagine what Grey Owl would say? I mean, we're like a secret within a secret, so gun battles with cops are …'

'Anathema?' the bald man suggested.

'*Anathema.* Good word, Mighty Oak. Exactly. I mean, I think we actually did really well just getting out of there without being detected.'

'Plus,' said the man with the square jaw, 'what did Grey Owl say just like a few hours before sending us in there? "Hit pause, keep quiet, wait for a call."'

'Although, to be fair, we did get a call,' said the bald man.

The old man said, 'But does Grey Owl say anything about this point that the target is warned and guided?'

'Not really. We'll hear back about that, apparently.'

'Wait,' said the bald man. 'You don't think …?'

'What?' said the woman in the fluffy jumper.

'No, it's dumb,' said the bald man.

'Mighty Oak,' she said, 'we're in a bar drinking beer after staying up all night shooting greenhouses. You're allowed to say dumb stuff.'

'Okay. You don't think Grey Owl could have called him, do you? I mean, who else knew we were on our way? Who else knows our tactics?'

'No,' she said. 'I don't think that. What would be the point?'

'Save his life,' said the bald man. 'Win his trust.'

'But what about killing him?'

'If he is what we think he is, and Knife-fish works the way we think it does, maybe he's a good weapon.'

'No way. Grey Owl wouldn't do that. What about the risk to us?'

'Maybe we're expendable?'

'Like I said: it's a bar, we're tired, we're drinking beer, so you can say dumb stuff tonight. But don't you ever say – or even *think* – that again. I know I can bitch about Grey Owl sometimes, but we're all on the same side. We're all working for the same thing.'

'Okay,' said the bald man. 'I was just thinking aloud. Like you said, we're all tired.'

'Okay.'

'So what's our next move?' asked the man with the square jaw.

'I think you can guess,' said the woman in the fluffy jumper.

They exchanged looks.

'No.'

The woman said, 'Hit pause, keep quiet, wait for a call.'

The man with the square jaw clapped his hands. 'Okay. So let's get shit-faced.'

Monday

46

The CIA were putting Lance up in a rented room in a family home, which – even after flying economy class – surprised him. He was used to being put up at vast expense whenever he travelled for work with MTV. Otherwise he put himself up in places that were on the lavish side of quirky and bohemian. He didn't know whether it was worrying or reassuring that the world's largest and best-funded intelligence agency was so budget-conscious.

Lance was staying in a room recently vacated by the family's eldest daughter. On the door was a sign that the father – a doctor at one of the hospitals – helpfully translated as, 'I am a girl! I may change my mind at any time.' This same girl had left all of her second-tier possessions in the room, so that it was completely full of the clothes, posters, stationery and cuddly toys that an eighteen-year-old judged too embarrassing to take to university. Lance found this all quite refreshing, and thought that it would make a very successful theme for a chain of expensive hotels in Japan.

What he didn't find refreshing was the bed, which was narrow and wedged beneath a sloping ceiling. The mattress was ridged and undulating like pleasant countryside, and the pillow was a large square, only about half filled with something completely insubstantial, so that he was at a loss to see how it proposed to fulfil its duties. In fact, as he gradually discovered through the night, it intended to shirk its duties altogether, leaving his head to support itself.

When he got up that morning with a sore neck and opened the window, clear spring sunshine poured in. He found himself looking out over what he at first took to be a park. On second glance, he saw it was a collection of small gardens, without houses but each with a neat little shed. It was as if the gardens had wandered away from suburban houses and huddled together for warmth during the night. Lance had never been to Germany before, and was already mystified by almost everything he had encountered in his short exposure to the country.

The phone he'd been given by Lizzie rang.

'How's the jetlag?' she asked.

'Fine,' he said. Then, 'Is Germany weird?'

'Yes. You ready to get going?'

'I've only just woken up,' he said. 'Let me just find the shower and a way to put some coffee inside me.'

'I'll be outside your door in ten minutes. I'll bring a coffee with me. You just focus on that shower. We're going to be sitting together in a confined space for most of the day.'

Lance discovered, in one of the downstairs rooms that he'd forgotten being shown last night, a mystifyingly foreign shower and a toilet with a little elevated shelf just above the water, presumably to allow him to conduct a detailed analysis of his poo before flushing it away.

Fifteen minutes later, he emerged blinking in the sunlight and climbed into Lizzie's car.

'You look great,' she said. 'Why aren't you jet-lagged?'

'I am,' he replied. 'It's just that I'm Lance Ferman.' He raised his eyebrows and shrugged helplessly.

'Well I'm Lizzie Morden and I always look at least as bad as I feel. Here's your coffee.'

'Thanks. What's the plan for today?'

'We're going to look at pubs.'

'Sounds good. Shouldn't we maybe try to find Jonathon?'

'You were saying yesterday that if Jonathon had a shock of some kind, and found himself alone in a strange place, he would "almost certainly go to a cosy but slightly down-at-heel cafe, if it was the daytime, or a cosy but slightly down-at-heel pub if it was the evening." We think it would have been the evening, so we've compiled a list of pubs and bars within a reasonable radius of his last known position.'

'Okay, take me to this reasonable radius.'

The car pulled smoothly away from the kerb.

'By the way,' she said, 'do you have those photos of Jonathon?'

He pulled them from his jacket pocket and handed them to her. He had only been able to find two. In one, Jonathon and Lance were in an Indian restaurant, both wearing Hawaiian shirts and garlands of flowers, for reasons Lance couldn't remember, while Jonathon bravely tried to smile through the pain of his costume and the food. In the other, Jonathon was standing by a tree in Central Park, wearing the world's largest coat, holding an incongruous hot dog and inconveniently blinking.

Lizzie pulled up at a junction and looked at them.

'Okay,' she said. She visibly tried to find something good to say about them, and just as visibly failed. She was saved by the lights changing.

'He's a hard man to photograph,' said Lance.

'But these are good likenesses, right?' said Lizzie.

'Sort of. It sounds weird to say, but there are other people who look more like Jonathon than he does himself.'

Lizzie gave him an uncertain smile and went back to driving.

She took them first to O'Malley's Irish Pub, the outside of which was painted green and festooned with shamrocks, leprechauns and references to the tremendous craic to be had within. It reminded Lance that, outside the British Isles and possibly Australia, anywhere that calls itself a pub is not to be trusted. And anywhere that calls itself an Irish pub will be as bad as a pub in Ireland is good.

'There's no way Jonathon went in there,' said Lance. 'He would sooner walk into a set of rotating blades.'

'Okay,' said Lizzie. 'That's why you're here.' And she pulled smoothly off.

The next place they went to called itself an 'Eck-kneipe', which Lizzie said meant 'corner bar'. Someone had carefully removed all traces of atmosphere from it by installing a long melamine counter, a dozen TV screens and a load of gambling machines. In it were three men, their skin ash-grey and hair like tarred string, all smoking and sitting as far away from each other as possible. Whoever you were, there was no way you could look at them without reflecting that perhaps your own life hadn't turned out so badly after all.

'Are there many of these eck-kneipes on the list?' asked Lance.

'At least a couple of dozen,' said Lizzie.

'Cross them all off,' said Lance.

They continued. Lizzie had a route worked out that took them past every one of the drinking places. It was plotted on a map that she'd given Lance, so he could navigate.

'This must have taken you ages,' he said.

'What can I do?' she said. 'I'm a map nerd. It was a little difficult to work out, because the Germans see beer as basically a soft drink – you can buy it almost anywhere. I mean, seriously, the state library serves beer. So I've tried to include anywhere that's open in the evening, and that wants you to come in just to drink a beer.'

They were able to glide past a succession of eck-kneipes, so that the next place to consider was called, in German, 'At the Little Market Hall'.

'This looks promising,' said Lance. The place looked ancient and picturesque, with a decorative wrought-iron gate at the front, along with old-fashioned lanterns. This time, they got out of the car and went inside. The bar was full of dark wooden panelling and huge old tables that looked like they had formed in some geological sub-stratum and been dug out, rather than made by humans.

Inside, the place was deserted, but a waitress in a fresh white shirt stood behind the bar.

'Hi,' said Lizzie. 'Do you speak English?'

'Of course,' said the waitress, in more or less the same insulted tone she might have used if Lizzie had asked her whether she brushed her teeth.

'We're looking for a friend of ours who disappeared on Thursday night,' said Lizzie, showing her the photos of Jonathon. 'Were you working then?'

'No,' said the waitress. Lance was expecting some kind of reaction or elaboration, but none came.

'Could we maybe talk to someone who was?' asked Lizzie.

'For this you should speak with the manager,' said the waitress, with a mild shrug.

'Thanks. That would be great. Could you get him?'

'He is not here,' she said.

After answering each question, the waitress went back to looking at them uninterestedly, as though she were waiting for a subway train and they were trackside posters.

'Do you know when he'll be back?' asked Lizzie.

'No.'

'Should we come back this afternoon?'

The waitress shrugged.

'Is there a day or time when he'll definitely be here?'

'No,' she said.

Lance kept expecting her to start polishing glasses or something, but she just stood there, looking at them.

'Are there any times when he definitely *won't* be here?' asked Lizzie.

'All the days in this week. He is on holiday.'

'Okay. One more thing: is there someone else I could talk to? Like, ideally, an American?'

'No.'

'Well, thank you. Have a nice day.'

The waitress frowned, as though she were not sure she could comply with this order, and said, 'Goodbye.'

Back in the car, Lance said to Lizzie, 'Well that was suspicious. It was like she was trying to hide something. Did you notice that she never volunteered any information? She just answered exactly what you asked, nothing more.'

Lizzie said, 'I'm afraid it's just how they are. Talking to Berliners who work in any kind of customer-service capacity can be a bit like talking to an oracle. You have to make sure you ask exactly the right question.'

'Wow,' said Lance. 'This is going to be an annoying day.'

'But what did you think of the bar?' asked Lizzie. 'Was that a possibility?'

'I don't think so,' said Lance. 'It looks nice from outside but it's a bit too daunting, with the gate and the path. I think he'd need somewhere with windows onto the street, so you can see what it's like inside as you pass.'

'Okay,' said Lizzie, crossing it out. 'This is great. We've barely started and I've already crossed off nearly half the places on the list.'

'It's kind of great,' said Lance. He was beginning to wonder whether there were any pubs in the whole of Berlin that Jonathon would even have thought of setting foot in. And beyond that, he was wondering how this whole thing was going to turn out fine with almost no effort on his part, which was how he was used to the world working.

47

Michaels was waiting. He was cold and tired, and his legs hurt. The place was dismal, windowless, with a low ceiling and harsh, buzzing lights. The floor beneath his feet was greyish tiles, just like the ceiling above and the walls all around. It seemed he had been there an eternity. Waiting. He hated German supermarkets.

The aisles were narrow, meeting at awkward angles, and the stock seemed to have been dumped on the shelves in a great hurry. It was almost as though the supermarket were trying to make itself look as bad as possible. Perhaps it feared that making any part of itself even slightly nice would lead to complaints: that the money for, say, better lighting should have been spent instead on further cheapening the potatoes, heaped up in huge sacks near the doors.

He moved on, idly contemplating the quark, potato salad and gherkins – German staples that barely existed in Britain. He put something into his blue plastic basket, feeling that he should. Looking down, he saw that it was herring salad, bright pink and seeming to throb gently in its jar.

He was moodily eyeballing some pickled eggs when he became aware of a presence beside him.

'Guten Tag, Michaels,' she said.

She was in her workweek attire: a long black coat over a black suit. In it, she looked more than ever like a gothic edifice, despite the blue plastic shopping basket in her gloved hand.

'Dame Margery,' said Michaels, impulsively taking a jar of pickled carrots from the shelf.

They drifted on, not looking at each other directly.

'Strange, isn't it,' he said, 'that Germany and Britain, both northern European countries, similar in language and wealth, should differ so fundamentally in their approach to buying food. I believe Germans see light, space and good design as fundamentally dishonest.'

'Whereas our supermarkets know that if you get those things right, your food doesn't have to be as good. The Germans have a point. We are a fundamentally dishonest nation. It's the source of our success.'

She stopped and took a tin from the shelf.

'Speaking of which,' she said, 'what brought you to Berlin? I imagine you didn't come here just to stock up on *Kichererbsen*, whatever they are.'

'Chickpeas, Dame Margery. And no. I came here because Mr Channon summoned Miss Palgrave here at short notice, in the middle of the night. I thought it the ideal opportunity to spend some time with him' – he picked up a tin of kohlrabi chunks and quickly put it back – 'especially since his urgency indicated that something must have changed, concerning Fairfax.'

She glanced at him.

'You needn't worry,' he added. 'I paid for the flight myself, and my hotel. There'll be no expenses claims. And I shall make up for my other work when I return.'

She looked at him again, sidelong, and moved on to the refrigerated section.

'And how much time,' she said, thoughtfully hefting a carton of

Schlagsahne, 'have you succeeded in spending with him?'

'Cream,' he said. 'And, well, none.'

'I see,' she said, taking instead a *Schmand*.

'Also cream,' he said. 'All these are: *Sahne, Kreme, Schmand, Rahm, Dickmilch …*'

'I see,' she said again. 'And the girl?'

'They need a lot of different types,' he explained, putting a small *Sprühsahne* into his basket. 'Miss Palgrave? She is confined to her hotel room, and a large American at her door insists she doesn't want to see anyone.'

'Have you tried telephoning her?'

They were moving again, slowly past many milks.

'On her British telephone? Our networks are so insecure, the Americans would be sure to hear every word. So yes, I called her but said nothing of any importance – and neither did she.'

He stopped, and they inspected a wall of pork.

'She is at least sensible then,' said Dame Margery. 'And you imply that she also has something other than a British telephone.'

She put a pair of *Schweinenacken* in her basket.

'The Germans,' he said, 'with their experience of the Stasi and Gestapo, now do everything possible to prevent electronic eavesdropping.'

He took a *Schnitzel* and they moved on.

'So you supplied her with a German telephone,' she said.

'Yes,' he admitted.

They were moving slowly down the aisle.

'*Teigwaren*?' she asked.

'Literally "doughware", by which they mean pasta.'

'I see. Your own idea, the German telephone?'

He paused, contemplating some *Bandnudeln*, and said, 'A suggestion of Ms Morden's, but I believe a sound one.'

She looked at him, taking the *Bandnudeln* from his hand.

'You've been in touch with Morden?' she asked.

'Yes.'

They moved out of doughware, past the huge crisps, heading for the vegetables.

'When was the last time?'

'Early yesterday morning. She called me as I was on my way to the airport.'

'So many potatoes,' she said.

'Yes,' he agreed. He didn't take any: the weight would be intolerable. He opted instead for a nearby *Kohl Jaroma*.

'This German telephone,' she said, 'has anyone called it?'

'I haven't given anyone the number.'

'Have *you*? Called it, I mean?'

'No. Not yet.'

She had in her hand a slice of turnip, a leek, and two carrots, a rubber band holding them all together.

'Channon has been in touch, you know,' she said.

'Oh?' He failed to keep a hint of fear from sounding in his voice.

'He is, understandably, unhappy that you're here. It looks like interference. This is American territory.'

He looked at her and glanced back at all the potatoes. 'It's German territory, isn't it?'

'You know what I mean,' she said, moving towards the checkout.

'Yes I do. But does that mean we intend to abandon Fairfax and Miss Palgrave here?' He made a gesture, but mistimed it, so that he seemed to imply they had mislaid the two young people in a pile of unusually coloured carrots.

She said nothing. They arrived at the checkout, and unpacked their baskets of cover shopping, putting their oddly miscellaneous collections of items on the conveyor belt. Dame Margery was silent a long time, standing behind a man with face tattoos and metal studs implanted in his scalp.

The tattooed man took his shopping and left, and the old lady behind the till gave them a stare of cold hatred, as she did all her customers. She muttered a venomous 'Hm' and set to ferociously scanning their shopping, throwing it down the shallow metal ramp so that it collected in a wounded heap at the bottom.

As Michaels began to pack the shopping into a bag, Dame Margery turned to him.

'Personally,' she said, emphasising her words with the elastically bound vegetables, 'I regret what is happening to Fairfax and Palgrave. I know you must too. But professionally our duty is very clear. Remember, we are the stagehands, guiding behind the scenes. We cannot afford to get caught up in what happens to the actors in any given scene. Britain's long-term interests depend on the CIA. That trumps the wellbeing of two individuals.'

The old lady behind the till said loudly, '*Five-and-twenty, sixty.*'

Michaels handed her thirty euros, which she took with a malicious glare and another 'Hm.'

Near the door, Michaels said to Dame Margery, 'But what about this possibility that Channon's a mole?'

'Michaels,' she said, 'it would be wonderful if you were able to expose a mole in a senior position among the Americans. But even that is a small thing compared with simply maintaining our course. Besides, as I said, I find the idea very unlikely. It is far more likely that almost anyone else is a mole, even me.'

'Even you?' he said, emerging, blinking, into the sunlight.

'I was simply making a point,' she said, and patted him on the arm. 'Now really, you've had your fun, you've played at spies for a bit. But now it's time to get back to London and the desk job.'

She handed him the bag of futile shopping, then turned and walked away, through the crowds in their anoraks and leather trousers. From far above came the rattle of the overhead metro line. Michaels stumbled on, hampered by the burden Dame Margery had bestowed upon him.

48

By five o'clock, Lance and Lizzie were more than three quarters of the way through their list and were visiting the places that opened later.

These seemed more promising – many cosy and candlelit, with home-made furniture and eccentric names. They had now been to three that Jonathon might have preferred to rotating blades. And in two of these they'd been able to talk to people who had been working on Thursday. Both said they sort of recognised Jonathon's face from Lance's photos. But since Jonathon sort of looked like everyone and sort of looked like no one at all, these vague statements of recognition didn't mean much.

Now they were pulling up outside a bar just off a wide, tree-lined, grittily urban boulevard. The spring sun still shone, though the shadows were long. This latest bar sat on the corner of the street, as did a large proportion of its clientele, chatting in German and English and straddling rickety wooden furniture. It was an unremarkable-looking place, with doodled-over white walls, brown-tinted windows and the word 'Travolta' written in large letters over the door.

As soon as they walked in, the man behind the bar said, 'Hey, what can I get you?' He had the fluency and diction of an American, but a mysteriously non-specific European accent.

'Hey,' said Lizzie, 'a friend of ours disappeared on Thursday night. We think he might have come to a bar in this area. Were you working that night?'

Lance glanced around at the long, brick bar, the solid, high tables that flanked the windows, the table football, the steel-legged barstools, the man in the corner wearing a dusty corduroy jacket, nursing a beer and a book. A tired old dog glanced back at him from the corner of the room.

'This is it,' he said.

'Are you sure?' said Lizzie.

'Yes, completely sure. Or at least, if he didn't come here then he should have done. Just look at it: ridiculous, unthreatening name, windows on two sides so you can see how cosy it is and tell whether there's enough space, plenty of tables where you can sit on your own without looking conspicuous, not horrible but clearly not designed at all. It's perfect.'

'Thanks,' said the man behind the bar. He was balding, tanned, and wearing an old blue T-shirt with a picture on the front that had faded almost to nothing.

'So, were you working Thursday night?' asked Lizzie.

'I work here every night – I own it – but I'm not always behind the bar. Dave, was I around Thursday night?'

The barman turned to the man he'd called Dave: red-faced, middle-aged, wearing a crumpled floral shirt and with hair exactly like someone had glued some hairbrushes to the top of his head.

'Thursday?' said Dave, looking up from his newspaper. He had an English accent, from the Midlands. 'Don't know.'

'Were *you* in that night?' Lizzie asked Dave.

'I imagine so,' he said, smoothing down his stiff hair, which immediately stood up almost vertically again.

The man behind the bar laughed. 'Dave puts in the same kind of hours as I do.'

'You work here?' asked Lizzie.

'No, just a regular, like,' said Dave, giving an embarrassed chuckle. 'Just while I get meself sorted, you know.'

'Which is, what, four years now?' said the barman.

'Three,' said Dave.

'Do you recognise this man?' asked Lizzie.

She showed him the photos of Jonathon.

'Maybe, maybe,' said Dave. 'There was a fella come in one night, could have been Thursday.'

'Did he talk to anyone?' asked Lizzie.

Dave looked at the man behind the bar, who folded his arms.

'Maybe,' said Dave, looking down at his paper.

'Listen, I'm pretty busy ...' said the man behind the bar.

'Is something making you uncomfortable?' asked Lizzie. 'Because we're only interested in finding our friend.'

The man behind the bar looked at her and seemed to be thinking.

'To be clear,' said Lizzie, 'we are not interested at all in whether you have the right paperwork for people working bar here. If you're employing, say, an American with no visa–'

'Is that what this is about?' said Lance, incredulous. 'He thinks we – he thinks *I* – work for the German government?'

'Hey, man, don't get–' said the man behind the bar.

'I'm trying to find my friend, whose life is in danger and who's lost his memory,' said Lance. 'I live in New York, I'm an MTV presenter, for God's sake – except I've come here when I should be filming, so I don't know if I am any more. Why would you think I work for the German ... I don't know ... tax department? Please, if you remember anything–'

'And,' put in Lizzie, 'if he talked to someone who works here, she could be in danger too.'

'All right, like,' muttered Dave. 'Keep your hair on.'

'Hey, man, I didn't mean to ...' said the man behind the bar, letting his sentence trail off.

'Sorry,' said Lance, sitting down on a stool. 'I didn't mean to lose my cool like that. I'm jet-lagged.'

'That's okay, man,' said the man behind the bar.

'Actually,' said Lance, 'could I have a beer? Is that okay, Lizzie?'

'Sure,' said Lizzie.

'Grosses or kleines?' asked the man behind the bar.

'A small one for me,' said Lizzie, 'but I guess my friend here will have–'

'A big one,' said Lance. 'Definitely.'

'Haake?' said the man behind the bar, tapping the handle of a pump.

'Is it a beer?' asked Lance.

The man behind the bar nodded.

'Then yes.'

When they had their beers in front of them – and the man behind the bar had taught Lance how to make eye-contact while clinking glasses so as to avoid seven years of bad sex – Lizzie turned to Dave and said, 'So, you maybe saw our friend Thursday?'

'There was a fella in here, Thursday-Friday time it would have been, talking to Karen.'

'Karen,' said Lizzie. 'You're sure of that name?'

Dave frowned. 'Am I sure Karen's called Karen?'

'Never mind. Please go on.'

'Well, Karen asked us if I knew the name of that film where the fella loses his memory. What's it called?'

Lance and Lizzie exchanged a significant glance.

'Do you remember what time he left?' asked Lizzie.

'It was kicking-out time, I think. Karen said he could stay at hers. She does that, like. Anyone with a hard-luck story.'

'Okay, and who is Karen?'

'She works bar here,' said the bald man in the blue T-shirt, 'but she hasn't been in since, uh, since Thursday night.'

'Okay. Can you describe her?'

'Karen? She's – I don't know what we're meant to say now – mixed-race, or something? Kind of darkish skin, dark-brown curly hair, one metre sixty? Early thirties, I guess. Light build. American.'

'Okay. And tell me about after Thursday?'

'She got someone to take over her shift Friday and Saturday, and then she didn't show on Sunday. I tried calling her, but no answer. You think she's okay?'

'Is it unusual for her to miss shifts like that?'

'She might swap a shift here and there, like everyone does, but she's probably the most reliable person who works here – including me.'

Lance and Lizzie exchanged another significant glance.

'We've got to stop doing that,' said Lance.

'Noted,' agreed Lizzie. Then she said, 'Did she call here, when she got someone to change her shift?'

'No,' said the man behind the bar, 'she just arranged it with Ingeborg. That's how we do it here. It's not a big deal.'

'Do you have Ingeborg's number?'

'Sure. Listen, it sounds like I should be worried. Should I contact the police or …?'

'You already have,' said Lizzie. 'Actually, I'm a couple of steps up from the police. Here, let me give you my card. It's a US number, but you can call me collect, any time of the day or night, if you think of anything else we should know. I'll take your number, and I'll be in touch as soon as I find anything out. Now, is there anyone else we should be in contact with about Karen?'

'There's her boyfriend, Boris, but I don't have a number for him.'

'They live together?'

He nodded.

'Okay, what's the address?'

49

'Sterling, you got a minute?'

Channon was standing in the doorway to his office with what was either a trick of the light or a faint friendly smile on his face.

'Sure, sir. Absolutely.'

'Great. Hey, Kerr! Could you bring us a couple green teas? One-eighty degrees.'

Kerr got up and headed towards the kitchen. Sterling called after him, 'Thanks, man. You want my thermometer?'

'I told him to get his own,' said Channon, ushering Sterling inside. 'So, sit down.'

'What can I do for you, sir?'

'I want to talk at you, Sterling. I can't ask for your advice, because you were born like two seconds ago. Not to mention you could be the mole–'

'You still think I'm the mole?'

'Nothing personal: I think everyone's the mole – to varying degrees of certainty. But whether you're the mole or not, you're a good listener. I mean, you listen and you talk as well, which is pretty rare: most people come down hard on one side or the other. Kerr, for example, is your classic non-talking listener. And Mason's one hell of a non-listening talker.'

'Thank you, sir. I think. What did you want to talk to me about?'

'Newman wants to meet me. Alone, unarmed, in a public place of his choosing.'

'Where? When?'

'Doesn't matter. And there's no room for tricks – at least, not about where and how I meet him. If I bring guys disguised as mailmen or whatever and he spots it, I could scare him away for good. And besides, the more support I bring, the bigger the chance the mole will find out.'

'And then Newman's dead.'

'And then *I'm* dead. Newman's an anomaly. Most of the guys who've been killed are like me: senior operations guys. I don't know what they want with Newman. But this is a bad time for a guy like me to be hanging out on his own, unarmed, in a public place.'

'Right. I hadn't thought of that.'

'Don't get me wrong. I'm not afraid to die, and I'm willing to lay down my life for my country. But we're pretty short-handed around here. There's not many guys left with experience and balls. A lot of my generation left in the nineties. And some of the best ones who stayed on have been killed. Of course, there's this hiring bonanza going on at the moment, but it just means the Agency's filling up with inexperienced dolts – guys who wanted to be in the Marines but thought they had too many degrees for it.'

There was a knock on the door and Kerr walked in, holding the cups of green tea carefully so as not to spill any on his perfectly pressed cargo pants.

'Thanks, man,' said Sterling. Channon nodded.

When Kerr had left, Channon took a sip and winced. 'Son of a bitch. He boiled it!'

'You want me to …?'

'Forget it. Pay attention to the anger and watch it dissipate like the steam from this fucking boiling hot cup of green tea. What was I saying?'

'Marines, too many degrees, your generation.'

Channon blew on his tea. 'My generation. I joined in 1965, straight out of Princeton, and my first big job was infiltrating the peace movement. That was a great time. I got to grow my hair long, listen to the music, drop acid, explore love and who I really was, and I got paid to do it. I got to drop out without the downside of having to find a way to climb back in.'

'We infiltrated the peace movement?'

'Sure. I know our charter says we're not meant to do that kind of thing in the US. But, you know, we're a country that gives people a lot of freedom, so it's only prudent to make sure it doesn't get too far out of hand.'

'I guess so.'

'After that I went to Latin America and learned the ropes with a couple of coups, and then back to Germany, where I'd done a year or so after basic training. Been here ever since, pretty much. Met my ex-wife here – she was in my team.'

Channon stared at the filing cabinet, lost in a reverie.

'So,' said Sterling, 'you're wondering whether the Agency can afford for you to risk all your experience for the sake of bringing Newman in?'

Channon snapped back into focus, looking directly at Sterling.

'Yes,' he said. 'That's exactly it. I'm not so much afraid of losing my life as of the Agency losing my experience. I mean, look at what's going on out there.'

Channon nodded out of the window, to where Farge Lacan and Chase Mason were comparing the size of their biceps, while Jerry Dempsey sat watching them in his shades.

'This may be way off the mark, sir, but is there a reason Newman's setting the timetable here? I mean, won't his position get worse as time goes by? He can't have much money left, and his curiosity about who he is will only grow, no?'

'He has plenty of money. I released a standard field kit to him, partly to win his trust. Plus, if he's penniless, he's on the street, just waiting to be picked off by the bad guys – or he has to go to the authorities. I persuaded him he's wanted by the police, but if he doesn't resume his MK-Ultra treatments, all his memories will gradually return, and then he'll know the truth. He could go public.'

'Is there no way of locating him without meeting? Surveillance cameras?'

'You don't know Germany yet, son. They hate surveillance cameras here. There's a handful in the whole city, with big signs to let everyone know they're there, and people smash them up the whole time.'

Sterling glanced out of the window, lost in thought, and saw that Dempsey was now trying to impress Farge Lacan and Chase Mason by doing one-handed pushups. Amy Wintergreen, the woman who always wore a fluffy sweater, walked past them. It was sky-blue today. She came to Channon's door, glanced in through the glass and seemed to change her mind about knocking.

'It's tough, sir,' said Sterling, as she walked away.

'Plus, I *need him* for the Reichstag session tomorrow afternoon,' said Channon.

'Well, that sounds like a lot of reasons for needing him back, sir. But if you go and the Agency loses you, it permanently loses its capacity to deal with other stuff as important as this.'

'Yeah, well, that's the dilemma. And I've got so much invested in this guy. I've sweated blood for him. The Congressional Oversight Committee got wind of Knife-fish and wanted to shut it down, so I had to reconfigure the programme to stop that happening. I mean, the paperwork alone …'

'I know you don't want advice, sir, but it sounds to me like there are a lot of short-term pressures that would skew your judgement in the direction of prioritising bringing Newman in now, rather than protecting your long-term value to the Agency. I mean, he's got you thinking of going outside without even a gun. The only other time you've left this building was to visit that British girl, and you took like five guys with you then.'

'That is kind of crazy, isn't it? But at this point I feel like I'd walk around Berlin all day long in my birthday suit if it would bring Newman in.'

50

'Then why's it called a currywurst,' asked Lance, climbing into the car, 'if there's no curry in it?'

They closed the doors and sat there side by side, each holding a little crinkled cardboard tray containing a chopped sausage and fries.

'I don't know,' said Lizzie, using her tiny wooden fork to amplify her shrug. 'I guess just because it's hot and spicy like a curry?'

'But it's actually just paprika sprinkled on top of ketchup, on top of a really cheap fried sausage?' he asked, continuing to eat the living hell out of it.

'Yup.'

'Then what makes it taste so good? Also – unrelated question – what are we going to do now?'

Lizzie delicately shovelled her last piece of sausage and the last few fries into her mouth, dabbed with a paper napkin and, still chewing, said, 'Beer.'

'Is that an answer to the first question or the second?'

'The first.' She carefully put her empty crinkled cardboard tray on the back seat. 'We have a lot to do.'

'Absolutely. I guess you'll want to get your agents involved, put a trace on Karen's phone, send a team to watch her address, have your computer guys hack the backchannel port into her email. Can I help with any of that? Can I watch?'

'*Hack the backchannel port*? Really?'

'Or whatever,' said Lance. 'I'm guessing at the details. But you'll want to do something like that.'

'I'll want to do something like that?' said Lizzie, annoyed. 'Listen, *I'll* tell *you* what I want to do, because I am actually a professional intelligence officer and you're just a guy who presents a minor-league cable TV show that's sort of vaguely related to the topic of spying.'

There was a moment of silence. *Wow*, thought Lance. *How long has that been building up?*

'Okay,' he said. 'Sorry. I didn't mean to be one of those men who, on the basis of almost total ignorance, nonetheless patronisingly explain to women how to do the things they're experts in–'

'There really should be a word for that,' said Lizzie. 'It happens all the time.'

'It's just that I'm worried about Jonathon, and now we have a lead and I've eaten a currywurst, I kind of … want everything to happen. But I get the feeling that there's a lot I don't know.'

Lance folded his currywurst tray into a neat square and posted it under his seat.

'Okay,' said Lizzie, 'I guess it's time for me to level with you.'

'About what?'

'The fact is that this whole thing of trying to find your friend … it's not entirely official.'

'Is that why we flew economy class and I'm staying in a room that says "I'm a girl" on the door?'

'Yes. This is coming out of my pocket, and I don't know how long it's going to carry on.'

'I'll pay my way. I want to find Jonathon. But why isn't it official?'

'You know how I told you Channon says there's a mole in the agency, passing information to the assassins?'

'Yes.'

'Well, I believe Channon *is* that mole. And if I can find Jonathon, not only will it save his life, it'll also give us our first evidence against Channon. You see, Jonathon's the only person so far to have survived an attempted hit.'

'He is?'

'Yes.'

'He's … even when you've known him a long time, he's full of surprises.'

'That's nice. You really like him.'

'Yes,' said Lance, and stared out of the window for a bit. Admitting to liking his friends made him uneasy.

'In fact,' said Lizzie gently, 'Jonathon has now survived three assassination attempts. I appeared suddenly outside your apartment at one in the morning because I'd just heard about the latest attack.'

'Jesus shit,' said Lance.

'Relax. It failed. But it came so soon after Channon learned where Jonathon was that it can't just be a coincidence. And I couldn't just stand by and watch it happen again.'

'So what's Jonathon doing now?'

'We believe he's somewhere in Berlin.'

'We?'

'I have a contact close to Channon who's keeping me informed.'

'Does Channon know where Jonathon is?'

'No. But they're in touch. A meeting's being arranged. And I think that meeting will be a trap. Jonathon won't survive it.'

'What? But … what? I mean … what?'

'At this point, Channon wants Jonathon for the same reason I do–'

'What, to save his life?'

'Okay, that's a point of difference between us. Yes, I want to save Jonathon's life. But, like I said, he's the only one who's survived. He can describe the assassins and their methods, and that's all we've got to go on, to track them down. Channon knows that too. So Channon needs Jonathon dead to make sure the identity of the assassins stays secret. Because one thing the CIA is good at is identifying people – we have a huge amount of footage and data from all around the world.'

'When you said in New York that Jonathon had lost his memory and was in danger, I thought you meant … you know, not eating properly, sleeping in parks. And then you casually mention assassins on the plane, and I thought, you know, hypothetically assassins could find him. But now it sounds like waves of trained, professional hitmen are repeatedly doing their best to … kill him. How has he survived?'

'I don't know,' she said, shaking her head. 'Maybe that's the reason Doug Channon recruited him.'

Lance put his hands over his eyes. 'I have a headache,' he said.

'That'll be the currywurst,' said Lizzie, sympathetically.

'And why,' said Lance, suddenly sitting up straight and looking at her, 'do you think the mole is this Channon guy?'

Lizzie paused. 'A lot of reasons. There's *signs*, but … the big thing is, I know him. I know what he's like. I … well, I used to be married to him. We divorced eight … no, what, ten? Ten years ago now. But I was in his team as my second assignment after joining the Agency, and I fell for him.'

'And what do you mean, you know what he's like?'

'I mean he loves the intrigue, the power, the action. But he doesn't care so much what it achieves. I think if someone approached him the right way …'

'… he would help them assassinate a load of his colleagues and friends, including someone he recruited?'

'That's a little … blunt, but yes. I mean, I found out a lot about the guy while we were married. One of his first assignments was infiltrating the peace movement in the US. It was his job to make friends with idealistic hippies and then blackmail them or have them arrested. After that he was in Latin America, having a whale of a time, creating private armies, torturing people, launching coups. I know him as well as anyone, and I know he's psychologically capable of this.'

'So have you told anyone else about your suspicions?'

'There's my contact in covert ops. And I have a few other … friends. But I haven't said anything officially. I have basically no proof. And I used to be married to him, which is really not a good look when you're accusing someone of something this serious.'

'That's true,' said Lance, who was himself unsure whether to believe her.

'Plus,' said Lizzie, 'Channon's really good at making the other person look stupid. It's one of the reasons I couldn't stay married to him. You say he could maybe – I don't know – put the trash out a little more often. And he starts talking very quietly and the next thing you know he's tied you in knots and you're crying and it just seems so unreasonable and irrational to ever think that he didn't put the trash out enough.'

'Wow. So he never has to empty the bins?'

'Never.'

'That's impressive.'

'That's Channon.'

'Why didn't you tell me all this on the plane?'

'I didn't want to alarm you. I thought I should let you into the craziness slowly.'

'And then suddenly smash me over the head with all of it at once over a currywurst in a rented Opel Rekord.'

She looked at him and smiled wryly.

'Yeah, something like that.'

'So what do we do now?'

'We go to Karen's address. Saturday night's attack happened in a village in northern Germany, but we believe they're now back in Berlin. There's a chance they've gone back to her apartment. I have a friend watching his apartment, so I know they aren't there.'

'Won't Channon be watching her apartment?'

'Channon doesn't know who Jonathon's travelling with. This lead is the one advantage we have.'

'Well, that's one thing. What about – and I realise this is entirely your area of professional competence – tracing her phone or reading her email?'

'Her cellphone is German, so we can't trace that – they have very strict data protection and privacy laws here. I mean, maybe I could if I had a certain kind of evidence, but I am not even officially in the country, so that's out of the question for now.'

'Okay,' said Lance, dejectedly.

'But her email address is a US one, so I might be able to talk to a friend at the NSA about that, get him to "hack the backchannel port."'

'Or whatever,' said Lance, patiently.

Seven minutes later, they knocked on the door of a flat with the nameplate, 'ASEFA, K'.

51

The man sat down next to Karen on the sofa, nervously jiggling his new phone from hand to hand.

'I feel as though something's about to happen,' he said. 'Something weird.'

'That's just because weird things keep happening,' said Karen. 'And then today has been pretty much non-weird all the way along. You're just not used to it.'

'You're right. That must be it.'

A loud knock sounded. The man looked at his phone.

'I think that's the sound doors make,' said Karen.

'You're right again. I'll get it.'

'Relax. Save your feet,' she said, getting up and looking pointedly at the man's bandaged feet in their large German orthopaedic sandals. They didn't compliment his baggy, patterned Indian trousers, his black vest or his ski jacket, all of which Karen and Boris had chosen for him. He suspected they were beyond complimenting, unlike the black overcoat he still wore, which was the only thing he liked. He hoped it would distract people from the rest of his clothes.

She walked around the neat little coffee table, across the shining wooden floor, and over to the grand door. This large, comfortable flat was Karen's great triumph, found and booked online the day before. It had an excellent toaster, and overlooked the canal and a beautiful old bridge.

She opened the door.

'These pizza guys, they are assholes,' said Boris, walking in with a stack of cardboard boxes.

'You say everyone's an asshole.'

'Everyone is asshole,' said Boris, 'except Mister. And sometimes you.'

He handed them each a box, flipping the edge up to check the contents.

'And this is garlic bread,' he said, putting an extra box on the table between them, 'and this one is profiteroles.'

'I love you,' said Karen.

Boris nodded, already eating.

The man picked up a slice of pizza and raised it to his lips.

DADDLE-AH DAA, DADDLE-AH DAA, DADDLE-AH DAA, DAA!

He dropped the pizza, wiped his hands, and stared at his ringing phone. 'Number withheld,' said the screen.

Karen nodded encouragingly. The man took a deep breath and pressed the green button.

'Okay,' said Channon's voice, 'we have a deal. I'll meet you. In public. Alone.'

'You'll tell me who I am?'

'Yes. If you'll tell me everything that's happened since you lost your memory, including descriptions of the people who tried to kill you.'

'Um, right. Yes.'

'So what's next?' said Channon.

'This is what I'd like you to do, please …'

52

Lance knocked again.

'Karen?' he called.

'Karen, honey, we're here to help, so let us know if you're in there,' said Lizzie.

They listened, silently, heads bowed. The building was silent, apart from the sound of a child practising a very small, or very distant, trumpet.

'What do we do now?' asked Lance.

'Oh, I'll just get all my "agents" on it and we'll go in via the back-channel port,' said Lizzie.

'Okay,' said Lance, evenly.

'Or,' she said, 'you could keep watch and I'll try to get us in through the frontchannel port. Also known as the door.'

'I like that plan better,' said Lance, taking up a position on the staircase, looking up and down, keeping an ear out for footsteps.

He glanced back at Lizzie. She had taken what looked like a credit card from her wallet, and was extracting from it, at some cost to her nails, what looked like very thin allen keys.

Lizzie crouched and began patiently inserting these slim pieces of metal into the lock, the tip of her tongue protruding from between her teeth. In the background, the tiny or far away trumpet demolished 'Au Claire de la Lune', leaving its wreckage hanging in the air as a kind of terrible warning. In one of the lower flats, a dog mourned. No one used the staircase.

When Lance next looked, the door was already open, and Lizzie was cautiously stepping inside. Lance abandoned his post and followed her in.

'Seems like someone got here before us,' said Lizzie, gently closing the door behind them. 'The place has been ransacked.'

Lance glanced around. 'I think this is just an untidy flat,' he said. 'This is what mine used to look like, when I used to think gnomes dirtied all the dishes every night so there was no point washing up.'

Lizzie looked at him.

'But then I earned some money, got married and employed a cleaner,' he explained.

They were standing in a small entrance area, looking into a living room and kitchen that were strewn with clothes, bedding and dirty dishes. Elsewhere, the trumpet, now thankfully even more minuscule or remote, was sadistically smashing god's living shit out of 'Happy Birthday to You'.

'It's not even that bad,' said Lance. 'Completely standard Bohemian mess.'

'Really?' said Lizzie. 'I guess I'm out of touch.'

'Lucky I'm here,' said Lance, strolling forth.

The sofa showed signs of having been slept on, as it was half covered with a dingy sheet and an unzipped sleeping bag. There was a dirty plate under it. The kitchen table was covered in bagel crumbs and coffee stains. In the bedroom there was a broken drum stand and a selection of cheap microphones. The bathroom was very clean but entirely overrun with shampoo.

'Hey, Lizzie,' said Lance, 'I think we–'

Lizzie, still standing in the middle of the kitchen and living room, was looking at her phone. She held up her hand.

'Just got a text,' she said, 'with some not-great news. It looks like Channon is almost certainly meeting Jonathon tomorrow.'

'Shit,' said Lance, sitting down heavily on one of the kitchen chairs.

'Don't touch anything,' said Lizzie.

'Don't worry,' said Lance. 'No one has my bottom-print on file.'

'Our time just got shorter,' said Lizzie. 'We have to somehow track this Karen Asefa down by, I guess, midmorning tomorrow – and pray Jonathon is still with her.'

'Why don't we just email Karen? Tell her what's going on, ask her to pass a message to Jonathon?'

'Great idea. I'd love to leave an electronic record that the NSA can read, proving that I'm in Germany with you right now, trying to interfere in a sensitive CIA case.'

'We don't have to reveal who we are,' said Lance. 'It's probably pretty easy to set up an anonymous German email account. We could buy a German phone and have her call us.'

'Yes. And let's say we're a Nigerian prince with a huge sum of money for her.'

'What? Oh, spam. Right.'

Lizzie pulled a thinking-about-it face, gnawing on the stubby antenna of her mobile phone.

'It could work. It's just, there's a ninety-nine percent chance it'd go straight into her junk mail folder and she'd never see it.'

'You're right. Shit.'

'I'm not saying don't try it,' said Lizzie. 'But it's not what we do first.'

'How long will your guy take to get into her emails?'

'I don't know. He didn't definitely say he would do it – it's totally against the rules.'

'Bloody rules.'

Saying this made him think of Piper, because it was exactly what she would have said. So it seemed slightly uncanny when Lizzie said, 'There's one other chance. I didn't tell you before, but Channon's brought Jonathon's girlfriend over. She's at the Adlon.'

'Piper's here? But I thought you said the CIA weren't going to involve her?'

'She's here. I … I lied. I didn't want you to try to contact her. And I didn't want to worry you, because she's in lockdown in her hotel room and Channon pretty certainly means to use her, one way or another, to trap Jonathon.'

'Oh, Moses fuck. Can't we call her? Warn her?'

'She has a UK phone, so we can't call on that, not without Channon hearing every word. Michaels, the British intelligence officer I told you about, he slipped her a German phone – at my suggestion. But he won't give me the number. I should ask again.'

'Can I talk to him? Maybe I could convince him? I really don't want anything bad happening to Piper.'

'I'll call him and tell him what's changed, and maybe he'll give up the number. If he does, we can try to figure out how to get her out of there. Then Channon wouldn't have anything over Jonathon. It'd all come down to whether he's managed to make Jonathon trust him or not.'

'Right. We've also got the number for Karen's barmaid friend. Do you think she might have a way to get in touch with Karen? Or maybe Karen and Jonathon are staying with her?'

'Seems unlikely,' said Lizzie.

'Well everything's unlikely,' said Lance. 'But something's got to work. Otherwise how will we inevitably save Jonathon – and now Piper – just in the nick of time?'

As if on cue, the tiny trumpet struck up 'The Last Post', underlining its bleak melancholy by solemnly strangling each note to death. Nothing survives, it seemed to say, not even music.

53

Piper had by this time spent the best part of two days cooped up in an almost unimaginably luxurious hotel suite in central Berlin. But the luxury seemed to make everything worse. A filthy cramped room would have more accurately mirrored what was going on inside her, and would perhaps have pushed her to overcome it. As it was, the unbearable sequence of hope, boredom, frustration, uncertainty and gloom seemed to thrive among the velvet and plush.

What was she meant to be doing here? They had said they needed her help, but no one had asked her anything. There had been a very brief call from Michaels, and a short visit from an extremely relaxed tense man with a white ponytail, but then his phone had rung and he'd disappeared.

Outside her door, at all hours, there stood a man in a black suit which visibly struggled to contain him. He said they needed her to stay where she was, as Jonathon would need her help very soon. His tone made it very clear that she had absolutely no choice in the matter. She was, she realised, basically in prison, but with room service.

She threw herself onto the bed, which yielded lovingly while also remaining reassuringly firm. God, everything was so *designed*. It must be hell being rich. She went and lay on the antique blue chaise longue, which was there just for show and thus had the decency to be uncomfortable.

She heard her phone vibrate in her bag and her heart leapt then dived. It was probably just Gus, her dad, offering his bloody love and support. She instantly felt guilty about this thought, and tried to become her best daughter self as she rooted through her bag.

Her phone was not ringing. The sound was coming from the mysterious cheap grey phone she had zipped into one of her bag's many unused special compartments.

'I feel like a shower,' she said, self-consciously trying to talk to herself the way she would have done if she hadn't been sure the room was infested with surveillance equipment. She felt like a terrible actor. If she'd been alone she would have made up a short song about it and done it in a stupid voice, but the CIA weren't to know that.

She headed into the bathroom, wondering if she should say something to herself about why she was taking her bag with her into the shower. *I'll just take the old bag, just in case.* That was the sort of thing she might genuinely have said to herself, but it suddenly didn't seem very plausible, so she kept quiet.

She turned the shower on, quickly undressed, sucking her stomach in when she got down to her bra and pants, then wrapped a towel around herself, took off her underwear with her back to where she imagined the camera to be, and answered the phone which she'd clutched to her bosom as she'd taken off the towel.

'Hello?' she said.

'Don't say my name,' said a voice at the other end of the line.

'Well that's easy,' said Piper. 'I've got no idea who you are.'

'What?' said the voice.

'Sorry,' said Piper, 'I'm in the shower, and not talking very loudly.'

'That's good,' said the voice. 'What did you say when I said, "Don't say my name"?'

'I said I don't know who you are.'

'Okay, well, when I tell you my name, promise you won't repeat it with a delighted squeal?'

'I promise.'

'It's Lance. Lance Ferman.'

'Oh. Hello.'

'Okay.' He sounded deflated.

'What? You said not to repeat your name.'

'I know, but I was expecting a bit more … Anyway, never mind. I'm in Berlin too, also with the CIA. How are you?'

'I don't know. A bit stir crazy? I've got a … a *goon*, I suppose – that's what they're called, isn't it? A huge silent man packed uncomfortably into a large silent man's suit. He stands outside my door and follows me down at mealtimes. Actually, I've been here for two days, so it can't be the same man, can he? There must be lots of identical ones doing shifts. Sorry, I'm rambling. My brain's gone a bit funny.'

'That's okay.'

'Have you got a goon?'

'No, I've got a lovely person called Lizzie who likes old-fashioneds and *It's a Wonderful Life*.'

'I should have guessed.'

'Listen, Lizzie's the one who gave Michaels the idea of slipping you a phone. And there's something you should know. She says the American CIA head guy who got you to come here, Channon, is a mole.'

'A mole?'

'Yes. He–'

'But that doesn't make any sense. A mole?'

'Yes, I know it's hard to believe, but–'

'This is insane. What do you mean, a mole? He's a man with a ponytail and a linen shirt.'

'Haven't you heard the term "mole" before?'

'The blind animals that dig up people's gardens?'

'Okay, well it also means a spy on one side who's actually secretly working for the other side. How have you not heard that before?'

'I don't know. I've never been interested in spy stuff. It just leaves me cold. Sorry.'

'You've never even watched a James Bond film?'

'Am I a twelve-year-old boy?'

'What?'

'Sorry, still talking quietly into a cheap phone in a shower. I said, "Am I a twelve-year-old boy?" It was rhetorical.'

'Okay, never mind that. The important thing is that Channon's working for the other side–'

'Which other side?'

'We don't know who they are. Maybe the Russians?'

'The Russians? Still? I thought that stuff finished in the eighties.'

'I know. The important thing is that Channon's the one behind all the attempts to kill Jonathon–'

'God, I'm so confused. Didn't he recruit Jonathon?'

'Yes. It's confusing. But the point is that he's using you to set a trap for Jonathon.'

'So the CIA recruited Jonathon and are now trying to kill him? Why would they do that?'

'Hey, their minds work in strange ways. Their way of funding right-wing groups in Central America is to sell weapons to Iran, their biggest enemy. The crucial thing is to stop giving Channon information.'

'But I haven't given him any information yet – not really. I just said that if Jonathon suddenly found himself in a strange city, he'd go to a low-key cafe if it was during the day or a low-key pub if it was the evening. Oh, and that if things got too much he might go to the countryside.'

'Oh. That's what I said too.'

'Well we are talking about the same person.'

'Have they mentioned, or asked about, a meeting between Channon and Jonathon tomorrow?'

'No. They keep saying they really value my input, but then not asking for any.'

'Okay, well if they do ask for any, try not to give it – but without making them suspicious.'

'How can I do that?'

'You'll find a way. Listen, Lizzie says that someone close to Channon shares her suspicions and is working to help her defeat him. She thinks it's getting too dangerous for you to stay where you are, so we've worked out a plan to get you out of there tomorrow, and hopefully reunite you and Jonathon.'

'Oh. Goodness. Right. What do I have to do?'

Part Three

The German Connection

Tuesday

54

Channon walked into the Curious Fox bookshop on Flughafen Strasse, took a book from the shelf and flipped through it while he surreptitiously glanced around. Everything looked fine, though he'd accidentally picked up *Little Women*, his ex-wife's favourite book. He was the sole customer in the shop's two smallish rooms. The only other person was a sensitive-looking woman with an asymmetrical bob, reading a book behind the cash register.

Over in the other room, on the far wall, he spotted the religion section. He replaced *Little Women* and made his way over, his eyes skimming the titles till he found the one he was after. He wondered why Newman hadn't used his standard-issue CIA hollow Bible. Perhaps he thought the risk of someone opening it was too high. After all, people do buy the Bible. Instead, he had gone for an ultra-safe choice: *Meditations on Scripture* by former president Jimmy Carter. Opening it cautiously, he found, in a neat cutout section near the spine, nestled a cheap phone. He turned it on, selected 'contacts' and called the one saved number.

'Um, hello?' said Newman's voice.

'It's Channon. You sound surprised to hear me.'

'Ah, no. That's what I thought at first, but then I realised it's just the way my voice is.'

'Okay. What now?'

'Could you go to the toilet, please?'

'Sure.'

'And stay on the phone till you meet me, if that's all right. Otherwise, I'll worry that you've called someone else, and then I won't be able to meet you.'

'Fine. Like I said before: whatever makes you feel comfortable.'

'Oh, I don't think I'll feel comfortable. I'm too worried about people killing me and things. Thanks though.'

Channon replaced the book on the shelf, then walked to the little corridor at the back of the shop and through the door marked 'Toiletten'.

'Okay, what now?' he said.

'Go into the one with a picture of a man on it,' said Newman.

Channon pushed open the door that bore a graffiti-style picture of a man with glasses and a Mohican. Inside was a toilet of the traditional German variety, with a shelf for viewing your doings. There was also a washbasin, a dirty-looking towel, and a large red holdall with 'Haspa' written on it.

'I'm in,' said Channon.

'Right. Um, good. This is a bit awkward, but could you possibly take off all your clothes?'

Channon took a deep breath. 'You have got to be kidding, son.'

'It's just that we're a bit worried you might be wearing some kind of tracking device.'

'I'm not wearing a tracking device.'

'Ah, yes. It's just that–'

'That's what I would say if I was wearing a tracking device?'

'Yes.'

'You could just get someone to frisk me. There are no tracking devices small enough to avoid detection by a pat-down.'

'But then one of us would have to come into the room with you, and you could kidnap them.'

'Okay. A little paranoid, which is no bad thing. And flattering that you think I could kidnap someone one-on-one from a bookshop men's room. But I see where you're coming from.'

'So, will you? You just need to take off your clothes and put them in the red bag. Then walk to the women's toilets next door where you'll find another set of clothes. We'll give yours back to you afterwards.'

'How will you know I'm not wearing a tracking device?'

'Someone will be watching you between toilets.'

'Son, you're lucky I've spent a lot of time in warzones and the Human Potential Institute in Esalen, that's all I can say. I'm comfortable with nudity.'

'Oh, good. Well done.'

Channon took his clothes off, folded them military-style, and packed them neatly in the red Haspa bag, wrapping his trousers around his neat little Taurus revolver. It felt bad to be leaving the gun behind, but he had a plan, and in the end a plan is worth more than a gun. He then walked out of the men's toilet, totally naked. Through the window from the little corridor he could see a man in a balaclava, watching him with furious eyes. Channon gave the man an ironic salute and walked into the women's toilets.

'I guess your guy's the one in the balaclava, right?'

'Maybe. Um, yes.'

'Well, he's seen me.'

'Oh good. Have you found the clothes in the women's toilet?'

'Yep,' said Channon, unzipping another red Haspa bag. 'I see you've been spending the agency's budget wisely: all Primark.'

'Sorry. It's just that it's only for one journey. We've included two different shoe sizes though.'

'Very thoughtful,' said Channon, checking the shoes. 'I get to choose between slightly too big and slightly too small.'

Channon put on the clothes and instantly felt much more German. He was wearing black trainers, white socks, jeans that seemed to be made of a cotton-cardboard blend, a striped aqua sweatshirt and an anorak so brightly orange that it must be visible from the moon.

'What now?' he asked.

'Walk out of the shop and turn right, away from Karl Marx Strasse.'

Channon did as he was told, walking along Flughafen Strasse, past yellowing six-storey buildings with pitched roofs above and unappetising bakeries below. He walked almost its whole length, past Turkish barbers and junk shops, kebab shops and betting places. He stopped at a crossing beside a huge block of flats, its windowless side painted with a sudden bright dreamscape of cartoon people. Then he crossed the road and walked on until he reached a swimming pool where Newman told him to turn left, down a narrow footpath.

He emerged onto Tempelhof, the vast former airfield which any other city in the world would have covered in executive apartments before you could say Jack Robinson, but which the people of Berlin had voted to keep completely empty. It was a shock, in a city, to emerge into a place where you could almost see the horizon. The field was perfectly flat: a sea of grass criss-crossed by disused concrete runways, interrupted only by the occasional tree, or an odd patch of shanty-allotments.

'I've got to hand it to you, son: if you want to check that someone's alone, Tempelhof's the place. You can see there's no one within a mile of me.'

'Oh, thank you. Yes.'

'I guess you've got people watching me and signalling you.'

Newman didn't reply, but directed him to walk along an old runway with stalks of grass sprouting from its cracks, then asked him to walk up to another main road, cross it and follow a rough scrubby street between the fenced-off edge of a park and a wild hedgerow. It was lined with big old vehicles, lived in by men smoking joints and women wearing tie-dyed leggings.

'Straight up the street and over, please,' said Newman.

Channon emerged into a sort of bourgeois fantasyland: more six-storey apartment buildings, but now immaculately white and ornate, like huge residential wedding cakes. On, towards a spiked church which looked like a rocket, as though the Germans had decided to blast themselves directly into heaven.

After this, the buildings became plainer, painted like old kitchen cupboards in faded orange and blue. Channon was walking beside a long, thin park, at the end of which the street opened out into an idyllic canal-side scene. He walked across some grass to a picturesque bridge that had somehow kept its antique street lamps and wrought-iron balustrades, despite all the terrible things that had happened since it had been built.

'Um, wait there, please,' said Newman.

The spring sun had come out, and Berlin was lit up. All around were cobbled streets and balconied buildings, with the canal flowing calmly and willows nodding their heads on its banks. On the bridge lounged some of the youngest and most beautiful people Channon had ever seen – which, since he was Californian, was saying a lot. They sat in little knots, strumming guitars as their hair floated languidly in the breeze.

Channon felt old. A bolt of regret hit him, that he had spent his life protecting his country and neglecting his guitar and his girlfriends. And then his meditation voice stirred in him, saying, 'regretting, regretting', and his attention moved to the sensation of the breath in his body. He accepted the regret, opening himself to it even as it dissolved, leaving him in the present moment, standing in the warm sunshine on a picturesque bridge surrounded by young, beautiful people playing guitars and no doubt suffering in their own ways.

'Um, hello,' said a thin man holding a cheap phone.

It was Newman. He looked terribly tired, with thick grey marks beneath his eyes.

'You must be Mr Channon,' said Newman. The way he spoke had subtly changed. He sounded much more British now.

'I guess I must be, son. What now?'

'Would you like a pizza?'

Channon looked at him. 'Not what I was expecting after all that. But I must have walked off at least two pizzas getting here. So yes, I would like a pizza.'

Newman led him over to a crowded pizza place, half inside one of the old buildings, half spilling out onto a terrace overlooking the bridge. At the brink of the crowd of diners, Newman hesitated and seemed to be trying to catch the attention of one of the waiters who walked busily about, shouting to each other and brandishing notebooks and pizzas.

'I think we just sit down, son,' said Channon, selecting an empty table near the edge of the eating throng.

Channon sat and picked up a menu. It had been a long walk, but he felt better for it – he shouldn't have let himself stay cooped up in the station for so long. The journey had reassured him that this wasn't a trap. The precautions they'd taken, the way they'd guided him in, it was the sort of plan that would be cooked up by a careful amateur, and didn't follow the MO of any professional organisation. It was fascinating to Channon which bits of Newman's memory had gone, and which remained: something he looked forward to studying in more detail.

'I'll take a pepperoni and a mineral water,' said Channon.

'Right. Er, well, I think I'll have the same thing,' said Newman.

'Now we just need a waiter.'

Channon looked around. The waiters all looked Italian, which was a good sign, because Germans, in his experience, were not cut out for customer-service roles. But these ones seemed to have gone native, charging around with their heads down, not looking at the diners, or, alternatively, standing chatting to each other behind the counter. Channon missed American service. And he realised that a tiny part of him expected the waiters to do better for this occasion, because it was his first time outdoors in a week, and he was trying to bring in a high-value asset.

'You okay, son?' he asked, looking into Newman's tired eyes, which were darting around after the waiters. 'You must have had a hell of a time.'

'Um,' said Newman, still distracted. 'Yes. Sort of. Yes.'

Channon waited for a waiter to pass, judged his moment, and held the man's arm, gripping it lightly but firmly, a Wing Chun technique.

The waiter got two syllables into something irritable and offensive before Channon clicked his tongue, silencing him.

'We're ready to order,' said Channon in English, and the waiter involuntarily took out his notebook. 'Pepperoni pizza, two.' He held up the fingers. 'And mineral water, two.'

The waiter noted it down, gave a curt nod, and charged off again, in the opposite direction.

'Wow,' said Newman. 'That was amazing.'

'Son, I just ordered lunch. It's what I've got to do next that's amazing.'

'Oh, what have you got to do next?'

'Win your trust and bring you in.'

'I, er, don't think I'm ready to come in. I just wanted to talk to you about who I am, why people are trying to kill me, and what to do about it.'

'Okay, well that's not a bad place to start winning your trust. By the way, if someone will leave his clothes in an English-language bookshop, show himself naked to a guy in a balaclava, dress up like a German, and then walk several miles to meet you, that's a pretty strong sign you can trust him.'

'Oh,' said Newman, sounding surprised again. 'Is it? Doesn't it just mean that you trust me?'

'Son, I am taking a huge risk coming here. I am meant to be in lockdown at headquarters. That's what protocol says. And if the guys who've been trying to kill you saw me here … bang, I'm dead.'

'Sorry.'

'No problem. It's nice to be out. So, okay, who are you? Let's start there.'

55

'Am I under arrest?' she asked.

'What, for covering someone's shifts? No, honey, of course not,' said Lizzie.

Having got nowhere with any of their other leads, and having found nothing helpful in Karen's flat, Lance and Lizzie had, that morning, finally managed to get hold of Ingeborg – the barmaid who'd covered Karen's shift – and were interviewing her in her flat.

'We're just trying to find Karen,' said Lance. 'She's disappeared and people are worried about her. I mean, if you disappeared for four days, you'd expect people to worry about you, wouldn't you?'

Ingeborg looked at him with that disconcerting absence of expression he was finding so many Germans were able to achieve.

'No,' she said.

'What? Why not?'

'I disappear often. Everyone will just to think I am clubbing.'

'Clubbing? For four days?' said Lance.

She looked at him blankly, as though he had just said, 'Breakfast? In the morning?'

'Of course,' she said.

'But how?' he asked, forgetting all about Karen.

'I am young,' she said simply, 'and this is Berlin.'

'But even so …'

'One must just to stay hydrated, and keep several pieces of fresh fruit in the backpack.'

'Wow,' said Lance.

'Let's get back to Karen, shall we?' said Lizzie, brightly.

'Yes, does Karen go clubbing for four days straight?' asked Lance.

'She is old, so–'

'She's thirty-three,' said Lance, defensively. He had found her passport.

Lizzie turned to him and said gently, 'Could you maybe … shut up?'

Lance turned this over in his mind and had to concede that it had certain advantages. He nodded.

'Sorry, honey,' said Lizzie to Ingeborg. 'Carry on.'

'Karen maybe does not go clubbing this long, but I do not know,' said Ingeborg.

'Okay, so if we put this whole clubbing thing aside' – Lizzie looked significantly at Lance – 'if Karen disappeared for four days–'

'And definitely didn't go clubbing,' put in Lance.

'Do you know where she might have gone instead?' ended Lizzie.

'No,' said Ingeborg.

There was a silence.

'Okay,' said Lizzie, brightly.

RURR-RURR-RURR

Lizzie looked at her phone.

'Okay, I gotta get this,' she said. 'Lance, could you make Ingeborg a coffee and not talk to her about clubbing while I take this?'

'You wear the trousers,' he said cheerfully, springing up and grabbing the coffee pot from Ingeborg's machine.

'Jake, hi,' said Lizzie to her phone. 'That's great! That's amazing! Thank you so much. Could you text that address to this number? Awesome.'

Lance looked expectantly at Lizzie as Ingeborg took her coffee pot from his hand and began filling it with water.

'NSA,' said Lizzie. 'We got an address – a holiday apartment Karen rented yesterday by email.'

'Great,' said Lance. 'But what if she isn't there, like yesterday?'

'We'll just have to make another plan. I'm praying Piper manages to get away.'

They effusively thanked Ingeborg, who maintained her total absence of facial expression, and hurried off.

56

By now, Piper was very seriously regretting that she hadn't packed anything to do – not even a book to read. When you're woken in the middle of the night and told the CIA need you to take the next flight to Berlin, you naturally assume that what follows will be wall-to-wall excitement and non-stop action. How could she possibly have known she would be spending the next three days on her own in a hotel room?

She badly missed the calming effect of embroidery, especially since her boredom here was accompanied by a cold and fizzing anxiety – about whether she would be reunited with Jonathon, whether he was going to survive, and now whether she would succeed in the escape plan Lance had described over the phone the day before, while she'd pretended to have a shower.

At least she had now got used to the idea that the CIA were watching and listening to her every second of the day. Like people on reality TV, she had gone from being excruciatingly self-conscious to totally oblivious in a matter of hours. That was why she was, at that moment, passing the time by doing made-up and poorly executed martial arts moves on a hotel pillow while singing 'Un-break My Heart' by Toni Braxton, in a Russian accent.

She had just delivered the pillow a solid punch in the face when she caught sight of the clock. Unaccountably exempt from the luxury everywhere else, it was a completely standard bedside clock with square red numerals. They said '11:57'. If she was going to regress to weird childhood bedroom pursuits, she should do it quietly, so she could hear the three vibrations of the concealed phone that would be her signal to begin the escape attempt.

Piper dragged her bag under the bedcovers, which was no stranger than anything else she'd been doing over the last three days, and checked the cheap grey phone. No missed calls. She crawled back out and lapsed again into her almost hallucinatory state of disinhibited tense boredom.

What could she do that was quiet? She should meditate. She needed calming and, after all, how hard could it be? All you had to do was sit with your legs crossed and think no thoughts.

She sat on the floor beside her bed, looking out to the office buildings across the square. There was more street noise than usual, but the thick windows reduced it to a whispered roar. She closed her eyes and resolved to clear her mind, looking for calm.

Almost before her eyelids had closed, her mind was set upon by thoughts. *Is Jonathon still alive? Is Channon really trying to kill him? Was Lance wrong? Why didn't I encourage Jonathon to get a proper job so he would never have gone to that interview? Am I going to die alone?*

Her eyes flipped open. She was sweating and breathing hard. *Is this what a panic attack feels like?* she thought. *Why can't I catch my breath? Is there a paper bag I can breathe into?* She jumped up and began looking in drawers. *Why were paper bags meant to help anyway? Would a plastic one do? How about a suitcase? Am I really contemplating breathing into a suitcase?* Even with her eyes open she was overrun with thoughts. They were everywhere, thousands of them. No wonder the Buddhists hated them so much.

RURR-RURR, RURR-RURR, RURR-RURR

The phone. The signal.

All at once she realised she didn't need to breathe into anything. She was ready. She'd been apprehensive of Lance's plan, but now anything seemed better than being trapped in this thought-infested room.

She put on her jacket, grabbed her bag, dabbed the sweat from her brow with a tissue and checked her reflection in the mirror. It was stupid to care whether she looked all right for an escape attempt, but she couldn't help it. She fluffed her hair slightly and eased open the door.

The corridor was clear. Her goon had gone. Just as Lance had said.

Now all she had to do was reach the cleaners' cupboard two floors down.

Her room was at the end of the corridor. She closed the door quietly behind her and walked briskly, passing five doors. None of them opened and no CIA thugs leapt out. She was nearing the corner where the corridor turned left. Her heart was beating hard, as though it was trying to jack-hammer its way down into her stomach. Should she stop and peer around the corner? Wouldn't that look suspicious? It would, so she simply walked briskly around it into the next corridor.

A large man was standing there, looking directly at her, a knife in his hand.

Piper stopped, transfixed. Unable to move or speak, staring at him.

The man, wearing a white shirt and black waistcoat, glanced down at a large silver dish on the trolley in front of him. Then Piper noticed he was also holding a fork. He carefully placed the knife and fork on either side of the silver dish, and minutely adjusted a napkin.

Walk, she told herself. He's a waiter, delivering room service.

The man looked up at her again. Was he waiter, or just someone dressed as a waiter? She had to coach her legs through each step. Had she just done two steps in a row with her left foot? *Don't look down*, she told herself. She looked down. *Don't act suspiciously in front of the man who's either a waiter or is just disguised as a waiter*, she told herself. Looking up, she stared at the tiny recessed ceiling lights. *Now you've over-corrected*. How would she have walked if she weren't escaping? She had no idea. Would she have instinctively given the man a tiny smile, sympathising with his having to push trolleys around for rich people all day? She tried it, and felt a ghastly leer creep over her face.

'Good morning, madam,' said the waiter, in accented English.

'Good morning,' she said, surprised at how normal her voice sounded. She steered herself laboriously past the trolley, the whole experience suddenly reminding her of high-stakes pretending-not-to-be-drunk when she was a teenager.

She was past the trolley. Ahead of her, the corridor opened out into a bank of lifts, a flight of stairs running down beside it. *You've made it*, she told herself. *Don't look back*. She glanced back, and saw that the waiter was looking at her. *Oh god*. Was it because he was an agent? Or was it just because he'd never seen a woman walk down a corridor so badly before?

She kept going, trying not to feel his eyes on her back. The stairs were clear; now she just needed to–

Bing!

The lift doors opened and there stood Bill Drummond, stuffed into his suit like a package of sausage meat left in a car on a hot day.

'Ms Palgrave,' he said, seeming taken aback to see her. 'Good morning.'

'Good morning,' she replied in a voice that sounded tight and scared, quickly adding, 'Mr Drummond.' She noticed there was a shirt-end sticking out of his flies. Had they got him away from her door by giving him a … laxative? What other explanation could there be?

He said, 'I take it you received the message that we have to get going?'

He held up his phone.

'Oh, er, yes,' she said, patting the spot in her bag where her phone was.

Her earlier doubts returned. Why didn't he seem angry to see her out of the room? *Was* Lance wrong about what was going on? Was Channon exactly what he seemed and not a mole at all? Had she been kept in the hotel room just – like they said – so she'd be on hand to help Jonathon?

Bill Drummond put his hand over the lift door to stop it closing and held out his arm.

'Please,' he said, 'step in. Allow me to escort you. My apologies that I was … briefly called away from my post to, uh, help a member of staff.'

Piper looked down the stairs? Should she run? Could she make it? No. She was wearing a skirt, like an idiot. Who escapes a building in a skirt? And her shoes, like all her shoes – like all women's shoes ever – were completely wrong for it.

She gave Bill Drummond a tiny smile and stepped into the lift. Now it had all gone wrong she felt surprisingly composed.

'So,' said Bill Drummond as the doors closed. He clasped his hands in front of his body, the way large men in suits do, which had the effect of covering that shirt-end. 'I, uh, I guess you must be pretty pumped?'

'Oh yes,' she said, 'ever so … pumped.' Piper was, by some reckonings, half American, and yet all her sensibilities were English. She hated the whole idea of being pumped.

'We are expecting to make contact with Jonathon Fairfax' – Bill had one of those slow American accents which ring out a name syllable by syllable, like a row of bells – 'presently. We're not quite sure where we'll be meeting him, but we need to get ourselves over to the right area. There are big demonstrations starting up around here and over by the Reichstag' – again both syllables rung out – 'so we need to set off right about now.'

'Yes, of course,' she said weakly.

'And we don't want you and Jonathon Fairfax' – *Bong-a-bong Bong-bong* – 'kept apart a moment longer than is truly necessary.'

He smiled at her, a surprisingly sweet smile, and she suddenly felt that he meant it.

They were going to drive her to Jonathon. She felt herself flush. Could it be true? She had no idea who to believe, and – in any case – no option but to accompany this enormous man to the car waiting outside.

57

Michaels checked his watch. He had been waiting in this fourth-floor cleaners' cupboard for nearly twenty minutes now, and was beginning to suspect that something had gone wrong. But then, finally, the door opened.

'Miss P–' he began, then said, 'Ah.'

'*What make you then?*' said a woman carrying a mop and a bucket of water. She was wiry, with tired eyes and a sharp nose.

'*I search the toilets,*' he improvised. '*How find I them?*'

'*Not in the cleaning-materials room,*' she said, eyeing him narrowly.

'*I have a mistake made,*' he said.

'*Clearly.*' She looked out, down the corridor, and called, '*Colleague!*'

'*That is not necessary,*' he began.

'*What?*' said a voice from the corridor.

'*We have a man in the cleaning-materials room.*'

'*A man? What makes he?*'

'*He says that he the toilets searches.*'

'*The toilets? In the cleaning-materials room?*'

'*That have I said.*'

Michaels, who had been standing uneasily beside a shelf full of Frosch for longer than he would have liked, took a deep breath. *Right,* he thought, *you asked for this.*

'My good woman,' he said, switching into English. 'Please stand aside. I would like to see your manager.'

58

'Who are you?' repeated Channon. 'Well, let's take that step by step.'

'Okay.'

'First step: are you sure you want this? You actually don't need a name or a life history to know who you are. You are the part of you that's aware. You're not your thoughts, or your memories, or your emotions. Those things change second by second. Your awareness is the only constant. The name, passport number and life history you think you have is kind of irrelevant.'

The man thought about this. Over on the bridge an American girl with quite a good voice started singing about summertime, and how easy the living was. He imagined living in Berlin, near his friends Karen and Boris, becoming Mister permanently: Mr Mister.

But he would always be curious about who he had been. He would always be dogged by this yearning for someone – someone he couldn't remember but wanted to. And, presumably, he would also always be dogged by people wanting to kill him.

'I want to know who I am,' he said. After all, the girl on the bridge, having lightly touched on the way fish jump, was now urging him to spread his wings and take to the sky.

'Okay,' said Channon. 'As long as you're going into this with your eyes open. So, until about a week ago, you were Adam Newman, a British national with US citizenship, in Berlin as part of a programme to give foreign graduates experience working in the German parliament. Your interests were confined to German politics and keeping fit. You had no friends, did not read for pleasure, and rarely listened to music. Reactions?'

'What made me so ... *boring?*'

'We did, son. You're also part of a top-secret and highly experimental programme, sponsored by the US security establishment. We prepared you for your role by inducing amnesia via a combination of hypnosis, operant conditioning, and drugs, allowing us to create a whole new identity for you. We turned you into the ideal intelligence officer: one with no messy personal life, one who could remember no life other than your cover identity and no goal apart from your mission. I guess that sounds pretty heartless, huh?'

'It sounds horrible.'

'Well, you know, I also had a philosophical interest in this. I thought that if I steered you away from books, thoughts, and music that had any inherent interest at all, you would be happier. You know, I read and I think, I'm devoted to the work of musicians such as Leonard Cohen and Joni Mitchell, and I've come to suspect that – interesting though it all is – it's probably, overall, a bummer. People are happier without all that stuff, all those thoughts and feelings.'

'Thanks,' said the man, unconvincingly. 'But it seems like a lot of trouble to go to to test out a psychological hunch and get a new employee for the German parliament. What was my mission? And why did you choose me?'

'Well, those two things are linked. You see, your job as an intelligence officer was an unusual – and highly unorthodox – one. The programme you're part of is codenamed Knife-fish. You know what a knife-fish is?'

'No. But that's not really the bit of what you've just said that I was most curious about. Is it like a fish-knife?'

'No, a knife-fish is a type of eel that uses its electrical charge to stun and disorientate the fish around it, rendering them vulnerable to attack.'

'Oh, right. Well, that's that cleared up.'

'We consulted with the writer and thinker Nicholas Emir Brunsengett, about his notion of "natural disruptors". These are individuals whose mere presence – like the knife-fish's – profoundly disrupts their environment. Brunsengett believes natural disruptors interfere with normal patterns of causation, radically changing the status quo in ways totally counter to the intentions of all those involved. These are people who aren't even trying. In fact, they often react to their powers by trying not to be disruptive. But they can't help it, it's almost supernatural: wherever they go they disrupt the status quo.'

'But that's insane.'

'Any sufficiently novel idea sounds insane. In the CIA, we aim to adopt ideas at exactly that stage of maturity – that's our competitive advantage.'

'And what's this got to do with me?'

'We looked back at inflection points over the last ten years or so, where there have been these radical changes in the status quo, and we compiled a list of potential natural disruptors. Your name was on that list.'

'What, Adam Newman?'

'No. Your name before that: Jonathon Fairfax.'

At the mention of this name, the man felt like a small train had just driven through his solar plexus.

'Oh,' he said.

This felt entirely unlike all the other times in the last few days that he'd been told what his name was. This time, it was true. He knew it.

'I'm Jonathon Fairfax,' he said.

'That's right,' said Channon. 'You remember anything about that now?'

'No, the name just feels right in a way that Adam Newman never did.'

'Right. That must feel good.'

'But how did I go from being Jonathon Fairfax to Adam Newman?' asked the man, and suddenly realised he should now be referring to himself, in his own head, as Jonathon.

'Well, we solicited your co-operation through British intelligence – it's professional courtesy. They interviewed you and said you were keen to get involved. But after we'd initiated you into the programme, we discovered that you thought it was all just an unusually elaborate briefing for some freelance illustration work. However, by the time we identified that fact, you already knew way too much.'

'So what happened?' said Jonathon.

'So that's when we moved on to the induced amnesia and operant conditioning, and got Adam Newman's retrospective consent for the whole thing.'

'But what did you tell the people who I knew?'

'We did not consider it advisable or appropriate to tell them anything. After all, it could have jeopardised Adam Newman's operational effectiveness, and his safety. You see, Adam Newman was our employee: we owed him a duty of care.'

'So Jonathon Fairfax just disappeared?'

'You could say that.'

'Did … Was … I mean, had … Um, was I in, er, in love with anyone?' asked Jonathon. He was afraid of a 'no', afraid that this terrible yearning that blew through him like a cold wind was just the way he was, or that he was yearning for someone whom he had merely glimpsed once on a rainswept jetty long ago. He hadn't known himself for long, but that seemed like just the sort of thing he would do.

But Channon said, 'Yes. You were in love.'

'Who with?'

'Her name's Piper Palgrave.'

'Is she all right?'

'She's fine. In fact, she's right here in Berlin. We brought her over for you. You want to see her? I can call her right now on this phone. I memorised the number. You want me to?'

'Of course,' said Jonathon Fairfax.

'Okay,' said Channon, picking up the phone.

59

Piper was escorted by Bill Drummond through the crowd outside the Adlon hotel to a conspicuous black car – one of a pair of big truck-like things with blacked-out windows. It was the sort favoured by shadowy government agencies, drug dealers and footballers, and it had the word 'Suburban' picked out satirically on the side in silver. She got in and Bill Drummond heaved himself after her. In the driver's seat, she was surprised to see a black agent – she must have assumed the CIA would be too racist to have any – wearing a bright blue shirt that she thought would suit Jonathon. Beside him was a standard white agent, with very short hair, wearing a polo shirt and ironed cargo trousers.

'Where are we going?' she asked.

'Please keep your cellphone ready, ma'am,' said Bill Drummond.

She pulled it out of her bag, careful not to disturb her other, secret phone, safe in its compartment.

The huge black car pulled off, inching forward through the crowd. Pedestrians had reclaimed the road, and were ambling along, ignoring the cars, forcing them to walking pace.

'Where are all these people going?' she asked.

There was silence.

'I won't tell anyone,' she said.

The driver turned and said, 'There's an anti-war protest today, ma'am. Germany's parliament is going to debate a motion to oppose the US-led invasion of Akkad.'

Someone in front of them unfurled a banner that said, 'No to America's war!'

'They'd all be speaking German if it wasn't for us,' said Bill Drummond, and Piper couldn't tell whether he was joking. Silence settled again inside the car.

They continued to creep along the broad, tree-lined street. It was full of imposing old buildings, and had incongruous giant blue and pink utility pipes running down the boulevard in the centre.

'What's this street called?' asked Piper, just to break the silence.

'This here is Unter Den Linden,' said Bill Drummond. *Bong-bong Bong Bong-bong.*

'And what's going on with the buildings?' she asked. Some of them had been covered with sheets bearing life-size illustrations of the structures beneath.

'They're restoring them, ma'am,' said the driver, 'after the communists left them to crumble. My first day off, I kept turning up at these historical monuments from my guidebook and finding they were still under construction.'

'And what are these big coloured pipes?' she asked.

But by this time the crowds had thinned enough for the car to have picked up speed, and the driver wasn't listening to her any more. She noticed there was a curly wire leading from the neck of his bright blue shirt to his ear, and he was texting with his right hand.

Piper whispered conspiratorially to Bill Drummond, 'No one knows what the pipes are for.'

'I believe they're water pipes, ma'am,' he said, not matching her whisper.

Directly ahead of them, in the distance, was the iconic building that looked like an olive on a cocktail stick. Beside them was a dirty, squat churchy building that resembled an evil gothic toad. They took a right, past a big red building covered with heroic bas-reliefs of men, possibly the proletariat, working in factories, making speeches and playing the trombone. And then the streets widened and the city opened out. They passed through a long expanse of nothingness: industrial buildings, underpasses, scrubby vacant lots, an area flying a pirate flag. After some more nothing, the driver glanced at Piper in his mirror and said, 'Here's the last surviving stretch of the Berlin Wall, ma'am.'

They were driving beside a very long stretch of concrete, doodled over with tags, scribbles and patches of colour. Here and there something solid emerged: a sequence of stylised cartoon heads, what looked like a Picasso, two middle-aged men kissing, a crocodile. It was like peering into the city's dreaming brain. And then it was over and they were crossing a river on a red-brick bridge that looked like a castle.

They drove along another long, wide street, this one with an elevated metal train track running along its centre. They passed a huge spaceman painted on the side of a brick building, but Piper was now too tense to ask about it. The traffic was thickening, glooping around a huge roundabout beneath the train track, then sludging along a wide road. 'Kottbusser Damm', said a sign. Eventually, they pulled off and drew up beside a small shady park where some youths were playing basketball.

'This is where we wait for the call,' said the driver.

60

Lance and Lizzie ran down the many stairs from Ingeborg's shared flat, Lance inwardly cursing Berlin's lack of lifts, and emerged onto Karl Marx Strasse, which seemed to commemorate the founder of communism's great love of traffic and cheap Turkish food.

'It's going to be quicker to run,' said Lizzie.

'They'll be expecting us to do the quickest thing,' said Lance. 'Why don't we outflank them by doing the easiest?'

'Who's "they"?' she asked.

He shrugged.

'You know, everything you say is total horseshit,' she observed affectionately. 'Come on.'

She set off at a run and he had no option but to follow, across the dual carriageway with its many slowly moving cars, and through a large square dominated by a shop called Karstadt, housed in what looked like an enormous nuclear bunker.

Lizzie's phone buzzed and she slowed to glance at it.

'Fuck!' she said.

Lance raised his eyebrows at her in a mute question, breathing too hard to speak.

'Piper didn't make it.'

'What happened?' Lance managed to say.

'I don't know. My friend says the diversion worked, but I guess Drummond wasn't away long enough.'

'You don't think your friend …?'

'Betrayed me? No. I don't.'

'And is Piper okay?'

'Seems like it. But they're bringing her to this area, which is bad news. Channon must have a way to signal where the meeting's happening. Come on, this address is all we have now. Everything depends on this.'

They set off running again, through a little outdoor market of jerry-built stalls, Lance almost knocking over a rack of plastic sandals. Emerging on the other side of the square, they passed a mattress shop and a dozen cheap bars. Lizzie kept getting texts as she ran, but now barely slowed as she read them.

They left the main road, passed a little park where some kids were playing basketball, and ran through a pleasant neighbourhood with little shops selling liquorice and handicrafts. Lance's feet slapped annoyingly on the pavement as he jogged along in expensive shoes designed mainly for use in restaurants.

To Lance's relief, a text arrived that stopped Lizzie in her tracks. She slowed to a walk and made a call.

'Yeah, hi, it's me,' she said. 'No, we don't know exactly where Channon's going to meet Newman. Just come to Kreuzberg, anywhere in the area, and I'll tell you when I know.'

She looked back at Lance, checking he was keeping up.

'Reichenberger? Sure. You're all together, right? And you have … equipment for this?'

She squinted ahead.

'Great,' she said. 'No, the escape didn't work out. But we have an address for Karen Asefa – we hope. We're on our way now. Yeah, bye.'

She started running again, and Lance's legs followed suit, though they were asking him to stop hurting them. He and Lizzie turned right into a long, wide street with a narrow strip of park running down its centre. Off ahead, tantalising in the distance, was a picturesque pizza restaurant beside an even more picturesque bridge, thronged with beautiful young people playing guitars, no doubt as a prelude to going clubbing for four days straight.

'That's it,' said Lizzie, pointing to a pale blue building opposite the pizza restaurant. They ran across the top of the park, reaching the building just as a postman left, managing to get in the front door before it locked.

'The name on the door is Reynardi,' said Lizzie.

They jogged up the stairs, checking the nameplates on each floor. At the very top of the building, Lance took some time out to catch up on his breathing while Lizzie found the Reynardi nameplate and knocked.

Through the door, Lance could hear the radio softly playing. The smell of coffee percolated out, but the door remained shut.

'Hello?' said Lance.

There was silence.

'Karen, honey?' Lizzie called through the letterbox.

'Yes?' answered a voice from inside.

'We're here to help.'

The door opened and there stood a woman with very curly black hair, golden skin and a worried expression.

'I didn't mean to answer,' she said. 'But you sounded like my mom. Who are you?'

'My name is Lizzie Morden, and I am … well, I'm not old enough to be your mom. This is Lance Ferman. He's a friend of Jonathon Fairfax, the guy who walked into your bar five days ago with no memory. We know all about the people who have been … after you. I believe they're controlled by a man named Doug Channon, and that Channon's meeting Jonathon today somewhere. We've been trying to find you so we can make you all safe and bring Channon to justice.'

Karen, the woman with curly black hair, looked at Lizzie for a long while. Then her eyes moistened and she wordlessly stood aside, allowing them in.

'Mis– I mean, the guy with no memory's at a pizza place, meeting Channon. We don't trust Channon, but we made sure he came alone and we made him change his clothes in case he was wearing a tracking device – I mean, we don't even know whether you can wear a tracking device, but … Anyway, Channon promised to tell Mister who he really is.'

'It's okay, honey,' said Lizzie. 'It's almost over now. I'm going to take care of this Channon guy and you're all going to be safe. You know the name of this pizza place?'

'It's Il Something …' said Karen.

'Honey, can you remember that second word?' asked Lizzie. 'It's just that all pizza places are called Il Something.' Her phone vibrated and she read something on the screen. 'Okay, just got the answer: Il Cas–'

'Casolare!' said Karen. 'Il Casolare.'

'Hey,' said Lizzie to her phone. 'Yes. We have a location. Oh, you heard. That's right. Pizza restaurant, top of Grimm Strasse, right by the canal.'

'You can see it from the window,' said Karen. She led them to the window overlooking the square and pointed.

'They're down there,' she said. 'Can you see them? Channon's wearing a bright orange coat.'

'I see them,' said Lizzie, then to her phone, 'Okay, Channon's in orange this season.'

Lance peered down into the square, struggling to find them among the diners, beside the bridge-based guitar-players whom he suspected of being on the verge of four-day clubbing sprees. Then he saw them. Jonathon, wearing a black overcoat, was holding a phone in one hand and a slice of pizza in the other. He was sitting at a round white table on a little terrace, opposite a man wearing a bright orange anorak.

Lizzie said, 'My guys are on their way – they're just on the other side of Kottbusser Damm. When they get here, they'll park around the corner and wait for my signal. We need to go down there right now, and you two need to make sure Jonathon knows we're on his side. Okay?'

She looked them in the eye, first Karen, then Lance. Each of them nodded.

'Only I might be doing a lot of talking,' Lizzie continued, 'so you might have to do it mostly with signals – with body language, your eyes, your faces. Do you think you can do that?'

'Okay,' said Karen.

Lance conveyed his assent with his body language, eyes and face.

'Lance, have you got that?' Lizzie repeated.

'Yes,' he said. This was going to be harder than he thought.

'And one more thing: don't believe anything I say to Channon. I will say absolutely anything to convince him to come with us when my guys arrive. Whatever I say, know that I am on your side and I am working to save Jonathon. Okay?'

'Okay,' they both said.

Lizzie took a very small black gun from her breast pocket and cocked it.

'I hope,' she said, 'that I am not going to need this. But Doug Channon is an unbelievable horse's ass.'

Lance and Karen exchanged a glance. Then, suddenly self-conscious, both looked out of the window.

'Oh, look,' said Karen.

61

For at least twenty minutes, Piper had been sitting in the huge black car in the little parking spot beside the park. The basketball players had gone, and she felt oddly bereft.

She had asked earlier if she could get out of the car for a bit, but Bill Drummond had said, 'We don't advise it, ma'am.' Now, bored by the repeated carousel of her thoughts and driven almost insane by staring at the neck of the agent in front of her, she opened the door and stepped out.

There was another black car beside this one, with three men in it, all wearing different varieties of casual wear, yet all conspicuously unlike anyone she'd seen on the streets of Berlin. Two of these conspicuous men got out of their conspicuous car and came to stand conspicuously beside her. They were joined by Bill Drummond, straining the seams of his suit.

The men stood there, flanking her, not overtly threatening, but penning her in between the two cars.

'Nice weather we're having,' she observed to them brightly, knowing they wouldn't reply.

They stood with their hands clasped in front of them. One, wearing a black leather jacket, shades and immaculate new jeans, was chewing gum.

But it *was* nice weather they were having. Berlin had been transformed from a dreary grey place of concrete and inexplicability into a beautiful Eden, just by the sun coming out.

'Who wants to play charades?' she asked, the impulse arriving from nowhere.

'Charades?' said the man in the leather jacket, pronouncing it the American way. 'Yeah, I'll play.'

Piper felt a thrill of surprise at having got a reaction from him.

'What's your name?' she asked.

'Chase. Chase Mason.'

'I'm Piper. Do you want to go first?'

'Sure. It's a movie. What's the sign for a movie?'

She held one hand in front of her face and rotated the other.

'You sure?' He took his shades off sceptically. 'How's that a movie?'

'I think it's an old camera,' she said.

'Like a wind-up camera?'

'I suppose so. I've never really–' she began, but was interrupted by her phone ringing. It was happening: the thing she'd been trying to distract herself from.

'Hello?' she said.

'Hi,' said a voice. 'This is Channon. You free to talk to Jonathon? We're at a pizza place. You want to join us?'

She couldn't say anything. Her voice wasn't working. Every thought seemed to have left her head. Her brain was an infinite void. The world around – the blue sky, the suddenly idyllic streets, the still-sceptical Chase Mason – loomed over her. She thought she would faint.

Bill Drummond opened the car door. She got in automatically and he closed it behind her.

'Hello?' said Channon.

The car backed slowly out of the parking spot and pulled off.

'Yes, I'm here,' she said. She tried to say, 'Yes, I want to talk to Jonathon,' but nothing came out. Finally, she managed just, 'I do.'

'Okay, you tell the driver – guy by the name of Sterling – to get over to … Il Casolare pizzeria, by Admiral Brücke, top of Grimm Strasse.'

She repeated what he'd said to the driver.

'Okay, good,' said Channon. 'Passing you over.'

'Hello?' said a different voice.

'Jonathon?' she said.

'Um, I think so,' he said. 'I think that's who I am. Who … I mean, um … who are …?' It was definitely and incontrovertibly Jonathon. A little door in her heart opened up and air poured in.

'Who am I? I'm Piper.' She heard her voice thickening, felt her eyes leaking.

'Ah. Hello, Piper. Is that an unusual name?'

'It's American. My mum's American and my dad just wanted to call me something that would make me sound like an oil rig.'

It was her standard line for explaining her name. But she felt it didn't matter what she said: every word meant every possible thing, and he would understand it all.

He said, 'Um,' and she knew exactly what he meant.

'Yes,' she said.

'I don't know what to say,' he said. 'I'm sitting in a pizza place next to a poetic-looking bridge, and Mr Channon's sitting opposite me wearing a really orange coat.'

'I'm driving along a really, really pleasant street where all the shops sell charming handicrafts. Oh, there's a liquorice shop! How does anyone manage to make a living from a shop that only sells liquorice? And at the end of that street I can see the big one with the railway running above it. I don't know why they've put a railway on top of a street.'

'The world's an odd place,' said Jonathon. 'I can only remember the last five days, but people seem to do lots of inexplicable things.'

'Yes,' she agreed. 'I'm afraid that's going to keep on happening. That's what it's always like.'

'Are you all right?' he asked.

'Yes, I think so. I keep thinking I'm going to faint, but I'm probably fine.'

'Are you ill?'

'No, it's just you. Hearing you, coming to see you after all this time. I've really missed you.'

'I've missed you too. I mean, I can't remember anything at all, but I've missed you anyway, even though …'

She leaned forward, so that her tears would fall to the carpeted floor and not make her eyes puff up. She had put on so much weight, and her face was already twice its normal size from crying. And then there were the huge bags under her eyes because she couldn't sleep. He had been gone for two years and she had turned herself into a monster.

But it didn't matter. She suddenly realised it didn't matter. He wouldn't mind. It had just been easy to funnel some of her excess worry into what she looked like.

'How are you?' she asked him.

'I don't know,' he said. 'I really don't know. My feet are bandaged, and I … maybe I should warn you that I look stupid.'

'I don't care,' she said. 'I just want to see you.'

'Hey, Piper.' It was Channon's voice again. 'We're gonna have to hang up now – our pizzas are here. But we'll see you in a few minutes, okay?'

She nodded her head, again unable to speak.

'Okay,' said Channon's voice, and the phone clicked and fell silent.

She kept it clasped in her hand, staring out of the window but barely seeing anything – even when they passed a man with several live crimson parrots perched on his bike. They reached some traffic lights and turned right, up a cobbled street with a long thin park in its centre. At the end of this street was an open area with trees and an ornate cast-iron bridge. It was covered in young people with shining hair and guitars, relaxing in the warm sunshine, the city suddenly alive and beautiful all around.

The cars stopped, and Chase Mason opened the door for her. She got out, the phone still clasped tight in her hand. There were some tables not far from the bridge, a couple of waiters carrying pizzas. And then she saw a man standing at one of the tables, holding a slice of pizza, wearing an overcoat on top of a ski jacket. A sudden shy smile. It was Jonathon.

62

'What?' said Lance.

'Down there,' said Karen, pointing.

Two identical black Secret Service-style Chevy Suburbans had pulled up by the side of the road and a woman was walking from one of them towards the pizza place. She tripped on the kerb and righted herself. Then she began to run. Over at his table, Jonathon had stood up and completely failed to realise that this was the moment for him to put his slice of pizza down. Now he and the woman were hugging.

'It's Piper,' said Lance. 'Jonathon's girlfriend,' he explained. 'He's completely devoted to her.'

'Really?' said Karen. 'Okay.'

Lizzie's face was set hard. She made a call.

'Where are you?' she asked the phone urgently. 'What? Well, how long's it going to take you?'

Down in the square, Piper was looking into Jonathon's face, saying something urgent.

'Yes,' said Lizzie to her phone, 'I understand how traffic works. But they've already arrived.'

Jonathon was gesturing with his crushed slice of pizza.

'I know he said he would try to slow them down,' said Lizzie to her phone, 'but I guess there are limits.'

Jonathon and Piper were looking at Jonathon's feet.

'Our guy, the girl and five other guys,' said Lizzie to her phone.

Piper was saying something.

'Well, I have no idea how I'm going to deal with the situation now,' said Lizzie to her phone.

Jonathon and Piper were walking, hand in hand, towards the picturesque sunlit bridge.

'They're walking away!' said Lance.

Lizzie ignored him. 'The second you get here, you text me, okay?' she said to her phone.

She hung up and put her phone in her pocket, then walked decisively halfway to the front door and stopped. She looked at Lance and Karen, who looked at each other.

'So, what are we doing?' asked Lance. 'Going down there?'

63

As the black car pulled up and the door opened, Jonathon was poised, mouth open, about to insert his first slice of pepperoni pizza into his face. But it never reached his mouth – because at that moment, there emerged from the car the most beautiful woman he had ever seen in his five-day life. He stood up.

The strumming of the guitars by the picturesque youths on the bridge seemed to cohere again into music, and someone started to sing 'Here Comes the Sun'. The breeze picked up the chestnut tresses of Piper's hair and the light chimed on its dark gold filaments. Time slowed, the world somehow switched itself into higher definition in order to convey the beauty of her upper lip. She gracefully tripped on the kerb, then righted herself, looking around. He stood, his mouth still open, the drooping pizza slice in his hand. She saw him and ran towards him. And then he was hugging her, slices of pepperoni dripping from the pizza slice that was crushed in his hand.

'It's you,' she said into his shoulder, into his ear.

He decided that if this woman tried to assassinate him, he would just let her. He would be too transfixed by the way the light played on her features to bother trying to escape.

His brain was having trouble dealing with the situation and had begun cycling through random words. *Matador, Blenkinsop, delphinium, boomerang jam*, it said. It was not calibrated for dealing with the sudden appearance of the universe's most beautiful being at the same time as a wave of love smashed through his heart, crashing into longing, regret, happiness, embarrassment and, so far as he could tell, most other emotions that a human being could feel, all at the same time.

'Rgcufenachu,' he said, nonsensically. His face had gone red.

She pulled away suddenly, looked up at him and said urgently, 'I'm sorry I'm so fat and my face has gone like this.'

'What?' he said, suddenly finding he could speak again. 'You're not. You're the most beautiful woman in the world. I'm sorry about my ... person.'

He gestured at himself with his crushed slice of pizza: his bandaged feet in their chunky sandals, his baggy Indian trousers, his embarrassing black vest, the thin cyan and purple ski jacket beneath his formal black overcoat.

'Shall we go home?' she said simply.

'Yes,' he said.

Channon, who had been calmly eating pizza throughout their reunion, looked up and said, 'Sit down.'

'We'd love to,' said Piper, 'but we have to be getting off home.'

'Yes,' said Jonathon. 'Sorry.'

'You know, you're still an employee of the Agency, and the Reichstag, come to that.'

'Oh right,' said Jonathon. 'In that case, I resign.'

Piper took his hand and they turned, strolling towards the bridge, towards the rest of their lives together.

64

'I don't want to go down there without backup,' said Lizzie, running her hands through her fiery hair. 'This is what we call a "fluid situation" and I am trying to adjust my plans accordingly. I mean, I had hoped we would be able to rescue the girl and intercept Jonathon before he met Channon.'

'Ah,' said Lance, 'but–'

'But neither of those things panned out,' said Lizzie. 'My next plan was to get down there to Jonathon and Channon and keep them talking till my guys could get there. But my guys are on the other side of Kottbusser Damm, and traffic's worse than usual because of the protests.'

'Oh,' said Lance, 'can't they just run?'

Lizzie ignored that. 'Meanwhile, it looks like Channon used Piper to get Jonathon to reveal his location. Now Channon's backup team has arrived: two cars full of armed ops guys. One of them is my guy, and I think I can rely on him, but there's basically nothing he can do in this situation except tell me where they are.'

'But it's okay,' said Lance. 'Jonathon and Piper are walking away.'

'No they're not,' said Lizzie, not even needing to look out of the window.

Lance looked out and saw that Jonathon and Piper had stopped.

'Oh,' he said.

They turned, and began walking back to the table where Channon sat.

'Oh,' he said again.

'Like I said, I don't want to go down there without backup,' said Lizzie. 'But I don't want to just watch your friends go off with Channon, because that's game over.'

Karen flinched at the words, as though she'd been slapped with something wet.

'Sorry, honey,' said Lizzie. 'But that's the situation.'

'I thought you said this was almost over,' said Karen. 'Why can't you just call the cops on this Channon guy?'

'Because I have basically no evidence against him. Sorry.'

Karen said urgently, 'But what does it how then that do some …? Wait. I'm making no sense. Fuck. Fuck.'

Lance said, 'But why would they go with Channon?'

'Yes!' said Karen, excitedly. 'That.'

'He's not going to get his men to drag them out of a crowded restaurant, is he?' said Lance. 'Not in broad daylight, in Germany's capital city.'

'I doubt it,' said Lizzie. 'But he'll find a way to make your friends go with him. I know it. Like I said, I used to be married to him. The guy's an unbelievable horse's ass, but he's a persuasive one.'

'So what are we going to do?' said Karen.

'Let me think,' said Lizzie, rubbing her forehead with her palm. 'God, I need my guys to just get across that fucking road.'

65

'Hey!' called Channon. 'I thought you were the kind of guy who kept his promises.'

Jonathon stopped. He hadn't thought about this. Was he? It had never really occurred to him to not keep a promise. What was Channon talking about?

'What are you talking about?' he called to Channon, who was all of six paces away.

Piper had stopped too, though she stood further away from Channon than Jonathon did. She looked from one to the other.

Channon said, 'I thought we had a deal. I tell you who you are; you come in.'

They did have a deal. He had completely forgotten.

'Actually,' he said to Piper, 'we do have a deal. I'd completely forgotten. Sorry. But it's not what he just said. I'll sort it out.'

'Let's go home,' she said, 'and sort it out from there.'

There was nothing Jonathon wanted more than to go home with the most beautiful entity in the history of the multiverse. But it seemed likely that he was, as Channon said, the kind of guy who kept his promises.

'I really want to,' he told her. 'But Mr Channon's helped me, and has kept all his promises so far. And I think, at this point, that it probably hasn't been him who's been trying to kill me. I'd better just sort this out. It won't take long.'

They walked reluctantly back to the table and perched on their chairs.

'Um, yes,' Jonathon said to Channon. 'We do have a deal. But also no, I'm not coming in. I just said I'd tell you what's happened to me since I woke up five days ago, and describe the people who tried to kill me. I'll do that now.'

'Great,' said Channon, 'but a lot's happened to you. We can't go over all that in a pizza place. We need to record it, get photofits, go back over stuff that's not clear. It's not a lot to ask. You know, I saved your life two nights ago, I gave you fifty thousand euros, and now I just laid your whole life story out for you on a plate. A few hours' debriefing is not a lot to ask in return.'

'Well …' began Jonathon.

'Wait a minute,' said Piper, 'no one would have been trying to kill him if you hadn't somehow accidentally recruited him into the CIA. And since then his brain's been wiped–'

'Actually, Mr Channon just said that he did that,' said Jonathon.

'Well then of course we're going home,' said Piper.

Channon raised his eyebrows.

'Also,' Jonathon pointed out to Channon, 'if I come in, you could just wipe my brain again.'

'Okay, well, I promise I won't,' said Channon. 'I take promises very seriously. Have I ever broken my word to you?'

Piper turned and asked Jonathon, 'Two years ago, did he promise not to steal two years of your life? Oh wait, you can't remember – because he wiped your brain.'

'Can we stop talking about my brain being wiped?' asked Jonathon.

'I'm sorry,' said Piper. 'But if he's trying to change the deal, then it's off. Let's just go home, like we said.'

'Yes,' said Jonathon, rising from his seat.

'Okay,' said Channon. 'In that case I have to tell you something you're not gonna want to hear, though it's for your own good.'

'Oh God,' said Piper. 'Now what?'

'I've poisoned you,' said Channon, with the casual lack of emphasis people usually reserve for statements like, 'I've brought dips.'

They were silent for a few seconds as Piper and Jonathon looked from one to the other and then back to Channon.

'Um, what?' said Jonathon, glancing at the uneaten pizza in front of him. 'You've poisoned me?'

'Not you, son. How could I have poisoned you? No, her. In her tea this morning.'

'You … *dick*,' said Jonathon, with feeling.

He found he'd picked up his knife and fork instinctively, seeing that the restaurant had thoughtfully supplied weapons. But stabbing Channon in the neck with a fork would not unpoison Piper.

'Relax,' said Channon. 'There's an antidote. I'll give it to her – if you come in.'

'But he doesn't want to come in,' said Piper. 'He wants to come home with me. You've already stolen two years from us and made me fat and a pit of grief.'

'You're not fat,' said Jonathon.

'Ma'am,' said Channon, 'we don't always get what we want.'

'I don't believe you,' said Jonathon. 'You wouldn't poison her.'

'Why would I lie?' said Channon. 'It's a fact that we're putting her up at the Adlon Hotel, and that she drank tea this morning.'

Piper nodded reluctantly.

'I guess you both know that poisons exist,' continued Channon, 'even if you have no episodic memory of them. And you know that some of those poisons have antidotes. Think about it: if I've got the resources to put someone up at the Adlon and hand over a case with fifty thousand euros in it, then I've got the resources to buy and administer a poison.'

Jonathon and Piper exchanged glances.

'In case it jogs your memory,' said Channon, 'this poison is called batrachotoxin. It's a steroidal alkaloid produced by South American poison dart frogs. Untreated, it causes ventricular fibrillation, resulting in cardiac arrest.'

'We'll just–' began Piper.

'The poison,' cut in Channon, 'and its antidote are unknown in Europe. If you go to hospital and tell them what's happened, they'll give you activated charcoal, which will do nothing. However, the poison can be counteracted by tetrodotoxin – ironically a poison itself, secreted by puffer fish. But it's only effective if administered within seven hours of the BTX – that's what we call batrachotoxin, in the business. What time did you drink your tea?'

'I don't know,' said Piper. 'Nine?'

Channon checked the time on Jonathon's phone. 'Okay, so we've got three hours left. That's enough for this guy to show us he's serious about helping us out.'

Piper looked at Jonathon, who looked at Channon.

Channon looked at both of them and said, 'I guess maybe you're thinking, "This guy Channon seems okay, would he really poison the nice lady?"'

Piper seemed like she was about to contradict him, but changed her mind.

'You must know the answer is yes,' Channon continued. 'I'm a high-ranking officer in the CIA. I've fought dirty wars in Latin America. I was here in Berlin at the height of the Cold War. So you know I have it in me to kill someone – even someone who's personally innocent and poses no danger. So then it's just, "Is he evil enough to do it?" That's what you're thinking, but it's the wrong question. It's wrong for two reasons. Firstly, I'm not the one who decides whether she lives or dies.'

Channon paused, almost unnaturally still.

'You are, son,' he said, looking deep into Jonathon's eyes. 'You come in, she lives; you don't, she dies.'

Jonathon took Piper's hand.

'Secondly,' continued Channon, 'I'm giving you this choice for a morally good reason. Bad things are going to happen if you don't come in – things that will be very bad for a very large number of people. So I'm making this personally real for you.'

Channon took a sip of water.

'And that's how I can poison your lovely girlfriend and still be the good guy,' he concluded. 'So, you coming in?'

'Um, yes,' said Jonathon. 'But I'm really annoyed with you.'

'I can live with that.'

'And how do I know you'll give her the antidote if I come in?' asked Jonathon.

'Because if you come in and I don't give her the antidote, are you going to co-operate?'

'No.'

'Exactly. Besides, if I don't give her the antidote then I have the hassle of disposing of a body and keeping it quiet. I can live without that. And also, I'm a good guy: I don't *like* killing people. But I'm a *really* good guy, so I'm responsible and pragmatic enough to be prepared to kill people if it'll make the world a better place.'

Channon's eyes were clear, blue-grey, and his stare so still and unwavering that it was impossible to doubt his sincerity. You had to hand it to him: he was convincing. Even Jonathon was beginning to feel that surreptitiously poisoning the tea of the woman he loved more than anything in the world could be a noble and selfless act.

'So what happens next?' asked Jonathon.

'Good question. All business, I like that. What happens next is that the three of us get into that big black car over there, and we head over to a debriefing location, where you tell us every single thing you remember from the past week. Once you've done some remembering, we give your charming girlfriend the antidote she needs.'

There was a silence. Channon drank the last of his water. Piper clutched Jonathon's hand. Jonathon knocked a spoon onto the floor.

'Okay,' said Jonathon, 'and what about after the antidote and telling you everything I remember?'

'Yes, when can we go home?' asked Piper.

'Let's not get ahead of ourselves,' said Channon. 'At this stage of the negotiations, all that's on offer is your lives.'

'But–' began Jonathon.

'Son,' said Channon, 'when I asked if you wanted to talk to her' – he nodded at Piper – 'and you passed me your phone, some part of you knew the price.'

Jonathon and Piper looked at each other.

Channon dabbed his lips with a napkin and stood up. 'I'd get the check,' he said, 'but you have my pants.'

Jonathon entirely failed to get the attention of any of the waiters, so he left a fifty-euro note under the ashtray.

Channon gestured towards the waiting cars. Two men stood beside them, hands clasped, wearing crisp leisurewear and neat hair. In this part of town, they would have been less conspicuous if they'd been wearing elephant costumes and on fire.

Jonathon and Piper stood up, hugged and, even though they'd only just met, he shyly kissed her. They looked into each other's eyes, knowing this was the last moment they could guarantee they would both be alive, together, and standing in the sunshine. It would have been helpful if the guitars had started up again and the girl with the quite good voice had sung, but that didn't happen.

They held hands and walked towards the waiting massively conspicuous cars.

66

'They're getting in the cars,' said Lance.

'I knew they would,' said Lizzie, tapping at her phone. 'Fucking Doug Channon!'

Down by the bridge, Jonathon was climbing into one of the huge black Suburbans. As he did so, he looked up at their window and put one hand over his eyes.

'That's the signal,' said Karen. 'It basically means it's all fucked up, so get out of here.'

Channon, in his bright orange anorak, was getting in the front seat. He slammed the door and the car pulled slowly off, manoeuvring around a man on a bike who held a guitar as as his lustrous hair waved gently in the wind. The second Suburban, equally large and equally black, followed.

Lizzie's phone made a noise. She looked at it and quietly said, 'God love you, you're still my guy.' She made a call.

'Just heard from our guy with Channon,' she said to her phone. 'Can you get to the big roundabout at Kottbusser Tor in five minutes? They'll pass through there. Great. I'll intercept the first car and come up with something that gets the three of us into it. You work to detach the second car. Okay?'

She clicked the button, put the phone in her pocket, and turned to Lance and Karen.

'Okay,' she said, 'I guess we're going to have to do this. I need to get to the roundabout at Kottbusser Tor, and I need you two to come with me. Will you do it?'

'Of course,' said Lance.

'Yes,' said Karen. 'Let me just get my–'

'No time,' said Lizzie, opening the door and sprinting out.

They ran downstairs, out of the building, across the bridge, through knots of beautiful young people whose strumming chords and floating hair were briefly disarrayed by the runners' harsh vibe. Lance tried to pretend he was on a treadmill at his artfully shabby gym in Greenwich Village, watching a point-of-view music video made to accompany an unusual minimalist track that consisted of the up-tempo rasping of an ex-smoker's breathing and the pattering percussion of feet running over cobbled streets.

What would they do when they intercepted the huge black Chevrolets full of armed CIA men? What would Lizzie say? Would her backup team arrive this time? Lance elected not to think about it. Everything was going to be fine.

Lizzie, in her trouser suit and sneakers, was by far the most effective runner of the three of them, her bright hair always bobbing an inconvenient distance in front of Lance as the old balconied stucco buildings gave way to decaying modern ones. They ran through a little square where statues of men with telescopes stood atop a huge concrete hourglass freckled with graffiti, but Lance was so intensely focusing on keeping his feet moving and trying to get enough air into his body that the thought 'What the fuck is that all about?' barely flashed through his mind. On they went, towards the grey ramparts of the elevated train line running above the street.

'That's Kottbusser Tor,' said Lizzie, breathlessly. 'This is the roundabout.'

She stopped and looked around, patting near her armpit, where she kept her gun.

67

Jonathon and Piper were in the Chevrolet's third row of seats, where there were no doors. He sat in the middle, with Piper on his left and, on his right, a gum-chewing CIA officer wearing a new black leather jacket, shades and immaculate jeans.

The charming sunlit neighbourhood, with its little bakeries and antique bookshops, already looked remote through the tinted windows, as though it were a far-off memory of better times.

It was a memory that would soon be gone, along with the woman who sat next to him, holding his hand. This car journey would probably be the last time he'd be with her. Soon, they'd make him forget again who he was, and he'd go back to being Adam Newman, doing what he was told and very occasionally listening to the music of Crowded House. But if that was the only way to keep her alive, it was fine.

There was nothing he could say to her, not in this car full of CIA officers – one loudly chewing gum beside him, another occupying much of the row of seats in front of him, challenging the seams of his suit, and then, in the front, the driver with the blue shirt and the curly wire in his ear, and Channon in his orange coat, playing with his phone.

But despite the silence and the fear, he felt close to Piper, as though they were two lakes, side by side, their waters mingling. He looked at her, suddenly afraid that she'd overheard him thinking of her as a large body of inert water. She looked at him at the same moment and smiled, squeezed his hand, and he realised she would see past the stupidity of any metaphor.

He needed to make this journey, this moment, last as long as possible. All he had learned in his five days of life was that there is never anyone coming to rescue you, things are exactly as bad as they look, and if you happen upon a good moment, you should pay it as much attention as possible.

The charming neighbourhood was long gone. They'd crowded along a wide ugly road, reached a roundabout with a huge grey train track running overhead, and were now driving in its shadow.

Jonathon looked again, shyly, at the woman beside him and clasped her hand in both of his.

68

'Hi,' said Lizzie to her phone. 'We what? How is that even …? Man!'

To Lance and Karen she said, 'We just missed them.'

She glanced up at the train line above them. A train – a tiny yellow thing, thin as a sardine tin – was approaching.

'Okay, guys!' she said, eyes blazing. 'Change of plan. We're going to get on that train!'

She said to her phone, 'We'll intercept them at Schlesisches Tor: traffic lights right before the bridge.' And then she set off running again.

Lance followed Lizzie up the concrete steps, past huge grey riveted girders, his thighs burning and his knees requesting that in future he restrict his exercise to trademarked classes run by women called Bethany with very white teeth.

Barp-barp, went the train doors as they began to close.

'*Soog-nak varshowerstrasser,*' said a distant, incomprehensible announcement. '*Iyn-shtaigen bitter.*'

Lizzie jumped into the nearest carriage, hands ready to hold back the doors, and Lance jumped in a moment after her, ducking to avoid hitting his head on the doorway, Karen colliding with his back and pushing him uncomfortably against a metal pole as the doors sealed behind them.

'Good job, guys!' said Lizzie, her face bright red but her breathing much more under control than Lance's or Karen's. 'We get off at the second stop. I'm gonna need you two to be down those steps and in that car in, like, four seconds. You did great, by the way. Now you just need to do that one more time.'

Lance had his hands on his knees. Sweat was pouring off his face and dripping onto the floor. He was heaving quantities of air in and out of his body in a way that constituted exercise in its own right.

However, his lungs were telling him that the stuff in this U-Bahn carriage was not exactly air. Looking around, he saw that what he was breathing in had already been breathed out by the other passengers, who were mostly either grey-faced smokers or dogs. They stared back at Lance with blunt curiosity, as though looking at a rare species in a zoo.

Karen had taken a phone from her pocket and dialled. Lizzie shot her a look and said, 'No calls!'

'What?' said Karen. 'Oh, it's just–'

'Really,' said Lizzie. 'No calls. I need you to hang up.'

'Okay,' said Karen, pressing the button to end the call.

'Thanks, honey,' said Lizzie. 'I'll explain later.'

The brakes whistled as the train rounded a corner. Then the first stop came, and a new cohort of passengers got on the little train, loaded down with youth and backpacks. The doors closed, and the train moved off.

Lance was standing now, mopping his brow with his sleeve. His breathing had passed the critical stage. In the background, the engine sounded a faint noise like someone softly blowing a mouth organ. And, on both sides of the train, huge old apartment buildings swept past, painted pink, blue, orange, cream.

'Have you ever seen *The French Connection*, with Gene Hackman?' he asked.

Karen said, 'I was just thinking how great it would be to have a little movie chit-chat. This is the perfect time for it.'

Lance ignored her sarcasm. 'This just reminded me of that famous scene where he chases the overhead train in his car, hitting loads of metal bins. It was really tense, because you were wondering how he was going to keep up with the train. But now I'm in pretty much the same situation, and I see that Gene Hackman had an easy job. It's much harder chasing a car in a train.'

Lizzie looked out of the window, silent and focused.

'We *will* intercept that car,' she said, her eyes doing their blazing thing again.

Like runners at their starting blocks, Lance, Lizzie and Karen arrayed themselves at the carriage door. The second station's black mouth was rushing towards them, its metal body shining in the sun. The doors clicked and pulled themselves open.

The three of them bunched together as they squeezed through the opening doors, out onto the nearly empty platform. Lance and Karen collided, then saw which way Lizzie was running. They followed her, Lance's heart pounding again, breathing hard, the sweat in his shirt cold against his skin. *What about tickets?* he suddenly thought, running past a battered yellow vending machine. But there were no barriers, no staff.

Down the stairs, through the station. He saw the road, the traffic lights. Two ranks of cars were just moving off as the lights changed. There it was, in the far lane, at first almost obscured by a large grey Audi: a big black Chevy Suburban with an orange anorak in the front passenger seat.

Lizzie was a dozen steps ahead, out onto the pavement, waving her arms. The traffic was picking up speed. Lizzie reached the traffic lights and was watching the back of the black Suburban as it receded into the distance. She looked after it.

'Shit,' she said.

'Fuck,' said Karen.

'Bollocks,' said Lance.

69

There was so much Piper wanted to tell Jonathon: about the cat, her dad, her work, the house, people who he wouldn't believe had got together and others who had split up, gone to China, or unexpectedly become very serious about boring things and grown rich but not quite themselves anymore.

But she was stunned into silence by what had just happened. And so she just held Jonathon's hand and occasionally glanced at him, marvelling at how tough he now looked, like – she thought – a very thin and uncertain Bruce Willis. She tried to concentrate on the sense of togetherness she felt, tried to hold onto it, and to the hope that all would somehow be well.

Outside, there passed an endless graffiti-freckled parade of tall buildings, plain and ornate, interspersed with empty spaces like pulled teeth. The frontages chimed in the sun: pink, blue, orange, cream. Overhead, the train line loomed, like a bank of iron-dark cloud.

To her left, a big grey Audi full of people in wigs and dark glasses dropped back. She looked behind them and saw a woman with red hair waving. More inexplicable Berlin stuff, which everyone else in the car seemed to have got used to.

Channon was tapping out a text on his phone, restored to him by one of his agents. The driver with the nice blue shirt kept his attention on the road. Bill Drummond sat stock still, and Chase Mason, on the other side of Jonathon, chewed distractedly and stared out of the window. Neither he nor she was in the mood for charades now.

They were making their earlier journey again in reverse. She watched as the cityscape passed by, with all its epic grandeur, tatty flats and train stations. And then their route changed, and they passed a huge Renaissance palace that claimed to be a post office, a gigantic ruined building in which people seemed to be living, an enormous old concrete building covered in bullet holes. On the pavements were people with signs and banners, all heading in the same direction. The people grew more concentrated, spilling onto the streets, slowing the traffic.

The car eased over a bridge that sat beside some white buildings which looked like grotesquely oversized washing machines. Here they slowed to a crawl, because there was a solid mass of people walking in the road, with banners and megaphones, walking slowly towards the Reichstag, with its big glass dome, which had been hiding behind the washing-machine building.

'They wouldn't be able to protest if we hadn't saved their asses from the Nazis and the Commies,' said Bill Drummond.

'True,' said the black agent, nodding his head.

'Won't even support us in this one war.'

'It's fucked up,' said the agent in the leather jacket.

The car had slowed to walking pace. People were glancing at it, perhaps noticing how neatly it represented everything they disliked. The crowd, festooned with banners, placards and balloons, stretched off into the distance, merging with Berlin's eccentric city-centre forest. The whole of the huge space in front of the Reichstag was filled with people.

'Is the CIA office inside the Reichstag?' asked Piper.

'What?' said Channon. 'No. We're here to do a little sightseeing first. Just me and Mr Orthopaedic Sandals here. You'll wait in the car.'

'I'm coming with Jonathon,' said Piper.

'You're waiting here,' said Channon, 'so that this guy has one more reason to come back out of the Reichstag with me, and not try to slip off or tell tales. Me and him are taking a tour.'

'But why?'

'Broaden his mind,' said Channon, straightening his ponytail. 'It's a fascinating place, and an unmissable chance to see Germany's parliament in action.'

As Jonathon climbed over Piper to get out, she hugged him, and he went red and kissed her awkwardly, stymied by the car's ceiling and the fact that both of them had noses immediately above their mouths.

'Come back,' she said.

'I will,' he said. 'I promise.'

Lance was standing with Lizzie and Karen by the entrance to Schlesisches Tor station, making all the drug dealers uncomfortable.

'Stay on their tail,' said Lizzie to her phone, 'but make sure they don't see you, okay?'

Lance had taken one of his shoes off and was massaging his foot. Karen was staring at the ground, so he asked if she was okay.

'Me?' she said, sounding surprised. 'I'm fine.'

'I'll work something out,' continued Lizzie. 'Just keep me up to date with where you are. My guy with Channon doesn't know where they're headed, but I guess it must be the Agency station in Berlin.'

Lance realised Karen was looking at him with concern, and that while she looked more or less as she had when they'd first met, he was now drenched in sweat and couldn't keep his shoes on. That was the problem with having genes that made him look slim and athletic without having to do any exercise: he very rarely did any exercise.

'Yeah, I'll work something out,' said Lizzie again to her phone. 'There is absolutely no way Doug Channon is going to win this thing. I've just got to think like him.'

She put her phone in her pocket and turned to Lance and Karen.

'Okay,' she said. 'Who–?'

Karen interrupted her. 'Can we *please* call the cops now?'

Lizzie sighed. 'And say what? Channon hasn't committed a provable crime. But you're living and working here illegally. I'm here unofficially in a way that my superiors will not enjoy. And this guy' – she gestured to Lance – 'is a minor TV presenter.'

'My show's in the top–' began Lance.

'*Okay,*' said Lizzie, with a tone of finality. 'Listen, we *have* to stop Channon getting your friends to the station–'

'What,' said Karen, 'the train station? Hauptbahnhof?'

'No, the Agency station. CIA bases are called stations.'

'Oh. Weird.'

'We could go back and pick up the hire car?' suggested Lance.

'I think,' said Lizzie, 'it's going to be quicker just to steal one.'

Jonathon was led by Channon towards the enormous square glass building. The American's hand was on his shoulder in a way that probably looked paternal, but the thumb was sharp against a nerve in his shoulder.

Jonathon walked slowly, trying to think of some alternative to meekly accompanying a killer into a faceless glass building. He was in a difficult position. The only way to save the woman he loved was to leave her in a car with some armed men while he went off alone with a total dick who wanted, on the most benign interpretation, to wipe his brain. This did not seem like a great thing to be doing. But the alternative was, unfortunately, impossible.

The alternative consisted of escaping, attracting the attention of the crowd, explaining the situation to them in shouted German, getting them to overcome their pacifist principles for long enough to smash their way into the huge black car and rescue Piper, then find a puffer fish, break into a laboratory and manufacture an antidote. All in – he checked his watch – two and a half hours. That sounded pretty impossible, even if Berlin had a really world-class aquarium and very lax laboratory security.

They arrived at the building's glass doors. Off to their right, only about a block away, stood the Reichstag. The crowd over there was much thicker, like a dense German soup. Most of the demonstrators looked terribly bored, standing in front of a building, holding banners and being shouted at by many competing people with megaphones. He strained to pick out what they were shouting, but *against the war* was the only thing he could make sense of.

The glass door opened, and Jonathon followed Channon inside the six-storey high cube of glass. They were in a huge open atrium, bordered by glass-walled offices stacked one on top of another, in which people in spectacles stared into screens or sat in groups around glass tables.

If there was no CIA office on the premises, what were they doing here? Was the German government in on this? Had they supplied a secret underground room where Jonathon could be quietly killed or – maybe worse – just turned back into Adam Newman?

'What are we here for?' he whispered to Channon.

'Nothing you need to know about. Now shut up.'

A tall man with a ginger beard was walking towards them, a pass around his neck.

Channon leaned in close to Jonathon's ear and whispered, 'If you say anything, she dies. That's just what happens. Automatically. You get that, don't you?'

Jonathon nodded. This was just about the only thing he wasn't confused about.

'Mr Channon,' said the man with the ginger beard. 'I am Matthias Gottwald, deputy director of the Reichstag secretariat administration. We have met once before, but I see you are now dressed bizarrely.'

He indicated Channon's orange anorak and Jonathon's ski-jacket-vest-sandals-overcoat combination, and smiled.

'This is very fun,' Matthias continued. 'I presume you are on holiday and having much enjoyment.'

'Something like that,' said Channon. 'And thanks for obliging us with this unofficial visit.'

'Of course. But I must just to check with a colleague that these leisure garments are suitable for wearing in the chamber.'

Chamber? Was that a high-tech brain-wiping chamber?

Channon's jaw tensed and he breathed out through his nose. 'Sure,' he said. 'There's a dress code?'

'There is no specific dress code but all attendees must uphold the dignity of the parliament.'

So, the Reichstag's debating chamber. Unless this was some sort of complicated bluff.

Matthias bustled off, and Channon muttered to Jonathon, 'You better pray there's no problem.'

'Um, okay,' said Jonathon, but he was too ambivalent about what was going on to actually follow through with this.

They waited there for some time, during which the muscles in Channon's jaw put on a tensing masterclass and he did something complicated with his breathing which didn't appear to prevent him getting more and more angry.

At length, Matthias returned, now accompanied by an elderly security guard with a moustache and a blue jacket. The security guard looked them over with a sort of mild severity, taking in Jonathon's vest and Channon's vastly orange anorak.

'Medical?' he asked, looking at Jonathon's orthopaedic sandals.

'Medical,' confirmed Jonathon.

The security guard, old enough to have grown up in an era when everyone wore ties and hats at all times, sighed sadly. He mimed to Jonathon to zip up his ski jacket so as to cover his embarrassing vest. This done, he gave them a last sad look and shuffled off.

Matthias now gave them passes to hang around their necks and ushered them through a little glass security gate.

'Please follow me,' he said. 'We must go through an underground tunnel to the Reichstag building, which is unfortunately surrounded by a large angry crowd today.'

At the mention of a tunnel, a chill passed through Jonathon's body. Was this where Channon meant to kill or brainwash him?

Matthias was already walking ahead. Channon took a few steps, then turned and stared impatiently at Jonathon, who had frozen to the spot. Channon made a little gesture, like drinking something from a very small container: *the antidote*. Jonathon reminded himself that there really was no choice.

Jonathon followed them down some stairs and along a brightly lit corridor. Channon put up with Jonathon's trailing behind, though he kept tensely turning to check he was still there. At no point did he or Matthias set upon Jonathon. Instead, they walked through the underground corridor without incident, and emerged into a waiting area in the Reichstag building, where the plaster had been cut away from the wall to reveal smooth stone blocks scrawled over with illegible writing. Matthias explained that this was graffiti left by Soviet soldiers in the war. He seemed hopeful that they would ask him about this, but Channon gave Jonathon a warning glare.

'You know,' said Channon, 'I'm really looking forward to my friend here seeing parliament in session. What are they discussing?'

'You do not know?' said Matthias. 'Today they discuss whether to support your country in this war.'

'Oh, right, right. That's today?' said Channon, glancing at Jonathon from the corner of his eye. 'Great.'

It looked like they really were taking him to the parliamentary chamber. Was the whole German legislature going to set upon Jonathon? Had Channon, perhaps, hypnotised him to do something there? Would he find himself assassinating the German Chancellor? He felt there was nothing too extreme or weird for Channon.

Matthias led them up some steps and they emerged in a huge, high-ceilinged lobby, this time made of stone. In front of them were tall glass doors, through which Jonathon could see out to the crowd that filled the open square and stretched off into the trees beyond.

Beside him, there was a counter full of Reichstag-branded mugs, pens and tote bags, attended by an elderly man with glasses and a moustache, sitting and reading a newspaper contentedly.

'Come,' said Matthias, 'I take you into the debating chamber.'

He led them through a glass door guarded by another elderly man with a moustache, and they emerged into the chamber.

It was lit from above by a circle of glass panels that seemed to concentrate the daylight and beam it into the huge room. On the opposite side of the room, at a raised lectern, stood a slim man wearing a blue suit. He was tanned and groomed, and used artificial-looking gestures, as though demonstrating them for students. This meant that his speech entirely bypassed Jonathon's facility for paying attention.

Matthias led them quietly up some steps to one of the viewing galleries suspended around the walls of the chamber. The gallery's tiered seats were crowded, but Matthias led them to three chairs on the front row, reserved by pieces of paper. Each had a bottle of fizzy mineral water on it, along with a glass and a small packet of peanut flips. It was easier to see the chamber now, with its blue seats arranged in curved rows surrounding the raised lectern.

Down in the chamber, a slightly scruffy white-haired man in a brown jacket was standing up at his desk, asking a question with an air of great annoyance. The man at the lectern waited patiently, and then answered with the same attention-defying confidence and fluency as before. Jonathon tuned in to what Matthias and Channon were whispering about.

'I didn't catch that,' whispered Channon. 'What did Baumberg ask?'

'This white-haired Baumberg asks, on behalf of the socialist government which has introduced the motion opposing the war, why Jens Metz, the conservative who is speaking, is being such a ... silly person.'

'Right. I heard *arschloch* – asshole – but the rest was kind of a blur.'

'Baumberg speaks quickly because he is very passionate on this point. Metz, in the blue suit, argues that Germany should stay close to America and support the war. But you see from the large crowds that this idea is not so popular in Berlin.'

'There's plenty of conservatives outside Berlin,' said Channon. His hands rested in a relaxed way on his thighs, but the muscles of his jaw were once again tense.

Jonathon too felt formidably tense, despite the fact that absolutely nothing was happening. The blue-suited man's speech continued, as boring as ever. Channon was doing his breathing exercises again, and very occasionally glanced at Jonathon out of the corner of his eye. He was clearly waiting for something. But what?

Jonathon tried to calm himself by focusing on the eagle, painted white on a glass wall, that overlooked the proceedings. It was surprisingly podgy and domesticated – the eagle equivalent of the elderly man at the souvenir stand. Jonathon found himself wondering whether he could draw it in an even more passive and unmilitary way, perhaps by adding a pipe, spectacles and a waistcoat. Was there a pen around?

Did he dare ask Channon if he had one?

He decided to have a drink of water while he plucked up the courage. He eased the bottle's cap around, as slowly as he possibly could, knowing how annoyed Channon would be if he made a noise. Moving it in one-degree increments, he managed to avoid the hiss of carbon dioxide releasing. Even the breaking, one by one, of the little metal filaments joining the cap to its collar was almost noiseless. He angled the glass and poured the water silently into it.

He glanced at Channon to see if he had noticed, but Channon was still tensely watching the man with the blue suit as he gave his unending speech. Jonathon raised the glass to his lips, but as he did so he managed to catch its rim on the bottle's base, spilling the water all over himself. He leapt from his seat, and the bottle and glass rolled hard and clanked against a post supporting the barrier in front of him. Then, in slow motion, the glass gently pivoted around the post, toppled through the gap beneath the barrier and fell to the floor below, where it smashed.

Every single person in the chamber turned to look at him. The man in the blue suit stopped talking and squinted up at Jonathon. And the white-haired man in the brown jacket also glanced up at what he must have seen as a damp-vested poltroon deliberately disrupting proceedings.

With the attention of the entire German government on him, was this Jonathon's chance to expose Channon? Surely they must have a puffer fish tucked away somewhere, mustn't they? He opened his mouth.

But it was too late. Something about Jonathon seemed to have inspired the white-haired man to act. He marched to the podium, a glass of water in his hand, and threw it in the face of the blue-suited politician. There was the sound of a lot of people breathing in all at once. And then the white-haired man was shouting, '*No more war!*'

and the chamber erupted in noise.

Matthias, hand in front of his mouth in horror, turned to Channon and said, 'Martin Baumberg has thrown a small quantity of water onto the face of Jens Metz! Nothing like this has ever happened before. I apologise that you see this.'

People were standing up all around, everyone was talking, some had taken up the shout, *'No more war!'* And then a recorded announcement sounded from speakers high on the walls, *'Very honoured gentlemen and ladies, we regret–'*

'They are clearing the chamber,' said Matthias. 'The vote has been postponed until tomorrow because of this outbreak of violence. Please believe me that this is an unprecedented disruption of our democratic norms.'

'Hey, don't worry about it,' said Channon, smiling, his jaw relaxed.

Then Jonathon felt Channon's hand on his shoulder. Channon, grinning, whispered, 'Way to go, champ,' and they joined the crowd filing slowly out of the chamber.

72

Piper sat in the back of the huge black car, watching the door of the glass building into which Jonathon had disappeared. She kept having to remind herself to breathe, and to ignore the sound of Chase Mason chewing gum. She wished she had her phone, but they'd taken her bag.

The protestors continued to flow past, every now and then giving the car a dirty look. *It's not me,* Piper wanted to tell them. *I'm on your side: I also try to prevent wars by going and having things shouted at me.*

At length she said, 'Do you know Channon's poisoned me?'

None of the three men in the car answered her, so she added, 'Chase? Bill? Other man?'

Chase Mason said, 'Hey, kid … you know … I …'

Bill Drummond stepped in. 'Listen, ma'am, whatever's between you and Channon is between you and Channon. We wouldn't know. We're just doing our jobs.'

'But your jobs involve standing by while innocent people get kidnapped and poisoned.'

'I have no specific knowledge related to that, ma'am,' said Bill

Drummond. 'Final word here: there are two types of people in this world – those who stay home and try to have a nice life, and those who get their hands dirty fighting for what they believe in.'

'Are you seriously comparing poisoning women to … just *needing to wash your hands?*'

'I've said all I'm gonna say on this, ma'am.'

'Channon said I only have another two hours or so before this poison …' She trailed off, trying to remember Channon's words, not wanting to say 'kills me' for fear of upsetting herself too much. '… causes ventricular fibrillation. What if he's in there for ages? Jonathon's co-operating.'

'Don't worry, ma'am,' said Bill Drummond.

The driver, who had seemed not to be listening, turned and held up a briefcase that had been in Channon's foot space.

'We're trained and authorised to administer anything that may be in this briefcase, ma'am,' he said, 'including antidotes.'

'Which does not constitute an admission that we have knowledge of the briefcase's contents,' added Bill Drummond.

Piper looked again at the protestors all around them. Chase Mason tapped the ceiling and said, 'Soundproof,' then went back to his noisy chewing.

At that moment, Jonathon emerged from the glass building, followed by Channon, who was looking pleased. Jonathon had his hands in his coat pockets in a way that only he could do, and Piper was suddenly grateful to him for not forgetting this, and amazed that she could be so overwhelmed with love because of such a small thing as pockets.

Drummond leaned over to open the door and fold the seat down, so Jonathon could climb awkwardly into the back with Piper, reaching instinctively for her hand. He said nothing, just glanced shyly at her and then out of the window. He looked frazzled, as though his mind might be breaking under the strain. She wondered how he would have dealt with the situation if he'd still been himself, and realised that the question didn't make sense: the situation would have been impossible if he'd still been himself.

'So, are we going to the CIA office now?' asked Piper, wanting to stay engaged, not just passively go where they were taken, though that was clearly their role.

'We call it a station,' said Channon. 'Berlin station.'

'That's weird. Like you're a fire brigade or … some trains. Except with poison.'

'That's right,' said Channon, tolerantly. 'And no, we're not going there. I'd have to be crazy to take a natural disruptor of *his* talents into the nerve centre of our European operations.'

Jonathon, sitting next to her in the back seat, pulled exactly the same face as he used whenever people said he was good at drawing – a kind of instantly disavowed pleasedness that made his face stiffen and flush.

'What's a natural disruptor?' she asked.

'Never you mind,' said Channon.

There was a wedge of silence during which the car did a severely hampered three-point turn on the bridge and pulled away through the thinning crowd.

'So where *are* we going?' she asked.

'Never you mind,' said Channon.

It soon became clear that where they were going was back – again – the way they'd come, past the enormous stone washing machines, over the bridge, past the tatty grandeur. They passed again the remains of the Berlin wall, and then they were back on the bridge that was also a red-brick castle. They drove on, beneath the overhead railway line, past the huge picture of the spaceman, then parted company with the train track, driving along a cobbled street and stopping outside a large yellow building with a huge anarchist sign near its front door.

'Here?' said Jonathon.

'No one else is using it,' said Channon.

Jonathon answered Piper's raised eyebrows, saying, 'Waking up outside this building is the first thing I remember. And then about three days after that I came back here and found the flat where I lived when I thought I was Adam Newman.'

'Again, doing you a favour,' said Channon. 'Jonathon Fairfax was a nobody. Adam Newman is a talented and effective CIA officer, working to protect the free world. Okay, enough of this. Let's get up there, do a little debriefing and, if you're good, take an antidote.'

Bill Drummond and Chase Mason climbed out and stood beside the car's rear doors. Then an agent in a Hawaiian shirt and the one in neatly ironed cargo trousers went to the building's entrance, one standing looking alertly around, eyeing the rooflines, as the other unlocked the door. Piper thought that it must be exhausting having to do things their special way all the time.

After a few minutes, the driver turned and nodded to Channon. Channon nodded back, and the driver said something softly into his left shirt cuff.

Channon got out, and then the agents standing beside the car opened the back doors. Bill Drummond took a firm grip on Jonathon's left arm, at the wrist and just above the elbow. Chase Mason gripped Piper's arm lightly but firmly above the elbow. She couldn't help feeling a little aggrieved that she didn't warrant a wrist grip, but then she remembered that she would die of poisoning if she didn't go up into the flat with them.

As they were marched up the green lino stairs, Piper wished she had walked just a little bit faster down the corridor that morning. If she hadn't run into Bill Drummond, she would have escaped, Channon wouldn't have been able to blackmail Jonathon into giving himself up, and Lance and his friendly CIA agent – now clearly the goodies – would have prevailed. Her only hope was that Lance somehow managed to rescue them in spite of all this.

73

Boris was hiding behind a wall, breathing heavily, smoking a furious cigarette. His hand tapped on the wall, beating out the drum part of East Infection's signature track, *Storm of Fucks*. The fury of it calmed him.

It had been an unusual day. After waking up in their pleasant holiday flat, he had breakfasted, showered, dressed, and then gone and stood in the corridor of a bookshop and looked angrily at a naked man whom he despised. After that, he had carried the man's clothes around in a red Haspa holdall, visiting a series of vantage points and checking that the naked man – now clothed and wearing a stylish orange jacket – was not being followed. He was not.

In this way, Boris had eventually reached Admiral Brücke, where he concealed himself among the trees and bushes on the bank of the canal, beside the bridge. The feeble and insipid guitar-playing of the young and unformed ones made him seethe with rage, so that he longed to run among them shouting 'fools!' and smashing their weak guitars. Instead he had remained hidden and watched Mister talk to someone on the phone and cry, which had made Boris angry. He wanted to weep himself, and to rip apart the person who had made Mister sad.

But then a woman had arrived in a big black car and Mister had cried again and hugged her. And Boris had seen that Mister was not unhappy but aflame with a love that could consume a man's soul. They had failed to eat any pizza, argued heartily with the dog Channon, cried again and then trudged with broken hearts to the waiting cars, which had taken them away. Boris saw that Mister was, deep in his heart, a Russian, that he suffered like a Russian with this very sad love affair and this mysterious persecution that was visited upon him like the curse of a dybbuk.

Throughout all this, Boris had been watching out for the wave of Mister's hand that meant, 'bring the red Haspa holdall, Boris.' It had not come. Instead, just as he was getting into the huge black car, Mister had given the other signal, the hand over the eyes that meant, 'All is lost, lost and ruined; try to save your own life, Boris.'

Boris had stood and walked, sorrow in every step, back towards the pleasant holiday flat that Karen had rented. At the thought of Karen his heart hurt with angry love. But then he had seen Karen rush out of the building's front door, fear in her eyes. She followed a big woman with glowing pink cheeks and hair of flame. Behind her was a man in foolish person's clothes, with hair falling over his eyes like a woman's, and Boris had felt rage in his heart.

He had followed them, like a protective spirit watching over Karen. She ran willingly, but something was wrong. Why had she not called him? At the back of his mind was the thought that if he could save her, she might stop mentioning how he had left her waiting at a service station for six hours when she was being pursued by killers. He knew he had been right: a man must never corrupt the sacred bond with his art. But she was a woman and could never know what truly lay in a man's heart.

Boris had waited until they went up the stairs at Kotti station, then he had run over the road, subduing with his eyes those who drove the cars, so that they stopped in his path. At the top of the stairs he had found the platform was empty, the train gone, the tracks thrumming in its wake. The fury in his eyes had made a man cringe and a child weep.

Then his phone had rung. He had answered and Karen's voice had said, 'What? Oh, it's just … okay. But–' And then the call had been over and there had been silence.

He had taken the next train. At the first stop a text had arrived: 'hi pockft text cant cbll i'. And then no more. He had looked out of the train's window but in the streets he could not see Karen or the woman with the hair of flame. The sun had shone but Karen was nowhere and Boris was lonely.

He had ridden the train further. Then he had got out and walked, not knowing where, needing only to walk.

He had sat by the river and opened the red Haspa holdall. There were clothes, a wallet containing two hundred euros, and a small snub-nosed gun, which he had put in the pocket of his ski jacket.

Later, another text had arrived: 'marianen n reichenberger yelo bldng top flr name newman cal 7olice guns k love'.

There was much in it that he had not understood, but he saw that Karen was telling him to come to the top floor of a yellow building on the corner of Mariannen Strasse and Reichenberger, and to bring a gun. Boris had then done something that he had once vowed he never would. He had taken a taxi.

Now he was hiding behind a wall, watching the yellow building on which he and Jochi had once sprayed a huge anarchy symbol. In the doorway stood two men, one dressed in neat casual wear, the other in a suit. Boris did not trust men in neat casual wear or suits. He watched, waiting for his chance.

74

Piper was sitting beside Jonathon at a large characterful old wooden table in a large characterless modern kitchen, with the sun pouring in through the French windows behind them. Jonathon kept glancing at the balcony beyond and flinching, or glancing at a little drawer in the table and flinching in a different way.

It was terrible what they had done to him. Not that he had ever been entirely free of distracted flinching, of course – especially when he had to do his accounts – but nothing like this. Her eyes filled again. She tried to wipe the tears away before anyone saw, but they kept dripping down her cheeks. The agent in the nice blue shirt moved a box of tissues over from the worktop, putting them in front of her, nodding.

'Thank you,' she said, taking one and blotting the tears from her face, the handcuffs on her wrists tinkling gently as she did so.

Channon, who had been sitting across the table from them, sifting through papers, now looked up.

'Okay,' he said, as though he had managed to sort out the administrative side of poisoning her and wiping the brain of the man she loved, and was now prepared to tackle the practicalities.

He put the papers aside and flipped open a slim briefcase. From inside he took a small glass phial, which he held up between thumb and forefinger.

'Here's the antidote,' he said. 'It needs to be administered within the first seven hours to avoid organ damage. So, we've got an hour and a half left for you' – he looked at Jonathon – 'to convince me you're fully playing ball. Okay?'

Jonathon nodded. 'I would never only partially play ball,' he said.

'Okay,' said Channon. And then, as though struck by a sudden doubt, 'Are you fucking with me?'

'I'm not fucking with you,' said Jonathon, glancing at the balcony and flinching.

Channon eyed him narrowly, as though, despite this assurance, he still suspected Jonathon might be fucking with him.

'He's not fucking with you,' said Piper, to allay his suspicions. She held the damp tissue tight in her hand, and hoped he couldn't see she had been crying.

He looked at her with the same distrustful expression.

'You're just as bad, little lady,' said Channon.

'Please don't call me little lady,' said Piper.

Channon frowned at her but seemed to decide not to pursue it. He reached into the briefcase, bringing out a small shiny black device which he laid on the table.

'Recorder,' he explained, pressing a button. He said his name, the date and Jonathon's name, and then, 'What is your first conscious memory?'

'Um,' said Jonathon, 'I remember lying on a street made of stones and a man wearing orange clothes holding up his hand and saying, "How many fingers?" And then … Oh!' Jonathon slapped his forehead. 'I understand that now: he just wanted to check if I could see properly.'

Piper wished she could squeeze his hand, but she didn't want to hear the sound of her handcuffs clinking against his. And besides, the agent behind Jonathon was eyeing her threateningly, the one in the immaculately ironed cargo trousers.

An hour later, Piper had listened tensely as Jonathon had recounted his whole story. She had then watched him produce photofits of the three assassins he had seen clearly: a woman with bobbed hair, an old German man with a kindly face, and a man with a square jaw and stubble.

When they were finished, Channon called, 'Hey, Chase!' And the agent with the leather jacket came in from the hallway.

'Pretty clear who these three are, no?' he said.

'Wintergreen, Stotz and Picketty?'

'Has to be. And driving a grey Audi. Give me your sat-phone.'

The man in the leather jacket pulled out a surprisingly chunky mobile phone and handed it over. Channon dialled a number.

'Nelson?' he said. 'Bring in Wintergreen, Stotz and Picketty. They're the moles. I don't want a fuss, but get on it right away. We can't afford to have them out there.'

Channon handed back the phone and turned to Jonathon. 'Now, just to confirm, I need you to remember the licence plate of this grey Audi.'

At that moment, the doorbell rang. Channon looked at Chase, the agent in the leather jacket, who put his hand on the gun he kept in the small of his back and went to the flat's front door.

Both the agent in the nice blue shirt and the one with the immaculately ironed cargo trousers took out their guns and moved the top bit back so that it clicked – a thing Piper had seen on TV but never understood. She would be useless with a gun if she had to remember to click the top bit every time before she could use it.

Channon held up his hand to pause Jonathon.

Piper could hear two voices talking quietly at the door, but couldn't make out any words.

The agent in the leather jacket returned, handed Channon a card, and said, 'A Lizzie Morden, sir. Plus two muggles. She says it's urgent. Straight from Langley.'

Piper realised she had stopped breathing and had to force herself to start, supervising the in-and-out business to make it look natural. Was this the person Lance had talked about? The one who had wanted to help her escape the hotel? Or was it someone else, come to make things worse. Maybe Channon had a boss who didn't think he was poisoning hard enough. She stole a look at Jonathon, who was staring at the drawer again and restraining a flinch.

Channon looked hard at the card.

'Lizzie, huh?' he said. 'Well, we're in protocol five here. Tell her they need to surrender any weapons and submit to a search.'

The agent left, and a couple of minutes later a woman appeared, large and windblown, with rosy cheeks, glowing red hair and a tan trouser suit.

'Doug,' said the woman, nodding at Channon. 'Been a while.'

'Lizzie,' he said. 'What are you doing here?'

Then Lance walked into the room, and Piper's heart leapt. If he was here, this must be the rescue party. The small, unarmed rescue party, walking into the flat full of armed men, handcuffs and poison.

Lance was followed by another woman, whose curly black hair and caramel skin did absolutely nothing to balance out all the guns, poison and ruthless cruelty. She waved shyly at Jonathon, who waved shyly back. Piper wasn't sure how she felt about this, but it was pretty far from being the worst thing going on at the moment. She glanced at Lance, determined not to let on that she recognised him.

'What's up, Piper?' he said.

'Oh, hello, Lance,' she replied. 'Imagine seeing you here.'

'I'm imagining it right now. It's so vivid it's like it's really happening.'

Channon looked from Piper to Lance with a frown. 'Would you guys shut up?' he said, as though genuinely curious to hear the answer.

'Yep,' said Lance.

Piper mimed zipping her lips, catching a bit of Lance's jaunty nonchalance.

'Who's this?' Jonathon asked Piper.

'Has he really forgotten me?' said Lance.

'Lance is one of your best friends,' Piper told Jonathon. 'I mean, by the amount you like him, he probably is your best friend. By the amount you see him he's probably about number nine. He lives in New York.'

'Oh. Hello, Lance,' said Jonathon. 'Sorry I've forgotten everything. It's …' He made a hand gesture that encompassed Channon, the agents and the general weirdness of everything.

'Hey, no problem, Double-O Jay.'

'Please don't call me Double-O Jay.'

'No problemo.'

'Okay,' said Channon, 'I'd like it if you guys would shut up now. Your accents are making my ears hurt.' He looked at Lizzie. 'What are you doing here? How long have you been in Germany? And why have you brought this shampoo-commercial guy?'

He looked at Lance, who pointed at himself and raised a quizzical eyebrow.

'It's all over, Doug,' said Lizzie.

'What is?' said Channon.

'The way you operate. Trying to topple Germany's government, Knife-fish, assassinations. It's over.'

'We know you're the mole,' said Lance.

'Shut up,' Lizzie told Lance.

'*I'm* not the mole,' Channon said. 'These guys are.' He gestured to the photofits on the table. 'Wintergreen, Stotz and Picketty. They're officers here in Berlin station. They tried to kill this guy.' He pointed at Jonathon.

'Lis–' began Lizzie.

Channon cut her off. His voice had an icy calm to it. 'You know, it's really not a good idea for you to be throwing accusations around. You have no authority here. So, if there's something I'm doing that you don't like, then you need to go through the proper channels.'

'I have,' said Lizzie, angrily. She took out her phone and pressed a button.

'Okay,' said Channon. 'I don't have time for this. I need you to le–'

WHUMF. DOOF.

There was a loud noise from the front door, followed by a thud.

In the doorway stood a large man wearing a black helmet, goggles, and a bulletproof vest over jeans and a sweatshirt. In his hands was a machine gun, which he pointed at Channon. Behind him was another armoured man, older and fatter, pointing his gun at the agent with the immaculately ironed cargo trousers. Another agent crouched in the hallway behind, also covering Channon.

There was a tense silence. The armoured people in the doorway adjusted their stances. Piper moved her eyes very gently leftwards, and saw that the agent behind Jonathon, the one in the cargo trousers who had clicked the top bit of his gun a while ago, was aiming it at the figures in the doorway. In the other corner of the room, near the kettle, the agent in the nice blue shirt was aiming at Lizzie.

'Hi,' said Channon to the new arrivals. 'We were just talking about you.'

Piper found she had stopped breathing again. Jonathon was sitting very close, so close he was in danger of pushing her off her wooden chair. He flinched and she squeezed his hand tight in hers, not caring any more about the awkwardness of their handcuffs.

Channon's jaw was clenched. He moved his eyes from the armoured figures in the doorway to his own two agents.

'Looks like we've got a stalemate here,' he said. 'It's almost like being married again.'

Lizzie said, 'Nice try, Doug. But this is pretty far from being a stalemate. Tell your guys to drop their guns.'

'I'm assuming,' said Channon, 'that none of our guys will fire unless one of us gives the signal. But if either of us does that, we'll be the first to die, since we both have a gun pointing at us. If the shooting carries on till one side's dead, then *maybe* there'll be one left on your side. But that still means each of you three guys' – he addressed the gun-toting new arrivals – 'has a two in three chance of dying: not good odds. That's what makes it a stalemate.'

Lizzie nodded at the agent in the nice blue shirt behind Piper. He switched his aim from Lizzie to the man in the ironed cargo trousers.

'Sorry, Kerr,' he said.

'Fuck sake, Sterling. Really?' said the other. 'After I tipped you off about the way things work?'

'I am sorry, man. Thanks for your help. Really. But this is bigger than you or me.'

Channon gave the agent in the nice blue shirt, Sterling, a hard stare and clenched his jaw.

'Fucking son of a bitch,' he said.

'Sorry, sir,' said Sterling.

'That fucking green tea. The mole is always the guy with the biggest incentive not to put a foot wrong. Which is why, if you're the mole, it's smart to do something a little bit wrong. You don't have a fucking thermometer so you can get the boss's green tea the exact right temperature. That was my thinking. That's why I had you down as just a fifteen percent chance of being the mole. I got it wrong.'

'I just did what I would have done if I hadn't been the mole, sir. Details are important. Besides, I want you to enjoy your tea. I like you, sir.'

'Right.' Channon gave a bitter laugh. 'And that's why you're betraying me.'

'No, that's a separate matter, sir. That's because I disagree with your values. Like I said to Kerr, this is bigger than you or me.'

Channon shook his head and muttered, 'Imbecile.'

'Okay!' said Lizzie brightly. 'Moving on. Now, no one's pointing a gun at me. If – what's your name? Bart?'

'Bart Kerr,' said the cargo-trouser man.

'Okay, Bart Kerr, if you fire or switch your aim to me you have a one hundred percent chance of dying. Doug, you'd die right away too. But my guys only have a one in four chance of being hit, and they're wearing body armour. That's why this is a checkmate, not a stalemate. And that means, Bart Kerr, that you need to very slowly hand your gun to Sterling, then turn around, put your hands on your head and sink to your knees.'

Kerr paused, then un-clicked his gun and held it out to Sterling. Piper was very glad Sterling had turned out to be a goodie. She clutched Jonathon's hand all the tighter as the gun was passed over their heads, and Sterling leaned in to take it. Then Kerr put his hands on his head and knelt down, facing the corner. Piper couldn't help thinking about what kneeling would do to his neatly pressed cargo trousers.

'Well congratulations, son,' said Channon to Jonathon. 'Thanks to you I left my gun in a bookshop restroom. Now we're both going to die.'

This didn't make sense to Piper. Jonathon wasn't going to die – not if someone shot the man who had ruined his life.

Channon turned to Lizzie. 'I may not have a gun, but I administered batrachotoxin to this little lady here. I have the antidote' – he held the glass phial upside-down – 'and I can flip the top off it before anyone can shoot me.'

'So?' said Lizzie.

'So I poisoned her. Without the antidote, she dies.'

'Well, no offence, honey,' said Lizzie to Piper, 'but I can live with that. I've been trying to kill your boyfriend for a week now.'

Piper felt a surge of alarm. But Lizzie must be bluffing. Lance's expression told her that. All that mattered was whether Channon believed it.

Channon sat there, thumb on the stopper. Lizzie shrugged, held out her hand, and one of the armoured figures by the doorway – a petite woman wearing a fluffy teal jumper beneath her bulletproof vest – put a gun in it. Lizzie clicked the top and pointed it at Channon's face.

'Flip the top off your little bottle if you want,' Lizzie said to Channon. 'But afterwards you need to hold out your hands to get cuffed.'

Time stopped. Piper's life was in this man's hands.

75

Boris stayed hidden behind the wall. He put his hand in his pocket, gripping the little revolver. He looked again at the building, at its huge red anarchist symbol.

The door to the building was now clear. The man in casual wear and the man in the suit had disappeared inside. They had gone in with a short woman who wore a jumper that was fluffy.

Shortly afterwards an old man and a young one had jumped out of a big grey Audi and run into the building after her, carrying black bags.

Should he really try to solve this problem himself? Or should he do something he had sworn he would never do, and call the police? How much of an anarchist was he?

76

Jonathon watched as Channon weakly let the antidote slip from his fingers onto the table, where it rolled to a stop against a pen.

Piper turned and hugged Jonathon – surprisingly effectively, considering the handcuffs – with both hands on one shoulder and her head on the other. She was crying with relief.

'We're safe,' she said. 'I can't believe it's over.'

Jonathon found himself making incoherent little comforting noises. He didn't know how to tell Piper that it wasn't over, that it had just got even worse. He wondered whether he had ever known how to tell a weeping beautiful stranger that they were both going to die. Perhaps there were etiquette classes in schools where they covered that sort of thing.

If so, they might also deal with another relevant question: what is the most polite way to push a weeping beautiful stranger off her kitchen chair so that you can leap over her and open a drawer in an old-fashioned table, snatch up what you hope is a fake bible and grab the gun which you desperately need to believe is concealed within, all while both of you are wearing handcuffs? That was a much more advanced question, probably only covered in university-level etiquette classes, if they existed.

Piper turned to him with large, shining eyes, and said, 'I love you, Jonathon. I really, really love you. And I'm going to take you home and you're going to meet everyone again: my dad, and Cess, and the cat, who's still called Hastings Banda. I tried to change it but …'

Jonathon tried to hug Piper back and join in with this moment, perhaps their last, while also looking surreptitiously around the room. Channon was being handcuffed by Amy, who had taken off her helmet. She caught Jonathon's eye and gave him a terrifying wink, before heading over to handcuff the CIA officer who knelt in the corner.

He heard her say, 'Man, why do you press your cargo pants, Kerr? It's literally the dumbest look.'

'It's called pride,' muttered Kerr, then, 'Ow.'

Jonathon needed to stay calm and watch for a moment when he could act without immediately dying in a hail of bullets. He was praying that what was in that drawer wasn't just a bible.

Amy returned from handcuffing the agent in the corner and stood beside Lizzie, machine gun cradled in her arms. She nodded at Jonathon and said breezily, 'Can we kill him now?'

Jonathon felt the blood rush from his face. Luckily, Piper couldn't see who Amy meant. She was still face-hugging him too hard.

Lizzie frowned, glanced at Lance and Karen, and said, 'Amy's joking.'

'Okay then,' said Amy, 'how do you want to play this thing? If you let the muggles go now, they have literally no reason to keep quiet about all this. This guy' – she pointed at Jonathon with her machine gun – 'already knows way too much, and could get the rest of his memory back any day.' She turned to Lizzie. 'So what's your plan?'

Lizzie sighed. 'This is my plan, kind of. I guess the take-out from this is, "Never make a new plan while running." My original, better plan was to intercept Jonathon before he could tell Doug everything. But then Doug's backup guys arrived while you were stuck in traffic. And I had to bring these two with me to make sure they didn't talk to anyone else.'

'Well,' said Amy, 'it's fine. We've ended up in total control of the situation. We can work with this.'

Channon, seeming to emerge from a trance, said, 'If you're thinking of killing just me and saying you found me already dead, you should know I put out a call for you three' – he glanced at the photofits on the kitchen table – 'to be arrested. No one's going to believe a story like that now. So I guess you have to kill us all.'

At this, Jonathon felt Piper's head twitch as she looked at Channon.

'Wait a minute,' said Lance to Lizzie. 'So it really *was* you trying to kill Jonathon? I thought that was a ruse.'

'What? No. This is real,' said Lizzie, wearily. 'You better cuff these two as well,' she said to Amy.

Jonathon felt Piper's jaw drop open against his shoulder. She turned to look at Lizzie and Amy.

'But why were you trying to kill him?' persisted Lance, putting his hands up as Amy turned her gun on him.

'Shut up,' explained Lizzie.

Amy handcuffed them as Lance's mouth worked, as though he were expecting words to come out and was surprised to find that wasn't happening.

'Okay,' said Lizzie, 'you two better sit over there at the far end of the table, in that space between Channon and the guy who just won't die.'

'I thought you'd never ask,' said Lance, making his way over and manoeuvring one of the wooden kitchen chairs with his feet. He sat down, and Jonathon thought that having your hands cuffed behind your back was actually quite stylish. His own were cuffed in front, which suddenly seemed really dorky.

There was silence for a few seconds as the room settled into its new configuration of handcuffed people sitting at one end of the kitchen, around the table, and heavily armed people standing at the other end, by the oven and the work surfaces.

'Tell me why, Lizzie,' said Channon.

'Did you ever read the Plack Report?'

'I don't know. Maybe? What is it?'

'I worked in a team led by Bulmer K Plack, former Deputy Director of Central Intelligence, and we did a complete review of the CIA's operational history, right back to the SSO days. We analysed every intervention, from Italy to Afghanistan, and we drew practical conclusions.'

'Okay, this is ringing a vague bell. I think it sounded a little … out there, so I steered clear.'

'Exactly. That report was supposed to set the future direction for the whole Agency. But it was buried because its conclusions were not what the Agency wanted to hear.'

'Or maybe the conclusions were wrong.'

'You think we wanted to come to those conclusions? No way. I used to be just as sold as you on the value of covert ops and intervention. I bought that whole "heroic defence of democracy" thing.'

'I guess that's why you dropped operations like a hot rock as soon as you got the offer of an easy job in analytics, back in Langley.'

'Okay, first of all, it was far from an easy job. I did eighty-hour weeks for five years while we put together that report. We looked at every single intervention. What I jumped at was the chance to get away from you.'

'Is that what this is about? I am sorry I didn't pay you enough attention when we were married. Lizzie, we are protecting the free world. It's kind of difficult for one person to be more interesting than that for a sustained period of time.'

Lizzie laughed. 'Surprisingly, Doug, this is not all about you. I know that must be tough to get your head around.'

'So what is it about?'

'It's about facts. The record clearly shows that CIA interventions – coups, assassinations, vote-rigging, blackmail, guerrilla warfare – have made America weaker, poorer and much less respected. And they haven't been great for the places where we've intervened. Plus, it's all been illegal and unconstitutional: the CIA's only legally mandated role is to collect intelligence. And the Plack Report said that's exactly what we should do: stop covert interventions altogether. That's why the report was buried and forgotten.'

'It sounds like you're saying CIA interventions have all been failures, bu–'

'Since nineteen forty-seven, eighty-six percent of interventions have failed to achieve even their short-term objectives. Ninety-eight point one percent failed to achieve their long-term goals. And over seventy-five percent achieved exactly the reverse of their objectives.'

'You know, where we haven't necessarily succeeded, a lot of that will be down to undiagnosed natural disruptors, like this guy. But I can think of dozens of successes. What about Chile? That was my first operation: total success.'

'We successfully brought down the socialist government of Salvador Allende.'

'Well there you go.'

'In his place we installed Pinochet, who abolished democracy, killed and tortured thousands, collapsed the economy and died with at least twenty-eight million dollars in secret foreign accounts. By the end, half the population were in poverty.'

'Who cares about the standard of living in Chile? That's small stuff. What about the big stuff? Like defeating the Soviet Union?'

'The CIA played no part in that. All our estimates of their military strength, their nuclear strength and their intentions were wrong. Over the whole course of the Cold War, we had exactly three Soviet agents who provided secrets of any value. All of them were arrested and executed. Meanwhile, even in the years right before the collapse of the Soviet Union, our head of counterintelligence and the head instructor of our training school were Soviet agents. There were dozens more. And that's just the ones we know about.'

'My mistake,' said Channon, ironically. 'I thought the Soviet Union collapsed and we won. I guess I got that the wrong way around.'

'I'm not saying we didn't win. I'm saying the CIA had no part in it. The Soviet economy was just too bad and its political system was unpopular. That's why it collapsed. It might have happened sooner if it was obvious who the good guys were. But people struggle to tell that you're the good guys when you've covertly ended democracy in half a dozen major countries.'

'You're missing the point. Do covert interventions sometimes make bad stuff happen? You bet. But the alternative is to just stand there and wait for good stuff to happen all on its own. That's not good for a country. If the world sees that's what you do, they try to take advantage of you. And that's why I will always believe in the value of covert US intervention.'

'Even if the evidence overwhelmingly suggests it doesn't work?'

Channon nodded gravely.

'And that,' said Lizzie, 'is exactly why we're here. It became obvious that only extreme measures would change CIA culture.'

'And now it comes out,' said Channon. 'So who are you working for?'

'I'm not working for anyone. Or you could say I'm working for everyone. The CIA isn't short of talented idealists who are ready to sacrifice themselves for the greater good. I assembled a network of them, dedicated to changing the culture of the Agency through a controlled programme of highly targeted assassinations. And yes, *believe me*, I am aware of the irony.'

'Highly targeted assassinations? Like this guy?' He pointed to Jonathon.

'Hey, our targets were almost entirely senior CIA leadership with the most pro-interventionist instincts. That's why you're on the list. He's an anomaly.'

'You got that right,' said Channon.

'We needed to stop you using him to collapse the German

government. It's one of the few that acts the way governments should: boringly responsible. The world needs boring government, Doug.'

'I can't believe you would do this, Lizzie. This was all your idea?'

'Pretty much. I may have had a little help.'

There was a soft cough from the doorway, and everyone turned to look.

'I do apologise for intruding,' said a fat little man with a sparse moustache, wearing a small grey hat and a large grey overcoat. He stepped into the kitchen. 'Good afternoon, Ms Morden. Everyone.'

77

Of all the shadowy figures, thought Lance, *who have ever dramatically entered a room, he has to be the least impressive.* The man was tubby, with a beaky little nose and a pendulous jowl a bit like a pelican's. His overcoat was shiny, his hat was silly, and his upper lip was sweating.

'You have got to be kidding,' said Channon, neatly echoing Lance's own thoughts. 'Him?'

'What?' said Lizzie. 'No. He just happened to arrive at that moment. Hey, Michaels. Glad you could make it. No, it was Plack who helped me with the idea. But he's at a conference in Michigan, so I guess he won't be stepping into the room.'

'Good afternoon, Ms Morden,' repeated Michaels. 'I came as soon as I could.'

So this was Michaels, thought Lance. He didn't look much like he had an exceptionally sharp mind, as Lizzie had told him. But then not everyone obligingly looked as amazing as they were, like Lance.

Michaels seemed on the point of saying something, but was interrupted by the attractive agent in the fluffy sweater – Amy – sticking her machine gun in his face. Michaels put his hands up.

'What's that in your hand?' asked Amy.

'What? Oh, a hanky.'

'A what?'

'A handkerchief?' said Michaels. 'I have a cold.'

'Well, whatever you call it, drop it,' said Amy. 'Hands on your head.'

Michaels did as he was told, flattening the ill-judged little grey hat he was wearing. He looked surprised and a bit put out as Amy patted him down with one hand, keeping the other on her machine gun.

She passed his wallet and phone to Lizzie, then told him to turn around, and cuffed him, his hands still on his head.

Lizzie said pleasantly, 'You mind standing over there in that corner, Michaels? We've kind of got a situation going on here.'

'Oh,' he said. 'Of course.'

He nodded tensely to Piper and took his place in the empty corner, a short distance from Channon and Lance.

'And keep your hands where I can see them?' requested Lizzie pleasantly.

'Indeed,' said Michaels. 'May I remove them from my head?'

'Sure. But, you know, slow.'

Michaels took his hands from his now quite badly misshapen grey hat and held them awkwardly just above the level of his belly button, which added to his air of being a troubled vicar.

'May I ask the nature of this, er, *situation*?' he enquired, his nose beginning to run.

Channon answered him: 'She's the one who's been killing our guys–'

'It was a controlled programme of highly targeted assassinations,' said Lizzie, 'dedicated to changing the culture of the CIA's top leadership.'

'She was trying to kill *him*' – Channon pointed at Jonathon – 'and now she's psyching herself up to kill everyone in this room. Isn't that right, Lizzie?'

'Oh,' said Michaels, whose glasses had steamed up. 'Oh dear.' He seemed to be swaying slightly, as though all the energy that he might otherwise have used to stand up were being diverted to taking in everything he had just heard.

'Okay people,' said Lizzie. 'Stay calm. No one's going to kill anyone.'

'Oh yeah?' said Channon. 'What happened to the guys on the door downstairs? And Chase, upstairs?'

'I mean,' said Lizzie, 'no one's going to kill anyone *else*.'

Piper gasped quietly, and said, 'Chase.'

'Well,' said Channon, 'we can't stay here forever and you can't let us go. So now Michaels is here, I guess that's it. You *have* to kill us.'

'Don't tell me what I have to do, Doug,' said Lizzie. 'Don't ever do that.'

A hush fell over the kitchen, as well it might.

Then Michaels stepped hesitantly forward, his hands visibly shaking in their cuffs.

'At this juncture,' he said, 'I should perhaps mention that I antici-pated this … this, er, eventuality. The building is surrounded.'

He looked around the room uncertainly, licked his lips, and added, 'By the police.'

Everyone in the room looked at everyone else in the room, as though by prior arrangement. Then they all looked at Michaels, whose nose was still running.

Michaels went on, his voice unnaturally high and wavering. 'There would be certain advantages for you' – he looked at Lizzie and her small gang – 'in surrendering to … to myself, rather than to Mr Channon or the German police.'

'Oh,' said Lizzie, politely inclining her head. 'Do tell.'

'Well,' said Michaels, speaking fast, as though he wanted to say everything before his voice gave out. 'If you were to surrender to Mr Channon here, he would, er, kill you. Whereas surrendering to the Germans would mean you'd get a public trial in Germany – their con-stitution forbids extradition if there's a possibility of the death penalty.'

'Oh, that's good,' said Piper.

Channon gave her a dirty look as Michaels continued.

'The whole world would talk about – and broadcast – such a trial. And you would have considerable public sympathy for rescuing a young man forcibly recruited and brainwashed by the CIA, and reu-niting him with his charming girlfriend.' Michaels looked shyly at Piper and added, 'People would hear about CIA activities – such as accidentally starting both the Iranian revolution and al Qaeda – and this would create the best possible chance of returning the CIA to its proper role.'

'That's why we should surrender to the Germans,' said Lizzie. 'What intrigues me is why we should surrender to you.'

'Oh, simply because surrendering to me would draw the British government into the whole thing and create diplomatic confusion. That would produce all sorts of advantages for you.'

'Such as?'

'Well, it would create an argument about where the trial should be held, whether in Britain or Germany, which would ensure immediate publicity, making it harder for the Agency to assassinate you while you're awaiting trial.'

'And what if Britain won the argument?'

'Oh, that wouldn't happen,' said Michaels. 'German law is very clear on the subject, and British law is rather unclear on almost every subject. Also, no British government has won an international argument about anything since 1934.'

Channon said, 'I think you're skating over the part where Lizzie and all her guys spend the rest of their lives in a German prison, eating potato salad and gherkins.'

'I apologise,' said Michaels. 'I had no intention of obscuring that. They would indeed have to spend a long time in prison. But since they were prepared to risk death for their goal, I imagine they are also prepared to spend time in prison for it. Especially since, unlike American prisons, German penal institutions are actually preferable to death.'

Lizzie raised an eyebrow.

'They're less violent and inhumane,' he explained, 'and offer excellent educational facilities. You would have no problem earning a PhD, for example, during your prison term. Prisoners get private rooms, with Scandinavian integrated furniture. And since German prisons are based on the idea of rehabilitation, you would be released once the authorities were sure you were no longer likely to begin another programme of targeted assassinations.'

'Interesting,' said Lizzie. 'I almost wish the building really was surrounded. Sounds like it would solve a lot of my problems.'

'Can't you just pretend it is?' suggested Lance.

'Lance, I kind of need you to continue to shut up,' said Lizzie.

'But,' said Michaels, his voice shaking again, 'the building *is* surrounded. I assure you.'

Lizzie went to the French windows and peered out.

'It doesn't *look* surrounded,' she said, her brow theatrically furrowed.

'N-no,' he agreed, his nose running even more furiously. 'The Germans … insisted on that. Didn't want to alarm anyone. Might I use my handkerchief?' He pointed to where it lay on the floor.

'You can blow it out of your ass,' offered Amy, turning her machine gun on him.

'As you say,' he replied, shying back. He glanced around and then wiped his nose discreetly on the back of his hand.

'So when I called you a half-hour ago,' said Lizzie, pacing like a lawyer back to her position by the cooker, 'and gave you this address, you had a team of very subtle German police with you, and they invisibly surrounded this apartment building. Then, even though you'd guessed my role in all this, you thought it would be a good idea to come here alone.'

'Yes,' said Michaels, looking down. 'Something like that. I mean, "surrounded" is perhaps putting it strongly. There–'

'Would "not surrounded at all" be more accurate?' Lizzie asked this in a neutral tone, kindly even, but while pointing her gun at his head.

'Ah,' said Michaels, staring down the barrel of the gun. 'Yes it would,' he admitted, crumpling. He took off his glasses and wiped his eyes.

Lance was horrified to see that Michaels was crying. His shoulders were shaking, and his cheeks shone with tears that came faster than he could wipe them away. He sank down to the floor.

'Oh, god,' said Michaels, rocking back and forth, 'I don't want to die. Why did I ever join? I've made such a mess of my life.'

'Jesus, Lizzie,' said Channon, 'just kill us all. Don't wait for everyone to have a breakdown.'

And that was when it hit Lance that he was going to die.

Until then, he had assumed something would crop up. There'd be a last-minute rescue, or he'd manage to talk his way out of it. But none of that was going to happen.

What are you meant to do when you're about to die? He started to pray, which was difficult because he hadn't done it since he was nine, and his hands were cuffed behind his back. He sat forward on his chair, his chin on his chest, and closed his eyes.

Please, god, don't let me die, he said silently. *I'm sorry I didn't believe in you, or didn't think about it, but I'm not bad. Don't let me die. I'll give up everything: New York, MTV, everything. I'll shave my head. I'll work with the poor. Or something. Whatever you want.*

'Doug,' Lizzie asked, 'why do you *want* me to kill everyone?'

'I don't want you to, Lizzie. But I've reached a point in my meditation practice where I'm at ease with the idea of death. And I can't see what other option you have. I mean, everyone who knows anything incriminating about you is in this room, handcuffed. You have guns with silencers fitted. You kill all of us, seal the apartment, and walk away.'

'But you said you gave the order for them to be arrested,' said Lance, seizing on this one tiny chance. 'So there'll be people looking for them. No one will believe they weren't involved.'

'I was lying,' said Channon.

'But I was here,' said Piper. 'I heard you. And then the man in the leather jacket passed the order on – Chase Mason.'

'Big deal,' said Channon. 'So they'll be arrested. All the evidence and witnesses against them are in this room. You guys just need to get your story straight before interrogation. Or just disappear – go to Africa, Russia, I don't know. Make yourselves new identities. Keep going with the assassinations.'

'I can't believe it,' said Michaels bitterly, red-faced and smeared with snot. 'You're trying to save the bloody CIA. You know that if they kill all of us, the CIA will keep going exactly as it always has. We'll be reported as some mysterious killings, which the German police will never get anywhere with investigating. Lizzie and her friends will escape or not, but they won't manage to assassinate their way to changing the CIA. And we'll all be dead. Dead. I've put my stupid bloody loyalty to the service aside, why can't you? At least I chose *people* in the end. At least I tried to help *her.*'

Everyone looked down, embarrassed by Michaels' bitter outburst.

So this was how he, Lance Ferman, was going to die: not in the course of some spectacularly weird sex thing, as he'd always assumed, but as a way of filling an awkward silence. It was the least fitting end he could possibly imagine.

78

Boris had seen movies. How he despised them: narcotics for people who needed to wake up. But from movies he knew that, with a revolver, you must flip out the cylinder, spin it and see that there is a bullet in every chamber. This revolver had five bullets, lying there like fat oligarchs in gold jackets, and one empty chamber.

Boris clicked the cylinder back into place and pulled back the hammer. Now the revolver was ready to fire. He put it in his pocket, kept it there in his hand, his finger on the trigger, as he walked to the front door.

The door was locked, of course. Rage seared through Boris's heart. Everything was locked to him. The world was all doors, all closed and bolted.

And yet the little fat man in the shiny coat had entered only minutes before. How? Boris had no idea. He angrily lashed out at the number pad beside the door that kept him from the woman he loved, smashing at it with the revolver's handle.

EEEP!

It was the speaker beside the number pad.

'*Yes, what?*' said a woman's voice, fuzzy as though coming from deep in the building's chest.

It took Boris a moment to summon up his few words of German. He was not accustomed to being addressed by a building.

'*My girlfriend is there,*' he said. '*She is in danger.*'

'*She is on the contrary not here,*' said the voice.

'*She–*' There was a click and the intercom went dead. '*Hello?*'

Ice stole into Boris's heart. Burning, fiery ice that soon turned to rage. He lashed out again at the number pad, beating it with the revolver's handle.

The voice spoke again.

'*You must not all the bells sound. That goes completely not.*'

'*My girlfriend is in danger!*' said Boris.

'*What?*'

'*My girlfriend is–*'

'*Louder. I can not good hear.*'

'*MY GIRLFRIEND IS–*' he shouted, but was cut off by a loud tutting from the speaker. There was a click. The voice of the building fell silent.

A rage passed before Boris's eyes, filling his head and his heart. He beat the number pad mercilessly with the butt of the little revolver. Then he looked desperately around. The door was at the top of some steps, and the windows of the lowest flats began higher than the head of a tall man. But if he could smash one of those windows, he could jump across from the top of the–

The door opened.

There stood an elderly woman, wearing glasses and a thick pink dressing gown.

'*I can not good hear,*' she said crossly.

'*My girlfriend is in danger,*' said Boris, pushing past her and racing upstairs, the revolver in his hand.

'*Stop!*' shouted the elderly woman, angrily. '*That goes completely not!*'

But Boris was storming up the stairs towards Karen, dark and angry as a doomed raven.

79

Jonathon had been standing there pointing the revolver at Lizzie for quite a while before anyone noticed. Then Lance did a double-take, and this caused a little ripple of glances in Jonathon's direction until finally, without anyone changing position, they were all looking at him. He felt himself blush furiously.

'Um,' he said.

Michaels' outburst had given Jonathon the opportunity he'd been looking for. The movement had begun as a cringe of embarrassment, but this had given him the impetus he'd needed. He finally had the courage to rudely snatch his cuffed hands away from Piper's, scootch over into her chair, pull open the little drawer in the table, flip the cover of the bible, silently thank god it wasn't real, and grab the loaded revolver concealed within – identical to the one in the Hamburg deposit box.

'Er,' he continued.

Taken altogether, he was not making a brilliant job of the talking side of holding someone at gunpoint. But he must have been holding the revolver quite convincingly because no one jumped in to interrupt him. In fact, the revolver felt perfectly snug in his hand. The stance felt natural: right arm straight but not locked, left hand supporting his right, a clear line of sight from his dominant eye along the gun's sights to a point right between Lizzie's eyes. He still couldn't believe she'd been trying to kill him. She seemed so nice.

Piper, lying on the floor since he'd scootched into her chair, said, 'Have you clicked the top bit?'

'You don't need to on this kind,' he said. 'It's a double-action. Thanks though.'

'No problem.'

His cheeks were still burning with embarrassment at this tricky social situation, but – thanks to Piper – he had at least begun speaking.

'Let, er, let go of us,' he told Lizzie, 'or I'll shoot your head.'

'You'll "shoot her head?"' said Amy. 'Man, that is the dumbest way to say that I've ever heard.'

'Oh yes?' said Piper defiantly, still lying on the floor. 'What should he say?'

'I don't know. "I'll blow your fucking head off?" And "let go of us?"

Do you mean "let us go?"'

'Let go of us,' Jonathon repeated in a steadier voice, determined not to be browbeaten by his murderous fake ex-wife, 'or I'll shoot her head.'

'I can't do that,' said Lizzie, gently. 'If I let you go now, Doug will use you to bring down the German government. And then he'll come after me. I'll spend the rest of my life on the run from the CIA, which will stay exactly the way it's always been.'

'Then let everyone go except me and Channon.'

'Nice,' said Channon.

'And I suppose the rest of them will never breathe a word about this?' said Lizzie. 'Lance, for a start, needs to explain why he hasn't been at work for the last two days.'

'Actually,' said Lance, 'I've been thinking about that and I've decided not to work for MTV any more. It's sort of a deal I've made with god.'

'Lance, honey,' said Lizzie, 'I like you, but you've been really kind of annoying me ever since we got here. Would you just stop saying stuff?'

Lance looked at the many guns in the room and nodded.

Lizzie said, 'If I let everyone else go, then I'd have to go on the run – me, Amy, Otto and Ken. And the CIA would never change. I'd have failed. I mean, I would have the satisfaction of killing Doug, but that's the only advantage.'

Amy said to Jonathon, 'We can't let any of you go. So shoot Lizzie and we'll shoot you.'

Lizzie gave her an annoyed glance.

'And then what?' said Jonathon.

'And then,' said Amy, 'we'll kill everyone else. Channon's right: we have to.'

Lizzie said to Jonathon, 'See? If you kill me, all your friends will still die, and so will you. It won't change anything. So put the gun down.'

Channon said, 'Killing her won't change anything, but it's all you can do. So do it. Teach her a lesson.'

The trigger was cold and hard under Jonathon's finger. He instinctively knew how little pressure it would take to fire the gun, to kill Lizzie. There were three people holding machine guns standing right next to Lizzie, all very deliberately not moving even a micron. He knew that would change the millisecond he pulled the trigger.

He suddenly realised that, though he was standing motionless, he was soaked in sweat. He was acutely aware of every nerve fibre in his right index finger.

From the floor, Piper said, 'Don't listen to Channon. It's really a choice between six people dying and seven.'

He thought of all the perfectly good guns he had thrown away, and the terrible environmental impact of it. He thought about lying in the German hospital, listening to things go beep, waiting to be asked again what a pen was, and wondering who he was – whether he was a nice person, what the terrible yearning inside him meant. Well, this was probably where he would find out who he was, really. And Channon was right, he had never needed a name to do that.

He suddenly felt a great sense of lightness and space, as though he was infinite. You'd think being infinite would be inconvenient, but it wasn't. He found himself smiling.

'Piper, did we ever talk about monkeys on a train?' he asked.

'Yes!' she said. 'It was our first proper conversation.'

'I think it's coming back to me. Just too late.'

Channon said, 'Are you going to teach her a lesson or not?'

'Yes,' said Jonathon. Everyone tensed up another notch. The trigger under his finger felt as big as the room. But he was infinite, so that didn't matter too much.

He put the gun down on the table. If all the good people were going to die, it was probably best if the bad people saw that killing really was, in the deepest sense, optional.

And then he closed his eyes and smiled. He felt fine, actually. It was all fine.

80

Boris was on his knees, crouching beside the elaborate old door, clutching the cold metal of the handle.

After two flights of stairs he had stopped running. Instead he had stalked, furious, watchful, out of breath, like a tall, dark bulldog.

Now he knelt here. Beside the door was an old-fashioned letterbox. '*Letters and newspapers*' it said in Gothic script, as though there had been a time when postmen would climb to the top floor. Postmen. How he despised them.

The door had been forced, splintering the doorframe around the lock, and then swung closed. Now, soon, he must fling the door open, charge in and shoot dead those who would dare threaten Karen and

Mister.

He had never fired a gun before. He had no training. All he had to guide him was his spirit, and his love for Karen. If he failed, he would have given his life for love. That was the subject of a song he had written long ago: *Frontal Sex Abattoir*.

But even to have come this far was a victory.

81

Jonathon heard Lizzie breathe a sigh.

'Okay,' she said, 'and now I'm going to give myself up.'

Jonathon opened his eyes.

Amy laughed.

'I'm serious,' said Lizzie. 'Mr Shampoo Commercial over there's right.' She nodded at Lance. 'Why don't we just pretend like we're surrounded by police? There's nothing to stop us getting the benefits of it. I think Michaels was right about what would happen if we surrendered.' She looked at Michaels, who was quietly weeping in the corner. 'And I really can't face killing a room full of innocent people, plus Doug.'

'You're making a big mistake,' said Channon.

'Channon's right,' said Amy. 'I'll do the killing. I don't mind. We all know you're not really at the killing-people end of the business. You're all about the strategy – Grey Owl. Why don't you just go to the bathroom, and when you come out, it's done. You don't even have to see it.'

'Hey, I've killed people – I used to be in covert ops, remember? It's not just that I can't face personally killing a room full of innocent people. I can't face it, period. The thing that made the assassination plan possible was that we were inside the CIA. Do you really think we'll be able to carry on with it if we don't have that advantage?'

'Sure,' said Amy. 'I mean, it'll be more difficult, but we'll find a way.'

'Okay, what do you guys think?' asked Lizzie.

She turned to the kindly looking old man with white hair who had tried to kill Jonathon in a car, and the man with the square jaw and stubble who had tried to kill him while dressed as a policeman.

'Because,' she continued, 'trying to kill this guy' – she jerked her thumb at Jonathon – 'has made me feel like this whole programme of targeted assassinations is a total pain in the ass. I want to do a PhD in a private room with Scandinavian-style integrated furniture.'

'I have to agree with Grey Owl,' said the kindly looking old assassin. 'I join with you because I feel so guilty about all what I have done when I was in the Stasi. But now if we are killing many innocent people and it does not stop the CIA employing a murdering drug dealer like Manuel Noriega, I feel I am really back in the Stasi. Also, I need to slow down. I cannot be on the run. I have these appointments for my hip twice per week.'

Amy shook her head. 'Come on, Ken, back me up,' she said, looking at the stubbled assassin.

'Amy, I think you're awesome. You know how I feel about you–'

'And that's why you're backing me up,' she said, jaw jutted.

'Sorry, I'm with Grey Owl on this one. For me, this is all about resolving one of the big things that stops the world making sense: the fact that the good guys are assassinating democratically elected presidents and selling arms to terrorists. I'd do anything to end that. And I think this whole trial idea has a lot more chance of working than going on the run and keeping on trying to assassinate our way to success. I mean, as Lizzie says, we were all aware of the irony of that.'

'Man,' said Amy.

'Sorry,' said the man with the square jaw.

'Fine, fine, call the cops. Let's just abandon our control of the situation and all go to jail.' She threw her gun down in disgust and ran her hands through her hair.

'Channon said, 'I can't believe I'm hearing this. What kind of an organisation did you guys think you were joining? The CIA intervenes – robustly. It's in our DNA. Nothing will change that: not killing us all, and not a big public trial.'

'Yeah, well, with all due respect, sir,' said the man with the square jaw, 'we think the trial option is our best shot.'

'Oh yeah?' said Channon, 'well maybe this trial won't work out so well if one of the main witnesses is dead.' He looked at Piper and held out the small glass phial containing the antidote, his thumb again poised to flick out the stopper. 'Which brings me back to my earlier threat.'

82

It suddenly occurred to Piper that she didn't need to carry on lying on the floor. She stood up, smoothing down the skirt which she was now regretting almost as much as this renewed threat to her life.

Michaels had also stood up and was sheepishly wiping his eyes and nose with the heels of his hands. He said, 'What's in that bottle isn't an antidote.'

Channon turned to him. 'You think it was always my plan to let this little lady die?'

'Don't call me a little lady,' said Piper.

'You never poisoned her,' said Michaels.

'You think I'm not capable of poisoning someone?' said Channon, looking insulted.

'Of course you're bloody *capable* of it,' said Michaels. 'That's why they have to assume you've poisoned her, whether you actually have or not. Which is why you haven't.'

'But you know we have poisons, right?'

'Yes.'

'So why would we not use them?'

'Because so much can go wrong – dosing, metabolism, how long it takes to get the information from Mr Fairfax. And tea is served in pots at the Adlon – bloody expensive ones at that. You'd have to know in advance how many cups she'd drink.'

'What can I say?' said Channon. 'Life's a gamble. Besides, she's British. She's going to drink all the cups of tea.'

'The fact that life's a gamble is what makes it so unwise to add extra gambles on top of it.'

Channon looked angrily at Michaels and said, 'You know, y–'

He was interrupted by Jonathon leaning across the table and dextrously snatching the phial from between his fingers, though the effect was somewhat spoiled by Jonathon's fumbling it immediately afterwards, so that it rolled to the floor.

Channon jumped forward, Michaels leapt on him from behind, and both crashed into the table. Jonathon was on his knees hunting for the phial, and Piper suddenly realised she had a clear path. She launched herself across the table, grabbed Channon by his ears, the chain of her handcuffs biting into his mouth, and smashed his face down into the table top as hard as she could.

At this point Amy stepped in, grabbing Channon's head from the table, punching him efficiently in the face and much harder in the stomach, then putting him on the floor with her knees on his back while she did something Piper couldn't see.

'You okay, Michaels?' asked Lizzie.

He nodded, breathing hard, and not making eye contact with anyone. Lizzie stepped around Channon and his overturned chair, gave Michaels his handkerchief and undid his handcuffs, then handed him her phone.

'Time to call the police,' she said.

Michaels blew his nose, wiped his eyes, then sat down and dialled with a trembling finger. The call was conducted in German, which meant that for Piper it was a cloud of noises with the occasional intelligible word poking out, like 'handy' or 'American'.

After a couple of minutes, he put the phone on the table top and said, 'Done.'

Lizzie took a deep breath, sighed and nodded. She sat down, looking suddenly tired.

'Well,' she said, 'I guess this means—'

But what she guessed it meant never became apparent, because at that moment the front door banged, and an aggressively bearded man stormed into the kitchen, clutching a gun.

A wall of sound appeared from nowhere, stood impregnably between Piper's ears and instantly disappeared, leaving a deep trench of silence filled with the loud ghost of sound.

83

For Boris, there was nothing. Then there was something. Just a hardness against his back, against his head. Voices. A tightness around his chest. Then light, blinking in under his eyelids. A burst of colour.

A voice, '*No A problem current. No B problem. I have a good radial pulse. No C problem.*'

He opened his eyes. Beige uniforms with hi-vis strips surrounded him. Someone was trying to put pieces of metal underneath him.

Where was Karen? He tried to ask for her, but heard himself say,

'Hggmuhgf.'

A head appeared above a beige hi-vis uniform: a thin face with thin hair. There was a baggy blue rubber glove, two fingers extended.

'*I am emergency doctor,*' said the thin-faced man. '*Be two fingers on left hand, please?*'

Boris nodded.

'*If you deep in and out breathe, goes that good or somewhat sore? Get you good air?*'

Boris breathed, coughed. There was no pain.

'*Good,*' he said.

He felt the bits of metal on either side of him again.

'*Okay,*' said the doctor. '*We make under you a stretcher together.*'

'*I need no stretcher,*' said Boris. '*Where is Karen?*'

'*One, two, three,*' said the doctor, and Boris felt the two bits of metal click together under him.

'*Where is Karen?*' asked Boris again.

'*Now put we you on a bigger stretcher,*' replied the doctor.

'*Where is Karen?*' asked Boris, grabbing the man's arm and looking intently into his eyes. There was a burning feeling in his shoulder, like the devil had hit him with a hot spade. Boris gritted his teeth as the pain arrived all at once. He tried not to show it, but couldn't help allowing a very small scream to escape his lips.

The doctor put a hand on Boris's unwounded shoulder and asked, '*How call you?*'

A man in a beige hi-vis uniform said, '*They speak all English. Ask,* "What is your name?"'

'*No,* "What are you called?"' corrected someone else.

'Boris. It's Boris!' It was Karen's voice. There she was, her face red and puffy from crying, her eyes shining, black hair all over the place. He had never seen her look so beautiful.

The drum part from 'Shit Out Your Heart' started up in his mind. *Bang! Bang! A-bang-bang bang bang. Smash!*

'Please be careful,' said the fine-haired doctor in English. 'The shoulder must not be disturbed. Please do not embrace him.'

'Boris,' said Karen, reaching her hands out but stopping just short of touching him.

'Karen,' said Boris, and winced. He had never realised that he used his shoulder to talk, but now pain ran through all the network of muscles and nerves around the upper-left part of his body. Luckily, this physical difficulty in speaking seemed to ease the emotional difficulty of saying his next words. Or perhaps it was just the opioids kicking in.

'I love you,' he said, quietly.

Karen's eyes filled with tears. She leaned in.

'I lo–' she began, and then her face was obscured by a large beige hi-vis arm.

'*One, two, three,*' said someone, and Boris was lifted and placed on another, more substantial, stretcher.

'We take him to the Urban hospital,' he heard the doctor say to Karen. 'Will you ride in the ambulance with him?'

'Yes!' he heard her say, from behind a huge beige fireman.

A face appeared from the other side of the fireman, looking at Boris. It was a scrawny man with sunken cheeks and a blue uniform, a policeman.

The policeman turned and asked the doctor, '*Can he questions answer?*'

Boris heard the doctor reply, '*The best is him in the emergency room to get. His shoulder is by a bullet smashed and he blood lost has.*'

'*Okay,*' said the policeman. '*Wait once. I get a policeman with him to go.*'

Boris heard the policeman say to Karen, 'I am sorry. You must to wait here a little longer.'

Boris was suddenly sad and confused. He had a dim memory of rushing into a kitchen with a gun, hoping to save Karen. What had happened about that?

The stretcher began to move.

'What has happened?' called Boris desperately, through the wall of beige hi-vis uniforms. 'Have we lost?'

'No,' he heard Karen call back. 'We've won. Kind of. I think we've kind of won.'

84

The late afternoon sun was pouring through the French windows that led to the balcony where all the trouble had begun. Jonathon was still sitting at the kitchen table, but now he wasn't handcuffed and was wearing one of those exciting shiny blankets around his shoulders. Piper, having taken the antidote, was with him, along with Lance and

Karen. The others had been taken away by the police, accompanied by Michaels, still sweating heavily and with a running nose, but otherwise much more composed than he had been.

The police had taken statements – in English, fortunately, so Jonathon didn't have to try to remember the words for 'amnesia', 'assault rifle' or 'fake ex-wife' – and were now treating the four of them as victims of a crime. Two slightly less gruff and impassive police officers had even supplied coffee, which everyone fell upon instantly, and cold potato salad, which they had all ignored. These victim support officers had put one of the Crowded House CDs on too, and there was something about its ubiquitous blandness that Jonathon was surprised to find quite soothing.

He sat there, staring at the mug of steaming coffee between his hands.

'Well,' said Piper, 'that was a weird … two years.'

'Yes,' said Jonathon. 'I only remember five days of it, but that was enough.'

There was a silence while they all stared again at the steam rising from their white mugs.

Then Jonathon said to Piper, 'Who am I?'

'Didn't Channon tell you?'

'I want to hear it from you.'

'You're Jonathon Fairfax. I don't know where to start. You always stir your tea anticlockwise? You have several pairs of stripy socks? You really like toast and marmalade?'

'And what do I do? Am I a hired assassin?'

'You're not any kind of assassin. I don't think you've ever hurt anyone, much less killed them.'

'Am I an import-export specialist?'

'What? God, no.'

Jonathon felt a sigh of relief fall from his mouth and a weight drop from his shoulders.

'No,' said Piper, 'you're a self-employed illustrator. You specialise in pen-and-ink animals wearing Edwardian clothes. You're good. Though you don't always have quite enough work, and then you start looking worried and playing Minesweeper too much.'

'Oh, thank god,' said Jonathon. 'I'm ordinary.'

'You're not ordinary. You're a very special person. Did I not mention the way you stir your tea? And you stand on one leg when you're confused. You've done it since you were a child.'

It was as though she had cut a tight band that had encircled his chest. He breathed again.

'So I don't do any pretty sweet deals?' he asked.

She shook her head.

'I'm not in the CIA and I've never killed anyone?'

Again, she shook her head.

'I'm just a person,' he marvelled.

'Yes. You're definitely a person.'

'And where do I live?'

'You live with me, in … well, in a slightly unrealistically beautiful small cottage in Hampstead. It's really nice, and we wouldn't ever be able to afford it, but we ended up with it without having to buy it, thank god. It's all a bit complicated, but I'll explain it one day. We have a dog called Cess and a cat called Hastings Banda. I tried to change it, but …'

'Do we really live together?'

'Yes.'

'But that's … amazing. That makes my next question a bit easier.'

'What's that?'

'I wondered if, er, if … would you like to go out for a drink some time? I mean, if you aren't busy. You're probably busy.'

She looked at him for a long time. 'You mean like a … date?'

He blushed and looked down. 'You're probably busy.'

She laughed. 'No, I'm not busy. That would be … nice. I'll even give you my phone number if you like. You know we've been on dates before, don't you? We share a bed. We're not just housemates.'

He blushed again. 'I'm still only five days old. I haven't been on a date yet. I've only just met you.' And then, without any advance warning, his brain blurbled out, 'I've fallen in love with you at first sight. And I don't know what the etiquette is for asking someone out when you've fallen in love with them at first sight but are already in a long-term relationship with them.'

Later

85

Piper felt a presence behind her.

'Hello Michaels,' she said without turning.

'Good afternoon, Miss Palgrave,' he said.

They were standing on Parliament Hill, a big grassy mound on Hampstead Heath from which you can somehow look down on the whole of London all at once, as though it were in a glass case in a museum. Off to the left was Canary Wharf, off to the right the Post Office tower, and in the middle St Paul's Cathedral, all surrounded by spindly cranes.

'I always see the cranes as needles,' she said, 'embroidering on top of all the patterns that are already there.'

'That would make a terrible mess of London's fabric,' he said.

'It does. I wish someone would just declare London finished so they could stop work on it.'

'That would–' he began.

'I know,' she said. 'But I wish it anyway. I've wished other impossible things that have come true.'

'Indeed,' he said. 'You're aware that the formal dissolution of the CIA comes into effect tomorrow?'

'Yes,' she said, turning to look at him for the first time. 'It's amazing that it all turned out exactly as you said: the row between Britain and Germany, the trial in Berlin, the reporting of all the ... well, the weird shit the CIA's done, and then everyone – even the Americans – realising that it's completely untenable for a freedom-loving democracy to have an institution that secretly doses people with LSD to see if they'll throw themselves out of a window. How did you know?'

Piper had done well to get through a speech of this length and coherence because at least half her brain was occupied with processing Michaels' appearance. When she'd turned she had seen that he was no longer wearing his familiar long coat and small trilby, but a deeply ill-advised yellow Hawaiian shirt with a red denim jacket. He had retained the sparse moustache, but his grey hair was spiky and gelled.

'I didn't know,' he said simply. 'I was just saying the first thing that came into my head in an effort to stay alive.'

'Well,' she said, 'I think sometimes the first thing that comes into our head is better than anything we could work out if we had weeks to do it.'

'Indeed,' he said. 'A lack of resources can force us into being intelligent. It often seemed to me that the CIA's practically unlimited resources was one of the reasons it was so immensely stupid.'

'Is British intelligence much less stupid?' she asked.

'Oh yes,' he said, 'substantially so. You may consider it misguided, but it is not stupid.'

'But you said British intelligence had decided it should support the CIA at all costs. That doesn't sound very intelligent.'

'Well,' he said, 'British intelligence – indeed the whole deep state, of which I could be said to have been a part – did believe in supporting the CIA, but not for the obvious reasons.'

'Oh, what were the reasons?'

'For centuries, Britain's foreign policy has been based on maintaining the balance of power. To do that, we would identify the strongest country and try to weaken it, usually by paying other countries to fight it. When America became the world's dominant power, we conceived of the "special relationship" as a cheaper alternative – a uniquely flexible means of constant subversion that didn't expose us to attack.'

'Er, what?' said Piper, still preoccupied with Michaels' hair.

'We used our weakness as an advantage, sticking close by America's side in an effort to trip it up – our tiny army making its wars more difficult, our arrogant diplomatic support wrecking its foreign policy. America's real power has always come from being liked, and the CIA is the institution that does most to destroy that advantage. That's why we've always supported the CIA.'

'Oh,' said Piper, rather stunned by this revelation, but finding it made sense of a lot of things that had always puzzled her. 'So what will you do now the CIA's gone?'

'I've no idea,' he said. 'I've left the service.'

'Is this why …?' she gestured to his clothes.

'Yes,' he said. They had by now begun to walk down the hill towards the trees. From behind his back, Michaels produced a small but delicately arranged and neatly tied bunch of sweet peas, anemones, jasmine and yellow roses.

'I've opened a florist,' he said, 'in Kentish Town.'

'Gosh,' said Piper. She had no idea what to say. 'What's it called?'

'Barry's Flowers,' he said. 'My Christian name is Barry. You might call me that, if you liked.'

After having a cup of tea and a scone with Barry in Hampstead – at one of the nice cafes this time – Piper returned to Jonathon, who was playing a game with the cat involving the sofa and a piece of scrunched-up newspaper. The dog watched them indulgently.

Jonathon didn't have enough work at the moment, and yet he hadn't played Minesweeper once – he didn't seem worried at all. When she had asked him about it, he had repeated what he'd said in Berlin: 'I don't do any pretty sweet deals and I haven't killed anyone. I'm just a person. Everything's going to be fine.'

'I've just been for a walk with Michaels,' she said, after they'd kissed.

'Oh. How is he?'

'He's a florist,' she said. 'A furtive and shifty yet oddly noble florist. He's called Barry and he wears a Hawaiian shirt.'

'That's wonderful news,' said Jonathon, deftly outwitting the cat with the scrunched-up newspaper. 'Have you packed for Berlin yet?'

86

Doug Channon stared morosely out of the window on his way to prison. The train's metal walls were painted a dispiriting brown, and through the window passed Berlin's dreariest suburbs. The faces of the few other people in the carriage were closed and downcast. Finally, the train clanked into the station. Channon got out and took a cab the rest of the way.

The prison was actually more pleasant looking than the East German concrete slab apartment buildings that surrounded and adjoined it. There was a yellow, nineteenth-century part and an orange modern part, with not a shred of razor wire. He collected his pass from reception and went to the visitors' room on the second floor. It was decorated like a showpiece suburban youth centre, complete with pot plants, notice boards and ping-pong tables.

Lizzie was already waiting for him at an oak-veneer table. Her red hair was tied back and she wore a white shirt and jeans.

'Hi Lizzie,' he said, taking a seat in the orange plastic chair.

'Hey, Doug,' she replied, putting her book aside.

'What are you reading?' he asked.

'*Strategies for Institutional Reform* – it's for my PhD.'

'Good for you. It's great you're doing that.'

'Thanks. I got the Scandinavian integrated furniture too, just like Michaels said.'

'That's great,' he said.

There was silence for a few moments, which both of them broke at once.

'You know I–' he said.

'Doug, listen, I–' she said.

'Sorry,' he said. 'You go.'

'I just wanted to say sorry that I was going to kill you. I mean, I'm legally required to show remorse for what I did, but I really am sorry.'

'Forget it,' he said. 'I was trying to convince you to kill all of us just so you'd be hunted down and killed.'

'Do you think there was maybe some bitterness between us about the way our marriage ended?' she asked.

He looked up at her and smiled. 'Could be,' he said. 'Could well be.'

Someone stopped by with a drinks trolley and he took a couple of coffees, handing one to her.

'So,' he said, 'how are you doing?'

'Great,' she said. 'I wish I could have checked myself into a German prison years ago. You get so much *done*. I don't have to deal with my cellphone going the whole time and a million meetings at Langley, while trying to do my job and co-ordinate a worldwide programme of targeted assassinations on the side. How about you?'

He made a face. 'Not so good.'

'Missing the Agency?'

He nodded. 'I guess I kind of never noticed that I didn't have a life outside of it. Feels difficult to start one at sixty-two.'

'Sixty-two's nothing. You'll figure it out. Still meditating?'

He shook his head.

'So,' she said, 'what are you doing back in Germany? Vacation?'

'No, I live here. I got my pension and a lump sum and I was planning on retiring to Palm Beach – get away from German winters and customer service. But I missed this place – it's so *serious*, in a way nowhere else is. It kind of gets under your skin. You know what I mean?'

'Doug, you're talking to someone who is mandated to stay here for at least another nineteen years, so no, I don't entirely know what you mean. But, you know, it's nice to hear there are Americans who choose to be here.'

Channon stared down at his coffee. He had the sudden feeling that he was managing to bring down a woman serving a life sentence.

'I hope you don't mind me coming to visit you,' he said.

'Are you kidding? I spend most of my time with German serial killers. It's good to see you.'

Another silence fell.

'Hey,' she said, 'you want to play table tennis?'

'Sure. Why not?'

She turned to a nearby guard.

'*Excuse you please,*' she said. '*Is the table tennis free?*'

The guard said, '*Evidently.*'

'*May we it use?*'

'Hm,' agreed the guard, in the tone of a supermarket cashier allowing someone to use a bag.

'We're good to go,' Lizzie told Channon.

They got up and moved over to the ping-pong table in the middle of the room, watched by two serious-looking prison warders in their slightly oversized uniforms.

'I always knew Germans were obsessed with table tennis,' said Lizzie, serving, 'but I never dreamed it would be such a big feature of their prisons. Yesterday I beat a woman who killed five postal workers in Wilmersdorf.'

'That's great,' said Channon. 'I can see you're really flourishing here.'

'So how long have you been retired?' asked Lizzie.

'They retired me right after I finished giving evidence at the trial.'

'My trial,' she reminded him.

'Yeah, officially your trial. And yes, I know you got sentenced to nineteen years – not that you'll do anywhere near that – for conspiracy to murder, but we all know it was really a trial by media of the CIA.'

'Exactly like Michaels said. Not just by media – by public opinion too.'

'Exactly. Where does the public get off on having an opinion of the CIA? And all these know-nothing pundits coming out and giving their two-cents worth. And Henry Kissinger! Henry Kissinger is suddenly saying he's always been a critic of the CIA, that every president thought the Agency was useless and embarrassing–'

'He said the Agency's always been five years and several billion dollars away from being fixed, which – you've got to admit – is something everyone's always said. I heard the president felt it was a relief to have an excuse to close the Agency down, replace it with something simpler, cheaper and more useful, that won't keep secretly giving billions of dollars to people you later have to invade.'

'We did what we had to do,' said Channon, putting a little too much vehemence into his return, so that the ball bounced off the ceiling.

'See?' said Lizzie, collecting it. 'There's a lot to this game, once you start playing.'

Channon quietened down and tried to concentrate on beating Lizzie at ping-pong.

Later, once she'd beaten him in five straight sets, they took up their seats and their coffees again.

Lizzie said, 'If you're feeling like, "I would have gotten away with it too if it hadn't been for those pesky kids", I'm right there with you.'

'How do you mean?'

'I mean, it was hearing about Knife-fish and the way you recruited Fairfax that opened the floodgates to the stories about how insane the Agency is.'

'Right,' he said. 'Which is weird, because the one thing I'm still sure of is that natural disruptors are real. I mean, look what one did to me.'

'What I'm trying to say, Doug, is that the Fairfax guy saved your life. Think about it: he's what halted my programme of targeted assassinations. If you hadn't recruited him, my plan would have succeeded. You'd be dead and I'd have reformed the CIA from within.'

'I hadn't thought of that.'

'You're only alive because of that guy.'

'I guess.'

'So the question is, what are you going to do with the life that you've been given? It's like, here's a free gift of a life, beginning at age sixty-two.'

'You're right. I can start again. I can leave it all behind me.'

'So, is there anything you'd like to do?'

'Well, now I come to think of it, this whole business has left me wanting to do one thing, which I think is kind of important …'

87

The man was running hard, the air cold on his cheeks and penetrating the thin cotton of his shirt. Beside him, the traffic roared along Skalitzer Strasse, while above him the trains rattled and clanked. He turned right, still running, past a little stack of kebab shops, and looked around. There it was, to his right, dirty brown but safe and warm. The man pushed open the door and walked in. *Jonathon.* He still forgot sometimes to think of himself as Jonathon.

'Hey, Mister,' said Karen from the table by the window.

'Um, hello,' he said. 'You were definitely right: it was too far to go without my coat. I had to run back.'

'And that's why all people should listen to Karen on the subject of coats,' said Karen.

'And the cash machine was exactly where you said it would be.'

'Did you think I would lie about that?' asked Karen.

'No, but …'

'ATMs are migratory,' put in Lance. 'You never know where they'll be next.'

'What is "migratory"?' asked Boris.

'It means they move around, like herds of gazelles,' said Lance.

Boris shook his head sadly.

'Even when I understand your words,' he said, 'I do not know what you are talking about.'

'I feel exactly the same,' said Arlene. 'And I'm married to him. This guy's conversation is, like, ninety-seven percent nitrogen.'

'Thanks,' said Lance. 'Nitrogen's a great fertiliser.'

'So's horse shit,' said Arlene, affectionately stroking his newly bald head.

She turned to Piper, glanced at Lance, and asked, 'What do you think?'

'It looks good,' said Piper, staring at Lance's unbelievably elegant skull. 'What made you do it?' she asked him.

'I told God I would,' he said. 'You know, when we were all going to die and I suddenly believed in him. I haven't – yet – done any of the other things I promised. This seemed like the easiest place to start.'

'Well I love it,' said Arlene. 'He's set off this, like, epidemic of bald-ness in New York. I swear, we walked into a restaurant and this one guy went and shaved his head *between courses*. Can you believe that?'

'Um, yes,' said Jonathon, handing everyone their little bundles of bank cards and cash. 'It's Lance.'

'Well,' said Piper, 'now we have some cash to pay for these drinks in this resolutely non-card-accepting city, let's toast Jonathon on the anniversary of his waking up in a bin, and the beginning of his return to real life.'

They all raised their enormously heavy glass mugs of beer.

'To Jonathon, bin day, and real life,' said Piper, and they all clinked glasses and ostentatiously made eye contact with each other.

'So,' said Arlene, 'do you think you really are a natural disruptor, like the CIA thought?'

Jonathon wrinkled his mouth and said, 'I think everyone's a natural disruptor. I've spent the last few months re-learning and remembering everything, and it just seems like everything in the world constantly goes wrong, all on its own. I think it's the nature of things. But that's a bit difficult to accept, especially if you're as powerful as the CIA. So it seemed easier to kidnap me and wipe my brain rather than deal with it.'

Everyone looked down and nodded, the way people do when someone suddenly says what they really think.

'So you remember me now, right?' asked Lance.

'Jonathon remembers nearly everything now,' said Piper proudly. 'Even you.'

'Yes,' said Jonathon. 'The bits involving Lance are hardest to believe. I keep remembering things you've done and thinking, "No, surely no one would behave like that." But then I tell Piper and she says, "Yes, he really did that."'

'And that's the reason I do things that are hard to believe,' said Lance. 'I had a hunch you would one day lose your memory and would need help proving that you'd regained it.'

'Anyway,' said Jonathon, 'to all of us, including Lance, but especially Piper.' She smiled and they kissed. 'Also especially Karen,' he continued, 'who kept me alive when all those people were trying to kill me.'

'You're welcome,' said Karen.

'And Boris, who burst into a flat full of heavily armed CIA officers to rescue us.'

'Yes, this is heroic, but I am shot by an old man,' said Boris.

'And Lance, who dropped everything to travel halfway around the world to try to find me.'

'What can I say? I'm just this amazing guy,' said Lance, as Arlene punched him playfully but hard on the arm.

'And Arlene, who made it possible for Lance to drop everything.'

'Yeah, okay, I've done least here,' she said.

'And Lizzie, who didn't kill us all, and also Channon, who has apparently started teaching meditation to underprivileged children.'

'Really?' asked Lance.

Piper nodded. 'Michaels told me so. I mean Barry the florist.'

'By the way, have you two got permanent residence now?' Piper asked Karen and Boris.

'We have,' said Karen. 'We just got a letter one day with these certificates in it. I don't know how it happened.'

'To residing permanently,' said Lance, and everyone clinked glasses and once more made ostentatious eye contact with every other person.

The End

A note from the author

Like many people, I've always found the world quite a difficult and confusing place. So, ever since I learned to read, I've been escaping into books. I've read and enjoyed lots of different sorts of books. But there's a particular kind that has really helped when the world has been at its most baffling and intractable.

I was nine or ten when I read *The Hitchhiker's Guide to the Galaxy* by Douglas Adams. It immediately made me think, 'Oh, maybe it isn't all my fault. Maybe it's just that nothing makes any sense.' It was a huge comfort and relief.

And then when I was in my mid-twenties and had a horrible corporate temping job, I found a 1932 *Jeeves Omnibus* by PG Wodehouse in a second-hand bookshop. I read it to soothe myself when I woke in the night, dreading the next day. Since then a few other books have worked the same magic. They include *Augustus Carp By Himself*, by the excellently named Henry Howarth Bashford, *Three Men in a Boat* by Jerome K Jerome, and *The Understudy* by David Nicholls.

There aren't many of these books, but I love them. To me it feels like the authors are whispering reassuringly that, if we're finding things difficult, it may well be because the world is senseless and absurd.

I would like to convey the same thing, however incompetent my whispering technique may be. I just want to write something that would have made me feel better if I'd read it when I was twenty-four and sitting full of dread on a District Line train.

I hope it worked for you. But in any case, thank you for reading.

Christopher Shevlin

To get in touch, find out how this book relates to reality, or sign up for my newsletter, please visit:
www.christophershevlin.com

What to do now

If you have enjoyed this book and are at a loose end, please:

1. Write a review on Amazon or Goodreads – each one makes the author feel like he isn't a complete idiot for up to 24 hours, and convinces 11 more people to give his books a try.
2. Sign up for the author's newsletter (at christophershevlin.com). You'll get a free copy of *The Deleted Scenes of Jonathon Fairfax*, and other things too.
3. Tell everyone you have ever even vaguely liked to get a copy of *The Spy Who Came in from the Bin*, as well as *The Perpetual Astonishment of Jonathon Fairfax* and *Jonathon Fairfax Must Be Destroyed*.
4. Leave a note on your fridge, reminding yourself that this book is attractively priced and, for the right person, makes a supremely adequate gift.
5. Sit back and bask in the author's gratitude and admiration. You are a good person, if somewhat misunderstood. Cup of tea?

Thank you again.

Novels by Christopher Shevlin

The Perpetual Astonishment of Jonathon Fairfax

Jonathon Fairfax Must Be Destroyed

The Spy Who Came in from the Bin

Printed in Great Britain
by Amazon

25012018R00169